ASHES OF ONYX

SETH SKORKOWSKY

CITY OWL
PRESS

ASHES OF ONYX
By Seth Skorkowsky

CITY OWL PRESS
www.cityowlpress.com

Cover Design by Mibl Art. All stock photos licensed appropriately.

Edited by Tee Tate.

For information on subsidiary rights, please contact the publisher at info@cityowlpress.com.

Print Edition ISBN: 978-1-949090-57-4

Digital Edition ISBN: 978-1-949090-58-1

Printed in the United States of America

PRAISE FOR THE WORKS OF SETH SKORKOWSKY

For Jorge Soto, who not only encourages my weirdness, but enables it.
Thanks, brother.

1

PINHOLE IN A PARADE FLOAT

Kate needed a fix. Three days since her last scrape of dust, and the withdrawals were creeping along the base of her skull like a hundred needle-legged fleas. Normally, she could endure it, but sitting and waiting only made the itching worse.

Desperate for a distraction, she rose from the leather chair and approached a locked display against the office wall. A modest collection of Outer World artifacts proudly rested beneath museum-grade lighting. Careful not to let her breath fog the tempered glass, she leaned closer to inspect a Hollit globe, a jeweled orb not much larger than a softball. Etched bands of red and whitish metal wove between the multicolored stones along its surface.

She'd seen a half-dozen such puzzle spheres before. Albeit smaller, Vegner's was superb in its craftsmanship. It was definitely the crown jewel of this collection. She could get a few hundred bucks for it with a single phone call. More if she had a week to shop it around. But why sell it for cash when she could trade for dust? Two, maybe three ounces if she played it right. The other artifacts were quite banal—a Dhevin gallows mask, a slender ivory ladle cut from the horn of some strange animal, and a bronze ring bearing an angular coat of arms she didn't recognize.

None of them were magical that she could detect. But Vegner would be a fool to display magical artifacts near a tempting window, even here on the nineteenth floor of this Baltimore skyrise. No, Kate decided, these

artifacts were here for her. That explained why he was late to this appoint-
ment, allowing her time to explore his office alone and see for herself that
he truly was a collector. Kate didn't care one way or the other—as long as
the money was good.

One of the two oaken doors opened, and Claudio Vegner stepped
inside, a waft of expensive-smelling cologne swirling in his wake. "I'm
sorry to keep you waiting, Miss Rossdale." He extended a hand, the manicured, square nails buffed to a high gloss.

"No problem at all," Kate said, delivering her lines in this needless play.
She accepted the hand, hoping he didn't notice how bad hers were sweating. "I was just admiring your collection."

He nodded his thanks. "Please sit."

Kate lowered herself back into one of the two chairs opposite Vegner's
desk, its inlaid surface preserved beneath a plate of beveled glass. She
scratched the back of her neck, chasing away the imagined fleas.

Vegner took his seat. His combed-back, blond hair gave an impression
of speed, disrupted only by his prominently jutting ears. The strong jaw
and deeply clefted chin were something movie stars would envy. His build
was that of a former athlete, a softening that still told of the muscles
beneath. "I trust you're doing well."

"I am," she lied.

"Good." He gave a hollow businessman's smile, tight lipped and devoid
of warmth. "I've had the opportunity to add to my collection a particular
piece of some value. But before I complete the transaction, I want to be
sure it's authentic."

"Always pays to be sure." Kate set her hands across her lap to calm
their trembling. It had been two months since her last job. She needed
money for a fix, and maybe food, worse than she ever had. Money hadn't
been an issue at first. She'd had plenty after Master Boyer's death, but time
and bad decisions had whittled that away. "You know my fee?"

"Of course," he said with a smile of very white teeth. Vegner withdrew
a stack of crisp twenty-dollar bills from his drawer and set it on the desk.
"Two thousand in advance. We can't have a disappointing answer muddle
our incentive to pay, can we?" He placed a small glass vial of red crystals,
like crimson rice, atop the bills. "And this is a little gift. Consider it a tip."

Kate's hands tightened, but she maintained her impassive smile. *Fuck
you*. She'd hoped her...dalliance wasn't widely known. Accepting it would
make her the junkie they believed her to be. No. She'd leave it here and
score some of her own the moment this meeting was over, but Vegner

wouldn't get the satisfaction of witnessing her need. "Thank you." She cleared her throat, fighting the urge to stare at the vial. The itching grew sharper. "And the artifact?"

Vegner was still smiling, the mean victory gleaming in his shit-brown eyes. He pressed a button on his desk phone. "You may send him in, Jodie."

The second oaken door into Vegner's office opened. A gray-haired woman in a flowing blouse stepped inside, a bald man with wild eyebrows and a navy suit behind her.

A loathsome dread settled in Kate's stomach. Terrance Dalton. *Jesus Christ.*

"Miss Rossdale," Dalton said. "It *has* been a while." His eyes flicked to the glass vial, and his lip curled. "Keeping yourself busy, I see. Claudio, why's she here?"

"I've hired Kate as my authenticator."

Dalton snorted. "Claudio, if you wish for authentication there are several impartial towers that I could recommend."

"No," Vegner said. "Too many back deals and alliances between towers. Covens bring their own baggage. Muddy things up. Miss Rossdale has no such loyalties, and that is the reputation I've hired. But if you wish to soil her neutrality, please, keep talking."

Dalton swallowed and lowered himself into the seat beside Kate's. "If this is your wish. I've no doubt she'll verify what I've said."

Kate forced a courteous nod. Lack of loyalties also required she not rock the boat. The Amber Tower held a lot of influence, not just in Maryland, but the entire east coast. The subtle glyph on Dalton's pinky ring showed that he'd achieved the rank of Magister Lex. Her equal now, though with a different focus. He could make life very difficult for her if she didn't play nice.

Dalton opened a briefcase and removed a flat, black-lacquered box. He slid an ornate bronze pin from the latch and held the box before her. Kate accepted it, surprised at its weight. Her face reflected in the shiny surface like a polished obsidian scrying mirror. Vegner watched her with passive intensity, his fingers laced before him as she set it onto the desk and carefully opened the lid.

An elaborate medallion of greenish gold rested inside atop burgundy velvet. A pale blue gem, as large as a quarter, crowned its center, nested in weaving bands of metal. The ceiling fluorescents hadn't even gleamed off its cut facets before Kate had determined there was no magic in it. But such news couldn't be delivered right away. Simply declaring it roused questions of competence. She had to at least *pretend* it was difficult to spot.

Gently, she lifted the amulet from its cushion, drawing the long chain from a hidden pocket. "Torban gold," she mumbled as if to herself. The artifact was definitely not of this realm. She couldn't identify the stone, but gemology had never been her forte. Most likely, it too came from Torba, but no different than any ordinary stone of its kind. Tiny glyphs ran the lengths of the golden ribbons, so small she could barely make them out. She opened her attaché and removed a folding loupe. Peering through the lens, she followed the intricate symbols around the gem, each one warping into full clarity under magnification before sliding away. The glyphs revealed this to be a ward, repelling elementals and lower hexes. The craftsmanship was superb, each tiny symbol crisp and precisely placed. Yet it didn't work. There had to be a
—*There!*

Hidden beneath the stone, she spotted a single symbol like a curved V, but the glyph was inverted. That one error, a half-millimeter engraving, had made an imperfect seal, allowing the power to escape.

"It's authentic," she said, closing the loupe, the trembling returning to her hands. "Torban, excellent quality, but..." She shook her head. "There's no magic in it."

"What?" Dalton laughed.

Vegner seemed unmoved.

"Claudio, she's mistaken."

"Are you mistaken, Miss Rossdale?" Vegner asked.

"No," Kate said.

Dalton huffed, still looking at Vegner. "Magus Eli Gregor learned the spell from that *very* amulet. That would be *impossible* if it wasn't enchanted."

Vegner opened his hand to Kate, asking for an explanation.

"I'm sure he did," she said. "It likely held the enchantment for years, but an imperfection in the spell's binding allowed it to escape. Slowly, like a pinhole in a parade float. But it's gone now."

The muscles in Dalton's jaw rippled. "Claudio, I assure you that the amulet is the real thing. You can't take this woman's word for truth. Her own Master died from her incomp—"

"Don't you speak of him," Kate growled, her face growing hot.

"Or what? You have no tower, no magic. Everyone knows that the once great Kate Rossdale, Magister Arcanus, is nothing but a worthless blood duster."

Kate shot to her feet, fist clenched, and attaché falling to the floor.

"That's enough," Vegner said, flicking his hand up. "Miss Rossdale, I'm satisfied with your findings. You've earned your fee. Thank you." These last two words were delivered in the same tone another man might say *fuck off*.

Kate opened her mouth, ready to tell Mr. Terrance Dalton exactly what he could do with his amulet, but stopped. *Not worth it.* She released a breath, rage cooling.

Dalton was grinning at her, the corners of his ugly-ass eyebrows upturned, obviously anxious for whatever she planned to say.

Forcing down her anger, she slid the spilled books back into her fallen attaché, scooped the vial and money off the desk, and shoved them into her purse. She'd earned this dust. "Thank you, Mr. Vegner."

"Good day, Miss Rossdale."

Dalton was glaring at her, an expression that said, *This isn't over*, but Kate was already moving toward the door.

"So, Mr. Dalton," Vegner was saying, "I'm no longer interested."

"Claudio, please."

"And it seems that you owe me two thousand dollars."

She shut the door behind her, missing whatever came next. The secretary, Jodie, looked up from her computer, a muted click closing what appeared to be a game screen. Heart still pounding, Kate gave her a perfunctory smile and made her way out of Vegner's office suite.

The mixture of anger, self-loathing, joy of cock-blocking Dalton's sale, and getting paid stoked her gnawing need for a fix. She stopped on the third floor and located a bathroom. There, tucked into a stall, she tamped a few of the tiny red crystals onto a compact mirror and crushed them under a credit card until they were a chalky pink. With the help of a rolled, fresh twenty-dollar bill, Kate snorted a bump up each nostril.

The blood dust burned, a sweet honey smell, undercut with roses and a bitter metallic tang. Warm tingles spread out from the space between her eyebrows, coursing down her veins with the electric hum of magic, a long-absent friend. She licked the last traces of powder off her mirror and card, her tongue going numb with the acrid taste she now loved. Her back popped as she rose from her seat, the tension fleeing her muscles with a dramatic crackle of vertebrae. She opened and closed her hands, sensing the unseen power arcing between her fingers. It wasn't more than what a simple Initiate wielded, but to her, it was a quenching river coursing through a desert. Teeth singing in their sockets, Kate emerged from the stall, the mounting high taking hold.

———

She forwent beating the traffic home, deciding instead to visit Whittaker's. The bar itself had operated for nearly two-hundred years, taking a short vacation under the name Lee's during the Prohibition Era. But that was only the front part. The upper floor, the *real* Whittaker's, had gone unchanged that entire time. It hadn't been a speakeasy. Those were secret with passphrases and hidden doors. The tavern had continued on with the absolute certainty that it was safe from discovery by anyone who didn't meet the qualifications. The businesses on either side had burned during the '68 Riots. The first floor had been looted, but even rioters hadn't braved the stairs. Probably never noticed them.

Still riding the buzz from her first bumps, their numbing taste dripping down her throat, Kate stepped inside. Giant mirrors, dingy with decades of cigarette smoke, covered two walls, making the narrow room appear far larger than it really was. No one had smoked here in years, but Kate always imagined the haze and stink of tobacco, a memory, but not hers. The bar's memory. A few people nursed their afternoon drinks, eyes transfixed on the televisions near the ceiling or on their phones. A pair of women in business attire whispered conspiratorially as they sipped colorful martinis. Kate nodded to the barman, a skinny guy she didn't recognize, strode to the back, down the narrow hall past the bathrooms, and headed upstairs.

The tingles started the moment she mounted the first step, like invisible spiders scuttling up her spine. The old wards hadn't faded with age, but Kate had never been able to determine where exactly they were hidden. There were eleven of them, but that was all she could tell.

The familiar smells of sage and old wood greeted her as she pushed open the door at the top of the stairs. A half-dozen patrons occupied the second floor—two at the bar, three chatting in the old wingbacks near a window, and Mr. Lacroix reading by himself in the same corner as always. He lifted his chins toward Kate in salutation and returned to his book.

"Well, what do we have here?" a woman with thick, tortoiseshell glasses and faded violet hair asked from behind the counter. "Long time, no see."

"Hey, Tisha." Kate slid onto one of the stools, resting her feet on the old brass bar rail. "Glenlivet. Double."

"Oh." Tisha cocked one eyebrow above the thick eyeglass frames. "Appears you intend to catch up for lost times."

Kate sniffed. "It's been a great day."

"Evidently." Tisha plucked the bottle from the shelf behind her and poured the drink. "So what have you been up to the last few months?"

"Whole lot of nothing." Kate dropped a twenty on the faded bar top, branded with a thousand interlocking rings from wet glasses. "How's it been here?"

"You know how it goes. More of the same. Few new faces wandered in. Few more forgot where the door was."

Kate sipped her scotch, the warmth blooming in her stomach like her temporary magic. Whittaker's was a haven, a magical sanctuary where deals were struck and contacts established, only noticeable to those receptive enough to see the stairs. Most were young, their minds still flexible and hungry. As age hardened their elasticity, many forgot about it or felt the discomfort that the wards emitted to those not attuned. The result was that a regular surge of youth kept the place from getting too stodgy. She'd wandered in herself on her twenty-first birthday, wide-eyed and desperate to learn. Much had changed in the seventeen years since.

Tisha leaned close. "Bit of rumblings in the Amber Tower, I hear."

"Really?"

"Mm-hmm. Too many chiefs. Sounds like they might actually split."

"They've been saying that for years. Master Boyer said it had been that way since he was an Initiate."

"Yeah, but they sound serious this time. Dissolution of the Onyx Tower pushed a lot of people under one roof."

Kate hid her frown behind another sip. Onyx hadn't dissolved. It had shattered, the leadership wiped out in a single night. She'd been one of the only two survivors of that failed excursion, and the blame landed squarely on her. It had been her Magus test, after all. Many reasoned her resulting disability was cosmic justice. Some went independent afterward. Others moved away, joining different towers. The rest had gone to Amber. It appeared the shockwaves from that night were still sounding. "Well, best luck to them. Who's their Ipsissimus?"

"No clue." Tisha glanced at the two men drinking at the edge of the bar and whispered, "There's about to be a lot of power shuffling. So you might want to keep your head low."

"They can't do more to me than has already been done."

"Believe it or not, girl, you've got a *lot* of influential friends in Amber that have kept you protected after everything. The next leadership might not be so forgiving."

Kate snorted. "Little late now."

Tisha cocked her head. "What's that mean?"

"Well." Kate lifted her glass before her. "You're talking to the girl that just humiliated Terrance Dalton and probably cost him two grand." She knocked it back.

"What?"

"True story." Kate coughed. She clacked the empty glass back onto the bar. "Just half an hour ago. Called him an asshole, too. It was great."

"Really?" Tisha asked, not seeming to appreciate the joy. "You show up after three months of hiding out, and the first thing you do is kick Dalton in the nuts?"

Kate shrugged. "It's my gift. I'll take another."

"How did this happen?" Tisha refilled the glass.

"I got a call from that collector, Vegner. He wanted me to authenticate some amulet. Ends up it was a piece Dalton was selling. Something that used to be Magus Gregor's. I told Vegner the amulet had no power. Words were exchanged. Now I'm here."

"So they're selling off Gregor's effects now?"

"It *has* been a year since anyone saw him," Kate said.

"You mean since the Spire got him."

Kate scratched her nose. "Doesn't have to be witch hunters. Maybe he just realized he was surrounded by assholes and ran off. Can't blame him." She turned to the wall of photos beside the bar, some so old they were printed on glass, their names long forgotten. Magus Elliot Gregor stood in the middle of a group shot on the upper right, probably taken in the seventies, judging by their hair and awful attire. She toasted the long-absent sorcerer.

Tisha rolled her eyes. "And the two grand?"

Kate sipped her drink. Maybe it was the blood dust, but the first glass was already taking effect. "That was my fee for ruining the sale. Sounded like Vegner was going to make Dalton pay for it."

Shaking her head, Tisha put the bottle away. "You know why he was selling Gregor's effects, right?"

"Pay for an eyebrow wax?"

"No," she said, her voice dropping to a whisper. "Because they're collecting money to fund a new tower. Now they have even less than they did before you came strutting in."

"It's not my fault he was selling a broken artifact." Kate sniffed again. "It was just a job."

"And where do you think their anger is going to..." Tisha leaned close, her magnified almond eyes peering into Kate's. "Why do you keep sniffing?"

"I'm not." Right on cue, she did it again, a Freudian sniff.

"Are you dusted?" Tisha hissed.

"What?" Kate laughed, too sharp to be believable, her smile forced.

"Your pupils. They're big as plates, and you're too damned happy for this conversation."

"Relax," Kate said. "I'm celebrating, and don't act like you've never enjoyed it."

"Don't you even try to pull that card with me. I've talked to you about this. Everyone already calls you a blood duster without you pissing off a tower and then strolling in here high."

Kate sighed, her gaze dropping to the scarred bar top. Christ, she'd just wanted a drink and her old friend. Why the hell was Tisha pissing on this? "Fine. I'm sorry. But I need this."

"Uh-huh."

"I'm serious. I need it. I don't give a shit about the rush or the buzz. I need it to feel the magic. Do you have any idea what it's like to lose that, to lose everything that I was? It's like...like I'm paralyzed, and every day I see joggers running past my window, ones I trained, and I can't even walk. I need it to feel human again."

Tisha's scowl softened a little at the corners, but her eyes remained hard, pinning Kate in that judging glare.

"I'm not like one of those mundies that learn a bit and leave. They're lucky. They forget about magic. I can't."

Tisha shook her head. "I don't like where this could take you. Remember Jess?" She pointed without looking at one picture on the wall. There, Jessica Chadwell, a hefty girl with straight black hair, sat grinning at a table beside Heather and Candace, their glasses lifted in an eternal toast, all of them now dead. "She used to justify it, too. Help her through the pain after Onyx."

Kate swallowed. Last time she'd seen Jess, the woman's skin had looked like tissue, mottled with yellow bruises, and that beautiful hair was coming out in clumps. Not that Jess had had to see that. The veins in her eyes had blown, leaving her blind. She'd died weighing under ninety pounds. "It's different," Kate said.

"How?"

"She did it to escape emotional pain. I'm not." Kate looked at her glass. Why would she bring up Jess? It was Kate's fault Onyx broke and that put Jess' fall on her too. "Look, oxygen gets people high. They have bars for it. But if you see some grandpa with an oxygen tank, you don't accuse them of being a junkie. I don't enjoy having to do this, but I need it. Please." She meant it. Every word. The smidge of magic it gave her was barely enough to levitate the glass to her hand, maybe light the Scotch on fire, but that would use it up. Truth was, knowing she could, that feeling of being a sorceress again, no matter for how brief a time, was worth the comedown.

It was near midnight before Kate left the haven. The amphetamine of the blood dust had made her a little horny, and she decided that it was best to extract herself from that situation before hormones and alcohol tricked her into making another regrettable decision. Keeping her promise to Tisha not to use in the bar, she managed to wait until after she'd left before tooting another bump behind a furniture store and then caught the bus back to Highlandtown.

There, in a ratty bus seat, watching the city lights glide past, the renewed drip began at the back of her throat. Kate sniffed.

A skinny woman with wild curls of dark hair looked up from across the aisle, a feral hunger beneath probing eyes.

Paranoid, Kate looked away, pretending to watch the streets. Sniffles outside of winter was like blood in the water for addicts. Might as well throw up a sign announcing, "I have drugs." *Probably shouldn't have taken that last hit*. She was going to be up all night now. *Might as well get some cleaning done*. Her tiny bit of magic could go into a charm. Nothing too powerful, but probably enough to cover the cost of the dust it took to make it.

But the idea of being alone didn't sound like fun. She still felt the itch. Maybe she could call Scott. He was about as dumb as rocks and about as mundie as they got, but he was always good as a distraction. He didn't know her past and didn't care.

Knowing it was a bad idea, she pulled the phone from her purse. Four missed calls. She'd put it on silent before her meeting with Vegner. Not that anyone called her, but if they were going to, it would have been then.

All of them were from a blocked number. No messages. Probably a collector.

Sighing, she turned the ringtone on and dropped the phone back into her bag, Scott forgotten.

Tisha's right. I need to get my shit straight.

Six blocks later, she exited the bus. The hungry-eyed woman stayed on, thank God, and with a pneumatic hiss the door shut, leaving Kate alone on the nighttime streets. Soft wind coursed down the trench between brick row houses. It stank of exhaust, soured garbage, and the faintest hint of burnt bread. Music thrummed from an open window, yelling voices from somewhere far away, and the rumble of tires on shitty asphalt. She barely registered all of this as she followed the sidewalk past slender trees.

A muffled rendition of Joan Jett's *Bad Reputation* erupted from her purse. She drew her phone.

Blocked number.

Shit. It was near midnight. Wasn't there some law against collectors calling so late? Kate pressed *Ignore*.

She turned right at a grease-caked dumpster and entered a narrow alley, just wide enough for a single car. During her time as Magister Arcanus in the Onyx Tower, she'd practically lived at Master Boyer's palatial Guilford home. Her final four months, preparing for the ultimately doomed test for Magus Viator, she'd made it official, commandeering one of the guest rooms. After the incident, and her funds dwindling far faster than she'd anticipated, Kate's current residence was a renovated basement. It didn't even have a number, and her mail simply went to Mrs. Cecilia Knorr, who rented the two-story house above. It was the sort of place for transients, former convicts, and those who had fallen between the cracks.

Her phone chimed with an incoming text. Not slowing her pace, she lifted the phone still in her hand.

Blocked Number. "*You're in danger.*"

2

COLLECTIONS

Kate froze, paranoia launching into overdrive. She glanced over her shoulder. The alley was empty. Danger? From who? Dalton? Surely he wasn't going to actually do anything.

She typed, "*Who is this?*" but deleted it. Dalton wouldn't do anything, nothing that could come back on him, but she wouldn't put crank calls beyond him. Kate replied, "*Wrong number,*" and dropped the phone back into her purse. *Asshole*.

Near the middle of the alley, she tucked behind a plastic trash can and descended the steps. Her phone chimed again as she unlocked her door.

"Leave me alone, dickhead," Kate mumbled, stepping inside. A faint pressure washed over her as she crossed the elemental ward she'd inscribed into the frame while dusted. If Dalton or anyone else were going to mess with her, they'd summon something to do it for them. She was safe here.

At least. that was her assumption until the wooden floor creaked behind her.

Kate whirled. A man, his face hidden beneath a tan stocking, lunged from the darkened living room. He swung a black-gloved fist. She tried to dodge but stumbled over the drying rack she used for slushy boots. The fist slammed between her shoulder blades, and Kate went down, keys and purse flying from her hands.

The attacker closed in. Kate stumbled to her knees, but a hand grabbed her hair, pulling her head up. Screaming, she twisted around as the man reared back, fist rising for another blow.

Kate wove her fingers in the air, drawing her power. With a loud, "Ka!" like a karate strike, she released the spell.

The man jolted back like he'd been kicked, lifting into the air before slamming into the closet door. Kate scrambled to her feet as he rose, anger blazing in his eyes.

Summoning the last of her power, Kate threw her hands out again. "Ka!"

His clothes fluttered as if hit with a summer breeze. He twisted his neck, eliciting a crackle of vertebrae. The last of her magic was spent. The man stood between her and the exit, so she ran deeper into the darkened apartment.

"Fucking bitch!" he screamed behind her.

Her foot kicked something hard, sending small objects clattering. The living room had been trashed—drawers dumped and cushions thrown about. Clomping footsteps pounded behind her. Kate rushed into the bathroom to her left, slammed the door, and locked it.

Panting, she flipped on the lights and looked around. The cabinet and towel closet were open, contents dumped into the tub and sink. A strip of square, glass bricks near the ceiling served as the window and couldn't open. There weren't any exits. She should have gone to the kitchen, grabbed a knife or a pot, something to defend herself. She'd used up all the blood dust's magic. Why in the hell had she cast a push? An emerald lance would have brought him down for good. What was she supposed to do now, fight him with a toothbrush and safety razor?

No. She wasn't helpless.

The door thudded.

Kate pulled open her attaché and found the worn Bible nestled between her other books. Dennis had given it to her after she'd been robbed fifteen years ago. Dennis, whose final screams still haunted her nightmares after the verl hounds had torn his jaw from his face.

The door thudded again, wood cracking.

Hands numb with adrenaline, Kate pulled the bible open, its cover held with an inset magnet.

A third blow and the bathroom door flew open, a splinter of wood sailing into the mirror. The masked man stood panting in the doorway, tall and lean, his hair smooshed smooth beneath the pantyhose hood.

Kate lifted the pistol from the hollowed book and pointed it at him.

The tiny .32 didn't even have sights. A "belly gun" Dennis had called it. The intruder's eyes widened as the light gleamed off the stainless barrel, but he didn't have time to escape before Kate fired.

The boom was deafening in the tiny bathroom. Its kick stung her hand.

Crying out, he dove into the shadows as Kate fired again and again.

Ears ringing, Kate blinked. A chipped hole in the white-enameled door frame showed that even at the close range, her shaking hands had caused at least one terrible miss. Pistol out front, she sidestepped to get a better look into the darkened apartment. Had she hit him? Had he left or was he hiding in the shadows?

"You better run, motherfucker," she called, her voice nowhere near as confident as she'd hoped. Her breaths were coming heavy to match her racing heart. The haze of gun smoke filled the small room with the smell of firecrackers. Pistol before her, she carefully stepped out into the living room.

She could barely see anything in the darkness, only shapes of black and gray. The front door was still closed, which meant he was still here. Had she locked it? No, not yet. Maybe she could get to it and get outside. Realizing she was a silhouette in the bathroom door, Kate stepped to the side and scanned the room again.

A faint scratching, like paper rubbing together, came from the left. Kate spun, the gun trained on the shadows. The vague form of her sofa dominated that half of the room. Removing one hand from the pistol, she slapped the wall beside her twice before finally finding the switch.

The lights flipped on, revealing the ruin of her apartment. Everything had been strewn about, even pictures removed from the walls. Their blankness emphasized the tiny bullet hole in the sheetrock. Another miss.

Three drops of bright, fresh blood speckled the worn floorboards. She'd managed to hit the asshole after all.

Just get to the door. Call for help.

Only thirty feet to the door, then up the steps. Should she stop for her purse? Yes. Her money was inside. That and the blood dust.

Drawing a breath, she bolted for the front door. Kate leaped over a pile of spilled books and veered around the coffee table. The door was close. She made it into the entrance hall, her eyes locked on the green leather purse. Movement shot to her right as she reached the foyer.

Crying out in surprise, Kate turned, the gun swinging. A hand seized her wrist. The pistol boomed, and a gloved fist smashed into the side of her head.

Dazed, she stumbled back Her shoulder slammed into the wall as she fell. Her vision cleared in time to see the fist coming down again but she knocked it aside. The man's weight pressed her to the floor. She screamed and kicked, but couldn't hit him. The hand clutching her wrist slammed it into the floor over and over, trying to knock the gun free. Kate gripped the pistol tight, and another blow caused her to squeeze the trigger. The slide raked painfully across the webbing below her thumb. She howled, and the next blow knocked the gun from her fingers.

Her attacker leaned close, his forearm across her chest crushing her down. His hot, stinking breath panted across her cheeks. Gritting her teeth, Kate slammed her head toward him, smashing his nose with her brow. She felt the cartilage crunch, and he screamed.

His grip loosened and Kate slithered partially out. She hit him atop his head. Blood spread across the stocking over his nose, but he didn't relent, his arm grasping for hers as she desperately slapped and punched as best she could. Gloved fingers pawed her neck, trying to grab hold.

Throwing her head back, Kate spied the metal drying rack. He must have sensed her intention, as his weight shifted, scrambling up toward her arm. Stretching her body beneath his bulk, Kate managed to wrap her fingers around one of the cast iron posts. She batted it down, slamming the rack into his arm.

He howled, and Kate drew back, readying to brain the bastard with the next swing.

The door flew open. A man rushed inside. "Stop!"

The man atop Kate froze, his masked eyes wide.

"Get off her," the newcomer said. "Now. Slowly."

The masked man released her as the newcomer backed away, a square, black pistol in hand as he closed the door behind him.

"Stay on your knees. Hands where I can see 'em." The newcomer looked to Kate still on the floor. She didn't recognize him. "Are you hurt?"

Kate blinked. It took a moment for her to realize the question was for her. "No." That was a lie. Her head hurt like hell, and her hand stung from where the slide had bitten it.

"Good. You can stand. Sit if you need a minute. But kick the gun toward me."

Eyes locked on the stranger's pistol, still pointed at her attacker, Kate scooted into a sitting position, her back against the wall. She still clutched the metal rack, but kicked the little .32 toward him with her toe. She'd lost a shoe in her fight but hadn't noticed.

"Take off your mask," the stranger ordered.

Grunting, the man on his knees reached up. Blood coated his lips and gathered on his chin in thick clumps. More blood covered his chest, spreading from a tiny hole above his right breast. He peeled the stocking from his face and glared up at the newcomer.

"Do you know this man, Miss Rossdale?" the newcomer asked.

Kate studied the man's face, trying to see past the bent nose and blood. Dirty blond hair, wide-set eyes. He looked maybe twenty-five. There was something familiar but... "No."

"All right. Slowly, and I mean *slowly*, take out your wallet. No sudden moves or I swear to God I'll kill you. There's enough evidence that I'll get away with it, too. So don't think I won't."

The man's sneer faltered, realization seeming to dawn. He winced as he carefully reached his right hand behind him and removed a brown leather billfold.

"Toss it to her," the newcomer said.

He flicked the wallet to Kate, who managed to catch it. Opening it one-handed, she found the Maryland driver's license. "Gerald Hippler." She knew that name. Jerry. He used to frequent Whittaker's, or at least back when she did. "Amber Tower?"

"Who sent you?" the newcomer asked.

Hippler didn't reply.

"Talk, asshole."

"Dalton." Hippler swallowed. "Dalton sent me."

A terrible weight settled in Kate's chest. Yeah, she'd pissed him off, but this? "Why?"

"Get his money back," Hippler said.

"Looks like you've earned a bullet for your trouble. Hold still." The stranger closed in. With his free hand, he patted Hippler down and peeled back his shirt. Hippler howled through bared teeth.

"Nuthin' but meat. Probably broken rib. You'll be fine if you get to a doctor soon." Right hand still on the pistol, the stranger stepped back and drew a phone from his pocket. He held it up and snapped Hippler's picture. "This is what you're going to do. You're going to drive away and get to a doctor. Don't recommend a hospital. Too many questions. Maybe your boss knows someone. Got it?"

Hippler nodded.

"Miss Rossdale, you want to hit this guy for good measure?"

"No," Kate said, a bit taken aback by the question.

"Okay." Pistol still trained, the man opened the door. "Now run along. Tell your boss that Miss Rossdale is off limits. She's protected."

Hippler didn't move for two full seconds, but another waggle from the stranger's gun sent him lurching to his feet and out the door.

The stranger shut it behind him and turned to Kate. "You planning to hit me with that?"

Kate eyed his gun, gauging her chances.

Not good.

She dropped it to the floor with a metallic thud.

He lifted the back of his shirt and slid the pistol into the waistband of expensive-looking jeans. "You sure you're all right?"

"Who are you?" Kate demanded, still gulping air.

"Name's Evan Derian. I'd been trying to get ahold of you all night."

"You were the one calling me?"

"That's right." Evan knelt and picked up Kate's tiny gun. "Seecamp. Good piece."

Kate stood up. She looked at Hippler's wallet in her hand and the pile of his effects on the floor. "How did you know he was after me?"

"My boss wants to hire you. He received word that someone was after you, so he sent me." Evan cleared the sixth and final round from her pistol and offered it back. Stern, honey-colored eyes regarded her from beneath dark brows. "Should've used hollow points. You're lucky it didn't jam."

She eyed the empty gun. "Your boss?"

"Richard Harcourt. He sent me to collect you."

Harcourt? Kate didn't recognize the name. "Collect me?"

"He wants to meet with you. We came from New York this morning."

"This isn't exactly a good time." She accepted the proffered gun.

"Do you have a car?"

"No."

"You can ride with me. Grab your things, unless of course, you want to talk to the police. Someone might have called about the shots."

Kate looked around the ruin of her apartment. What the hell was she supposed to say to the cops? Her gun wasn't even registered.

"Do you have a passport?" Evan asked.

"Yes."

"Bring it. If you accept the job, I'm not sure you'll want to return here."

Kate swallowed. Not return? If the cops weren't coming, she knew Dalton was going to try something else. It wasn't like she had much anyway, mostly some books and knickknacks. Her furnishings she'd carefully selected from resale shops and junk people had thrown out. A job meant money. Money meant she could get out of town. So what if she didn't know this guy? He'd just saved her a beating, or at least tried to. She nodded. "Just give me a minute."

"Be quick."

3

QUID PRO QUO

Evan tossed Hippler's wallet into the dumpster as he led Kate around to a black BMW. The vehicle was clean, luxurious with its leather seats and burl wood trim. A sticker in the corner of the windshield indicated that it was a rental.

As they followed Eastern Avenue toward the giant buildings of downtown, the shock and fear from her attack finally swooped in like some nocturnal raptor. Heightened by the blood dust in her system, Kate's hands began shaking. Gooseflesh pimpled up her arms.

"Are you all right?" Evan asked.

"Fine." Balling her fists, she turned her attention to the window. *You'll be okay*, she thought, without believing it. The Amber Tower had sent someone after her—to rob her, beat her, maybe worse. And what the fuck was she doing? She didn't know anything about this man whose rental she was now in or this Mr. Harcourt who had come from New York with a bodyguard.

They rode in silence for the next fifteen minutes before pulling up to the Four Seasons. A valet quickly took the car away, and Kate followed Evan into the lobby. She felt critical eyes, real or imagined, crawling across her as they passed through the polished lobby. Her makeup was a catastrophe, and her hair looked every bit like she'd been out drinking and in a brawl. She noticed several drops of Hippler's drying blood on her sleeve and covered it with a hand. Afraid to see those knowing stares, she kept her eyes forward as they crossed to the elevators. Evan pressed the button for the seventeenth floor.

The corner penthouse smelled of fresh-cut lilies from a red glass vase and the coffee brewing from the kitchen. Tiny boat lights glided across the harbor below, its shores lined with docks and overpriced apartment buildings. Kate watched a crowded party barge glowing with Christmas lights and wished she could tuck away long enough for a fix. She needed a bump, a fresh shot of magic, but after the night's excitement, she wanted more than just that. She needed a full rail, but this wasn't the time. Business first. To go and sneak a fix would make her the junkie they said she was. Evan had disappeared into a side room once they'd arrived, leaving her alone. It was now the second time in one day she'd waited in a high-rise for a wealthy client.

She eyed the polished copper disk affixed to the window frame, its surface stamped with geometric patterns. A Red Gate, it was called—not the best ward, but portable. She'd felt the one at the door when she'd entered the room, a subtle pressure change as she'd crossed the barrier. That one was stuck to the upper left corner of the suite's door like a glued penny. Another icon hung beneath an air vent. If each entrance to the suite was marked, and Kate suspected they probably were, then they were protected from weaker elementals and all but the most capable scryer's eyes.

"Miss Rossdale," a man said, emerging from a bedroom's double door. He wore shiny gray slacks and a white dress shirt with a subtle striped pattern. His gray hair appeared to have been brown once and formed a sharp widow's peak. He was short for a man, looking her eye to eye. "Richard Harcourt." He extended a hand with a gnarled burn scar along the index finger.

She shook it. "Pleasure to meet you."

Harcourt smiled, revealing very small and very white teeth. "Might I offer you a drink?"

Kate knew she shouldn't. She'd already had quite a bit at Whittaker's and was still deep in the throes of an amphetamine rush. But after the night she'd had... "Please."

"Scotch. Am I right?" Harcourt asked, turning to a small wet bar.

"Yes," she said, then wondered how he knew that.

He removed a bottle of Johnnie Walker Blue from a cabinet and poured two fingers into a tumbler. "I hope this is to your satisfaction," he said, extending it to her.

"Thank you." The glass was heavy. Crystal. Expensive whiskey, expensive glass, five-star hotel, Bimmer—posturing. Either Harcourt was truly richer than God, or he felt some need to impress her. She sipped the drink, hoping his need would continue.

Harcourt gestured to a thick chair upholstered in golden brocade with a pattern something like bamboo. "Have a seat, please." He waited until she'd taken it before lowering himself onto a sofa opposite the glass coffee table. A slim briefcase rested on one side, the tabs of its twin chrome locks inset with mother of pearl. "It's a pleasure to meet you finally."

"Thank you," she repeated, unsure what else to say.

"Katherine Rossdale. Thirty-eight. Born in Maryland," Harcourt said as though delivering the opening to a eulogy. "Magus Viator to the late Onyx Tower. Reputable certifier of rare exotica. Sorceress without magic."

Kate forced a smile. "The one and only. Although, I never achieved Magus. I was only a Magister Arcanus."

Harcourt lifted his brows. His blue-gray eyes sparkled with a knowing mischief. "Perhaps I was misinformed."

"Sorry to disappoint." She sipped her drink again, its burn a fine simulacrum of the one she felt. For Harcourt to know so much about her and miss her final rank seemed unlikely. A more plausible answer was that he intentionally said the error to test if she'd correct him, even to her disfavor. After years of study, that failed final test for Magus had been Onyx Tower's downfall. That was hardly a secret.

"No matter. By your reputation, I gather you're more than capable for what I need." He rolled the combinations on the briefcase and popped the latch. "I'd like you to look at this."

"Before I do, there is the matter of payment. My consultation fee is upfront. No freebies or tests. No exceptions."

Harcourt opened the case, toward him, preventing her from seeing inside. "Quid pro quo?"

"You got it. Let's just say a bad experience made that rule rigid."

Harcourt smiled. He ran his thumb along his scarred finger. "And no credit for rescuing you? What was that worth?"

Kate blinked. Shit. This was going off script. "I guess that might—"

He waved it off. "It doesn't matter. This isn't the job. I'm well aware what it is." He removed a white cloth bundle from the case and unwrapped it to reveal a slender book, its leather surface mottled with stains and scars. "Please," he said, sliding it toward her. "Look it over. You need not comment on its authenticity if you don't wish, but I believe you'll find it most interesting."

Kate eyed the relic a full three seconds before setting her glass down. It wasn't a book as much as a hard-backed folder, the spine elaborately stitched and woven with green thread like the handle of a Japanese sword. The cover was blank, save a blotchy water stain and a glued rent along the upper edge. As she reached to pick it up, the faint tingle of energy skittered along her palm. Yes, this was magic.

She turned it over in her hand, inspecting it. The book was old. Centuries. Sixteenth, possibly fifteenth. She couldn't tell if it was Outer World or not, but suspected it wasn't. Not that sixteenth century was any less her world than Dhevin or any of the others.

Carefully, she opened the binding. Eight vellum sheets were stitched inside. Intricate symbols in lustrous gold and blue decorated the first page. The vibrant zaffre ink held a faint shimmer, some non-color that seemed strangely familiar like a half-remembered dream. While the pages themselves were of this realm, that ink definitely wasn't. Torba, most likely. The Latin text was crisp, each black letter framed with white, showing the scribe had gone over each at least twice with different inks. She turned a page, finding more symbols, the diagrams for casting a circle, the intricate glyph of a Magister Lex, four circles interlocking three squares within a triangle—the lowest rank capable of casting such a spell. But a supremely competent Magus Arcanus might suffice. The spell appeared simple enough, though absolute perfection was required in the circle and preparation.

Kate's hands began trembling as she read the spell's purpose. She flipped the page, a strange, nameless joy and terror roiling in her guts. Her numbing fingers threatened to drop it onto the table. "What is this?"

"I believe you can see that for yourself," Harcourt said.

She re-read it, her mouth going dry. "*Consana Maledictus*. Restoration of the Accursed."

"It is. But more importantly, Miss Rossdale, *this*," he gestured to the book, "is your offered payment. Complete restoration of your magical abilities."

Kate swallowed. "But... I'm not cursed."

"No? Your affliction appears to match the curse this one remedies."

"But no one cast a curse. It was just a...mistake that caused it."

"Hmm. Tell me, in your vast studies, have you ever heard of a sorcerer accidentally losing the ability to harness magic? It's not something you simply lose. You're tapping into reserves within you or in the world. Something is obstructing your access to it. A blockage."

"I agree, but what I'm saying is that no one cast a curse on me. It just happened. It's what we call a *unique* situation."

Harcourt leaned back into his seat, thumb stroking his scar. "When it occurred, did you experience a flash of color? Not just visible, but all your senses, taste, smell, etcetera?"

Kate looked back on that terrible memory of when the circle tore. Not the memories of the screams and blood, and the verl hound's snarls, but just before that. Her stomach clenched. There had been something, an explosion, blinding and deafening her for an eternal instant. "Yes."

"Was it," his gaze fell toward the book, "blue, perhaps?"

Kate looked at the blue ink, now recognizing that scintillant non-color. Her life had shattered with that color. It had been the entire world, her only sensations for two, maybe three agonizing seconds, and when it faded from her eyes and tongue, she'd witnessed the horror. Her words lost, Kate felt herself nod.

"Three years ago, someone cursed you, Miss Rossdale."

"Who? Why?"

"Ah," he said, raising a finger. "Quid pro quo. I'll answer your questions to the best of my abilities, but my initial offer is *that*." The finger dropped toward the book like a knight's lance. "Do you want to be cured?"

"Yes. But why would—"

Harcourt tutted. "One at a time. Like yourself, I want payment upfront."

Kate looked at the book again. The offset of the elaborate border told her that the pages had been torn out of something else. Stitched and preserved in new bindings. Whoever owned the rest of that book, the part with the curse, might have been the very one who'd afflicted her. All the deaths and the pain, the burden of guilt she'd carried, came crashing down in an avalanche as anger erupted from beneath it. It wasn't her fault. Someone had to pay. She set the book down and finished her Scotch. The insistent itching of those imaginary fleas danced along her scalp, screaming for a bump. "What do you want me to do?"

"Nothing you're capable of at the moment. First, we have to remove this enchantment. Would you care for another drink?"

"*Please.*"

Harcourt carried her glass to the bar and refilled it. Evan slipped out from the back room, exchanging a momentary glance with his boss. The old man nodded, the clandestine message received. He returned to his seat with Kate's refreshed drink and a tumbler for himself. Evan took a seat on the far couch.

Kate accepted the glass. "So when do we start?" she asked with the most professional smile she could muster. If there'd ever been a job she'd needed, *this* was it—the Big One, and here she was, stinking of booze, her makeup a ruin, and a man's blood on her clothes. *Just keep smiling.*

"As soon as we find someone who can remove that spell."

"You can't?" Her smile faltered.

"Me?" The old man chuckled, shaking his head. "Oh no. Unfortunately, I didn't begin exploring the Art with any sincerity until much later in life. Until now, my interest has been purely academic. If you were to test my circles and squares, I'd rate no higher than an Adeptus at most. I'm self-taught, so I have no tower allegiance."

Kate nodded. She'd assumed the old man a sorcerer. He carried himself like a Magus, but perhaps money had given him that specific breed of confidence. "Do you have anyone in mind?"

"That's a question best suited for you. You're the one who has to endure it. Do you have any suggestions, a Magister Lex you can trust entirely and without any relation to the Amber Tower?"

Shit. A Magister Lex that didn't hate her or hold her personally responsible for Master Boyer's death? That was a short list. "Jim Stevens."

Harcourt lifted his brow into a knowing question. "He was in Onyx?"

"Yeah. He was there when it happened. We haven't spoken in about a year, but I trust him and he's very capable."

"Where can we find him?"

"He'd moved to Scotland last I heard. Edinburgh. I can shoot him an email, see if he's up for it."

"Good. I'll arrange the flight."

"Well, let me talk to him first."

"Is he the only one you know who can do it?" Harcourt asked.

"Yeah."

"He must do it in person. And I think it'd be safer if we leave Baltimore, don't you?"

"But what if he's not there?" Kate asked, scratching her neck. "He might be on vacation or something."

"Then we'll wait for him in Edinburgh. The sooner we get you healed, the sooner you can begin your job."

"But you haven't told me what it is."

"Does it matter?"

Unable to answer, Kate swallowed a healthy gulp of the rich man's Scotch. How did he know about her curse? A curse no one else had ever heard of, and where the hell did a non-practitioner get a book like this?

Harcourt must have taken that as a no. He rose. "In the meantime, Evan has secured you a room here. I'm sure you are exhausted after today. Rest up, Miss Rossdale. Tomorrow will be a long day."

4

CRUISING SPEED

Kate shoved her coffee into Evan's hand as she wrestled with the pillow and plastic-wrapped airline blanket that had been occupying her chair. Where the hell was the seatbelt? She got back up, kicking the blanket onto the floor, and fished the strap out from under her. The other first class passengers shot amused grins at her obvious frustration, while the grumbling line pushed through the doorway behind her, shuffling their way toward coach. She clicked herself into place.

"You seem..." Evan coughed. "...off. You all right?"

Kate took her coffee from his hand. "I told you, I'm just tired."

He'd first voiced his concern that morning when he'd come to fetch her from her room.

After last night's meeting, the first order of business, once she was alone, had been snorting a healthy line of blood dust off the marble bathroom counter. While a small part of her *definitely* wanted the rush, she'd needed the magic more.

Once the buzz was good and strong, she'd drawn a concealment circle. Terrance Dalton had come after her, and she had no reason to think he'd stop. And while she was militant about disposing of any hair left in her brush or drain, there was no way to get it all. If he got his hands on some, he could find her, send another crony, or even an elemental. Kate had to hide, and without the time or magic to ward every single opening into her room, the ring would have to do. Hotel carpet wasn't the most accommodating surface for such things. Wood or tile were better for drawing circles, so she'd used the bathroom floor, inscribing as large a ring as she could with a piece of orange chalk from her bag. Years of use had made Kate skilled at drawing every bit of power from the dust, easily five times as much as she could when she'd first started taking it. Even then, she required a bump to finish it off. Once done, and still jacked up on the drug's rush, she fetaly curled into the cramped ring and lay awake on the hard floor. She'd finally nodded off some time after 6:00 a.m.

Memories of verl hounds plagued her dreams, their crystalline fangs stained with her tower mates' blood.

Evan woke her at 7:20.

Breakfast had been a laborious affair as she shuffled food across her plate. It was probably the nicest meal she'd had in months, but the dust had left her taste buds numb and with no desire for food at all. She'd killed three espressos while forcing herself to eat just enough tasteless sausage and potatoes to maintain life function.

Evan barely spoke their entire time in the hotel restaurant. He sat straight, alert, aware of newcomers, corners, windows. A cold predator awareness of everything at once, his mind filing it all away like a busy secretary.

Once back in Harcourt's suite, he told her that they had a flight booked for Scotland that night. "You can't bring your gun," he'd said. "But give it to me. I can arrange for it to arrive shortly after, or secure a replacement."

"It was a gift," she said, reluctant to part with the tiny pistol that had saved her life.

"I'll make sure it's safe," Harcourt said. "But it does us no good if Customs confiscates it. Trust me."

She didn't. But as with this whole arrangement, she didn't have much choice.

What followed was a whirlwind of shopping. New clothes, new shoes, and bags to hold them.

Harcourt had suggested that Kate change her hair, maybe dye it. Kate had no intention of changing her color. She loved her natural auburn and figured it would blend well in Scotland. But she did agree to a much-needed cut. The tutting stylist transformed her home-made Bettie Page into a nice wedge cut. The sudden lack of weight and hair on her neck felt weird, and she kept rolling her head and brushing her fingers through it just to feel the difference.

All too soon were the crowds and stink of BWI Airport—a miasma of many foreign smells mixed with frustration and fast food. It swept past like some dream set on fast-forward. Exhaustion was kicking in, as were the distant rumblings of the imminent comedown headache. A pair of overworked baristas in hijabs manned the bustling coffee kiosk. They looked more ragged than she did. Kate snagged a double-shot latte and had only nursed a few sips before boarding. Harcourt had taken his seat three rows ahead, saying that there weren't enough spaces at this last minute to seat them all together.

"What are you on?" Evan whispered.

Kate blinked, her attention snapping back to the present. "On?"

His goldie-brown eyes met hers. He leaned closer. "On. You're fidgeting. Sniffles. Looks like you're coming down. Was it coke? Crystal?"

"No." She suppressed a grin at *crystal*. No, her crystals weren't meth. She scanned the shuffling passengers for eavesdroppers. "Nothing like that."

"Something like that. Noticed it last night, before we got to the hotel. This morning you still looked a bit jacked. You made it through security, so I assume you're clean."

She lowered her voice even more. "It's nothing illegal."

"So what was it?"

Kate swallowed back a swig of her latte. "It's called blood dust."

He lifted his dark brows. "Never heard of it. One of those bathsalt drugs? Call it something else so the feds can't nail it?"

"No, not at all. It's used to boost magic, push the caster beyond their abilities. Gives an edge, even increases their threshold over time. The... other effects are more a side-effect than anything." At least that's how it was for her at any rate.

Evan grunted. "I don't like drugs."

"Me either," she said, a defensive edge sliding into her tone. "Not the bad ones."

His forehead crinkled with his arching brows. It was kind of cute.

"If I was looking to get off I'd go for something else. Dust is half as fun as blow and three times as much."

Evan's stare continued boring into her, making Kate want to look away. "And it's that expensive because it gives magic?"

She nodded. "That and accessibility. It's not from this world. Either a Magus Lex has to make it, or they have to import it across the Abyss, which inflates the price."

The corners of his lips curved down, his eyes going momentarily blank as if he were trying to understand.

Kate narrowed her eyes. "How long have you two been together? You and Harcourt, I mean." Her initial assumption had been that he was Harcourt's apprentice. But after the old man had confessed that he wasn't a practitioner she'd been too caught up in the revelations. Someone had cursed her, murdering Master Boyer, Dennis, Candace, Heather, and causing Onyx Tower's downfall and its blame on her. She hadn't had time to consider Evan's experience in the Art.

Evan's gaze darted toward the front, Harcourt's head invisible behind the high seatback. "I met him a year ago, but I didn't start working for him until last month."

"You're not a practitioner," she stated, the realization clicking through the fog of exhaustion.

He shook his head, confirming her suspicions.

A flood of new questions swirled through her mind, so many at once that she had to struggle to find a single one. How had Harcourt known about the book and the curse? Why was Evan even here? Why were they together? Had Harcourt hired a mundie? She knew nothing about these people who had saved her and were now flying her across the world on their dime.

"So..." she started, not entirely sure how to phrase it,"...what is it you know? About the Art, I mean?"

He shrugged. "Not much. When I was in Afghanistan, I saw something. Made me question everything. When I got back, I started looking into it. Learned a little here and there. Impossible to tell what was real or bullshit. Learned of wizards and these towers all around us. Then I found Richard, or he found me, and he hired me on."

"What did you see?"

Evan scanned the aisle. Most of the passengers were already seated, the buzz of a hundred whispered conversations an unintelligible white noise. "We were running a convoy through Nangarhar. I was way in the back. Couldn't see much, but I felt it when the gun truck in front of us blew." His roving eyes faltered, losing focus. "We filed out. Black smoke and dust everywhere. But in the middle of it all...there was this dude just standing there, completely on fire. No clothes. No nothing. Just...fire." He licked his lips, gaze locking onto some distant memory. "I saw him walk straight to our Humvee. No one even tried to put him out. Too freaked out. They said shrapnel must have hit our fuel line or something because when he got to it, it exploded, too. But that's not what I saw. To me, it looked like he walked through it like it just wasn't there. Half-way through the engine, it exploded all around him." Evan's right hand tightened into a fist, his left one sliding protectively over it. "No one ever found him or confirmed which grunt it was. Said he was vaporized by the blast. But I know what I saw."

Kate nodded. She'd heard that the Art had been employed by the Noqra Tower before its fall, lashing at all sides, the spastic kicking of a dying thing, uncaring of who it hurt.

"Fire elemental," Evan added with a bitter grin.

Kate didn't feel like correcting him. A vulcanus, or salamander as they were often called, was something more, far more than a simple elemental. They were sentient. "I'm sorry," she managed.

Evan's chin dipped, his version of a nod. "It's nice to have someone believe me."

"I can imagine it's been hard."

A handsome male flight attendant with charcoal skin and large eyes stepped into view. "May I bring you a drink?"

Kate knew she shouldn't. She should be getting sleep as soon as possible and not adding more chemicals to her body. But some booze might help her sleep better. Besides, it was free, and that was her preferred price. "Whiskey and Coke, please."

The attendant nodded. "And you, sir?"

"Just water."

"Very good." With a flash of very white teeth, the attendant was gone.

Kate downed the rest of her coffee and traded the returning attendant her empty paper cup for a full plastic one. They sat in silence as the plane began its slow taxi toward the runway.

"You said Harcourt found you," Kate said, trying to keep her tone conversational. "How?"

Evan shrugged. His eyes averted for just a moment. "It's what he does."

"Yeah, but how? Did he just walk up and say, *Hi, you want a job?*"

He smiled, a flash of perfect teeth. "Pretty much. But he'll have to explain." He turned his attention to the screen mounted in the seatback before him, ending that line of questions. Finally, he said, "I do have one question."

Just one? Three years as a Lumitor followed by her final four as Magister were spent teaching Neophytes and Initiates, learning infinite patience in the process. She adapted her warm *teacher's smile*. "Of course."

"Why call them towers? Like, are there actual towers?"

"No, at least not anymore. Used to be, there were. India had quite a few, and the Italians loved them. But now it's just a name for a coven. Sort of how..." She was about to say Masons, but remembered her audience, "... VFW lodges aren't actual lodges. They could be, but they're all called that."

He nodded, seeming to accept that. "So, there's no tower made of amber?"

"Sorry to disappoint. Amber Tower is really the upper two floors of a building in Mount Vernon. Very impressive, I hear, but I've never been inside. My tower, Onyx, was an old house up in Guilford."

"And who runs them?"

Kate sipped her drink. She coughed a little, not expecting the burn. They hadn't skimped on the whiskey. She glanced again, making sure the cough hadn't brought anyone's attention. No one was watching. "A council of Magi, those who have achieved the rank of Magus. There's often, but not always, an Ipsissimus, one who's achieved the highest level. No one knows who the Ipsissimus is outside the Magi, but it's not hard to figure out. Just pay attention to who the Magi follow."

"But they don't always have one?"

"No. It's very uncommon for someone to ascend to that rank. One is required to form a new tower and to declare war on another. But they're so rare that if your Ipsissimus dies, the tower just keeps going."

He frowned. "Is a Magus the same as a Magister? Harcourt called that Dalton guy a Magister Lex."

Kate let out an unintentional sigh. Master Boyer would have scolded her for that one. To show irritation at questions only encouraged ignorance. She hid the self-beratement behind another sip. *Jesus, Harcourt didn't tell you anything.* "Okay. There are seven ranks to the Art, the Seven-Fold Path. Neophytes and Initiates are the lowest. Most people can't pass beyond those no matter how much they try. They have some power, but not much. Then you get to your more experienced ranks: Adeptus and then Lumitor. They have the innate power, but also a good deal of training in order to harness it. They can shift energy or cast small charms. At the fifth level, Magister, the student begins one of two paths. There's Lex, which are...more rigid. Rules-based. They follow a set path. Then you have Arcanus. They're more free-form."

"What does that mean?" Evan asked.

"Leges are more focused on healing and ceremony. They make the best charms because they're the most precise. Arcani are more unpredictable. They're more offense than defense," she said, the long-recited lesson plan coming back to her.

"So, they have to choose which path to take?"

"The path chooses them more than they choose the path. That make sense?"

He nodded, but those golden eyes didn't seem to believe it.

"After Magister, you become a Magus. Leges continue on a straight line to the end, but a few Arcani split off into a third branch, which is Viator."

"And that's what you were?"

"That's what I was trying to be," she corrected, a bitter pang in her voice. "Viatores are the rarest form. Their power comes from the Abyss, the world between worlds. They're the only ones who can pass through the veil." She pushed on before he could ask her to elaborate. "After Magus, you get the Ipsissima, which as we discussed, are the grand poobahs of perfection."

Evan's lips tightened as if he were about to ask more, but simply bobbed his head. Kate needed to get him alone and figure out who this Harcourt was. The old man knew too much to be a simple mundie. Maybe Jim knew something. He hadn't responded to her email, which when she'd reread it after breakfast had looked more like drug-fueled ramblings than she'd wanted. There were just so many things she had to say, and they sort of all poured out in her message.

The engines revved, and Kate's body pressed into the seat with the rush of acceleration. By the time they'd reached cruising speed, she was fast asleep, half-finished drink in her hand.

5

COME DOWN

As the Boeing Triple-Seven soared across the Atlantic, Kate dreamed. Not even the white noise hum of the engines penetrated the memories replaying through her unconscious mind.

"Take your time, Kate," Master Boyer says. His normally piercing eyes have softened with the joy of their successful arrival, and hadn't waned in their five hours on Hollit. He idly winds the antique watch on his wrist. "We want to get back in one piece for your ceremony."

Candace and Heather stand off to one side of the carefully drawn circle, their yellow robes fluttering in the warm breeze as they inspect the baubles they'd acquired at the Arin Market. Jim is crouched on the opposite side, watching the twin moons rise above the distant mountains, visible beyond the stone pavilion.

Dennis whispers beside her, his voice so low she can barely hear it. "Don't worry."

Kate blows into the bronze brazier. The coals glow pale orange, the hints of flame dancing between their jagged edges.

"You got this," Dennis assures.

She focuses her energy into the bowl, her right hand weaving the intricate pattern. Distorted filaments of light lace with each finger stroke, forming a glyph. As she releases it, Kate drops a muslin bag of powder onto the hot embers.

A rainbow of sputtering sparks dance and arc across the coals, spilling onto the green jade floor. Smoke twists and rises in a straight column and mushrooms out a dozen feet above their heads as if striking an invisible ceiling. Cinnamon and the smell of rain flavor the air as the smoke descends around them, forming a large bubble within the fifteen-foot ring. The chalked symbols along the edges shimmer with silvery light. Kate blows again into the now multi-colored flames, expelling every bit of her energy into the breath. Deep inside, a mesmerizing blue outshines all the other colors and then fades.

Spent, she looks up, her eyes watering from the smoke.

The moonlight and electric lamps outside the ring dim, or maybe the brazier's light has overtaken them, she can't tell for certain. Blinking away tears, she sees that yes, the light beyond the wall is fading, the grand pavilion with its spiral pillars is no more than a vague form on all sides.

"Yes," Master Boyer says, the pride in his voice making Kate's chest swell. "You've done it. First try. It only took me three attempts, but you're a natural."

Blackness swells around them, not solid, but the swirling, liquid mist of aether. Kate's gaze falls to the floor, now an insubstantial mirror—a black disk, its only solidity being the intricately drawn glyphs and ring forming their vessel through this infinite space.

The travelers laugh and cheer at Kate's triumph. A new Magus Viator has been christened, or will be once they return. Less than thirty exist in the world, and Onyx now has two. Of the four known Ipsissimus Viatores in all the world, Master Boyer will now rule the most powerful tower in over a hundred years. Three Viatores in a single tower, two Magi, and an Ipsissimus. The deepest unknown regions of the multiverse will be theirs to explore.

"We're equals now," Dennis says, his arm around her in a comradic embrace. "I knew what you were the first day I saw you."

Kate licks her lips, swallowing away the sudden urge to cry. "Thank you." She shivers against the chill worming its way through the ring. She'll need to work on that.

Within minutes they're all huddled near the brazier, its heat chasing the prickling goose flesh from her thighs.

"I can't wait to get out of this thing," Candace says, her arms hugging across her, hands hidden beneath the bell sleeves of her robe. The dark shape of a hardened nipple presses against the thin fabric. Kate's eyes instinctively avert. They've all seen one another nude. Many times. But there is nothing sexual about that. It's simply the way of towers. Etiquette is to never stare.

"Ditto," Jim says, briskly rubbing his forearms.

Vague forms float past in the misty aether, some as small as cats, others like jagged misshapen skyscrapers.

Master Boyer points out features on the infant worlds, taking everyone's mind off the cold. He never runs out of stories.

A distant cry pierces the eerie silence, like the scream of some strange animal. Kate's head snaps to attention as all their conversations cease. She scans the aether, her palms now sweaty and tightened into fists.

"Nothing to fear," Master Boyer says, his voice calm. "It can't smell us."

Another shrieking howl answers the first.

They float in silence for a long time. Kate can't remember, but it feels like hours. The steady drain of her magic holding the circle makes her lightheaded. Had it been this bad on the initial trip to Hollit? She wants to sit but doesn't want to appear weak.

"Well, that killed the mood," Jim says. Everyone chuckles, the tension shattered.

Kate begins laughing. She doesn't know why. The joke wasn't that funny, but she can't stop herself.

"I don't know about you," Heather says, tightening her crossed arms, "but I plan on raiding the brandy the moment we return."

"Damn right," Jim says, giving Master Boyer a sidelong glance. "This calls for the good stuff."

Master Boyer's mustache lifts into a smile. "That it does."

"How 'bout you, Candy?" Jim asks Candace beside him, staring into the warm coals, her hands tucked into her silk sleeves.

Candace's mouth tightens into a forced smile. "Sounds like a plan."

Another cry pierces the blackness, followed by a howl from somewhere else. The fear comes flooding back as Kate searches the aether, unable to tell where it came from. Were they closer?

A squirming mass shuffles past, a writhing giant worm with human faces on either end. Kate stares at the elemental, but the creature appears indifferent or fails to notice them. She releases her breath as is fades again into the swirling black.

A new howl rings behind them, like a child's scream.

"It's getting closer," Heather says, wheeling to face it.

"Relax." Master Boyer sets a hand on her shoulder. "We're completely safe. Just a wandering pack. One time, when I was—"

Two more shriek on either side, one more animal than human.

A wet snuffling sounds somewhere behind them, like a bloodhound on a trail. Kate looks back, searching for but not wanting to see the verl hound.

Nothingness.

"Kate, if you wouldn't mind speeding it up," Master Boyer says, still calm, but the tension in his shoulders says otherwise. "I think we need to get home."

Clenching her teeth, Kate pushes more energy into the smoldering brazier. She motions her fingers, weaving a focus, and the coals brighten.

Dennis removes a bundle of dried asafetida grass from his bag.

More sniffing comes from around them, followed by barks and yips, sounding like madmen believing themselves dogs. They grow closer, the pack converging.

Kate weaves the spell faster, the lines glowing with tracers in the air. She peers into the flames, imagining home. Smoke pours from the bronze bowl, and she holds her breath, fearing she might cough and break the spell.

Tall shapes grow beyond the circle's edges, closing in. Not hounds or elementals, but walls. Ghostlike planks form beneath her feet, the polished floor of the ceremonial chamber. Lights swell from the thinning aether, and Kate can see the lamps against the far walls.

The hounds scream in fury, but it's too late. They're almost there, each heartbeat bringing the world to more solidity. The aetheric forms dissolve, giving way for the real world, but Kate notices one shape, like a human silhouette standing in the far shadows beside the bookcases. *Is it real?* she wonders. *Maybe one of the initiates waiting for us.* She squints to see if it was aether, but then a screaming roar sounds behind her.

Brilliant blue light explodes around her, through her. Deafened, she screams, but only blue escapes her lips.

Kate snapped awake, her seatbelt digging into her lap. Before her, a tiny screen showed a cartoon airplane following a yellow path above a digital city. Red and gold beams of morning light shone through the half-opened blinds, piercing the dim cabin. A hint of lavender-tinged air.

"You okay?" Evan asked beside her.

Kate blinked, the last traces of the dream fleeing away. Her head pounded like it was being crushed in a vise, the throbbing pain stabbing into the backs of her eyes. She nodded. "Yeah."

"Nightmare?"

She nodded again. Her mouth felt dry like it had been sprayed with some gritty film. She could taste her breath. The comedown had arrived. "I need to use the restroom," she croaked.

"Sorry. We've begun the descent. We're landing."

"Already?" she squinted at one of the half-shaded windows, hoping to see London, but couldn't see anything past the blinding light. Her bladder ached at the denial of relief.

"You've been asleep seven hours."

Kate shuffled through Customs like a zombie, staring down at her shoes most of the way because her eyes were still killing her. After emptying what felt like her bodyweight in piss, she gulped down a few glorious mouthfuls of cold water from a fountain. It did little to satisfy her growling stomach as her body reminded her that she'd barely eaten in the last twenty-four hours.

She needed a cup of coffee with like a million sugars, but more than anything, she couldn't stop obsessing about the insane desire for more dust. Just one bump. One bump would wash away the headache, stabbing stomach, and the itching fleas at the back of her skull. One bump would replenish the little magic that had seeped out since her last hit, her own pinhole. For most, the extra magic faded far faster, their ample stores overflowing, but nothing was permanent. One little bump would get her back on her feet.

But she couldn't. She wasn't a junkie with patchy hair and eyes red with hemorrhaged veins. She knew she wasn't because she could deny herself the tempting crystals buried in her bag. At least she could until after dinner...or breakfast or whatever you called this next meal. Kate needed food and time to recover before her next dose. Soon she'd have her own magic again, but until then she needed a bit more dust to keep her stores up.

As they wove deeper into the labyrinth of rope barricades leading to the agents, her mind wandered back to the dream. Was that blue in the coals the same one that had blinded her when her powers were stripped away? And what about that figure? Was that the attacker who cursed her, a reluctant elemental, or was it merely a product of her dream? Memories were never as trustworthy as people imagined, and once they blended with dreams, for no matter how brief a time, there was no separating them. So had she even seen the blue coals and the waiting watcher at Onyx Tower?

Kate had never thought of those details before, her focus on the terrible horrors that came next. She'd never considered anyone but herself to blame for what happened. Like everyone, she'd assumed it was her own ineptitude that had allowed the hounds to catch their scent and follow them from the Abyss and into this realm. But now...now she was dredging three-year-old memories for answers to questions she'd never imagined. Maybe Jim would remember something to help cement her recollection. Surely, he'd read her message by now.

Kate's stomach unleashed a gurgling growl and Harcourt turned to look at her.

"Unfortunate you slept through the meal." He smiled, showing those tiny little teeth. "Don't worry. We'll find food before the next flight. Any preference?"

"Whatever is fine. I don't care."

He nodded. "Easy enough."

Struggling to ignore her gnawing stomach, she returned to her thoughts, running the unanswered questions over and over, but getting nowhere. *A bump will help you focus*, the junkie in her whispered.

Kate ground her teeth until the voice silenced and Customs was done.

Once through, she found a little eatery and scarfed down a sandwich and an Orangina, a fruit soda that never tasted quite as good back in the States. She could have more, a lot more, but figured she'd at least give her stomach a few minutes to figure out it wasn't empty anymore before she ordered the entire menu.

On the flight to Scotland, she devoured a pack of crackers and a yogurt, washing them each down with a cup of water.

"Looks like your appetite returned," Evan said.

She shot him a *fuck you* smile, but he offered his own unopened crackers and was immediately forgiven.

The pudgy man standing in the terminal at EDI wore a black suit half a size too large and a matching flat cap. The tablet he held at chest height read, '*G. Thorne.*'

"I'm Greggor Thorne," Harcourt said.

Confused, Kate looked to Evan who gave a tight smile telling her to stay quiet and not to ask.

"Pleasure to meet ye, Mr. Thorne." He tucked the tablet under his arm, revealing a gold name badge that read '*Finlay*' beside an engraved crown. "May I help ye with yer bags?"

Harcourt, of course, wasn't carrying a bag, just a briefcase, but Evan relinquished one of the two large rolling suitcases he was managing.

Kate towed nothing more than a red, hard-sided Samsonite and her purse slung over her shoulder. Finlay took her suitcase as well and led them out to where a silver sedan waited. Bagpipes played above the traffic hum as a young man dressed to the nines in a kilt played for tourists' tips.

Kate slid into the leather back seat of a Mercedes that still held the fruity tang of a previous occupant's perfume. They rode for half an hour, passing little houses nestled behind stone walls and hedges, only their high roofs visible to curious eyes. Houses gave way to apartments and then they crossed a bridge into a tightly packed city with grand churches and stone facades. Most of the buildings appeared old, their mortar still stained with coal smoke from bygone days, but a few others, all glass and steel with sharp edges, appeared to Kate to be trying too hard at defying the old-world ambiance.

She'd never been one for culture shock. She'd crossed the Abyss and walked on three separate realms with alien skies and bizarre defiances of Earthly physics. Yet the subtle difference of driving on the opposite side of the road always gave her a strange sense of wrongness that she couldn't shake.

Eventually they stopped before a palatial building with a clock tower. The gleaming brass sign beside the door read 'The Balmoral Hotel' beneath a crown.

A kilted doorman hurried to the car and led them inside to the fanciest hotel Kate had ever seen.

Once checked into her room, Kate savored an extra-long hot shower to wash away the airport film. Evan was in an adjoining room, while Harcourt enjoyed a stately suite on the floor above. Jim had finally replied to her messages. It was curt, simply telling her to meet him at Cù-Sìth at 10:00 that evening. Just the name of that haven made her skin crawl. Memories of those awful screaming howls rose to the back of her mind. How could he even enter a place named after those things?

After telling Harcourt about the meeting, she ordered room service. The old man still hadn't explained why they called him Thorne, and Kate was beginning to wonder if his name was even Harcourt. Once the modest meal was done, she sprinkled a pinch of blood crystals into a piece of toilet tissue and folded them up like one of those paper footballs the boys in her middle school would flick between each other's outstretched fingers. She washed it down with the last of her juice.

Ingesting the drug this way released it slowly. Not the hard, fast rush that snorting did, but it avoided the sniffles and therefore Evan's judging eyes. She was rested and fed, and if she was going to face Jim, especially in the oldest haven in Scotland, let alone a fucking place named after those god-dammed monsters, she needed to be sharp. She almost convinced herself it was for the magic, but deep down knew that was only a secondary benefit at the moment.

Tonight, either Jim would agree to help her, or she'd be straight out of options.

The need for a bump had won.

6

GABRIEL HOUNDS

K ate and Evan left the hotel at a quarter past nine. Jim's message hadn't included directions or an address, but Kate wasn't worried.

She knew the haven was somewhere along the Royal Mile, a strip of ancient buildings running between the hilltop castle and Holyrood Palace in the oldest part of the city. It made sense. The placement in what was once the most prestigious line of real estate in the capital city would be the only location for the haven. Practitioners of the Art were always in the middle of things. It was the same in Baltimore and New York. While mundies burned witches in the backwater outskirts, they never imagined that the real circles of sorcerers were safely nestled in the highest centers of law and culture.

They followed North Bridge past Market Street and reached High Street. The crystals she'd eaten earlier had now fully dissolved, and the electric buzz of magic tingled anxiously across her skin. Damn, she wanted to cast something. Tourists wandered up and down the thoroughfare, snapping pictures and debating which pubs to visit next. Between the dust-buzz and hopping five time zones, everything felt wrong. To her body, it wasn't even 5:00 p.m., and dust always left her living in a state of non-time, which gave the evening streets a surreal edge.

"Which way?" Evan asked.

Kate looked up and down the hill. The castle stood at the top but wasn't visible through the curving canyon of building fronts. *Would they place it closer to that or to the palace?* She scanned around, spying a hint of luminous blue across the brick street in front of an old, converted church. "Let's check the sign."

Evan followed her across, and Kate stopped before a symbol drawn onto the gray stone walkway. The curving glyph resembled a Japanese kanji, the ink glowing with ghostly light. At its heart, a greenish arrow pointed upward toward Edinburgh Castle.

"What's that?" Evan turned his head a little, squinting at the mark,

She'd wondered if he'd see it. The glyph was invisible to those not attuned, yet mundies could still sense them. A passing group of middle-aged women sauntered by, their feet all somehow missing the symbol as if some deep unconscious part of their brains recognized it as something alien and best avoided.

"Roadmap." Kate nodded up the street. "That way."

Following the wide sidewalk, she noticed another marker scrawled onto a wall beside an alley. Like many former walled cities, Edinburgh had compacted in on itself. The buildings on either side of the lane had grown over it, creating a tunnel. It stank of vomit, piss, and spilled alcohol. Music thumped somewhere above. They followed the narrow passageway, descending steps until it opened up on the far side of the building.

Black wrought-iron lamps illuminated the street, still too narrow for more than bicycle traffic. A few doors lined either side. The windows were dark. Someone had scrawled '*Carcosa Awakens*' across one wall, the bright gold paint no more than a few days old.

"There," Evan said as Kate's eyes found the bluish light, this time above an oaken door. It had no number, simply a horseshoe nailed to its smooth face. He paused. "That's weird."

"What?" Kate asked, turning toward him.

"It's just... I didn't see the door there. I saw the glowing symbol and then a moment later the door just sort of appeared."

"No, it was there. Been there for years, but no one notices it. Not unless it's pointed out or you're in tune."

His brow tightened. "So, am I in tune?"

"You're working on it. Most people lose it early. Though a close and personal encounter with magic can rip away the blinders they've made. It gets easier. Then eventually you forget that mundies can't see them."

"Mundies?" Evan asked, the eyeroll audible in his voice. "That like muggles?"

"Careful with that word," she warned. "Lot of people, especially the older crowd, hate anything dealing with those stories. But yeah, same thing. Mundanes, mooks, there's a lot of acceptable terms for those not attuned."

"Mundane. Don't know if I should be offended by that."

Kate shrugged. "Well, you can see the door, so obviously you're in the club now." Tingles danced across her flesh as she ascended the three worn steps. Shallow glyphs etched the brass handle, their magic making it warm as she pushed the door open.

She stepped inside, finding herself face to face with a giant painting of an enormous red wolf beast with a baby's bald head grinning stupidly back at her. '*Cù-Sìth*,' it read in plain black letters with an arrow pointing up a long staircase. Her already quickened pulse thumped faster in her ears, the blood dust ramping her response.

"The hell is that supposed to be?" Evan laughed behind her.

Kate curled her lip as she met the painting's white-pupiled eyes. Obviously, the artist hadn't ever seen one for real, otherwise it wouldn't look so damned friendly, or even have eyes at all. "It's a Cù-Sìth. Sometimes they call them Gabriel Hounds, or Cŵn Annwn. We always called them verl hounds."

"It's weird."

She grunted. "They're awful."

They followed the creaking stairs up toward the muted buzz of voices. Kate sensed nine wards as they ascended. The fourth one felt noticeably weaker than the rest, its magic fading.

Evan groaned.

"What?" Kate asked, stopping at the door atop the steps.

He shook his head. "Dinner must not be sitting well with me."

"It'll pass," she said. Evidently, he wasn't as attuned as she'd hoped. If he believed the discomfort would go away, then maybe it would. Otherwise, he'd be sitting outside.

She pushed open the door to the smell of pipe smoke. The haven was maybe sixty feet long, broken into three rooms with open doorways between them. The entrance was in the middle one. Everything but the floor was dark wood: paneled walls, carved oak columns, massive ceiling beams, the elaborate bar in the room to her left. In contrast, the floor was covered in an intricate pattern of tiny polished tiles snaking their way across the tavern in some path Kate couldn't quite understand. Save for a pair of cluttered bookcases in this central room, the walls were decorated with a wide collection of items pertaining to the Art, clustered together to give each booth and corner their own theme. Tarot cards shingled one corner, many of them hand painted and yellowed with age. Various grinding mortars, some chipped and cracked, completely covered one booth's walls like graven barnacles. Kate's gaze lingered on one wall decorated with candles and photographs. A painted image of a broken dagger with a clover-shaped pommel crowned the memorial. Evidently, Baltimore wasn't the only place the Spire had attacked.

Maybe thirty patrons laughed and talked at their little tables. Kate scanned their faces, searching for one in particular. An uplifted hand drew her attention to the rear corner, and she spied Jim's smiling face. He appeared the same as she remembered, save for a neatly trimmed stubble beard. The light above his table cast shadows down from his thick eyebrows and sharp cheekbones. His slightly hooded eyes carried an Asiatic edge, the product of his Korean mother and Caucasian father.

A girl seated beside him followed his stare, intense dark eyes beneath sculpted brows. Her short, bleached hair was done in a sort of crest, its tips dyed an eggplant-black. She looked no older than twenty-five.

"Katie." Jim slid from his seat and wrapped her in a lukewarm hug. "Long time."

"Too long," she said, breaking the embrace but keeping her arm around him. "This is my...colleague, Evan Derian."

"Good to meet you," Jim said, thrusting his hand out. "Jim Stevens."

"Evan," Evan grunted, obviously not feeling well as he accepted the hand. He cleared his throat. "Nice to meet you."

Jim gestured to the young woman studying Kate from her seat, her slender brows a flat line. "This is my apprentice, Nate."

"Natasha," the woman said, extending a slender hand. Rings adorned every finger. "But everyone calls me Nate." A Slavic edge tinged her Scottish accent, making it awkward to follow.

"Pleasure to meet you," Kate said, uncomfortably aware at how sweaty her palms were.

Nate's lips, painted the color of dried blood, pulled into a mistrusting smile. Kate wondered exactly what Jim had shared about her to earn that look.

"So," Jim said. "Have a seat. Tell me all this wild news and what brings you halfway 'round the world at a moment's notice."

Kate smiled. "Of course. Evan, could you please get me a Scotch?"

Evan swallowed, still looking like he might hurl. "I'm not supposed to leave you."

"Nothing to fear. This," she said gesturing around them, "is about the safest place I can be. Nothing'll happen here. Besides, it's a straight line of sight between here and the bar. I'll be fine."

Evan's honey eyes moved to Jim and then back to her, seeming to register the hint. "All right. I'm sure you two have a lot of catching-up."

"Thank you." She drew a breath, trying to calm the swirl of thoughts and emotion. She had one shot at this.

"Who is that guy?" Jim whispered the moment Evan left. "He screams newbie. And why do you need a bodyguard anyhow?"

"That's why I'm here." Her eyes unconsciously flicked to Nate staring at her, the corners of the young woman's mouth tight with mistrust and curiosity. "Jim," Kate continued, "the night of the test, when everything happened, before it happened, was there anything strange you remember, anything that just wasn't right?"

"The part when the circle tore."

"No," Kate snapped, a little harsher than she intended. She licked her lips and tried again. "Before that, just before. Think. Did you see anything strange, something you might not have thought about before?"

Jim held her gaze for several long seconds. "What are you getting at? And what's this curse you were rambling about in that message?"

"That's what I'm trying to tell you." She wiped her sweat-slicked palms across her jeans. "It wasn't a mistake. Someone attacked us—attacked me!"

Jim drew a long breath. "Are you dusted?"

"Looks dusted," Nate said. "Sounds dusted."

"God damn it, listen to me," Kate said, struggling to keep her voice low. "This guy, Harcourt or Thorne, I'm not a hundred percent sure, he's got this book, and it says I'm cursed and how to fix it, and you're the only one I can trust to do it. And then I can do a job for this guy, and he'll tell me who killed everyone and blamed me for it. Fuck, don't you understand? Someone tried to murder us."

Jim raised his palms. "Slow down."

Kate heaved a breath. Her heart was pounding so hard she wondered if he could see it through her shirt. "It's really import—"

"Are— You— Dusted?"

"Have you not heard anything I've said?"

He only looked at her, those dark eyes boring into her in that way only he and Master Boyer could do.

"Yeah, I'm on some dust, but that's just because I need—"

"Fuckin' hell." Nate stabbed a ringed finger toward her. She turned to

Jim. "God-damned junkie." Those disgusted eyes rolled toward Kate. "Probably rob us."

"Hey," Jim said. "This is my friend and my old tower sister. Careful what you say here."

Nate blinked, seeming shocked by her mentor's scolding.

"She's been through things I hope you never have to see. So quiet." Jim sipped his beer. "So, you're still dustin'."

"Because I need the magic. But this isn't some hallucination, Jim. Someone cursed me. They killed everyone, and I took the blame."

"Katie, look, I know this has been hard for you—"

"No." Kate's finger shot up. "You don't believe me, fine. Fine. Then explain to me how I have a fucking mundie bodyguard, I flew across the ocean with only a few hours' notice, I have a room in the Balmoral, and some guy that's richer than Jesus who knows more about me than I'm comfortable with. If I'm delusional, then please explain how I worked all this very real shit into my fantasy, and I'll listen. But that guy..." She glanced across the pub, seeing Evan's back at the bar. "...*he's* real. Now, you know I couldn't afford flying here and fancy hotels, so you tell me how *this* is all in my head."

He looked over at Evan and back.

"I'm in trouble. I'm with these people. I don't know who in the hell they are, but this guy has a spell, and you're the only one I can trust to cast it. *That* is real."

"This Harcourt fella?" Jim asked.

She nodded. "He's back at the hotel. He wants to meet with you."

"Balmoral?"

"Yeah."

He smiled, though there was nothing warm to it. "Tell me about this person who attacked you. You said you'd shot someone."

"That? Um, yeah, that's a different story. I sort of pissed off Amber Tower."

"Well, this just keeps gettin' better and better."

Kate shook her head. "It's fine. Evan chased the guy off. I can worry about that later."

Evan was heading back now, a glass in each hand.

"Jim," Kate whispered. "I know you don't fully believe me, but please. Please, will you just look at this spell? Hold your judgment until then. Just look."

"So how's the reunion?" Evan asked, setting the drinks onto the old table.

"Fine," Kate said, taking her glass and scooting over to make room.

Jim was staring at his half-finished drink in his hand, seeming to consult it like some trusted mentor. He drew a breath as if to speak, but held it. His gaze flicked to Kate, a decision in his eyes. "Drink up. Let's go see this book."

7

ANGEL KISS

K ate paced up and down her hotel room, hands clenched into fists, alternatingly tightening and loosening them. She stopped at the door, eyes flicking across the Emergency Exit diagram affixed there, and then tromped back past the four-poster bed to the window. She stared out, seeing but not really registering the tall spire monument atop Calton Hill.

Harcourt had insisted on meeting Jim alone; a separate business transaction, he'd said. And without any further explanation, he'd sent her back to her room like some scolded child while her parents discussed what to do with her. But why wouldn't she be allowed? The spell in question pertained to her. Jim was her friend, her old tower mate. Yet Nate was allowed to stay. She was an Initiate, an Adeptus at most. Kate deserved to be in there a thousand times more than that novice.

She might be a novice, but she has more magic than you, that little voice in her head whispered. *The real sorcerers are talking. You're just a junkie, and Nate tagged you for it in under a minute.*

Kate clenched her teeth, willing the self-hate away. It always came out a few days into a dust-binge, and she always seemed to forget how much she hated it between fixes. Another bump, a real one and not just swallowing it, would quiet that self-pity. Everyone knew she was using, so she might as well live up to their expectations. Besides, it would help ease the hell of waiting.

Kate removed the vial from her bag. She held the tube of crimson crystals up, letting the light flicker across the miniature facets. A quarter of it was now gone. But when Jim took the job, if he took it, if he cured her, then this would be the last vial she'd ever need.

She tamped a few of the crystals out onto the bathroom counter but stopped. No.

No, she needed to keep cool. If she came in all tweaked up and sniffling, then Jim might change his mind. Providing, of course, he was going to help her.

Of course, he'll do it. Kate carefully put the crystals back into the vial, screwed the cap on, and shoved the blood dust back into her bag. "I don't need you."

Saying it aloud helped her believe it, and she of all people understood that there really was power to words. A few traces clung to the marble counter—the *angel kiss* they called it, the portion one lucky winner got to lick up after the rest was tooted. She considered wiping it up with some toilet tissue and flushing the angel kiss away, but her conviction faltered. *Might make a good pick-me-up later.*

Exiting the bathroom, she checked the alarm clock. What in the hell were they even talking about? Surely Jim had read the spell. What was the holdup? Gnawing a thumbnail, she resumed her pacing. What if Harcourt decided to hire Jim instead of her, leave her out in the cold? No, Jim wouldn't do that. Would he? She ground her teeth, fighting down the paranoia.

The Red Gate would stop any scrying attempts, not that she'd ever been good at it. Maybe she should try it anyway. The old man might have missed an entrance, a little gap she might exploit. With enough dust, she might—

A door in the adjoining room thudded shut and snapped Kate to attention. She marched over to the connecting door and knocked.

She lifted her hand to knock again when the bolt clicked. "Yes?" Evan said, swinging it open. "You need anything?"

"Yeah. Answers."

He frowned, his chin dipping a nod. "They're still talking. Harcourt will call once they're ready."

"Yeah, I remember, and have been waiting, but that's not what I meant. I have other questions."

"Sure." He motioned his head. "Come on in."

Kate followed him inside. Though the same size, the floor plan of his room was wider. Hunter green and dark brown walls matched the bedspread and tasteful Chesterfield sofa, a sharp contrast to the blue and gold of hers. His black suitcase rested open on a wooden luggage stand, its contents neatly folded.

"Want anything to drink?" He opened a mini-fridge. "Water? Soda?"

"No, thanks."

Evan bent and removed a plastic water bottle. "So, what's up?"

"Harcourt?" she said, diving right in. "Is that his real name?"

He swigged his water, eyes considering her above the plastic bottle.

"It's not that it matters," Kate added. "I'm on board either way, but I want to know who it is I'm working for."

"It's not Harcourt. At least I don't think so."

"You don't think?"

"No." He shook his head. "No, it's not. I'm sure of that. I met him as Thorne, but he's also gone by Johansen. So maybe it's that. Maybe it's none of them."

"Why?"

"He told me that it's handy to have a few aliases."

"Is he a criminal?"

"No. Not in the normal sense," he added reluctantly.

"The normal sense? Come on. Spit it out. What are you talking about?"

Evan shook his head. "I'm not at liberty to talk about it. But no, he's not wanted by the law. He's simply keeping a low profile."

"Because someone is after him?"

He nodded.

"And that's why he needs me? To help him with that?"

"Sort of."

"What do you mean, *sort of*? Does he or doesn't he?"

"I'm not allowed to—"

"Talk about it," Kate said, finishing the sentence. If there had been any doubt Evan had been a soldier, this confirmed it. '*I could tell you, but I'd have to kill you*' bullshit.

"If it makes you feel better, he'll explain it once you're ready to do the task he needs," Evan added.

"And I'm guessing no hints about that?"

He shrugged. "Sorry."

She ran her fingers through her hair, still surprised by how short it was. "So is that why he didn't go to Cù-Sìth, and why he sent you after me? He's lying low?"

"Yeah."

There it was. Harcourt, or whoever he was, was hiding from a practitioner, maybe a whole tower. Evan had mentioned New York. There were three towers in the tri-state area and countless independents and small covens. That wasn't good. But why keep up the false identity here? He wasn't in New York. He wasn't even on the continent. So, whoever might be looking for him would have a long reach. They also didn't have any of his hair or nail clippings. Otherwise, the game was pointless.

But even if a tower was gunning for him, why her? What was it she could do when her powers returned that others couldn't? Tracking her down had probably cost a good deal. Money better spent on an actual sorceress. *Leverage*, Kate decided. Restoring her powers gave him leverage to demand something she might not normally agree to.

But that couldn't be right. Once he returned them, that leverage would be gone. Maybe he was relying on gratitude.

Not that it mattered, Kate decided, chewing at the ragged thumbnail. She'd lived as a pariah for three years, belonging to neither the magical nor the mundane worlds. Terrance Dalton and his flunkies at Amber Tower, or whatever tower they schemed to form, already hated her. She couldn't return to Baltimore without her powers, and there was nowhere else she had to go. So what if working for Harcourt pissed off another tower? If it meant getting her powers back and finding out who had killed her friends, then bring it on.

As if hearing her resolve, the phone in her room rang. Kate blinked and hurried to it. "Yes?"

"*Miss Rossdale*," Harcourt said. "*Would you come to my suite?*"

———

Jim opened the door when Kate knocked. Without warning, he wrapped his arms around her in a tight embrace. "I'm sorry."

Kate only stood there for a moment, unsure how to process this. What was he apologizing for? Sorry that he wouldn't help her?

"You were right," he said. "I'd been so mad at you over the years. Not directly, but it sort of built up. You tried to tell me, and I didn't believe you."

"It's all right," she said, the relief washing down. "You didn't know." She extracted herself from the hug and looked at him, her hands on his biceps.

Wetness framed the edges of Jim's eyes, threatening to become tears. "Can you help me?"

"Damn right I can." He stepped aside. "We need to talk."

Kate stepped through the invisible bubble of Harcourt's Red Gate. Her ears wanted to pop at the sensation. Nate was staring at her from a broad blue sofa, the hard edge gone from her eyes. The spell folder rested before her atop a claw-footed table.

"Please come in, Miss Rossdale," Harcourt said, his chair opposite the table. "There's much to discuss."

"So, we're in business?" Kate asked, too nervous to take the empty chair.

"Almost. There are a few details we need to complete first, but Mr. Stevens has agreed to help with those."

Kate glanced to Jim who was sliding onto the couch beside his apprentice. "Like what?"

"Before we begin," Harcourt said, "I require the Iron Word that you will complete the job."

"Does the job mean I find out who did this?"

"It does."

"Then why a geas?"

"Because I need the assurance that you will serve the entirety of the task until it's complete."

"Does it include killing them?"

Harcourt frowned. "Yes."

"Then you have nothing to worry about."

"Then agreeing to the Iron Word shouldn't be a problem for you, should it? Mr. Stevens and Miss Gadzinski have both agreed to it as well."

Jim and Nate nodded.

Kate drew a breath. "Appears like I get to learn your name, then."

Harcourt smiled, those little teeth peeking from behind his lips. "So it does. But not until the ceremony."

"We need to find out who did this," Jim said. "If he knows, then I'm on board."

Kate removed a tumbler from the wet bar and poured herself a whiskey on ice. The Iron Word was a serious spell, unbreakable once taken. It also ensured that none of them could knowingly allow any harm to befall whomever the word had sealed, a provision to ensure no one could weasel out of it. Many towers required it of any members above

Lumitor. The flipside was that Harcourt, or whoever he was, couldn't harm them either, which did have its appeal.

"Fine," she said.

"I can have the Iron Word ready by tomorrow night." Jim nodded to the book resting before him, its pages open to a five-layered circle. "But that'll take me a few days to get ready."

"How many?" Harcourt asked.

"Five, maybe six. I'll need to make some calls." His gaze moved to Kate. "But there's some prep you need to do."

"Hm?" she grunted taking the empty chair.

"You need to fast," Jim said. "No alcohol, for one."

Kate paused, looking at him over the rim of her half-tipped glass, the whiskey's aroma filling her sinuses. "You just had to wait until I sat down, didn't you?"

"Drink water. No meat, but a little fish is okay."

"I remember the process." Kate looked at her glass and held it out. "Anyone want this?"

Nate accepted the proffered drink.

"And no dust," Jim added. "You're clean as of now."

"What?" she blurted. Her eyes flicked to the room of people all watching her. Was he really doing this intervention shit here? "Jim, it's not recreational."

"Not negotiable, Katie."

"I need the magic."

"You're right, so if you want it back, you'll stop."

"Once I—"

"No, Katie."

"But a fast only needs to be three days."

"Maybe," Jim said. "But if you want my help, you're giving that shit up tonight. No discussion. I've sat by and watched you jam it up your nose for years, and I won't do it anymore. Boyer's death wasn't your fault. You were injured and abandoned, even by me, so my first order of business is getting you off the dust."

My fucking hero. She ground her teeth. Jim was right, she knew it, but living this final week having literally no magic and not even a drink...she really wished she'd taken that bump.

"How much do you have?" Jim asked.

"Only enough to get me through the week."

"Well, you're handing it over to me tonight. Do you have it on you?"

"It's in my room."

"Where?" Harcourt asked. "I can have Evan bring it up."

"I'll get it myself." Christ, this public shaming was bad enough without the thought of Evan creeping through her belongings. That was probably what he was doing right now, now that she thought of it. Shit.

"Good," Jim said. "Tomorrow night we'll do the contracts at my place. In the meantime, we'll get to work. Katie, if you want to stay with me, that's all right."

"And give this place up?" She snorted. "I can have at least one nice thing, can't I?"

"No, I get it." Jim lifted his palms in surrender. "I'd stay here too. Just remember, no booze, no red meat."

"Yeah, yeah. And Jim?"

"What?"

"Thank you. Thanks for believing me."

He smiled. "Sorry it took so long."

"Let me get the dust." Kate rose to her feet and headed down the hall. Evan wasn't in her room, and it at least appeared that he hadn't been inside. She removed the vial from her purse and shook it, watching all the tiny crystals twinkle inside. *Just sneak a couple out*, the inner junkie whispered.

No. While her resolve was still firm, Kate marched back and gave the tube to Jim, assuring him that was all of it. After all, the inner junkie reminded her, angel kisses didn't count.

8

ELEMENTAL IN THE NIGHT

K ate forced herself to bed just after 2:00 in the morning. Without the distraction of booze or dust, she decided to try acclimating to this new time zone. Her week of fasting and meditation would pass much faster if she could just sleep through it. With the heavy curtains closed, she lay in the cool darkness, blankets pulled up to her throat, and listened to her hammering heart gradually slow as the stimulant wore down. She got up to pee twice. Eventually, some time after 3:30, she nodded off.

The dream came quick, eagerly swooping in before she'd reached complete unconsciousness. Her world erupted into weird blue, and she found herself helpless against the onslaught of memory.

The blueness rips away like a stage magician's veil, leaving her sprawled on polished planks, all her senses rushing back at once. A horrible roar sounds to the left followed by a woman's scream. Fluid splatters her back and arm, so hot against the penetrating cold that she yelps, thinking it scalded her. It's blood, but not hers.

Wet slurps crunch and smack behind her.

Kate rolls to her knees. The silvery glow of the chalk ring flickers along the floor as misty aether hemorrhages through, swallowing the room's light. Hunched shapes scramble in the shadows like misshapen dogs with round, splotchy, red human heads. One hunkers above a fallen figure only an arm's length away. Blood soaks the figure's yellow robes, and Kate cries out as she recognizes Heather's brown curls.

The verl hound lifts its head, a loop of intestine coming up with the motion. The face is that of some giant deformed child with smooth, jutting brows. But it has no eyes beneath the ridge—only folded flaps of pink skin that open to reveal enormous nostril holes lined with bristling hairs. Heather's entrails drape from the beast's lipless mouth. Blood and gore squirt between crystalline fangs as it chews and smacks its horrible meal.

Fire erupts off to Kate's right. The orange glow through the vapor reveals it to be the asafetida grass. Dennis had dropped the bundle on the fire, and now sharp fetid smoke pours from the brazier. He kneels drunkenly beside Master Boyer as violet lightning crackles from the old man's hand. A verl hound wails in pain, the electricity skipping across its hide. The beast explodes, the pieces melting into aether as they sail apart.

Turning her attention back to the hound atop Heather, Kate's fingers dance to summon her power. This murderous beast will pay for what it's done. No sooner than she starts, a sudden pain explodes inside her skull. A wave of dizziness and Kate stumbles. She falls backward, retching as she hits the floor.

Dennis screams as a beast chomps into his face with a hideous crunch.

"No!" Kate cries.

Master Boyer is nowhere to be seen.

Growling, the verl hound above Heather snaps its malformed head in Kate's direction, the grotesque nostril-eyes flaring wide. Kate holds up her hand. Nothing happens but a fresh wave of nausea.

Her power? Where is her power?

The beast's jaws open wide enough to fit her head. Crystalline needles line the verl hound's throat. Dangling strips of Heather's torn flesh quiver as the hound emits a low growl. It steps over Heather's body toward her.

Green light pulses through the smoke and aether, but she can't tell who is casting.

Tears from sick and smoke cloud her vision. Blinking, she scrambles back, away from the closing beast.

The blind hound roars and lunges. Kate lifts an arm to defend herself, but then Candace steps above her, a spinning geometry of pink light unfolds before the incantatrix's outstretched hand.

"No!" Candace screams. The leaping verl hound hits the glowing shield and is knocked back. Claws clamor across the wooden floor, tearing splinters as it tries to right itself.

"You don't get her!" Candace shouts. The shield dissolves. Her fingers tut an intricate pattern and a golden beam streaks from her crossed thumbs and into the twisting aether. She looks down. "Are you hurt?"

"My magic," Kate coughs. "I...I can't..."

"Move that way, against the wall. Go!" Candace dives into the blackness. Shouts and human-like roars come from all sides. Orange flames erupt against the far wall. The house's smoke alarm blares its shrill beeping.

Half-blind from smoke, Kate crawls across the hard floor. She finds the paneled wall and huddles into the corner beneath a table, terrified and powerless to help.

The library doors burst open. Her tower mates come storming in. Ronny, a tall, slender Magister Lex stretches his arms, unleashing a wind. Smoke and aether swirl and the lights seem to brighten as the aether thins. The floor is aflame from the toppled brazier. A mangled severed arm blackens on the fire. Kate opens her mouth at the sight of Master Boyer's antique watch encircling the dead wrist, but no sound comes out. She's unable to breathe, her lungs simultaneously urging to inhale and exhale, a respiratory Mexican standoff.

Dennis' lower torso lies at the edge of the broken chalk ring, a red smear running across the floor. Shredded body parts and clothes litter the circle, the blood so bright that it doesn't look entirely real. Most of the remains are missing, pulled back into the Abyss with the banished hounds. Toppled bookshelves burn. Colorful flames lick between curling pages.

"Katie!" Jim cries, racing toward her.

Kate tries to answer but still can't breathe. She knows this is a dream, a horrible memory. This is the moment she passed out, but she doesn't have to again. She only needs to inhale. Forcing her lungs, Kate defies the memory and sucks a breath.

Kate awoke with a gasp, her lungs burning for air. Cotton sheets clung to her sweat-soaked skin. Breathing came difficult, like a weight was sitting on her chest. The room was dark, its only light the soft jade glow of the bedside clock. Heart still pounding from the vivid memory, she tried to sit up, but the pressure on her ribs shifted like a stubborn cat.

Quick wheezing breaths sounded inches from her face. Something slithered in her hair, brushing her ear, gooey with hard nubs.

In the green light, she saw the terrifying shape—pale, an emaciated torso, its hands pressing down on her shoulders. The heel of one palm squashed uncomfortably into the top of her right breast. But the head was wrong. The neck was slender, leading to a smooth, feminine jaw, but above that, where she'd expected an upper lip, nose, ears, eyes, there was only a long writhing tongue, like an octopus arm, a spiral of white nubs running its length. The tongue slid down Kate's cheek, smearing a fetid odor as it licked the sweat from her face.

Kate screamed.

She flung her arm, knocking the elemental off as she rolled away. Squealing, it tumbled off the bed and Kate came up in a tangle of sheets. She slapped the cherry wood base of the bedside lamp. Light would weaken it. She hit the switch, but only activated the first and lowest level before the creature hopped back up onto the bed.

The dim light seemed to penetrate its gray-mottled skin. It had no legs at all, the torso terminating just below the bony ribs. Twin rows of square, flat teeth spiraled up the three-foot tongue writhing above its chattering jaw. Walking on its hands, one with four fingers the other with seven, it scuttled toward her.

Kate stumbled backward, her feet kicking at the sheets as she wove her fingers in sharp, controlled strokes. Pale light threaded before her, the energy coalescing. The elemental leaped, the malformed hands outstretched. It struck, knocking Kate's arm aside as she released the spell. A green beam of energy streaked from her left palm and slashed the now empty bed like an invisible sword, throwing bits of pillow stuffing and memory foam against the far wall.

Climbing up her like a spider monkey, its enormous tongue snaked toward Kate's throat. A strange but calming odor flooded her senses—lavender and warm summer nights. An unnatural tiredness seeped into the back of her mind. She'd smelled that before—smelled it as she'd drifted off. It was trying to return Kate to her nightmares so it could feed on her pain.

Fuck you! She seized the monster by the neck and twisted her thumbs into the rubbery flesh. With her other hand, she took hold of one of its spindly wrists and pulled. Despite its size, she couldn't budge it. Locked together, they thrashed, knocking into the wall and Kate yelped as she stubbed her toe on a chair leg. The elemental's tongue dove for her open mouth, but Kate snapped it shut and pressed her lips tight. The nubby teeth slid across her face, bringing that tranquilizing stink.

Blinded by the sticky tongue slithering across her clenched eyes, Kate dove forward toward the lamp. Her knee hit the side table, and she heaved the creature toward it. The beast's grip weakened under the onslaught of close light. Wrenching its knobby wrist, she peeled its hand off her and forced it over the open top of the lampshade.

The elemental squealed as the direct light sizzled its flesh. Kate seized the opening and threw the beast across the bed.

Her last spell had sapped almost all of her power, only the barest traces remained, and not enough to guarantee another shot. The angel kiss was still on the bathroom counter, protected beneath a downturned glass. Without slowing to see where the elemental landed, Kate scrambled for the bathroom.

A crash came from behind her. She slapped the wall switch as she entered the bathroom, flooding it with white light. *Come on in here, asshole.*

Lifting the tumbler off of the traces of pink dust, Kate set it aside. She misjudged the distance, and it fell into the sink with a sharp crunch of breaking glass.

"Kate?" Evan shouted from inside the room.

A hiss and then Evan cried out.

"Jesus Chr—"

Kate stuck her head out the door to see Evan in boxers and a T-shirt. The elemental was on his back and its tooth-studded tongue around his throat. Its teeth clicked together as the coils tightened. The light streaming through the open door to the connecting room had weakened the creature. It was translucent now—smoky, but looked like it was going to make the most of the little time it had left.

Evan gasped, his eyes wide in terror, and the beast licked his fear.

"Hold still," she ordered. There wasn't time for the blood dust. She wove her fingers, summoning every drop of magic and unleashed the spell. The dull emerald beam was nearly invisible, but it struck home.

The elemental burst with a little pop, like a single cell of Bubble Wrap crushed between fingers. Its tattered pieces evaporated to aether and vanished, leaving only a faint scent like rotted flowers and unnamed bitter memories.

Kate's vision blurred. She swooned and caught herself on the door frame.

His hand to his throat, Evan rushed to her. "Are you okay?" He coughed.

"Fine." She hugged him, not from affection as much as relief and gratitude. This was the second time he'd rushed in to protect her. A faint tingle buzzed beneath his T-shirt. Magic? Was he wearing an amulet?

He broke the embrace and scanned the room. "What was that? I only got a glimpse of it."

"Elemental," she panted.

"What? No, it wasn't fire or water, it was... I don't know." His hand touched his neck again. "Awful."

"Nightmare."

"Nightmare's an element?" He stepped over to the slashed bed, white stuffing and yellow foam bleeding out from the blanket and mattress.

"Elemental emotion. Fear, lust, jealousy, anger." She'd been sleeping in only a short shirt and underwear herself and felt more than a little exposed at the moment. Her toe was still throbbing like hell, and she limped more than walked to her crumpled jeans and pulled them on. "If a dreamer enters the aether, their raw emotion can seed an elemental."

"I thought there were only four elements," he said. "I've never heard of this."

She shrugged as she pulled up the zipper. "There used to be five elements. At least in the west. Spirit, or Life. In the rawest form, they're aether. That couldn't be proven as an element, so science got rid of it. But that was an elemental, no less than a fire sprite or wind wyrd."

He pointed to the bed. "Did it do this?"

"That was me."

Evan pursed his lips, a question forming.

Kate wiggled her fingers. "Sorceress."

"Do you want to stay in my room? I can take the couch."

"Yeah. But you can have the bed. I don't think I'll be sleeping for the next month."

"Me neither."

Kate surveyed the ruin of her hotel room. Looked like she'd be crashing at Jim's after all. While she knew it had evaporated with the creature, she touched her face, feeling where the drool had slathered her skin. "Let me gather my things. Take a shower. Why don't you order us up some breakfast? And coffee. Lots of coffee."

"Are you sure you want to be alone?" he asked. "What if it comes back?"

"It won't. Sun'll be up soon."

He gave a reluctant nod.

"And Evan."

"Yeah?"

"Thanks for coming for me."

Before Kate had stepped into the much-needed shower, she'd licked the spilled traces of blood dust off the counter. Jim would have flipped his shit had he known, but she didn't care. Someone had sent an elemental after her, and if she hadn't had magic from her last bumps, the damage could have been far worse. Of course, Jim would have said that he'd invited her to stay at his place, which was surely warded against such things, but the truth was that Kate had really wanted to sleep in a bed for once that wasn't a couch or pulled from a dumpster.

She imagined his response, calling her silly. In a few days she'd have her power back and could sleep anywhere she wanted without fear. The ensuing imaginary argument lasted ten minutes and then she'd fumed for ten more after. But by the time she'd toweled off and gotten dressed, the barest traces of the angel kiss' magic was humming through her veins, and she'd forgiven Jim for the stupid, arrogant things he'd never actually said.

"Mr. Harcourt wants us to go to his room," Evan said as Kate emerged from the bathroom. The ruined sheets had already been stripped off the mattress and piled at the foot of the bed. A thick splinter of jagged wood jutted from the frame of their adjoining door, from where Evan had kicked it open. She wondered what story they could tell the hotel about the damage.

Her Samsonite was open on the stand, all of her effects that hadn't been in the bathroom with her neatly packed. Normally she'd have just shoved the bundle of dirty clothes and toiletries inside, but guilt obligated her to pack them proper. "How are you feeling?"

He shrugged. "Fine now. That...thing took a lot more out of me than I'd thought."

"They can't kill you, at least not little ones like that. But they'll sap you dry, even drive you insane."

"I believe it," Evan grunted. "So what was it doing?"

"Forcing me to relive the worst night of my life so it could drink up my fear. Little bastard." Kate zipped the suitcase. "Did you order coffee?"

"It's in my room."

"Good. Let me have that, and then we'll go see the boss."

9

WHEN DIPLOMACY FAILS

"What happened?" Harcourt asked as he answered his suite's door. "Are you all right?"

A cart heavy with covered platters stood beside the table. The weak effects of the angel kiss did nothing to soil Kate's instant hunger at smelling the warmed sausage and other breakfast food. "We're fine. An elemental, but I banished it."

"How?"

"Magic from the blood dust everyone keeps telling me to stop." She headed straight for the food cart. A fresh pot of coffee already rested on the table, thank God.

"No," Harcourt said. "I meant how is an elemental after you? Have you told anyone about what we're doing?"

"No." Bit of an odd question. "I'd bet money it was Terrance Dalton and his buddies at Amber Tower."

"Are you sure?"

"Not a hundred percent, but who else would it be?"

Harcourt grunted. "Please," he said, gesturing to the food, "help yourself."

Kate removed a plate and began loading it with little button mushrooms soaking in a dark sauce. She was about to scoop some eggs when she remembered the fast. *Shit*. That ruled out the sausage, too. Grumbling, she spooned all but three of the mushrooms back into the serving dish and loaded up on fruit and a yogurt.

She sat down at the table with the second-place breakfast, noticing Harcourt's briefcase on one end. No. That one had mother-of-pearl tabs, this one had black. How many cases did one man need? "Anyway," Kate said, dipping a strawberry in the yogurt. "It was my fault. I... For some reason, I assumed that leaving the country I would somehow escape them." *Because you were fucking high*, a little part of her brain said, but she ignored it with a bite of food.

Harcourt lowered himself on the opposite side of the table where his case and milky coffee sat. Evan began loading his own plate with breakfast.

"It wasn't the first attack, either," Kate said after swallowing.

"No?" Harcourt asked, his head cocking slightly to the right.

"On the airplane, flying here. I think it first got me there. I had a nightmare, a memory, and it was so...real. I'd chalked it up to all the other stuff, but now that I think about it, that was the first attack."

"I think I would have noticed that thing next to me," Evan said. "The world would have noticed it when someone else saw it and put it on YouTube."

"Doubtful." Kate ate another bite. "Mundies can't see 'em," she said, mouth still full. "They're like the street symbols."

"I saw those."

"Only 'cause I pointed 'em out. Nice shadowy airplane, lights off, people sleeping. I bet that little bastard curled up in my lap and nursed from me like a baby."

Harcourt's mouth curled. "Not a pleasant image."

"You should imagine it from my side," Kate said.

"Will it return?"

She shook her head. "Doubt it. Dalton, or whoever did it for him, would have to summon another and there's no real reason to. He made his point, and it was just two thousand bucks."

"You did shoot his boy," Evan said, setting his steaming plate down and taking a chair. Jesus, that sausage looked good.

"And you robbed him."

Evan paused. "You think he'll come after me?"

"He has no idea who you are. He probably got some of my hair or skin from something at my place."

"There's no guarantee he'll stop," Harcourt said. "Mr. Dalton has a vindictive reputation. He might do it again out of boredom. Will he know you banished it?"

She nodded. "He'd have felt it. Or at least the summoner. Leges can't call them themselves."

"So he might know you have magic."

"He knows I had the blood dust. He saw it."

Harcourt looked toward the window, his blue-gray eyes focused on nothing in particular, his thumb sliding up and down his scarred finger. "We can't afford this man's grudge to interfere with our task. Can you contact him?"

"Why?" she asked. "Ask him to stop, say please and sorry?"

"I was thinking money, but if you think apologies might work..."

"Money?"

The old man nodded. "He needs money. He's upset you cost him. Therefore, money should appease him."

"Fuck that," she said around a spoonful of yogurt.

"This isn't about the two thousand that you cost him. It's the potential thousands more that failed sale could have made. How much do you suspect Dalton was selling that amulet for?"

She thought about that. "Thirty, maybe forty. The gold and the gem are worth half that."

"Do you think twenty would appease him?"

"You want to pay him twenty? Thousand?"

"It's my money, not yours. Should that work?"

Kate snorted. "More than he deserves, but probably."

"Good. Don't tell him where the money is coming from. Only that you want to pay him. Get his account number, and I'll have it taken care of."

Kate didn't have Dalton's number but had a good idea where she could find it. Because her cell wasn't set up for international calls, Harcourt offered his hotel phone, and Kate paced the suite's second bedroom, its wall decorated with a painting of the Highlands, dusted with purple heather.

The phone answered on the sixth ring.

"*Hello?*" Tisha croaked, her voice heavy with exhaustion.

"Hey, it's me, Kate. Sorry if I woke you."

"*Kate? Christ, it's six-thirteen in the morning. Are you okay?*"

"Yeah, yeah I'm fine now, but I have something I need."

Tisha sniffed. *"Where are you? It says International."*

Kate peeked through the open door. Harcourt was sitting in the main room, listening of course. Evan had the briefcase open in front of him, peering inside. "It doesn't matter," Kate said. "I'm sorry, I forgot about the time zones. I just needed to get out of town. Have you heard anything about me?"

"No. Should I have?"

"No. No. Just wondering. Look, do you know how I could get ahold of Terrance Dalton?"

"Dalton?" Tisha laughed. *"Now I know you're in trouble if you're trying to get a hold of that prick. What's going on?"*

"It's best if I don't talk about it," Kate said, hyper-aware of Harcourt's listening ears. "But do you have his number?"

"Of course. Give me a minute."

Kate continued pacing while Tisha scrolled through her contacts list. She had just about everyone's phone number. If someone got a little too rowdy or drunk at the bar, she'd call their tower or coven-mates or their mentor to come deal with it. Running Whittaker's made Tisha and her family the most well-connected practitioners in Baltimore. Kate glanced back to Harcourt but noticed Evan lifting something from the briefcase, turning it over. The case's black lid blocked her view, but not the reflection in the mirror behind him. Kate almost dropped the phone. It was only a glimpse, a gleam of shiny metal, but enough to make her instinctively look away. *Holy shit.*

Had they seen her looking? Did they see the recognition in her eyes? Kate cleared her throat, a little reminder to them that she was still there as if they could have somehow forgotten that she was just thirty feet away.

"Almost got it," Tisha said, thinking the noise was for her.

It couldn't have been what she thought it was. A witchhunter blade? The only one Kate had ever seen had been Tisha's, a memento from a Spire assassin who'd somehow made his way into Whittaker's forty years before. Her granddad made sure he never came back. The forked cross guard, the clover-shaped pommel. That was it. No, if Harcourt and Evan were with the Golden Spire, they wouldn't just flash that in front of her. No, they couldn't be with them.

Kate risked another look. Evan was whispering something to Harcourt, and the dagger was no longer in his hand. Harcourt still watched her with the same passive attention he had only minutes before. Either he hadn't seen her spot the witchhunter blade, or he had and didn't think much of it. Maybe he didn't understand what it was.

"*All right,*" Tisha said. "*You ready?*"

"Yeah." Kate swiveling her head in search of the notepad she'd set down while waiting. Finding it, she rushed over to copy the number that Tisha had already begun to rattle out.

"*You're in Scotland, aren't you?*" Tisha asked.

"What?" Kate said her voice high and terribly acted.

"*You're visiting Jim. I was trying to figure out where you'd be and remembered he'd gone there.*"

"Yeah, you caught me," Kate admitted, glancing to the half-wall in case Harcourt might somehow hear that Tisha had figured it out.

"*Rekindling the old flame?*"

Kate snorted. "Nope. Just friends."

"*Tell him hi for me.*"

"I will. Thanks for the number. I'm sorry again about waking you."

"*It's okay,*" Tisha said. "*You take care.*"

"You too." Kate pressed the off button and walked back to where Evan and Harcourt waited. The briefcase was now closed.

"Got it," Kate said, holding up the pad with the number. She sipped her cooling coffee. "So you think I should wait and call him after eight?"

"Your decision," Harcourt said. "He woke you up early so if you want to wake him I see no problem with that. You'll be bearing gifts, after all."

A mean grin stretched across Kate's lips. "And here I'd thought you'd try to talk me out of it."

"*Hello?*" Dalton answered casually, as if a six-thirty call was nothing unusual.

"Mr. Dalton, Kate Rossdale," she said with a sugar-dipped smile. "I hope I didn't wake you."

"*Not at all,*" he said, his own pleasant tone withering with each word.

"Wonderful. Listen, Terrance, I have a bit of a problem, and I was hoping maybe you could help me with that. Someone sent an elemental after me. Can you believe it?"

"*Miss Rossdale,*" he said, voice sharpening. "*If you're accusing me of or any of my tower—*"

"No, no, no." Kate laughed reveling in the bitchy cheerfulness. "I would *never* accuse you of anything so..." She wanted to say competent, but held her tongue. "...petty."

Dalton didn't seem to have a response to that, so Kate continued.

"So, here's my proposal. Maybe you or one of your friends might know a spell or something to stop these little annoyances. But I'm willing to pay for your—"

"*Miss Rossdale, if you think this is some idea of a joke—*"

"No!" Kate snapped. "But here's the deal, Terry. Some asshole broke into my home. I shot him. I let him go, and I've never told anyone about that little incident. But he left something behind. Blood, a good deal of it and you know what can be done with just a few drops, right? Of course, you do. Now, I don't want to have to use that blood, that's a dark path, and I don't feel that anyone else needs to know about that intruder and who he said sent him, so I'm willing to pay you twenty thousand dollars if you can promise me that it'll stop."

"*Uh...*" Dalton cleared his throat. "Excuse me?"

"Twenty thousand. Just give me an account number, and I'll send it. Do we have a deal or not?"

Harcourt and Evan were watching this little exchange with rapt attention. Kate couldn't tell if the old man's raised eyebrow was amusement or terror in how the conversation had devolved.

"*A deal,*" Dalton repeated, but Kate couldn't tell if it was in agreement or a question.

"Yes. You'll stop the elementals if I donate twenty grand to your little cause?"

"*Do you even have that much money?*" Dalton asked.

"I do. I just need an account number."

"Does he need more?" Harcourt whispered, but Kate waved him off.

"*I'll see what I can do,*" Dalton said. "*Let me get it for you.*"

"Did you really get his blood?" Evan asked once Kate was off the phone.

"Not on purpose," she said. "I was too freaked out at the time to gather it myself, but he got some on my clothes during the fight."

"It wasn't a good idea to threaten him," Harcourt said. He was typing Dalton's bank information into a silver laptop.

"He wasn't really leaving much choice." Kate looked at the stocked bar. She really needed a drink right now, but she'd already broken one rule of

Jim's fast this morning and didn't think it smart to break another. "Diplomacy had failed, so I figured a threat might open his ears."

"There's no guarantee he'll stop," Evan said.

"No, but he's a Lex. They're pretty good about sticking to agreements. They're the dealers. Very rules-oriented."

"From my understanding," Harcourt said, "Leges are simply more inclined to twist their words. Lawyers each and every one."

"While us Arcani will straight-up lie," Kate added.

The old man closed the laptop. "That's why I put my faith in people, not titles."

"What about that Iron Word? You don't have faith in me?" She regretted the words the instant she said them, but it had been a shitty morning, and Dalton had her keyed up.

"It goes both ways, Miss Rossdale. It'll hold me to my word as much as you to yours. But since I don't trust this Dalton one iota, we need to discuss your sleeping arrangements until after your powers are restored."

"I'm way ahead of you. So unless you're inviting me to stay in here with you..." Kate motioned her nose toward the copper icon fixed above the window. "...I'll be staying at Jim's for the next few days."

"Correct. Mr. Stevens has made the offer, and I think it'd be best to take him up on it."

"You sure you don't want me here?" Kate asked. "I can be one hell of a great roommate. We'll paint our toenails."

The old man smiled humorlessly, like a patient parent. "Maybe another time. Evan will stay with me until we can begin your job."

10

IRONCLAD

Jim's flat occupied the upper floor of a renovated warehouse in Leith, less than three miles from the hotel. Renovated might have been a strong word, Kate decided, because the enormous room still looked very much like a warehouse. Wide, wooden panels, their edges stained with the oil of many hands, ran on tracks, allowing the room to be divided up into smaller ones. Many of these rolling walls were decorated with elaborate designs and half-finished murals, paint crackled with age. For the most part, these panels hung against the wall, save for two rooms at the back, a bedroom and a bath with an ancient claw-foot tub standing atop a gray marble platform.

The flat smelled of herbs and sweat, the latter Kate supposed coming from the weights and equipment in one corner. But more than anything, it smelled old—old wood, dusty pipes green with corrosion, antique furniture looking as out of place as a tuxedo at a barn dance. Black and stainless appliances made up the kitchenette, its polished counter probably cut from the same slab as the bathtub platform.

"And you'll be over there," Jim said, pointing to an overstuffed couch sitting before a modest television.

Kate sighed. "All right." She rolled her Samsonite over to her new bed. Several Outer World artifacts decorated a nearby shelf. Like Vegner's back in Baltimore, the majority were fairly banal. However, unlike the wealthy businessman, Jim had acquired these himself. Mementos from the past.

"Would anyone care for some tea?" Nate asked.

"Please," Harcourt said. He was admiring the carved and richly stained glyph mounted above the door.

Evan shook his head. "None for me, thanks."

"Coffee?" Kate asked.

Nate nodded. "Sure."

"Hold off on that," Jim said.

Kate shot him a questioning look, her eyebrow raised.

"You're fasting, remember."

"Bullshit," she laughed. "No. No, I'm not giving up coffee, too."

"You know the rules, Katie. You've done this before. Master Boyer always said..."

"The first cup after a fast is divinity," Kate said at the same time. She'd loathed those words when directed at her. But the malicious glee she'd felt from reciting them to Initiates, their eyes wide with the realization that a few days without Starbucks would be the hardest test for advancement, had never grown old. Kate wondered how much pleasure Jim was having at her expense. "Come on. I've had a hell of a morning."

"Chamomile?" Nate offered. Unlike Jim, she didn't even try to hide the mean amusement.

I'd rather drink piss. She managed to hold that in. Kate shook her head. *Eye on the prize*, she reminded herself. "Do you have Earl Grey?"

The young woman nodded.

"Please," Kate said. "Strong."

"Chamomile is fine for her," Jim called after Nate had vanished behind the kitchenette's half-wall. He shook his head at Kate. "What part of no caffeine is hard to understand?"

Kate's eyes narrowed. "This is a conspiracy, isn't it?"

"Huh?"

"You've gone native. They've turned you into a tea-drinker, and now you're trying to convert me."

Jim's mouth tightened into a half-smile, that grin he used to give back when they were tower mates with the whole world ahead of them. She'd missed that smile. "You got me."

"Well...it's not going to work."

"We'll see about that."

Near 10:00 Jim began the ceremony. The Iron Word was a simple affair compared to most other powerful enchantments. Many towers refused to teach it to anyone below the rank of Magus Lex. But Master Boyer had scoffed at the idea of denying knowledge to his students. He wouldn't have accepted them into Onyx had he thought them irresponsible. Any initiate that had earned their way to Magister Lex was taught it.

Master Boyer had trusted Kate, placed his faith in her ability to move them through the Abyss. Three years of self-hate that she had betrayed his trust was coming to an end. It was harder than she'd thought. Hatred, especially toward one's self, is a difficult thing to kill. Redirecting it was far more effective. And as Kate stepped barefoot into the ring of braided indigo rope, she stared into the eyes of the man who could tell her where that anger could go.

Harcourt stood straight, hands at his side. He'd removed his dark suit jacket and rolled the white shirt sleeves up to his elbows. Patches of pink burn scars spattered up his right arm like grease burns on a fry cook.

She didn't trust this man who hid the magic-thief's identity from her, holding it as leverage, this man who carried a witchhunter blade, this man whose name she didn't even know. But soon that last would be remedied.

Jim stepped into the circle beside them, a copper knife in each hand. She accepted one and Harcourt the other. While crafted from multiple parts, every piece was solid copper. No alloy, just pure elemental metal. With Jim's guidance, they pressed the cold blades to each other's throat, his fingers holding them in place.

Jim's lips moved in a silent chant. Then he nodded to Harcourt.

"I, Calvin Phillip Vogler, vow that in return for the spell to remove your curse, I shall require your full service of my intended task, but not to exceed one year from now."

Jim mouthed the words as they were spoken, and the knife in Kate's hand warmed. The final clause of one year meant Harcourt, or now Vogler, had no intention of divulging the exact job yet, but terms had to be set.

"I will not harm or allow any harm to come to you in that time," he continued. The blade grew hotter, threatening to burn her hand and his throat, but Jim held it firmly in place. "If I do not keep this promise, then this blade will take my life."

The sharp knife glowed as if heated in a great forge, but neither Kate's hand nor Vogler's neck burned at its touch, just that uncomfortable heat like sunglasses left in a car on a summer day.

Jim nodded to Kate.

"I, Katherine Julia Rossdale, vow that I shall complete your intended task to the best of my abilities for a time not to exceed one year from today." The hot metal stung against her neck. "I will neither harm nor allow harm to befall you in that time. If I fail to keep this promise, then this blade shall take my life."

Jim finished his silent recitation of her words, and Kate winced at a mild shock from her hand and the blade at her throat. The Iron Word was sealed. He removed the blades from their necks.

"So," Kate said. "Vogler, is it?"

"Harcourt, if you please." He touched the fading red line at his throat.

"You're the boss. But still no hint as to what this mystery job is?"

He shook his head. "Not until your powers are restored and our contract officially begins."

Kate smiled. Had Harcourt taken the path to sorcery, she had no doubt that he'd have not only become a Lex, but excelled at it. She stepped from the rope ring and returned to the table where her cold tea waited.

Nate was the next to enter the ring, and after the words were recited, sealed her allegiance to Harcourt for a period not to exceed the completion of the task or one full year. Evan watched the affair with rapt attention, his gaze locked on the glowing blades. Kate's first instinct had been writing it off as a mundie seeing real magic. For many, it took until reaching the third level of Adeptus before the marvel faded from their eyes. But then she remembered his story of the vulcanus he'd encountered, and recognized the hint of fear in those honey-colored eyes.

Once Nate was done, Jim performed the ceremony a third time, this one between Harcourt and himself. Kate continued to watch Evan's reaction to the glowing blades until she heard Harcourt say, "Five-hundred thousand euro," and her attention snapped back to the ceremony.

A half-million? What was he supposed to do for that much?

The Iron Word complete, Jim removed his knife from Harcourt's neck, three pink lines slashed across the pale skin. Jim exited the ring and sat on the overstuffed couch, sinking into it with an exhausted sigh.

"Very good," Harcourt said. He extended his hand to Evan who offered him the chrome and mother-of-pearl briefcase. "Per our agreement." Harcourt unclicked the locks and removed the slender book. "I will leave this in your care."

"Going back to the hotel?" Kate asked, accepting it.

"Yes. It's safer for me."

"So, who's after you? I can't betray you now." *At least not for another year.*

"Once your payment is complete," Harcourt said. "Only a few more days." He bid farewell to Nate, then to Jim, who was sitting with the thousand-yard stare one got after expending a great deal of power. He left, Evan at his side.

"A half-million," Kate asked. "That's what you're charging to get back my magic?"

Jim blinked. "No. That's for a one-year contract. For you, I'm doing it on principle."

"So, he's paying you five-hundred grand, and you're making me sleep on the couch?"

Jim smiled weakly. "You can have the floor if you prefer."

Kate's eyes narrowed.

"But you do get a zero-elemental guarantee." He rose to his feet. "I need to crash, I'm beat."

"Can we talk first?"

"About what?"

"About our new boss," Kate said, nodding to the closed door. "He has a witchhunter blade."

Jim froze. "Are you sure?"

"Saw it this morning. Evan was looking at it, but I don't think they saw me notice it."

Jim's lips tightened, moving like words were trying to escape but couldn't. Finally, "They can't be Spire."

"Spire?" Nate asked, looking to her master and then to Kate.

"Has he told you about them?" Kate asked.

The young woman nodded. "Everyone knows about 'em. Mundies. Inquisitors."

"Pretty much," Kate said. "But they're not total mundies. Fight fire with fire is their MO. Any practitioners, real or imagined, that fall under their radar, they come at them like the hashashins of old."

"So, they're witchhunters, eh?" Nate asked, nervously running her fingers through her spiky hair.

Jim shook his head. "No way. Spire wouldn't be asking us for the Iron Word. Harcourt must have gotten it somewhere." He marched toward the kitchen. "I need a drink."

Kate fought the growing need for a drink herself. "I don't know if they're Golden Spire. But he's keeping everything too close to the chest.

He has a Red Gate up in his suite. And Evan's got some sort of pendant, I think."

"Yeah, Nate spotted the gate icons before I did. Asked me what they were," Jim said, popping the top off a beer as he came back. "Witchhunters might use those, but so could anyone. What'd the pendant look like?"

"I don't know. I only felt it." Kate finished off the cold tea.

"Okay, so what does it do?"

"I don't know. But it was enchanted."

Nate cocked her head. "Then...how do ye know?"

"I felt it," Kate said. "After the elemental, I hugged him and felt the magic through his shirt."

"It'd have to be powerful as hell for you to do that," Jim said, lowering himself back down onto the couch.

Kate shook her head. "Not really. Not for me." She rose and headed to the kitchen for more tea.

Nate gave her a look.

"Katie, how sensitive are you?" Jim asked.

"How do you mean?" Kate asked, scooping a healthy dose of leaves into a stainless infuser.

"Just that." He swigged his beer. "I mean, you've always been sensitive to magic, but how much?"

"I don't know. More than I used to be. It's how I did authentications."

"But how much?" he pressed.

She sighed. "Um... Could you feel the Red Gate at Harcourt's or did you not know until you saw the icons?"

"Not till I saw 'em."

Kate frowned. "Really?"

"Really."

She poured the last of the hot kettle into her cup and strolled back to her chair. "Well to me they felt like...you know when you open the door to a really hot room or attic, and the air just feels thicker? It's like that. Can't miss it."

"Did you feel anything in the hotel?" he asked, turning to Nate.

She shook her head. "I didn' know what they were until ye told me later."

"Can you feel my wards?" Jim asked.

Kate blew on her cup. "Oh yeah."

"How many?"

"Three."

He lifted his dark eyebrows. "Can you tell me where?"

Kate rose and approached the door. "Well, there's the big wooden one there." She slowed as she neared, holding out her hand to feel the pressure change. "And one..." She moved her hand to the left, right, then back to the left toward the hinges. "Here." She touched an area low near the doorstop, a prickling beneath her fingertips despite the smooth enamel. "You hid it under the paint."

Jim's stupefied expression verified that she was right. "And the third?"

She moved her hands more, feeling the warm spongy ward but not the anchor. There! She reached up toward the carved icon. "It's under there, isn't it? Just below the first one?"

He lifted his bottle. "Color me impressed."

"I'll be damned," Nate said. "Ye didn' even tell me about tha' one."

Jim gave her a shrug.

"So do you believe me?" Kate asked returning to her tea.

"Oh I believe you're hypersensitive," Jim said. "Shit. This happened after your...curse?"

"Yeah. Slow at first, but the longer I went without magic, the more I could feel it."

"Damn." He swigged his beer. "So, your empathy is incredible, but that doesn't mean Harcourt's a witchhunter. Just means he has a blade. We also know he's rich as shit, so he could have just bought it."

"But why the secrecy?"

"I don't know. Rich people get paranoid. He's up to something, but no witchhunter would strike a deal to give an incantatrix back her power and demand the Iron Word saying that he can't harm her. If he or anyone in the Spire comes after us, he'll die too. That doesn't make sense."

"Well, I'd wish you'd shared this before we sealed ourselves to him," Nate said.

"I only saw it this morning," Kate said. "I've been under watch ever since."

"Really?" Jim asked, his voice oozing with sarcasm. "Not even thirty seconds to go, *Oh, Jim, can we talk in your room a moment?* Was that it, or were you just afraid that if I knew I'd back out."

Kate's cheeks blazed hot. She drew a breath, ready to lay into him for even thinking that, but paused. Maybe he was right. Had she kept it from him out of fear? A weight settled in her stomach. Releasing the breath, she glanced away. "You know I wouldn't do that to you," she said, hoping to convince herself as much as him,

Nate looked to her master. "So wha' do we do?"

"Nothing." Jim lifted his beer but seemed to think better of it. "We can't assume they're Spire."

Kate shook her head. "But I saw—"

"A knife. Lots of practitioners have 'em. Tisha, too, if I recall. It doesn't mean anything."

"It doesn't mean *nothing*."

"And we can ask him about it. The Word is done. It'll take an Ipsissimus to counter it, and I doubt they'll find one to do that. But you're coming off a dust binge right now. And you're getting paranoid."

"Paranoid?" Kate snapped.

"Look, I don't blame you. You've had a shit couple days, and this is definitely weird, but before we get all caught up thinking our new boss is a witchhunter, we have to remember perspective."

"That I'm just crazy?" Kate asked.

"That you've been attacked by an elemental and strung out."

Kate's hand shot in a sort of karate motion, chopping it on each word. "Jim, I'm not fucking imagining this."

"I'm not saying you are, but—"

"No." Kate stood. "Fine. Don't believe me."

"Katie..." he pleaded.

"Don't start that. You're on my couch. Get off. I'm going to bed."

11

THE TEN GATES

The second day under house arrest at Jim's was when Kate wanted to die. Between the comedown off the blood dust and the incredible caffeine withdrawal headache, she needed a drink and a bump more than anything in the world. Her stomach ached like she'd eaten a whole cactus, and food made her sick. Bright lights or any noise above a whisper and her skull felt like bursting at the seams. Motor skills were about nil and brushing her teeth had been a feat of sheer will.

The only solace she found was in the deep cast iron tub. There, somewhere between asleep and awake, half submerged in water the temperature of blood, her head back against the rolled edge and eyes closed, she prayed for the pain to go away.

The door knocked, rousing her from her trance. "Katie?"

Kate blinked. Shit, how long had she been in here? "Yes?"

The door creaked, and Jim stuck his head in. "You all right?"

"Fine. Do you need the toilet? I'm sorry... I—"

"No. I'm fine, just checking on you is all. Can I come in?"

The briefest moment of self-consciousness shivered down her back, and she lowered into the milky, soapy water. Jim had seen her naked before, not just as a tower mate, but those few times as lovers a decade before. Her legs were sticking out, suds clinging to the hair. She hadn't shaved in over a month, maybe two. She pushed herself up higher, submerging them. So what if he saw her breasts, they might take his attention away from the horror show below her waist.

"How are you feelin'?" he asked, stepping inside.

"Like someone held me down and beat me with a hammer."

He nodded, taking a seat on the toilet. "That's good. Means you're cleaning up. You drinking plenty of water?"

"Yeah." It wasn't a complete lie.

Jim scratched his stubbled cheek. "I've put out a few feelers. Nothing much, but so far no one knows anything about either a Calvin Vogler or Richard Harcourt."

"I thought you said I was paranoid."

"Paranoid doesn't mean wrong. It might take a few days to hear back from some people, but I am looking into it."

She nodded. "Thanks. You try Thorne?"

"Aye." The word sounded weird coming from him. Two years in Scotland had begun its subtle alterations to his vocabulary, even tinges had worked here and there into his already muddled accent.

Kate squinted to the narrow wedge of light spilling through the cracked door. "Nate here?"

"She's out running some errands."

Kate nodded, remembering when Nate had asked her through the door her preference for dinner. "Are you two screwing?" She hadn't intended that question, at least not like that. It just slipped out.

"So what if we are?"

"She's your student," she said, voice rising. "It's wrong."

Jim shrugged, the motion barely visible in the dim light. "That's a tower rule. I'm not in a tower, remember?" Kate frowned, about to reply when Jim continued. "But no, we're not. We have, back when we first met, but once I took her as my apprentice that ended."

"Oh. Well, that's good."

"Jealous?"

"No," Kate snorted, not realizing it was a lie until after she said it. Not that she wanted Jim in the slightest. But a nameless pang in the back of her mind assured her of her envy. "It's just I didn't want you to be like Larry Kelman or any of those people."

"The ones who took in all the cute novices to *show them the power*." He air-quoted that last part.

"Yeah."

"No way. I hated those scum bags."

She grinned, relief washing through her.

"God," Jim chuckled. "I hadn't thought about Greaseball Larry in forever. He still around?"

"Yeah, but not at Whittaker's. Tisha banned his ass on sheer principle."

"Good for her."

"Now he just trolls coffee bars and bookstores."

"There's always those types." He cleared his throat. "Anyway, I'm studying that spell, and while I don't fully understand how this curse was done, I figured out a little more about it."

Her attention snapped firmer than it had in two days. "What's that?"

"It's not that it blocked your power. It redirected it somewhere else."

"Where?"

"To whoever cast it, I assume. They stole it for themselves."

"Stole it? How?"

"I don't know. But it looks to me like they took all of your abilities, making them a Magister Arcanus."

"Son of a bitch." She ran her hand across her jaw. "But they wouldn't be trained."

"No, but they'd have the power and be attuned. Think about it, they could cast that on a Magus Viator, Lex, and Arcanus, and with a little training be all three at once."

She straightened, any traces of modesty forgotten "Holy shit. They'd be a tower unto themselves."

"Yeah, and think if they did it to three Ipsissima? But here's the deal. If you die, they lose it. So you have to stay alive for them to keep your power."

"That's a plus, I suppose."

"I guess. But when I break this curse, whoever placed it on you will know. They'll feel the loss and be on to us."

"Maybe they'll just think I died."

He shrugged. "Maybe. But maybe they'll feel the curse break. And if they do, they'll know you're onto 'em. They might try to take your magic back."

"Or kill me," Kate said, her gaze falling onto the edge of the tub, but not registering it.

"That's not going to happen."

It was near 11:00 on the sixth night when Kate emerged from the bathroom wearing nothing but a thin cotton gown. Her hair was still damp after her bath followed by a shower rinse. She'd scrubbed every millimeter of her body, paying special attention to the ten gates. A haze of frankincense filled the air, the smoke rising from a trio of black bowls set at the center of the room. The furniture had all been pushed aside, and her knees still ached from scouring the floors with Nate, removing any traces of dirt and grease that negative energies could cling to.

The blonde initiate now stood near the wall beside Harcourt and Evan, hands clasped before her.

Jim stood at the far side, also wearing a white gown, though with shorter sleeves. He extended his hand and Kate moved toward him, the smooth floor cold beneath her bare feet. Carefully, she stepped over the elaborate pattern of dotted lines in five colors of chalk and stopped in the open space in the center.

"Here," Jim said, and gently led her to the hard floor, positioning her feet and arms open like a star. Eyes forward, she stared up at the ceiling rafters.

Muttering a quiet mantra of concentration, Jim circled her clockwise, drawing the first ring in yellow chalk. He drew the symbols around the ring with infinite care and precision, all the while whispering the words.

A subtle buzzing started at her toes and fingertips as he completed the first ring. Kate held her breath, the anticipation mounting.

Nate brought him three cylinders of ice, each about the size of a large soda can, and Jim placed those around the ring before beginning the next circle in blue.

The fear that this wouldn't work wormed into the back of Kate's mind, but she pushed it away. This had to work. Jim had assured her that the spell was real and she trusted him with her life. If anyone could cast it, Jim could. Had Onyx not been attacked, he'd have been a Magus Lex by now.

The buzzing grew louder as the second ring closed. Its humming moved deeper along her arms and legs and began at her other extremities, ears, nose, lips, and nipples.

Jim placed quartz crystals along the next circle. Kate could no longer hear his whispered chant over the buzz. Three long tapers came next, and the fire ring was sealed. Her body trembled like a taut piano wire, the buzzing like a hundred million bees. Breathing grew difficult, but she remained still, flesh crawling. Jim continued his work, taking his time with maddening patience. Kate could no longer see him in the corner of her watering eyes.

The buzzing filled her world as the fourth ring sealed. Every inch of her droned, something between pain and numbness. She gritted her teeth, feeling them hum in their sockets like some overdose of blood dust. Was this how Jess had felt before she'd died?

Kate's body tensed, every muscle and sinew drawing tighter and tighter. The pain was growing too intense. Her eyes vibrated against the back of their clenched lids so hard she knew they were the only thing keeping them in. Redness flared, an unseen brilliance. A scream welled in her throat. She tried to stifle it but then—

Silence.

She lay there for several seconds, her body suddenly numb. Somewhere, a thousand miles away, she heard Jim's chanting voice. Kate opened her eyes. Six-inch flames jetted from the three tapers, filling the room with yellow light. Water rushed and flowed within the second ring, the ice-blocks had melted, but none had crossed the chalk lines.

High above, the ceiling rafters appeared the same, indifferent to the ceremony below. But no, she realized. They were darker, the shadows thicker. She stared up at the perfect circle of darkness above her, somehow immune to the candles' blazing light.

The darkness swirled and flowed, and she recognized it for what it was. Aether. It trickled down from those dark places above, reluctant strands curling and feeling their way toward her like a misty jellyfish.

That familiar smell like rain and warm spring ignited her senses. It flowed down onto her, through her hair, and beneath her gown, wrapping her in a soft cocoon. The aether laced between Kate's fingers, caressing like a reluctant but long-absent lover. Her taut muscles relaxed beneath the aether's touch and without warning, it struck.

The living fog surged between her lips and up her nose. It pushed its way through her eyes, ears, vagina, and anus. It assaulted all ten gates, pouring into her with an unrelenting flood. Blinded, deafened, and unable to breathe, she tried to struggle, to get up, claw at her face and her privates, but the misty strands encircling her arms tightened with an iron hold, locking her into place.

It filled her lungs and flowed into her veins, flooding each capillary with an electric warmth. Her hammering heart slowed, and her struggles ceased. The aether slid from her arms and legs, retreating inside Kate's body, but she couldn't move. It entered every muscle, every bone, every cell. It felt as though she might burst, but still more poured into her, snuffing out her senses until she felt nothing at all.

All at once, her joints popped. Not just her joints but everything. Ligaments, organs, eyes, blood all popped in one excruciating but orgasmic snap. It wasn't violation. A missing, long-absent piece of her clicked into place and what had occupied that void, the imposter, fought back.

Her body shook, every cell a sudden battlefield of control, yanking and tugging different directions at once. Blue haze filled her senses, struggling to burrow back in or tear her apart. Kate screamed, or tried to, but all she felt or heard was a tumult of blue, aether, joy, and agony. The deep-rooted invader ripped free and began to boil.

Liquid light poured from her like blazing quicksilver. It came from her eyes and ears and between her legs. It ran down her skin, evaporating into luminous fog.

Kate gasped as it fled her lungs. A cyclone of white light surged around her. She was floating several inches from the floor, slowly spinning. The candle tapers had melted away, but three-foot jets of blue fire shot from the places they had been. The quartz crystals glowed with some internal yellow brilliance. The ring of water surged and boiled into a column of steam, and beyond all of that, Jim chanted at the edge, veins bulging from his pained face. The others watched her in both awe and horror, Nate's mouth open and eyes wide. Evan looked as though he might scream. But Harcourt watched her with steady bombardier eyes, clenched fists at his sides.

The last of the light exited her body and faded. The crystals dimmed. Candles extinguished, and Kate fell to the floor with a hard thud.

An explosion like some unseen supernova erupted in the space between her brows. A river burst within her mind's eye and rushed through her with the fury of a broken dam. The other six energy hubs ignited in succession—her crown, her throat, her heart, and downward—all bursting with power. Each gasped breath fueled them harder, more magic than she'd felt in years, more than she'd ever remembered possible. The blood dust had only given her a taste, fooled her into believing that its pittance was anything but meager scraps. Her vision blurred and the room lurched drunkenly.

"Too much," she wept. "Too much."

Hands gripped her shoulders, gently urging her into a sitting position.

"There," a man whispered. "You're safe. You're okay."

Kate opened her tear-blurred eyes to Harcourt kneeling beside her.

Nate and Evan were helping Jim to his feet. His head lolled, but he smiled as he saw her.

"That was...something," he mumbled.

Kate smiled back. She looked at Harcourt. "We need...to talk. Now."

"We will. Can you stand?"

Waves of magic were still crashing through her. Every fiber in her body ached, but Kate nodded.

"Here." With one hand under her arm, the old man helped her up. He was stronger than she'd thought, lifting her more than anything until her feet were on the floor. Cold wetness squished between her toes. The melted ice ran across the planks, swirling with colors from the chalked lines.

The room warbled around her, and Kate closed her eyes. Was she high?

Harcourt helped her to the sofa and laid her down. "Do you need any water, anything?"

"Nah," she said. Evan and Nate were leading Jim to his room. His sweat-soaked gown clung to his bare skin.

"We'll talk in the morning," Harcourt said. "But you need rest."

Kate nodded absently. One more night wouldn't hurt. Right now she needed to savor what she'd feared she'd lost forever. She lifted her hand, feeling the magic arc between her fingers. "Thank you."

"No need to thank me." His thin lips curled into a joyless smile. "Quid pro quo, remember?"

"I remember."

He brushed her hair back, like a father and stood. "Rest up."

Evan returned from Jim's room and closed the door behind him. He looked to Harcourt, who nodded, and fetched the briefcase from the table against the wall. Opening it, Evan removed a folded gray cloth and a plastic box from the case and carried them to where Kate lay. "These arrived for you. I got you some hollow points for it." He unwrapped the cloth enough to show the polished stainless gun and then re-wrapped it. The box rattled as he set it on the end table beside her. Four rows of gleaming, nickel bullets appeared to float inside, suspended by a clear, perforated rack. "Wear gloves when you load it. That way there's no prints on the shells."

"Thanks."

He smiled, warm and delicious. "No problem."

"You're cute," she mumbled, her lips pulled into some approximation of a smile.

Evan's grin faltered, and the sudden horror of what she'd just said struck her like a fist.

Shit. She was flirting. Christ, what the hell was wrong with her?

Her realization must have been written all over her face because Evan seemed to brush his surprise off. "Get some rest."

Without another word he and Harcourt left, leaving Kate alone on the sofa, a melting ring on the floor, and power coursing through her.

12

TATTOOS AND HANDCUFFS

K ate awoke some hours before sunrise, though awoke was hardly the proper word. She found herself weightless, floating five feet above the sofa, staring down at herself.

Christ, she thought, *I look like hell*. It wasn't like looking in a mirror, eye to eye with a reflection. It was more like a photograph, that glimpse of one's self from the eyes of another, the angles different than one was normally accustomed. Her pallid skin was obviously unaccustomed to sunlight. But a faint dusting of freckles along her cheekbones told of brighter days. She'd lost weight, more than she'd thought, and her long, slender nose always surprised her when she saw it from any angle but straight on. The crease across her forehead had grown deeper these past few years, looking like a knife slash, but the smile hidden at the corner of her lips said that even in this state, she knew the ordeal was over. What had been a wasting drug addict not twelve hours before was now a sorceress, her body resting while her essence explored the magical realms.

It had been years since she'd projected, a feat she once considered simple, mundane even. Even some mundies could leave their bodies during sleep or times of incredible pain—childbirth, torture, the wreckage of a car accident. Most wandered blindly, believing it a fantastical dream. Practitioners, especially those of Onyx Tower, perfected the art. Her lessons to Lumitors were almost exclusively received outside her body.

Jim's flat was silent, a faint snoring coming from the bedroom. Outside, the rumble of morning commuter cars and the distant thrumming of an airplane high above. Tiny white specks floated down around her, like a light, downy snow. Unhindered by the physical sphere, it passed through the furniture and floor, continuing ever downward. She felt neither cold nor warmth, but a subtle breeze fluttered her non-corporeal hair and white gown. The garment wasn't real of course, and only existed because she'd remembered wearing it. Many travelers in this state found themselves naked, lacking the knowledge or desire to imagine garments.

Of course, being outside her body was not without its risks. Other wanderers might find her, even the occasional lone verl hound might smell her here, or an elemental might attack her or try to slither into her vacant body. But the wards sealing Jim's flat made it safe as long as she didn't leave. Even now she could feel their muted hum like electric wires beneath sheetrock. She could leave them but not re-enter, not without Jim's permission. Enjoying her current state, Kate decided a bit of exploring was in order.

Lowering herself to the floor, a meaningless act in a world devoid of gravity or walls, she approached the shelves, peeking into boxes and drawers. Searching in this manner had taken some practice. Unable to so much as lift a piece of paper, she couldn't open a book, and pages were too close together to read. But peeking inside closed spaces was rather simple. Darkness didn't hinder her. Light was only a requirement of flesh eyes. She perused the living room and kitchenette, finding very little of note save for a mouse nest tucked deep below the cabinets.

It took some time before Kate realized what she was looking for, the prize of this little quest—her blood dust. Not that she wanted it, per se, but it was something hidden.

He wouldn't have left it out here where I could find it, she thought, eyeing the rolling wall of his room. She passed through it as if it were no more than a misty veil.

Jim lay on his side, softly snoring. He still wore the ceremonial gown, crumpled striped sheets draped over his hip and thighs. Nate was curled behind him, swallowed by a sleeveless black shirt about four sizes too big. Bright colors shone along the back of her exposed shoulder, the image of a bent-necked crane, reds and golden yellows behind it. The tattoo didn't appear complete, its lower section devolving into traced lines. Kate moved for a closer look but met with a humming wall of resistance.

She peeked beneath the bed to discover a large painted circle protecting the sleepers. *Clever.*

Kate knew she should feel guilty for entering this room. She'd been taught and had taught better than that, but she was too excited to care about such things as privacy. With her magic back, she was a schoolgirl again, this renovated warehouse her personal playground. She checked the side table drawer, discovering a rolled baggie of marijuana and a couple of personal romantic items Jim would flip his shit if he knew she'd discovered. She'd never taken him for the handcuff type before.

A large armoire stood against one wall, serving as the closet. There, in the drawer beneath the big mirrored door, Kate discovered her vial of blood dust tucked beside winter gloves. Its magic hummed beneath her incorporeal fingers. To think she'd once considered its pittance of magic as a blessing. But now that she had her powers back, she wondered how its boost might feel, and desire rekindled.

Nate let out a groaning sigh, breaking Kate thoughts. Rising, she turned back to the bed and flinched as she met the apprentice's eyes.

Her hair tousled with sleep, Nate squinted directly at her, her face a mixture of puzzlement and surprise. She rubbed her eyes between thumb and forefinger, and Kate stole that moment to retreat backward, gliding through the armoire and out the wall into the bathroom.

"Hello?" Nate croaked from the bedroom.

Panicked at being caught, Kate shot back to her body and woke instantly. How could Nate have seen her? She'd read of, but never met anyone that could see incorporeally, but had no doubt Nate had done it.

The creak of someone rising from the bed sounded from beyond the door. Kate hopped off the sofa and hurriedly began to dress. She'd squeezed into a pair of jeans and a dirty tank top by the time Nate emerged from the bedroom.

"Morning," Kate said cheerily, arranging the cushions.

"I didn't know ye were up." Nate looked around as if somebody else might be there. The big T-shirt for some band Kate had never heard of swallowed her narrow frame.

"Yeah, been awake for a while. Sleep okay?"

Nate nodded absently. "Aye. And ye?"

"Fantastic. My fast is over, so I'm in the mood for coffee and greasy food. What do you say?"

Nate was looking at her, a question bubbling behind her unpainted lips. "Sounds good."

Kate smiled. "Great."

Nate retreated back into the bedroom. Kate release a sigh. From now on she'd be paying closer attention to Jim's apprentice.

13

LUMINOUS CLOCKWORK

"And how are we today?" Harcourt asked, emerging from his bedroom as Kate and the others crossed the Red Gate and into his suite. Fine pinstripes ran along his charcoal suit, offset by an electric purple shirt, by far the brightest thing Kate had seen him wear.

"Spectacular," she said. The caffeine from her quad-shot latte hummed through her veins, a long-absent friend.

Evan closed the door behind them, the latch clicking into place.

Harcourt smiled. "And...were we successful in last night's venture?"

Kate's lip curled into an impish smile. Scanning the room, she eyed a black plastic hotel pen resting atop a polished table. Hooking her middle finger, she twisted her hand open, thumb stabbing to the side in a quick motion. The pen launched from the table and sailed into her open palm. "I'd say so."

"Excellent," Harcourt said, not seeming as impressed with the display as Kate was. Not long ago, such a trick would have cost her fifty bucks worth of blood dust. Now, she barely registered the drain on her magical stores.

"Mr. Stevens," Harcourt said, looking to Jim. "I completed the transfer of funds last night. It should have appeared in your account by now. Would you like to check?"

Jim shrugged. "I trust it's there."

"Are you sure?" Harcourt asked.

Jim nodded.

Kate flipped the pen between her fingers. "Now that I'm up and running, you have some explaining to do."

"Of course." The old man extended his hand toward the sofa and chairs. The mother-of-pearl-latched briefcase rested on the coffee table. "Please." He waited until everyone had sat before taking a seat.

Once they were all seated, he claimed his own. He ran his thumb idly across his scarred finger. His lip twitched, a whisper of hesitation, and then he spoke. "As you now know, my real name is Calvin Vogler. For thirty-three years I belonged to the Brotherhood of the Golden Spire."

Nate sucked a hiss, her posture straightening. Her muscles tensed like every tendon had been replaced with stainless wire, ready to spring. Her eyes darted between Evan and Harcourt, but the two men remained impassive.

"Fuck me," Jim groaned. He shook his head. "You were right, Katie."

Harcourt's brow lifted. "You'd guessed?"

Kate swallowed, her mind racing. "I suspected it."

The old man sighed. "You have nothing to worry about. The Iron Word ensures I'll keep you protected."

Jim snorted a laugh. "Well, you're lucky I didn't know you were a fucking witchhunter." His hands tightened into fists. "You realize if anyone found out I took money and worked for the Golden Fucking Spire what would happen to me?"

"Then I would keep that to yourself," Harcourt said. "I, for one, don't plan to announce it. But if it is any consolation, I'm no longer with the Brotherhood."

"No?"

"No," Harcourt said. "In fact, I'd very much like to avoid them."

Kate grinned. *So that's who you're hiding from*, she thought, the pieces falling into place.

Harcourt looked at her. "I'm sure you have questions."

She ran her tongue along her cheek and nodded, then pointed her pen toward the wet bar like a stage magician's wand. "I need a drink," she said rising. "Anyone else want one?"

"Shit, yeah," Jim said.

Kate poured herself two fingers of whiskey. She took a long, healthy drink and coughed as the burn sizzled down her throat. "Do you know how many of my friends you've killed?"

Harcourt's expression remained stone. "I doubt I, or any of my associates, have killed any of your friends, Miss Rossdale. The kind of practitioners we target are among the worst kinds of human beings."

"Uh-huh." She clinked the bottle and three empty glasses down on the table and took her seat. "So, Magus Gregor, you know nothing about that?"

He shook his head. "No, and he was an Ipsissimus. That fact is well-known. But we had nothing to do with his disappearance."

"And Jason Truman? Lilly Yen? None of these ring a bell?"

"Not the Spire."

"Bullshit," Jim said, pouring a drink.

"We are not the bogeymen we are believed to be," Harcourt said. "Being what we are, unknown, we're accused of far more than we actually do."

"Really?" Jim said. "So the Spire never hunted us or tortured and murdered families?"

"Oh, that happened. I won't deny it. Any institution as old as the Spire has been guilty of atrocities. But I assure you that those days are far behind us. The Spire's no longer concerned with practitioners so much as practitioners who would harm our world."

Jim snorted and took a drink.

"You think of us as monsters," Harcourt said. "But who assisted with the death of Rasputin? He was an evil sorcerer if there ever was, but the Towers failed to act. And who burned the Nazi castle of Wewelsburg, where Himmler's cult resided? While the Towers fled and hid, we attacked."

"You didn't do that," Kate said. "Nazis burned it down themselves."

"Oh," Harcourt said, an amused edge to his voice. "Did they? And who exactly said that? What is your source? The Nazis?" He tsked. "You should find more credible witnesses. And the Order of the Silver Sun in Florence, the Loti of Argentina, and countless murderers and budding cult leaders. Those are who draw the Spire's attention. Believe me, I've no reason to lie about this."

"All right," Kate said, letting the argument lie, but still not believing it. "Then why is the Spire after you?"

The old man smiled humorlessly. "A disagreement."

"You refuse to murder someone?"

"No. There's someone I want to kill. And that, Miss Rossdale, is what this is all about. Your job is to help me."

Kate's jaw tightened.

"Don't worry," Harcourt said. "She's the same one who stole your powers and murdered your friends."

Jim froze halfway through his second drink.

"Who?" Kate growled.

"Let me show you." The old man leaned forward, reaching for the briefcase. The twin latches popped with a loud double-click.

Kate tensed as he reached inside, expecting to see that cursed dagger, but instead, Harcourt drew out a slender laptop.

"In the nine centuries the Spire has existed, we've collected many artifacts related to the Art. Our library of magical tomes is the greatest in the world. Even more than the Vatican's. Of course, it's not held all in one place, but spread out among our...or their...headquarters. The spell that was used to remove your curse came from the personal collection of the sorcerer John Dee."

"Dee?" Jim asked, sounding impressed.

Harcourt nodded. "Penned by his own hand." He opened the computer. "Many of Dee's volumes were housed in our Manhattan office. High security. Three years ago, that office was attacked. Sixteen members were slaughtered, and the archives raided."

Kate chewed her lip. She'd remembered some whispering about a Spire House being attacked, but nothing more.

"The Brotherhood employs state of the art security. Always has. But all of our electronic surveillance was knocked out during the strike. Except for a single camera, a relic from a time when it was the cutting edge." He clicked the keyboard. "It operated mechanically, sixteen-millimeter film. The archivist, Jeff, maintained it out of some fondness. That camera activated when the vault doors were opened, and is the only witness to that day." He rotated the computer toward them and clicked a button.

A video began, a widening crack of lights, a door opening to a darkened room. A white globe of light glided inside, illuminating the back of a vault door, racks of drawers, and hundreds of books. A figure stepped in behind it, face hidden behind the floating light between them and the camera. But the build and swaying walk revealed it to be female. The video was silent, and Kate watched the figure move along the aisle searching, removing tomes. The light floated higher, and Kate's hand went to her mouth.

"No way!" Jim breathed beside her, leaning close to the monitor. "Candy?"

Kate only watched, still not believing. Candace Cross appeared exactly as she'd remembered her—the short, upturned nose, the slender face, and chisel wedge of blonde hair.

Candace removed several leather-bound books and called out, her words unreadable. Another figure hurried into the vault, male, wearing a snug black shirt and his face hidden in shadows. The man gathered books and hurried out as Candace plundered a pair of wooden drawers. Within two minutes of her entry, Candace left, her arms loaded with her spoils. The floating light dimmed and faded away.

"When was this?" Kate asked as the video stopped.

"September twenty-eighth," Harcourt said. "Nearly two weeks after the incident that left you powerless and Onyx destroyed."

"That can't be," Jim said. "Candace died that night. I was there."

"Did you see her die? Did you see the body? My sources said no."

"What sources?" Kate demanded. "How did you even know about what happened?"

"The Brotherhood has many agents. Our duty is to watch. After the massacre in New York, we searched for who might have perpetrated it. The collapse of a Tower is heard around the world. We first believed our attack might be some misguided retaliation. Our agents asked the right questions, and over the years many pieces slipped out."

"So, what? You have spies in Whittaker's?" Kate asked.

Harcourt nodded. "Of course. And here and dozens of havens around the world. That's why I couldn't go there or to Cù-Sìth myself."

Kate's stomach roiled, imagining a spy in Whittaker's, listening to their conversations, buying drinks, and sharing stories. "Who was it?"

Harcourt looked at her.

"In Whittaker's? Who was it?"

He shook his head. "I'm sorry. If I knew I still wouldn't betray them."

"But you aren't Spire anymore."

"That's not the point. They're still my brothers and sisters, and despite my current situation, I'd never endanger their lives."

"What about Evan there?" Jim asked. "He walked right into Cù-Sìth and ordered drinks."

Evan shrugged. "I'm not with the Brotherhood."

Harcourt nodded. "I found Evan privately. My primary duty with the Brotherhood was recruitment. His encounter in Afghanistan drew my attention. I'd have brought him into our fold, but by that time I knew my future with the Spire was near its end." He turned the computer toward himself and clicked several buttons before turning it back.

"I was in Prague at the time of the attack. Otherwise, I'd have been killed as well." Images played across the screen, photographs of the dead, blood splattered walls, severed limbs, burned faces contorted with pain, a man seated in an engraved high-backed chair, his entrails piled at his feet like a loyal dog. "Finding the murderer became my only focus. I was obsessed with it. Her accomplice was a Brother. Andrew Bochenkov. He went missing at that time, and was feared among the casualties. I, however, investigated everyone.

"Andrew was one of our spies." An image of a young man, late twenties with dark hair and a Caesar cut, appeared on the screen. Large ears protruded from either side, and a pair of moles dotted his left cheek.

Kate frowned, recognizing the face from somewhere.

"Yeah," Jim muttered. "I remember him. Tony or Terry or something. Remember?" he said, looking to Kate. "Candy started seeing him in that last year."

Kate shook her head, only vaguely remembering her having a boyfriend. But she'd been so distracted with preparing for her test that she hadn't paid much attention to anything outside of it.

Harcourt nodded. "Baltimore was in his territory. Agents are forbidden any form of relationship with practitioners, but obviously... The codex that contained the spell used to curse you was sent from London to the New York house a full year prior, and was signed for by Bochenkov. It was never placed in the vault. He had forged the archivist's request for the book and must have given it to Miss Cross. The missing portion, the part with the counter-spell, was safely in our Vienna House."

"I still can't believe it," Kate said. "When could she have cast it? We were all right there in the circle together. We'd have seen it."

"Probably while we were watching you," Jim said. "It was *your* test. Master Boyer, me, we were all watching you and Dennis above the brazier."

Kate replayed that final night in her mind. '*You don't get her*,' she'd screamed at the hound. Kate had thought it bravado at the time, but no, if Kate had died, Candace wouldn't have been able to steal her powers. She remembered Dennis kneeling drunkenly beside the brazier as Master Boyer fended off the hounds. "She tried to steal Dennis' powers, too."

Jim's brow furrowed.

"When the hounds attacked," Kate said. "Dennis was just sitting there looking dazed, probably just like me."

"But Dennis died," Jim said. "I saw it."

"I don't think it was part of the plan. Candace drove the hounds away from me. She ordered them back."

"You can't control verl hounds."

"Dee claimed to," Harcourt said. "And so did the Ancient Egyptians."

"But why us?" Kate asked. "Why not Master Boyer?"

Harcourt shrugged. "I believe your master might have been too powerful for her at the time. But two Magus Viatores would have been irresistible. In the years since, nine Viatores have gone missing. Four more died, including an Ipsissimus. Only one of those was the Brotherhood responsible for."

"Who?" Jim asked.

"Amahle Nortje."

"Really?"

"She was a vile creature. Killer of children. But the others…" He shook his head. "That wasn't us. But many powerful sorcerers have vanished these past three years, and there's only two or three left who can cross the Abyss."

"But why?" Kate asked.

"To have it for herself," Harcourt said. "She'd need all the power she could to reach Carcosa."

Kate arched her brow. "Carcosa?"

He nodded. "Among the volumes she took was our entire collection on the city."

"Carcosa's a myth," Jim said into his drink.

"The Brotherhood told me the same thing. But I don't think it is. I believe she's seeking it and I want to follow her. So I hired a Viator of my own."

Snorting, Kate refilled her glass. "Then you're in for a disappointment. I already told you I'm only a Magister Arcanus."

Harcourt lifted a single brow. "Are you certain of that?"

"Uh-huh. Pretty damned sure."

"I was under the impression that you'd cast the circle taking you to and from Hollit."

She sipped her drink. "Yeah, but we never sanctified it. I never moved up."

"What does that matter?" Harcourt asked. "You cast it successfully. You don't need a ceremony to make you a Viator. The ceremony only acknowledges it."

Kate paused, the glass nearly to her lips.

"Prove me wrong. Show me your glyph. If I'm mistaken, please show me."

A sudden fear prickled along Kate's scalp. Was she? She set the glass onto the table and almost like she was watching it versus doing it, she extended her hand, weaving her fingers to gather her power.

Faint lines formed in the air before her, glowing with an orange light. The line twisted, bending into shapes, seven interlocking squares, the glyph of the Neophyte. The spinning pattern shifted. One by one, four of them unfolded and reformed into circles, the glyph of Magister. She awaited the Arcane Pentagram to weave itself among them, the living sigil of her rank. Instead, another square reassembled itself into a fifth ring, joining the dance. Her mouth went dry as a seven-pointed star laced itself into the pattern—the Viatoric Heptagram.

"Holy shit," Jim breathed.

Nate stared at the glowing glyph, rotating like luminous clockwork. "I've never seen one of those."

Kate only stared at it, the realization reluctant to come. She'd done it, but somehow it didn't seem real.

"You are a Magus Viator, Miss Rossdale," Harcourt said, watching her above the twisting glyph. "A Mistress of Worlds, the rarest form of practitioner and my only hope for vengeance."

"I still can't believe it," Jim said, watching the security film for the third time. "Candy was with us five years."

Kate absently nodded, her brain still wrestling with everything over the past hour. It wasn't that she didn't believe Harcourt's story. It fit too neatly into her own memories of that night for it to be wrong. '*You don't get her.*' She played the scene over and over, each time cementing her belief. '*You don't get her.*' Dennis on the floor, his head bent like he might throw up. Her own sickness at trying to draw power. But the most damning memory, if it was memory and not pure dream, was the shield spell. Leges cast the strongest shields, a net of interlocking geometric forms, each one precise and sharp. Arcani and Viatores could create shields, but nothing with the precision and strength of those created by a Lex. Candice was an Arcanus. There was no way she could have cast something strong enough to stop the charging verl. But she had and could only have done it by doubling her own power.

"She was a Magus?" Harcourt asked.

"She was," Jim said, finally breaking his gaze from the screen.

"Five years is a short time to achieve that rank."

"She was already a Lumitor when she joined," Jim said. "Been an independent down in Florida."

The old man gave a non-committal grunt. "We'd known of Miami, but I hadn't known she was a Lumitor. However…" He keyed the laptop and turned it back toward them. "…I did find this picture."

The screen displayed a black and white image of three people descending steps from a large building. One, a black woman with a short afro, another a stocky, tanned man with a neatly trimmed beard, not much longer than Jim's.

Kate leaned closer inspecting the third, a blonde with rounded, shoulder-length hair. Most of her was hidden behind the bearded man, and a knit cap covered the top of her head, but Candace's face was the same, possibly four or five years younger. "Where was this?"

"Chicago," Harcourt said. "Nineteen eighty-one."

Kate gave him a look. "She wasn't even born yet."

"The picture's real," Harcourt said. "She was going by the name Leslie Mills. The Brotherhood had taken an interest in those three, a small coven called the Disciples of Hali. Nothing incriminating, mind you, but they'd become quite active in the area. Their apartment burned down three months later. The man, David Dourif, was found dead inside. The other woman, Erica Margolis, was discovered in a motel the following week, apparent suicide." He clicked a button, and the screen changed to a yellowing photo of the afro-woman slumped in a bathtub, the water a dark red. "We never heard about Leslie Mills again."

"Chicago?" Jim snorted and shook his head in disgust. "We went there a few years back. Candy made it out like she'd never been there before."

Kate nodded, her mind wandering back to that weekend getaway, Candace and her getting lost and having to find a taxi. Their friendship had cemented that weekend. How many lies had she told? How many friendships had she faked?

"What about France?" Jim asked.

Harcourt paused. "What about it?"

"I don't know. We were drinking wine one night. She started talking about it. Said she'd spent some time there."

"Marseille," Kate added, another cherished memory withering. "I remember. Then we got onto *The Count of Monte Cristo* and Dumas."

"I'd thought she was talking about a school trip or something." Jim looked at Harcourt. "How old is she?"

The old man shrugged. "That was the only other photograph I found."

Jim hid his frown behind a swig of scotch. "So, she could be eighty or a hundred and eighty years old? She might have even known Dumas. How?"

"Magic is *your* specialty, Mr. Stevens."

"Stealing youth," Kate said, her lip curling. "It's possible, but evil as all hell. Take forty years of life from someone, give yourself twenty. If she stole magic, why not steal years?" She peered at the face of the woman she'd called sister. "So how did you know it was her?"

"The misty lake of Hali. The cloud shores beneath Carcosa," Jim said, a musical dreaminess to his voice, as if reciting a poem. "You found it by the name?"

The old man nodded.

"What the hell is Carcosa?" Nate asked. She'd been holding her whiskey, not drinking it, for the past twenty minutes.

"It's a lost city," Kate answered. "Standing at the eye of the Demhe, an old term they used to call the Abyss. I have no idea if it's real, but people are always trying to hock some bullshit artifact claiming it came from there."

"It was the capital city," Jim said. "Home of the emperor and hub of the multiverse."

"There's an emperor?" Nate asked.

Jim shook his head. "It's a story."

"Master Boyer called it El Dorado, a myth," Kate said.

"The Brotherhood had quite a lot on the subject," Harcourt said. "While most of the books themselves were taken, I do have scanned copies." He opened a folder with over twenty files inside, several of them huge.

Kate clicked one, *The Lost Kingdom*, written in Latin. No author given. She scrolled through the photographed pages, elaborately penned in multi-colored inks. "These spells are useless," she said, looking through page upon page of circles and incantations.

"All of them?"

"We need the original book to access the magic. The spell is cast during the writing, the written words simply bind it to the page. Otherwise, it's like we have instructions on how to fly a plane, but no airplane."

"It's all I have," Harcourt said.

"What about that Andrew fella?" Jim asked. "You ever find him?"

Harcourt gave a short nod. "In a New Jersey hotel, dead. A single hole burned straight through his head. The carpet had been torn up and the floor cleaned as if for a circle, but there wasn't one."

"If it was for traveling it would have gone with her," Kate said, still scanning the laptop. She sighed, stopping on a three-ring pattern for traveling to the fabled realm. "Well...at least it gives me an idea what to look for. Maybe the Athenaeum of Kell. If anyplace has the ritual, they would."

"If they'll let you in," Jim said.

"They'll let in a Magus Viator," she said, picturing herself at the great, black iron doors, the glowing glyph professing her rank for the eunuch librarians.

"Where is this Athenaeum?" Harcourt asked.

"On Dhevin," Kate said.

"How soon can we leave?"

She snorted. "That's the problem. I never learned the circle to reach Dhevin. I'd only cast the circle for Hollit and then back to Terra. So I can get us to Hollit, from there we could buy passage to Dhevin. Moving between those realms is common."

"How soon?" he repeated. "I'm eager to begin as soon as possible."

"Want to see the Outer Worlds, huh?"

"That and my brothers and sisters are after me. I'd like to move beyond their reach."

Jim refilled his glass, then poured the last of the Scotch into Kate's. She hadn't even touched it since making the glyph. "So one disagreement and now you're on their hit list? Yeah, they sound real pleasant."

Nate snorted a laugh.

"Not exactly," Harcourt said. "The files were not all that I took before leaving. I knew I'd need supplies, some artifacts, and funds to finance it."

"You robbed 'em?" Jim asked.

"I did."

Jim laughed and raised his glass in salute. "Well, then. That changes everything. So you're saying that you paid me with their money and not yours."

"I am. Your payment represents half of what I took, not counting the anti-curse, warding icons, two executer blades, and a few other effects, including all my files."

Kate's lips tightened. Executer blades...she preferred witchhunter blade herself. It sounded less self-righteous.

"Balls," Jim said, bobbing a finger at the old man. "Huge balls. No wonder you want to get out of town."

Harcourt smiled, displaying those tiny teeth. "Which once again I ask, when can we leave?"

"I'll need to get some supplies together for the circle," Kate said. "Nothing too much. Get some clothes for us." She motioned to the laptop. "We'll need to print everything we need. Crossing the Abyss does a number on electronics. So...three, four days."

14

CHANGE OF PLANS

A bell above the door tinkled as Kate emerged from the florist's, leaving behind the sweet aroma of blossoms. Clutching her bag beneath one arm, she opened her umbrella. The gray clouds had brought a cold drizzle, more of a mist, really. The kind of rain that one could ignore until they realized they'd gotten soaked without noticing it.

Nate stepped out behind her and clicked her own umbrella open. Short spikes of dark-tipped bleached hair poked out from under her burgundy knitted cap. "Great place, eh?"

"Perfect," Kate said as they started up the wet sidewalk. "I wouldn't have found it on my own. Thanks. Might have gotten a bit carried away." She shrugged. "Not like it's *our* money." The plastic bag at her side swung like a pendulum with each step, the contents a wide range of crystals and dried herbs she'd procured from the secret shop operating in the rear half of the store. The shop-owner, a skinny man with curly red hair framing a bald spot, had quickly escorted them back once he'd seen Nate, fluttering around her like an awkward schoolboy, while guiding them through his selection. Thankfully, he'd had jasper, which was honestly all she'd needed.

"Ye hungry?" Nate asked.

Kate shook her head. "Not yet, but if you are..."

"Naw. I'm fine," Nate quickly said. She'd warmed up to Kate in the last two days since their meeting with Harcourt, offering to help her at every opportunity. Whether that had to do with Kate being a Magus, or the realization that she wasn't going to steal Jim away, Kate wasn't sure. Jim seemed to be encouraging it, sending them off together while he readied his own affairs.

"We'll get something at the hotel," Kate said, side-stepping a huge puddle. "Get out of this rain and sift through some paper."

Nate's Doc Martins splashed straight through the shallow water. "I wanted to ask ye. I read that book last night, and is there really a yellow king?"

Kate shrugged. "Maybe." She'd picked up everything she could find on Carcosa, which to her surprise amounted to quite a lot. Bierce had been the first to write on the subject, a single story using names that all but the most well-read practitioners had never seen before. Chambers expanded on it with his book, *The King in Yellow*. Lovecraft penned his own interpretations, followed by countless more authors, their descriptions building on one another, each adding their own artistic flairs and mythology, both true and imagined. "The trick is separating the wheat from the chaff. Figure out what's real."

"Sounds like a waste of time, if ye ask me," Nate said. "Harcourt's files should be more reliable."

"It's not that easy," Kate said. "Just about everything written about the city is myth, Outer World or here. But beneath it's the truth, the nuggets gleaned from dream visions. It's like those sunken ships in *National Geographic*, you know. They're so encrusted with barnacles and coral that they're unrecognizable. We just need to scrape that shit off, separate the real from fantasy."

"But Jim said it's all myth."

"I love Jim, but let me tell you, he's not the best to ask about this. Leges don't believe anything unless they see it. That's just the way he is. Arcani and Viatores, we're less literal."

"So ye think I'm more an Arcanus?" Nate asked, a hopeful edge to her voice.

"No doubt. You're very..." she risked the word, "observant. You see things from other angles."

Nate looked away, focusing on the ground like it was suddenly fascinating. "So wha' do I do?"

"How do you mean?"

"If I'm to be an Arcanus and Jim's Lex, I'd have to find a new mentor."

"Eventually. But you're not even Lumitor yet. Magister is still a long way off. He's the best mentor for you right now. Leges are better at teaching foundations. You need that before the path divides."

"Oh, Christ," Kate said as she entered Harcourt's suite.

"Welcome to the print shop," Evan said, leading her inside. On one side of the main room, a shiny black printer hummed with rhythmic whirrs. Its cardboard box rested beside it, packed with a green and white mound of crumpled paper looking like it might soon spill over. The paper wrapping was from the tower of reams piled onto a dining chair.

"Good afternoon," Harcourt said, looking up from a half-filled three-ring notebook.

Kate surveyed the stack of colored binders already loaded, their spines labeled with blocky, black marker letters. "I hadn't thought it'd be this much."

"*Susurros Salis* took two and a half binders by itself," Evan said. "The *Liber*..." He squinted at the spine. "*Retnahla*, is looking to be four."

Harcourt worked a quarter inch of paper through the open, silver jaws. "I'm not sure how fast you can wear out a hole-punch, but I'm working on it."

"There's no way we can carry all of this," Kate said.

"I'm open to suggestions," Harcourt said.

Kate tongued her cheek. "There's no need to lug a three-volume book if it only has a dozen pages we need. So," she raised her hand, "who's good at speed-reading Latin?"

Nate grimaced.

Evan rolled his eyes as if saying, '*yeah, right.*'

Harcourt lifted his hand.

"Well that's a start," Kate said. "Let's order some food, and I'll get to work on a list of terms to search for."

"How 'bout this?" Nate said, extending a handful of loose pages.

Blinking, Kate looked up from *Confessions of Philippe*, the meticulous transcriptions of a seventeenth-century madman, translated from their original French. Accepting the pages, Kate flipped through several charts, converting the seasons for a dozen Outer Worlds for two hundred years.

The tables ended in nineteen twenty-five. "Perfect. We'll use this to figure out the weather for anywhere we're headed." She passed the pages to Evan. "Stick them in the Frankentome."

Evan loaded them into a red three-ring binder, a rainbow of plastic tabs along the edge labeled each section they'd piecemealed from other books.

In the chair opposite her, Harcourt rubbed his temple with one finger as he flipped through volume three of *Susurros Salis*, tagging each section he thought useful enough for Kate to review. Judging by the yellow Post-It notes, she guessed that to be about half.

The printer hummed and clicked against the wall, printing *The Lost Kingdom's* yellowed pages.

A knock came from the door.

"Christ, about time," Nate said, springing to her feet. "I'm starvin'."

"I'll get it," Evan said.

"Too late." Nate crossed the room and opened the door. "Come on in."

A lean man in a dark jacket pushed a dish-laden cart through the door. Kate's stomach grumbled instantly, and she set her binder on the blue armrest beside her. Evan was looking at the attendant, his eyes narrowing.

"Just right over here," Nate said.

The attendant's eyes were locked straight ahead, every muscle in his face rigid. Sweat beaded his forehead.

"Look out!" Evan shouted, springing to his feet and papers scattering to the floor.

A black tube appeared to be jutting from the side of the attendant's head, and then a man stepped around the doorframe, the silenced pistol in his hand now swiveling in Harcourt's direction.

The old man lifted the binder before him like a pathetic shield. Rising, Kate spun to face the gun-wielding stranger, power gathering in her hand.

The gun fired with a loud, metallic *chak* as Kate released the spell with a "Ka!"

The gunman's arm jolted to the side like it had been hit with a sledgehammer. The weapon fired again, blasting a hole through a cabinet before flying from the man's grip.

The terrified attendant dropped to the floor, scrambling toward the kitchen.

A second man entered the room, pistol in hand. His eyes zeroed in on Kate, filaments of light lacing between her fingers. He raised his gun, the muzzle swinging toward her like a black eye. Terror took hold, and Kate took an involuntary step back, her spell faltering.

With a primal scream, Nate lunged. She grabbed the cart and drove it forward, slamming it into the would-be killer's legs with a clatter of dishes and trays.

The gun fired, but the shot went wide as the man reeled. Nate reared the cart back and slammed it into him again knocking him to the floor.

The first gunman moved toward her, his broken arm twisted at an impossible angle, now tucked against his chest. He drew a slender witch-hunter blade from under his jacket and lunged toward Nate.

The young woman leaped back, dodging the first swing.

"No!" Kate cried. An emerald lance shot from her fingers, its brilliance lighting the room green. The beam bent mid-air, away from his head and into the slender dagger with an electric crackle. Unphased, the man lunged, dagger raised.

Three loud shots boomed, and the attacker crumpled, a red mist spattering the wall behind him. Compact pistol before him, Evan was up and around the spilled cart to where the first attacker was on his knees, spilled food all over him. The man lifted his head just as Evan's boot smashed into his mouth with a meaty crack of broken teeth.

Heart pounding, Kate watched the door as Evan peeked out.

"Miss...Rossdale," Harcourt groaned.

Turning, Kate gasped. The old man grimaced in his chair, jagged confetti all over him. The binder lay in his lap, a bullet hole through the lower corner. Bright red blood oozed between his fingers clutched across his stomach.

"Shit!" Kate hurried to him, kneeling before the chair. Blood wicked across his white shirt.

"They found me," he said, wincing as she moved his hands.

"I figured that part out." She tore open his shirt to see a ragged bullet hole.

"We have to leave," Harcourt said. "Now. They wouldn't have been alone."

"Hall's clear." Evan picked the silenced gun off the floor.

"I don't think we can move you," Kate said.

"You have to." Harcourt tried to push himself up. "Someone has to have heard the shots. Police, Brotherhood, either way, we have to go."

"I'll help him," Evan said, sliding his arm beneath the old man's. "Take what you can. Now! And towels from the bathroom."

Kate grabbed the Frankentome, shoving loose pages inside. "Get the daggers," she called to Nate, who was hurrying out of the bathroom. Nate handed off the towels to Evan before taking the fallen witchhunter blade from the floor and another from the unconscious man's open jacket.

Her arms loaded with binders, Kate followed them out into the hall. Evan was already moving Harcourt toward the elevators.

"My case," Harcourt wheezed, a bloody hand drunkenly motioning the way they'd come.

Kate hurried back to the room. The guy on the floor groaned through bloodied lips. She stepped on him as she moved inside. The jacketed attendant was curled in the kitchen, head between his knees. "Stay down!" she ordered to both of them. Kate scanned the room, spotting Harcourt's chrome and mother-of-pearl briefcase.

The elevator dinged outside, followed by two loud pops from a silenced pistol. Kate froze, scenarios racing through her mind—Evan and Harcourt dead. Nate alone. That image prompted her to move, the fingers of the arm clutching the binders instinctively weaving, readying a spell.

Nate was in the hall, unharmed. A crumpled form laid outside the open elevator—a woman with dark hair pulled back into a thick ponytail. Blood spread across the carpet beneath her.

Evan was helping Harcourt into the lift. "Hurry up."

Kate ran toward him, the briefcase rattling in her hand. Not looking at the body, she stepped over the red wet spot and into the elevator beside Nate. The doors slid closed.

"Can you magic this?" Evan asked, pressing a wad of hotel towels against Harcourt's gut.

Kate shook her head. "I'm not a Lex."

"Jim can do it," Nate said, buttoning the old man's jacket over the bulge of towels. "If we can get to him."

"We have to," Harcourt said, not moving his jaw.

They stopped on the third floor. Evan had holstered his gun and shoved the silenced one down his pants, the print of the suppressor looking huge there. Wedged between Nate and Evan for support, Harcourt held his stomach as they headed toward the stairs.

Evan held up a hand once they'd reached the door. He stepped inside, emerging a moment later. "Clear."

He took the front, fingers on his waistband near the pistol. Behind him, one hand gripping the railing, Nate assisted Harcourt. Kate maintained the rear as they made their way down in silence, pausing long enough for Evan to check each corner before continuing the descent. Their footsteps and huffs echoed through the stairwell, a beacon announcing their passage to any enemies above. Kate strained to hear any noises of pursuit.

The old man slipped as they neared the bottom. Evan caught him before Harcourt might have wrenched Nate down, sending them both sprawling.

It was still drizzling when they emerged onto the street, wet tires sending up mist with their passage. Evan peered around and led them west. His arm around Nate, Harcourt walked mostly upright, his colorless lips tightened into a pained grimace. Kate's eyes searched every face in every window and car, expecting some look of recognition or the black barrel of a gun, but no one seemed to pay them much mind. She pressed the binders against her, trying to shield the precious pages from the wet.

"There's no way we can walk to Jim's," Nate said.

"Just two more blocks," Evan called back.

After what felt like an hour, they stopped beneath a metal awning, tucked back from the street. Harcourt huffed each labored breath, his face pale. A faint pink tinged the water beneath his rain-soaked slacks, now clinging to his body.

"I have him," Evan said, leading the old man to a concrete bench. "Call us a ride. Kate, call Jim. Tell him everything."

"I don't have a phone," Kate said.

"Here," Evan said, almost throwing his into her hand.

Ignoring the bloody fingerprints, Kate scrolled through the contacts until finding Jim's number.

He answered after the fourth ring. "*Yeah?*"

"It's Kate. We have a problem."

"*What?*" he said, his tone changing to deadly serious.

"Spire. They attacked us at the hotel."

"*What? Are you—*"

"Shut up and listen. Harcourt's been shot. We made it out and are heading your way. They might be after us, they might be outside your place, but we need to go. Get everything ready and don't open the door for anyone."

"*How bad's he hurt?*"

Kate swallowed. The old man was lying on the bench as Evan peeked beneath the blood-soaked rags. They were whispering something.

"I don't know," Kate said. "He's bleeding a lot, and you'll need to help him. Maybe on the way to Hollit." She looked over her shoulder. There were no pedestrians on the street, thank God.

"*Hollit? You want to go now? Do...do we have everything?*"

"I got the crystals. We can go. They can't chase us there and neither can the police. There's...bodies."

"*Shit.*"

"Nate's calling someone for a lift. We'll message once we're on our way."

"*I'll be ready. Be safe.*"

Kate hung up. "How is he?"

"Not that deep," Evan said. "Notebook took the brunt of it, but we need to get him patched."

Harcourt smiled weakly. "I look...forward to seeing the Abyss...Miss Rossdale."

"You just hang tight and we will. But call me Kate."

His eyes lowered to the briefcase beside her. "I should have...clarified. The other case."

"What?"

"The other briefcase. In my room." He swallowed. "There went that plan."

"We got another dagger, if that's what you mean."

"That was a big part of it."

"See, no worries." Kate glanced back again. "No good plan has ever gone without a hitch. So that part's over with. Now we can stop worrying about what it'll be."

The old man chuckled, then winced.

Evan placed a hand on him and whispered something, too low for Kate to hear it.

Harcourt shook his head. "No talk of that. No time and we need you."

"No talk of wha'?" Nate asked, pocketing her phone.

Harcourt shook his head. "It doesn't matter."

"What doesn't matter?" Kate asked.

"It's nothing," Evan said.

"Bullshit. No more secrets. What's going on?"

"Let's get out of this alley first," Evan said.

Kate's lip curled in response. She looked back in time to see a young man glance toward them as he passed the alcove. "Nate, how long till that ride?"

15

WELCOME TO THE ABYSS

After fifteen agonizing minutes, Nate's friend, a bald black kid with a red septum ring, pulled up in a ten-year-old Honda Jazz. His name was Pegg, and his car smelled of French fries. Evan guided Harcourt into the hatchback's small rear bench, wedging the old man between himself and Kate.

"Thanks for comin'," Nate said, sliding into the front.

Pegg eyed the injured man through the rearview and grunted. "Aye. What shite ye gotten inta?"

"Nothin' ye need to worry 'bout."

"Tha' guy dyin'?"

"No," Evan said. "But five hundred pounds if you get us where we're going and stop asking questions."

"Ye got it." Tires squealed on wet pavement as Pegg hit the gas.

Thirteen minutes later they arrived at Jim's flat. The rain had picked up, now coming heavy and streaking the windows as Kate searched for any signs of pursuit. Evan had Pegg circle the block once before stopping.

"Here." Evan extended a fold of multicolored bills. "Forget you ever saw us."

The cash vanished in Pegg's palm with the smooth motion of someone well-versed in quick deals. "Already forgotten, mate. Take care, Nate."

Kate helped Harcourt out and into Evan's hold before following them out, case, bag, and Frankentome clutched to her chest.

Jim opened the door before they'd even reached the top of the stairs. "Hurry up," he said, eyes scanning the street.

The center of the room was cleared, save for a recently purchased wrought iron brazier. Kate's Samsonite and a pair of backpacks rested nearby along with a haphazard pile of food and other supplies.

"Over here," Jim said, leading Evan and Harcourt to the kitchen table, now completely cleaned. "Lay him down."

Nate bolted the door behind them.

Kate dropped her burden beside the other supplies and turned toward the black metal bowl. Brushing a hand across her wet hair, she mentally ran through the ceremony she'd recited a dozen times in the last two days.

"Eww, shit," Jim said, pulling back Harcourt's bloodied towels.

"Can you help him?" Evan asked.

"Yeah," Jim said after a moment. "I'm no Magus, so it won't be perfect, but sure. Nate, get over here."

Removing the five jasper nuggets from her bag, Kate approached the brazier. Jagged cubes of hazel wood filled the bowl. Drawing her power, Kate touched her thumb to her middle finger and blew through the ring they formed. The pale wood darkened beneath her breath. Faint smoke trickled up, and then the wood ignited. Kate blew more, stoking the flames until the heat became uncomfortable.

"What do you need me to do?" Evan asked across the room.

"You?" Nate asked. "Get outta the way."

Kate affixed a thick chalk stick to a string, carefully measuring it out to nine and a half pedes, just over nine feet. She looped the other end over a flat nail head Jim had installed for scribing circles, though he rarely needed the help, and she began drawing the first ring. Despite the mounting fear of witchhunters kicking down the door, she moved slowly, careful to make sure the circle was perfect.

"Hold still," Jim hissed through clenched teeth as he dug the bullet from Harcourt's abdomen. Blood was everywhere. The old man lay motionless, his eyes closed. Nate leaned over Harcourt, her forehead pressed to his, her fingertips splayed along the side of his head.

The first circle complete, Kate shortened the cord by six Roman inches and began the second ring, this time driving her energy through her hand and into the chalk. Her lips began mouthing, "Alla tehru. Alla tehru," over and over. The simple mantra was meaningless, nonsense words Master Boyer had taught her when she was still an Initiate to help her focus. She'd never lost the habit, much to her tower mates' amusement.

Now, as she silently recited it, Kate imagined him beside her, coaching and encouraging her.

Wood banged as Evan shoved a pair of chairs against the door.

Harcourt let out a pained grunt.

"Got it!" Jim exclaimed.

The second ring complete, Kate began inscribing the elaborate glyphs in the hollow space between them. Her hand moved in sharp, quick strokes. They weren't the precise and measured symbols of a Lex, but Arcane free-form, her magic pouring into each sweep of chalk. Knees against the hard floor, she drew counterclockwise around the great ring.

Jim was chanting something low in the background. The stink of anise and burnt sulfur wafted from his direction. Harcourt grunted, and gave a long high squeal that seemed to go on forever, but Kate continued her mantra, pushing the distraction from her mind.

"Alla tehru. Alla tehru."

Harcourt thrashed, the hard heels of his shoes banging against the tabletop.

Jim continued his chant, his voice rising.

"Alla tehru," Kate recited. She finished the first lap around the circle and began around the other way, completing each symbol as she went. "Alla tehru. Alla tehru."

"There," Jim panted. "It's not pretty, but it's done."

"Just in time." Evan was leaning over his barricade, peering through the door's peephole. "Car pulled up. Circled twice before stopping."

"Katie," Jim called. "How are we doing?"

Unwilling to break her concentration, Kate continued without answering, each stroke coming down with a sharp click. She was halfway around —too close for a fuck up now.

"All right," Jim said, seeming to take the hint. "Once she says go, everyone move everything into the circle we want to take with us. Step wide over the lines, don't drip on them, and keep away from the brazier."

"All right," Evan called. "Two of them. Man and woman. Don't see weapons, but they look pissed."

Gritting her teeth, Kate worked faster, her hand a blur of motion, the mantra an unintelligible rhythm. Her head swooned as the magic poured from her.

"Get back from the door," Harcourt ordered.

"Done," Kate cried as she finished the final stroke. She began positioning the jasper stones in place along the scribed rim.

The others didn't wait. Nate jumped over the rings and dropped the backpacks and was out again in almost one motion. Harcourt, his bloodied shirt open, carried in Kate's Samsonite and a pack of water. The old man looked like total shit—wet, ragged clothes, skin pale—but he moved with a speed she wouldn't have expected even if he hadn't just been shot.

"Jim," Kate called, moving to the brazier, "the herbs."

"Shit!" He looked side to side, then pointed to a brown wooden tea box with a brass latch. "There. Nate."

Nate dropped an armload of rolled blankets and grabbed the box off the floor. She rounded the circle that was now busy with bodies and stepped in from behind Kate, extending it out before her. "Here!"

Kate opened the lid. There, nestled in one of the compartments was the muslin bag she'd prepared the previous night. Thank God she hadn't procrastinated. Clutching it in her left hand, she focused her energy into the bowl. The hazel wood had burned down to bright coals. The fingers of her right hand began drawing an intricate pattern, threads of light weaving a jagged glyph.

A heavy thump sounded from the door. Then several shots tore through, spraying splinters of wood.

Beside her, Evan drew his pistol, bracing it in both hands.

Kate released the spell and dropped the bag onto the hot coals. The muslin ignited and burst, releasing multicolored sparks like miniature fireworks. A column of white smoke surged upwards, umbrellaing out a dozen feet above the floor and spreading back down in a wide bubble.

The smell of apples and milk filled the dome. Kate blew into the rainbow coals, expelling every ounce of power she could summon. The fire blazed, the colors swirling.

The door thumped again, harder, as if hit with a sledge. Wood cracked.

Eyes watering from the smoke, Kate looked up to see the door inch open with another bang. Shadows moved beyond it, but everything was losing clarity as if the lights outside were quickly dimming.

The door thumped again, and a head emerged through the gap. Something long slipped through, pointed at them. Evan's gun fired three deafening shots, but then the door, the room, everything was gone. Liquidy aether whirled around them, glimpses of dark infinity visible beyond its misty curls.

"What the hell?" Evan said.

Nate released a loud breath somewhere between a sob and a laugh. She was crouched behind the backpacks, wide eyes transfixed the direction the attackers had been. "Fuck me, tha' was bloody terrifyin'."

Ears ringing, Kate dropped into a sitting position.

Harcourt knelt across from her, looking up and around at all sides with childish wonder. A purple starfish of ugly scar tissue shone from his pale abdomen. "My God."

Kate smiled. "Welcome to the Abyss."

The old man nodded absently, as if unwilling to turn his eyes from the endless ocean of flowing aether.

"What the fuck is that?" Evan pointed through the mist. A greenish mass, about the size of a washing machine, glided past about sixty feet away—an eyeball-studded brain with stringy tendrils flowing behind it.

"Elemental, most likely," Kate said.

"But the one we saw was small." Evan shook his head, his knuckles white on the pistol's plastic handle, but his finger was at least off the trigger. "It didn't look anything like that."

"They're all unique. Little nightmare snowflakes. Eventually, enough of those bits of dreams and emotion all come together, and it becomes more. Don't worry, it can't see us in here."

"No?"

"No."

He seemed comforted in that, his grip relaxing just a little.

"What about tha' one?" Nate pointed behind them.

A weird shape, a gelatinous net made out of writhing worms, flapped behind them like a swimming ray. "Is it followin' us?"

"Nah," Kate said. "Probably sees our wake." She poured a little more magic into the brazier. The circle accelerated, leaving the wormy net far behind. She surveyed the infinite curls, feeling like she was finally home, a sea captain at the bow of her ship. Three years. How many times had Candace sailed the Abyss with Kate's stolen magic? Had she appreciated it, too, or was it just an ocean in need of crossing?

"What's tha'?" Nate asked.

Kate turned to see a towering, angular shape crowned with irregular blocks, like insane battlements. It was visible for only a few seconds before a rolling curl wall of aether blocked it from view. Once it had passed, the shape was gone.

"Dream reef, Master Boyer called them. They sort of float around. Eventually, they might join one of the worlds, break apart, or grow large enough to form a new world. Don't worry. They're not like icebergs. They won't hit us."

Jim was crouched near the circle's edge, gazing out into the darkness. As if somehow independent of him, his hands worked against one another like live things, rubbing away Harcourt's dried blood.

"Jim?" Kate asked.

He acknowledged her with a nod, but didn't turn away.

"You all right?"

"Aye," he said, his voice low. "Just...listening."

A shiver ran along the back of her neck. The memories of their last voyage through the aether rose to the surface. "They can't smell us."

"What can't?" Evan asked, the hard edge returning to his voice.

"Hounds," Jim said. "You were rushing the circle. I don't blame you," he added. "Bit under pressure."

"There's no cold. That means the circle is good. That last time..." Kate remembered Candace lingering near the edge, "...she tampered with it. She called them. But this circle is good."

"Those baby-headed things?" Evan asked.

Jim nodded. "This is where they roam."

"The circle masks us from them," Kate said. "Just keep your toes away from the chalk."

Evan's foot shifted away from the ring. "Good to know."

"We didn't have much chance for the pre-flight safety video."

"Anything else?" he asked.

"Not that you'd get any bars here, but your phones are probably toast."

"Damn," Jim said, breaking his focus from the aether to lean back and dig in his pocket. "I forgot about that."

"Take the batteries out if you can," Kate said. "Maybe it'll work when we return. Maybe not."

"Bloody shite," Nate grumbled, peering at her own black-screened mobile. She peeled off the back plate and removed a blocky battery.

"Same for watches or anything else with a battery."

Evan glanced at his black digital and grunted. "I liked that watch."

"I packed a pair of winders we can use," Jim said. "They'll help us track time between us, but Hollit has twenty-nine hour days."

"Self-winding." Harcourt lifted his wrist, displaying a gold Rolex.

Kate gave an impressed nod. "Nice."

The old man tapped the watch's cobalt face. "Little trinket I picked up after leaving the Brotherhood. Retirement gift. Speaking of which, how long will we be here?" He motioned a finger toward the swirling blackness.

"Couple hours," Kate said. "Hope you took a piss before we left."

"That long?"

"I could speed it up if I need to," Kate said. "It takes more magic to do it."

Jim turned toward her, his brow creased. "Can you? You just drew a circle and cast the gate. Frankly, I'm amazed you're even talking right now."

Kate shrugged. "Me too. I dumped a lot of magic into the ring, way more than the recipe needed, but even then I'm still pretty good. I'm a bit more...fuel efficient than I was before." At the thought of how she'd achieved such efficiency, Kate eyed the haphazard pile of gear scattered about the circle, wondering if Jim had packed her dust. She didn't need it now, but after the day's excitement, a little taste sounded pretty good.

"I say we use this time to inventory our supplies," Harcourt said, touching his clothes, still wet with rain and blood. "I seem to have forgotten my luggage. Does anyone have any clothes I could borrow?"

"Well," Jim said, rising to his feet. His voice was still low. "There lies a problem. I was supposed to be picking up some clothes for us this evening. We're going to stick out as is, but dressing local is always a good idea. I have my robes, but that's it. We'll need to hit the Arin Market as soon as we get there."

"Do you have anything I can wear in the meantime?"

He nodded and started for one of the packs. "Next problem is money. I have a few coins, but that's it. None of you happen to be stocked with some gold or silver by chance?"

Harcourt smiled ruefully. "In my other case. I thought I prepared for this. I'd packed a good deal of Outer World currency."

Jim unbuckled the top of a gray pack and began rummaging. "How much?"

The old man shrugged. "Don't know the value, but over eleven ounces of gold coins and even more in other metals. Even some flat green stones."

"That would've been nice," Jim said, shaking his head. "But without money, we might need to hock any jewelry or non-essentials. So I hope you aren't too in love with that watch." He pulled out a black T-shirt and a rolled pair of jeans and offered them. "Here. No dressing room. So hope you're not shy."

16

GOLDEN BEETLE

K ate pressed her knee against the side of her suitcase, eliciting a crinkle from inside as she zipped it closed. It had been decided that it was the most suitable to contain their meager food and other effects while Nate now carried Kate's clothes in her frame pack.

Inventory had come to four day's food and water—five if they were careful, some junk food, including two sodas, four books, including the Frankentome and the anticurse, a modest supply of herbs and crystals and other casting materials, a roll and a half of toilet paper, one crank-powered flashlight, three Red Gate icons, three witchhunter blades, two silenced pistols with eleven rounds each, Evan's .45 with twenty-three rounds spread between two magazines, and Kate's tiny .32 with an unopened box of twenty-five bullets. This was all in addition to one dead laptop, four dead cell phones, Harcourt's blood-stained clothing, and £732.62. None of which were terribly useful.

Jim's hoard of Hollit coins came to seventeen silver senyu—about as much as it would take to clothe them and buy a kabob. No mention of the blood dust, leaving Kate to the sad resignation that it was now in the Spire's hands. No need to grieve aloud, as Jim had likely just lost everything in his flat. She tried to push the gnawing hunger for a bump from her mind. It wasn't like she actually needed it anymore.

"That's it?" she asked. "No one's got any gold fillings we could pry out?"

The others chuckled humorlessly, Jim's a pity laugh. He wore a black, full-length smock, like a funerary muumuu, cinched with a braided silk belt. Bright, electric reds and blues lined the inside, visible through the wide sleeves or when he moved, and the slits along the front and back parted to reveal the colors beneath.

She looked to Evan. "What about that amulet of yours. You still have that?"

His brow creased. "I don't know what you mean."

"Under your shirt," she said bobbing a finger toward his chest. "Don't think I didn't know about that."

"Oh." His eyes darted to Harcourt, then back. "It's, um..."

"It's what? Sentimental? Filled with chocolate? Do you have it or not?"

Evan swallowed. His tough-guy persona softening. His goldie eyes moved back to the old man, seeming to ask for help and Harcourt gave an assuring nod.

Evan lifted his shirt. "It's not an amulet."

Kate's head cocked in surprise at the jeweled beetle planted in the center of his chest. She stepped closer, leaning in. Six gold legs extended out from a flat yellow gem and buried into the flesh above his sternum. The puckered skin around each puncture wasn't red or inflamed, but she couldn't tell how deep the spindly legs extended. The beetle's pincers were open into a wide, serrated V that flickered in the brazier's firelight. "What is that?" her fingers unconsciously moving toward it. "Is that a...a yeng beetle?"

"Really?" Jim said stepping over his pack to get a closer look. "I'll be damned. Do you know how rare these are?"

Kate met Evan's eyes, her lips fighting to form the words. "Why do you have this?"

"I gave it to him," Harcourt said. He looked almost comical in Jim's large T-shirt and jeans rolled up at the ankles.

"Why? He doesn't..." She peered at Evan closer. She'd found him handsome since they'd met, but had never *really* looked at him. He had no scars or blemishes, no crow's feet or any imperfections at all, just pristine skin over perfectly toned muscle, the kind of body that only existed on magazines or in darkened-room fantasies. "What happened to you?"

"I, uh..." He bit his lip, his gaze averting hers like an embarrassed schoolboy. He pulled the shirt down, hiding the powerful artifact. "I got hurt."

"Evan was injured during the war," Harcourt said. "Most of his body was burned. His right hand amputated."

"Jesus," Kate said. "So that story you told me...about the burning man?"

Evan nodded. "Shrapnel hit me. I went down unable to move as I burned."

"I offered him a second chance," Harcourt said. "It's the only thing keeping him moving and therefore not available to sell."

Kate swallowed. Yeng beetles were powerful, capable of healing even the most fatal of wounds. The cost, however, was high, shortening the patient's life depending on how severe the injury. A simple scrape might be a day, a broken bone a few months. Burns and regrown limbs would cost decades. *Does he know that?* she thought. *Does he even care?* No wonder Evan hadn't required the Iron Word to gain Harcourt's trust. The old man had given him a second life.

"That's what ye were sayin' in the alley," Nate said. "When Harcourt was hurt, ye were offerin' him the beetle."

Harcourt nodded.

A guilty pang needled the back of Kate's mind. She'd assumed the little secret exchange as proof Harcourt didn't trust her, proof of his dishonesty. No, Harcourt had been protecting Evan.

"The yeng beetle was the first relic I took from the Brotherhood. Once I did, I knew it was only time before I had to put my plan into motion." Harcourt sighed. "I just hadn't expected them to find me so quickly."

"Depending on how far they'd go for it," Kate said. "They'd just need some blood or hair to track you."

"The main reason I rarely left my suite. But the Brotherhood's trackers are extremely resourceful."

"They didn't find you," Evan said.

Kate gave him a look. "I'm pretty sure they did."

"No." He motioned to Jim with his chin. "They knew where he lived. Knew he was involved. No one followed us to Jim's place, but they still came. Means they knew where we'd go. Probably had eyes on it and called it in once we arrived. We were in the alley a lot longer, and that would have been a better place to hit us."

"The Brotherhood was looking at me?" Jim asked, palpable fear in his voice.

"Bet they tracked the money," Nate said. "Half-mil."

Harcourt shook his head. "That was off-shore. I insisted in case of something like that."

"I know what tipped them off," Kate said.

All eyes turned to her.

"We asked around about you."

Jim groaned. "Fuck me."

"None of the Brotherhood know my aliases," Harcourt said.

"They would have, when asked in the same sentence if anyone knew about a Calvin Vogler," Kate said.

"What?" The old man's eyes widened. "You asked about me? With that name?"

Jim finger-massaged his temple. "Aye."

"Why would you do that?"

"It's not like I knew the fucking Spire was after you. They don't concern themselves with mundies."

Harcourt's face flushed red. "You knew I was in hiding!"

Jim lifted a hand to quiet the raised voices. He scanned the aether. A small winged shape, like a butterfly with incredibly long legs hanging below it, fluttered past, apparently indifferent to any noise it might have heard.

"We wouldn't have done it if you hadn't been so damned secretive," Kate hissed, her voice low. "You think we weren't going to look you up? We took the Iron Word, and you still waited a week to tell us, *Oh, by the way, the Golden Spire is hunting me. And while I'm on the subject, I'm also a fucking witchhunter.*"

"I had to be sure the Iron Word was in effect. You hadn't been restored yet."

"But we told you it was. Even then you still could have said something to sway us from looking up just who we'd shackled ourselves to. But you just had to keep playing it close to the chest with this damned *Mr. Mysterious* act."

"If I'd told you who I was with before the Iron Word took effect, would you have joined?"

"Yes."

"Don't be so sure. I recall Mr. Stevens saying how lucky I was that he didn't know."

"And that was before you told us Candace Cross betrayed us," Kate said. "But no, I'd have stuck with you the moment you showed that you could cure me. I gave my word, and that's all there is."

"You'd have wanted the assurance that I wouldn't have harmed you."

"Damn right. I'd have demanded the Iron Word after that. But don't think the only reason I'm doing this is because I have to. And I can guess Jim feels the same."

Jim nodded. "If I'd known about Candy, believe me, I'd have joined on the spot. But I'd no idea that this would come down on us by my nosin'.""

The muscles in Harcourt's clenched jaw rippled. Finally, he said. "I believe you. If it were intentional, the Iron Word would have done its work. But if you had any lingering doubts as to my membership, I hope those are satisfied."

"No doubts on my end," Kate said. "But on the flip side, if you have any other little secrets or items you haven't shared, you need to trust us."

"Understood."

A quarter hour later the glowing chalk lines brightened, and the faint drain on Kate's magic heightened. She knelt beside the smoking brazier and peered into the coals, their multi-colored hues hidden in the tiny caves and crevices between them. "Fasten your seatbelts."

Peering deeper into the fire, without focusing on any one part, Kate opened the flow of magic. Deep in her mind's eyes, a vision formed, the pavilion beneath Kanotep. She hadn't seen the structure in years, her last glimpse had been on her doomed journey back to Onyx Tower. Kate held the image, filling in every detail, the smell of the evening wind, the tiny blooming flowers along the slopes, the stink of old goat shit. That's what it had been, but things had changed.

A second picture formed, overlaid atop it. Tiny weeds peeked up in the spaces between jade stones. Leaves rustled across the dusty floor. Kate allowed the second image to take hold. The opening appeared clear. Nothing in the way that might prevent their arrival. She blew into the flames and in her vision a breeze coursed through the empty pavilion, scattering leaves and sending tiny birds fleeing the rafters. Gating was so much easier to a prepared spot, one locked away and protected from intrusion, but with a little work, she'd scattered the few things that might cause problems with their arrival.

She wove her fingers and released a stream of magic into the burning bowl. They glowed brighter, a few dancing sparks popping free. And then the aether outside the ring thinned. Upright shapes materialized all around them. A stone floor solidified beneath her feet, sprigs of slender grass emerging from the cracks. A twisted stick appeared from beneath the ring's chalk lines, the white markings running across it as if they'd been spray painted there. A soft wind blew from somewhere behind her, carrying the smell of moist earth and grass. The brazier's smoke whisked away with the breeze and Kate looked up to see the jade pavilion and beyond that the sea-green sky.

"Amazing," Harcourt breathed.

A shaggy goat looked up from its grazing, golden eyes transfixed on the sudden newcomers. It bleated a cry and trotted away, the brass bell jingling at its throat.

Kate rose and breathed deep, savoring the mountain air. The pavilion was a little worse for wear—light peeked through a hole in the tile above, broken light bulbs, and bits of strewn trash. She stepped across the circle and scanned the horizon, finding the small moon hanging in the sky. A larger one, white and smooth like polished ivory peeked partially above the green slopes of Mount Kanotep. Turning, she spied a grove of twisted and ancient olive trees, each one older than Stonehenge. Far to the right, glinting in the light of the descending sun, a silver bullet raced across the grassy plain. "Welcome to Hollit."

17

THE ARIN MARKET

W hen Kate had purchased her red Samsonite, her motivations had been for practicality. The wheels and telescoping handle made sense, as did the hard, protective sides. The bright color would make it easy to spot in a luggage carousel. The price was also a plus because she wasn't the one paying for it. Kate had seen some cases that doubled as clunky, uncomfortable-looking backpacks. She'd rolled her eyes at the notion that she would ever want or need to forgo the quad spinning wheels and elect to strap it to her back.

By the end of the half-mile hike across the rock-littered grass, she swore she'd never get anything but the backpack option ever again. It wasn't as bad once they reached the road. The white concrete strip curved its way through the hills and up the far rise toward the distant glow of Arin. Relieved to have reached a flat surface, Kate almost threw the heavy Samsonite down onto the Roman concrete, so grateful for it that the clack and rumble of the rolling plastic wheels didn't even bother her.

Evan was the first to spot the spiral of elevated silver rails running off to the left, the fiery light of the setting sun gleaming off the mirror-polished metal. Hoop-topped uprights, spaced every fifty yards, held the triple helix in place. He'd seemed somehow skeptical when Jim had said it was a train track, but five minutes later a tinny whistling sounded in the distance, and the track-bearing hoops began to glow with pale light. They brightened as the train neared. It had no headlight of its own. Not even windows—just chiseled lines running from its bullet tip and down its length like some art deco rocket ship crafted from chrome and gleaming brass. It shot past, maybe a hundred feet away, with a high-pitched hum and a sound like rasping knives. The glowing hoops dimmed once it passed through them, taking a full fifteen seconds to fade away. The effect of rings brightening and dimming in succession gave the whole thing the look of a comet streaking up the far rise before plunging over the hill and out of sight.

"That was freaky," Nate said after the last of the lights extinguished. "Why don' we get those back home?"

Evan, still focused on the spiraling rails, now nearly invisible in the fleeting light, shook his head. "What I want to know is why they don't buckle under the weight. I mean, look how far apart those braces are. But it didn't even dip when the train went over them."

Jim grinned. "Physics."

"What? I'm talking about the physics. That shouldn't hold the weight. Is it the curve of the rails? It that why?"

"I'll tell you what," Jim said. "You have until after sunset, and then I'll tell you."

Kate suppressed a grin.

Evan looked back to the red glow still lingering at the edge of the horizon and nodded. "Okay."

They continued along the road, marching toward the rise. A few tiny cracks marred the concrete's smooth surface. It wasn't flat, but subtly angled, peaking in the middle to divert water to inset brass drains every few feet. Blinking fireflies rose from the grass and shrubs like green and orange stars, dancing to the cricket music beneath the twin moons. Still, in the distance, the red light of the setting sun continued to glow like the lava-filled caldera of a silent volcano.

Twenty minutes and one mile along the road Evan said, "The sun's not going to set is it?"

"Nope," Jim said, his robes swishing as he walked.

"So, are we near a pole or something?" Evan asked. "Six weeks of light, six weeks of night, all that?"

Jim grinned. "Oh no. Not at all. Hollit isn't a globe. It's flat."

Evan snorted.

"Dead serious," Jim said. "The sun will circle `round that way and come up on the other side in the morning."

Evan's brows tightened into an admirable *Don't bullshit me* expression.

"He's not making it up," Kate said. "We're on a flat world. If we had time, I'd take you to the ocean. *Amazing* view."

"All right," he said, cautiously. "So...if the world is flat...what's on the other side? Do the oceans just pour off?"

Kate shrugged. "Obviously not. But you can fall off it. Probably fall forever or eventually land on a pile of dumbasses who jumped off to see what was down there. The point is that the train rails and the flat world with its never-setting sun work here because that's how physics works here. Don't think of it like being on another planet. We're in another universe, and the rules don't work the same. It takes time to get used to."

"If you ever can," Jim added. "Honestly, it still weirds me out. Just wait until we get to one of the bizarre ones."

Evan's eyes flicked between them. "I'm still not getting the how."

"Because a long time ago, people dreamed of flat worlds," Kate said. "Each dream and concept built onto the other, altering the gestalt into something entirely unique. Butterfly effect on overdrive. After enough time," she gestured around with her free hand, "we get this."

"So the Flat Earthers were right."

"Maybe. Or maybe they visited Hollit in their dreams and mistook it for Terra. That's when we get into the chicken and egg argument, and you are *not* ready for that one."

Half an hour later the first distant sounds of civilization, a tolling bell, rang in the distance. Shortly after, they crested the large hill and the sprawling lights of Arin came into view, laid out like some sort of drunken grid-work along the valley below. A few pale lights shone along the farther slope beyond a calm lake glistening with moonlight.

Far to the left, a comet of glowing hoops raced along the valley floor, destined for Etop.

It was smaller than Kate remembered it. The term *city* was probably generous. Her first time it had seemed so huge, every inch of it filled with wonder and amazement, she'd somehow inflated it in her mind, expanding it to fit all the tiny details etched into her memory. Spotlights illuminated the smooth white dome of the Grand Kelsut. The city's largest building stood a good hundred feet high, the golden nipple-like cap at its peak making it look like some enormous tit from which Arin fed.

"First things first," Kate said. "Let's get a hotel. Somewhere with a wood or tile floor."

"And food," Nate said. "I'm already sick of protein bars."

Kate's stomach clenched, audibly groaning at the mention.

"You ate three of 'em," Jim said.

"Well, lunch got cut a wee short. So it was that or kill and eat one of ye. I wouldn'a thought peanut butter could taste like jellied ass, but those bars proved me wrong."

Kate switched her grip on the suitcase's handle. "Then let's get down there before we start cannibalizing each other or kill the rest of Jim's jellied ass."

The city of Arin was two towns conjoined together sharing a single heart. The main city was crescent-shaped, extending around its sibling in a protective embrace. The blocky buildings were old stone or stucco facades made to mimic old stone that rose, slightly tapering toward the top. Statues and stylized hieroglyphs decorated the first floor of most buildings. Glowing oval signs hung above many of the doors like neon cartouches, proclaiming the residents or businesses within. The Egyptian influence was undeniable, though Viatoren scholars had debated for millennia whether Hollit was born of the dreams of Egypt or the dreams of Hollit had birthed the Pharaohs' dynasties.

Elaborate obelisks lined the narrow streets, many capped with brass fixtures like melted crowns holding spherical street lights. Laughing voices came from a cafe ahead. A small crowd filled the wrought iron tables around a bubbling fountain. It silenced as they drew near.

"Eyes forward," Kate whispered as they walked. "Don't stare."

Through the corner of her eye, she watched the seated men openly staring, bright colors peeking from the folds of their black robes. The women, their hair done in complex sculptures like 1980's rock stars were more restrained in their ogling. Their clothes were the direct opposites of the men's—bright, swirling colors, so much that it was difficult to take it all in—their cheeks and hair painted to compliment. It appeared orange was in fashion. They made Kate think of flamboyant road cones.

A slender car turned down the street ahead, its single headlamp shining on them like a spotlight. It was a two-seater, one in front, the other behind like a jet fighter cockpit. Sweptback fins extended from the vehicle's back, glittering with rainbow hues like intricate stained glass or dragonfly wings. It slowed as it neared and the driver, barely visible beneath a blue-mirrored dome, turned his head as he passed.

"I feel a bit underdressed," Harcourt mumbled once the car rolled away, its engine entirely silent.

"No kiddin'," Nate said.

"Just get to the market," Kate said. "We'll stop by the first vendor we see."

A few blocks later, they passed from the old town and into the market. The twenty-nine-hour bazaar was both of and separate from the town itself. Elaborate pavilions and tents lined the winding streets, many of which had stood in the same plot for generations. An oily miasma of unwashed bodies, smoke, soured beer, and shit undercut the aromas of roasting food, sweet perfumes, and strange spices that flowed through the lanes. Tiny lights draped the stalls like strings beaded with glowing dew. Strange music, jingling bells, and boisterous hawkers called out above the white noise of commerce.

A slender woman emerged from between fringed tent flaps, her robes a beautiful metallic green and her oiled skin so purple it looked black. Wafer bells sang across her swaying hips as she closed in on Evan. "A strong man deserves good shoes," she purred in a thick accent.

He turned toward her, but Kate grabbed him by the bicep. "He's not interested."

The saleswoman grinned pearly teeth, clicking her tongue as Kate pulled him away.

"What was that?" Evan asked. "Latin?"

"Yeah. Can you speak it?"

"Not really. Just a little in high school."

"Good. Just let me and Jim do the talking here."

"Why do they speak Latin?"

Kate scanned for a clothier. "Because Rome conquered and explored more than just Europe and North Africa. Scholars, later on, kept it going. So now it's the major trade language." She spotted a huge shop with common clothes displayed behind barred windows. "Here we are."

Nate and Jim had taken a beeline to a cart, summoned by the fragrance of spiced meat. Smoke rose from a pair of iron, round-bottomed grills. Jim glanced back to where she stood and lifted a finger to say it'd only be a second. He didn't seem to register Kate's dagger eyes, and the sudden clench of her empty stomach assured her that maybe he had the right idea.

Two minutes later, they returned with several dangling strings of grilled meat and what appeared to be tiny, cherry-sized, green apples. Nate was already tearing into hers like she hadn't eaten in weeks.

He offered three of them out. "Here ya go."

Harcourt eyed the meaty hunks, dripping with brownish red sauce. "What is it?"

"Dehod," Jim said, impatiently shaking the stringers. "It's good."

Evan removed one of the kebobs. It ran a foot in length. Six apples, six chunks of meat, and a mushroom cap on the end. "What's a dehod?"

"You allergic to shellfish?" Kate plucked one from Jim's grip and began eating.

"No."

"Then shut up and eat it," she ordered around a mouthful of apple.

Evan and Harcourt accepted the proffered meal, and Jim tore into his own.

Harcourt took a tentative bite. "It's like..." He licked his lips. "...honey-glazed lobster."

"Not quite." Jim grinned. "Dehods are scorpions." He took another bite. "Big ones."

"Tasty ones," Kate added.

"Scorpions?" Evan's lips curled in revulsion.

"Big fuckers," Jim said. "Size of a spaniel."

Kate met Evan's disgusted grimace. "If you don't want it, give it to me."

Harcourt was already halfway through his, each bite eliciting a little moan of pleasure. Nate still hadn't come up for air.

Evan shrugged and began to eat.

The sign above the tailor's shop read 'Heiramon.' It was run by a skinny man named Theosh. Like all Hollitian fathers, he was completely bald, the purple skin atop his smooth head dotted with scars from years of razor nicks. He'd emerged from the rear of the cluttered shop with the swish of silk robes and instantly began doting on them with well-practiced efficiency. While humans weren't entirely uncommon, even ones with no apparent Hollitian ancestry, their wide eyes and strange dress tagged them instantly as foreigners. And as any salesman in any world knew, foreigners meant two things: Money and suckers.

With the broad sweeping gestures of a Hollitian merchant, he led them to several fine garments with intricate brocades and tiny beadwork. Jim, who was at least dressed like a local, acted as spokesman. He studied the garments for the time propriety demanded, complimented the quality craftsmanship, and then explained that their budget was rather limited at this time and requested something more mundane for now.

Theosh clicked his tongue at this, a sign of disappointment or polite apology, and led them to the even more cramped portion of the shop. "Where are you from," he asked removing a plain black tunic from a wooden hanger. Stripes of vivid green and purple lined the interior.

"Sar," Jim answered without missing a beat. "In Lumit."

Kate's jaw tightened at the lie.

"Ah, Lumit," the tailor said, though the tightness at the corners of his pale eyes said that he didn't entirely believe it. "Very beautiful."

"Have you been?"

He shook his head. "I have not, but I have heard many tales of the Hollow World." He offered the garment to Evan.

Kate's jaw relaxed. Lumit had been a gamble. She and Jim had gone there only once with Master Boyer. Unlike most of the Outer Worlds, Rome had conquered it entirely, the natives who had lived there before being squashed from memory. After the Empire's fall, the world fell into isolation. Humans only until maybe the last two centuries. Not much was known about the secretive realm, and that made it a good cover.

After an hour of dressing and redressing, they had made their selections from the humblest of Theosh's stock. Kate stood before a slender mirror, admiring her bright crimson robes. The fabrics were from different batches, and one sleeve was slightly darker than the rest of the ensemble, a slight error that resulted in its inclusion in the discount section. Velvety black lined the interior, some soft fabric that absorbed the light, giving the impression that between the flowing folds lay a black and infinite void.

Nate wore similar robes in aqua-blue, though hers lacked the silver piping. She twirled before her own mirror, the fabric blossoming out.

"Like it?" Kate asked.

Nate's lips pulled into a crooked grin as she gave herself a long, appraising look. "It'll do."

Harcourt had somehow managed to give his black robes an air of sophistication, fitting him like a designer suit lined with golden yellow. Kate couldn't tell if he'd fixed it in some way, tightening the braided belt and puffing the right spots, or if it was simply his posture and manner. Neither Evan nor Jim, even with his upscaled robes, looked anything more than mournful black-clad monks, but the old man looked like a Supreme Court justice about to meet the president.

Theosh must have noticed it as well, because the shrewd negotiator refused to negotiate the price as low as they'd hoped. "This is fine quality," he boasted, gesturing to Harcourt near the back. "People will say that is a man wearing Heiramon's, I promise you. These are no rags. They demand respect."

Round and round they went, each of Jim's counteroffers meeting with a disapproving click. Kate glanced at her suitcase, about ready to pull out her ace in a hole. She'd hoped to save it, but eventually Theosh reluctantly agreed to thirteen and a half senyu.

Begrudgingly, Jim counted out the hexagonal coins and dropped them into the smiling tailor's hand.

Theosh pressed his fist to his forehead and nodded, "Good transaction," closing the deal.

"Where to now?" Jim asked as they stepped back into the market streets.

Kate looked up and down the winding lane. Music and shouting voices filled the market. It appeared the night crowd had finally emerged, eager to enjoy the pleasures best suited for the darkest hours.

A pack of beggar children raced past. A man cried "Thieves!" behind them.

Kate's gaze lifted above the networks of strung lights to fall on the towering shapes of the old town, looming like a protective wall on three sides. "Now," she said, scanning the luminous cartouche signs, "we need a suitable hotel that can shack up five broke foreigners."

The Canboht House was a modest three-story along the inner edge of Arin Proper, in that gray zone where market and city merged. The exterior appeared ancient, walls caked with centuries, stained with pollution, and pockmarked from any number of conflicts. Inside was polished stone and gleaming copper. Blown-glass lamps of metallic blue lined the tiny lobby where a pair of long-eared cats lounged atop a cushioned bench.

The manager, a woman called Eshe, whose braided crest of violet hair arched up and out to the side like a hat, could house them all in a pair of adjoining rooms. Yes, the floors were wood, and spacious enough for their needs, though Kate had carefully avoided any hint of what those were.

"The rooms will be eighteen senyu," Eshe said.

Kate maintained a straight face, but Jim must have reacted because the manager's pale eyes flicked to him and her smiling demeanor dimmed.

"We are short of money for the next two days," Kate said. "But are you willing to trade?"

Eshe clicked her tongue. "This is not the market."

"I understand," Kate said. "But please, let me show you what I'm offering first."

"We only accept valid currency," the manager said through eerily white teeth. "If what you have is of significant value, then you may sell it in the market and return."

But Kate was already kneeling and unzipping the Samsonite, digging for her ace. She found it buried in a mesh pocket loaded with protein bars. "Not even this?" She set a 500ml plastic bottle of Coca-Cola onto the tiled countertop.

Eshe's eyes widened in seeming disbelief.

"Do you know what this is?" Kate asked.

A pink tongue ran across Eshe's purple lips. "The bottle isn't correct."

"They don't make 'em out of glass anymore, but it's technically bigger than those were. If you're not interested, that's fine. I can sell this in twenty minutes in the market, or we can simply strike a deal now."

Eshe eyed the bottle for some time, her desire barely masked. "One night."

"We need two nights."

"Then one room. Two nights."

Kate tapped the counter as if considering it. They definitely needed two nights and cramming all of them into a single room and still having floor space for a circle seemed pretty unlikely. She was straight out of Cokes, and her next option needed a bit of upselling. Kate turned to Jim.

His lips tightened into a hesitant look.

"All right," Kate said, crouching and reaching into the Samsonite. "For a second night, how about this?"

She set another soda onto the counter, this one a bright orange with a blue label.

"God damn it," Nate groaned. "I was saving that." If she was acting in order to add to the sell, she was doing a great job. But her not saying it in Latin meant that she was probably serious.

Eshe squinted at the bottle. "What is this?"

"They call it Irn-Bru."

"It is not Coca-Cola."

"It is, but a different flavor." Getting into the definition of brands was probably way more than a Hollitian could handle. Thanks to some creative

Magi back in the thirties, Coke was a rare and cherished prize. Master Boyer always brought a six-pack of glass-bottled Cokes whenever he came to the market. The empty bottles themselves sold for a full senyu. If Candace really had knocked out as many Magi as Harcourt had claimed, then it might have been a while since anyone here had seen one.

"It's not Coca-Cola," Eshe repeated as if the answer might change.

"No. This is actually rarer." Which was true if you weren't in Scotland, which they definitely weren't at the moment.

"I will give you five senyu for it," Eshe said.

Kate shook her head. "This is worth twelve."

Eshe somehow clicked and snorted at the same time. "I doubt that."

Kate shrugged and removed both bottles from the counter. "Then I'll sell them and see. We'll be back."

"No," Eshe said, smoothly, a little too smooth not to be forced. "No need to trouble yourself. We can come to an agreement."

Kate looked to Jim, as if conferring and set the bottles down. "Two bottles. Two rooms for two nights. And believe me, this is in your favor."

Eshe pointed a long finger at the Irn-Bru. "This is like Coca-Cola?"

"Yes, but not exactly. Still bubbles and still gives a buzz."

She seemed to consider it. Kate wondered what else she might need to barter with, but finally, Eshe placed her fist to her forehead and nodded.

"Good transaction."

Kate repeated the gesture. "Good transaction. And those will taste much better with some ice. I recommend you try it."

Eshe gave them the keys and directed them toward a tiny elevator sort of shoe-horned into the corner beside the stairs. There was something vaguely funereal about the lift's shape, like some over-sized coffin of cut glass and framed in bronze.

"I can't believe that worked," Evan said as he squeezed in beside Kate and Harcourt. There wasn't room for all of them.

"Never underestimate the power of carbonated caffeine." It took Kate nearly a full minute trying to figure out the elaborately decorated knob before pushing the stylized bird's head in and dialing it to three. The lift started smoothly, moving up along a pair of gleaming, smooth tracks.

The doors opened on the third floor with a faint hiss. At their room, Kate inserted a brass key, like an old-timey punch card, into the door lock and the bolt clicked.

The room was simple, fifteen by ten feet at most—polished wood floor, creamy blue plastered walls, a tiny bathroom with no discernable toilet, but a crystalline, Jacuzzi-sized tub. It smelled of jasmine, wafting from a bouquet of perfumed glass flowers in one corner.

She opened the door to the adjoining room. Each had a single window, light from the market outside peeking around the curtain. Two windows, two doors. "We'll place the Red Gate on the other entrances, but I'll ward this one. Also the door between rooms and the bathrooms as safeguards."

"How do we divide the rooms?" Harcourt asked.

"We don't." Kate motioned to one of the beds, which was nothing but an oversized mattress directly on the floor and covered in pillows. "We'll move this into the other room. We'll all sleep in there. Clear this one out and give me room to work."

Harcourt nodded. "I should warn you, I snore."

"From what I understand," Kate said. "I might have you beat."

18

BANK WITHDRAWAL

Viatoric traveling required two parts. First, the caster needed the proper components and glyphs to plot the course through the Abyss. The second was a clear mental image of the destination point. Without the first, chances of finding the correct world were nearly impossible. Without the second, the traveler risked any number of disasters, including appearing any distance above the ground or below it, materializing within a wall or other object, or arriving in the middle of an ocean, a thousand miles from anything. Because of this, inscribed spells included a mental image ingrained into their transcription, imprinting itself on the reader's mind, aiding them for their first journey to that location, a bullseye to aim for. But traveling to a destination the caster was familiar with was relatively simple, providing of course that it wasn't warded against entry.

Kate had visited Bern once before, accompanying Master Boyer as he conducted some of the Tower's affairs and visited with a friend. Though it had been a full decade since she saw Switzerland, she was confident that most of the locations were in relatively the same condition as they'd been before. The trick was choosing one where their appearance wouldn't draw attention. That ruled the bulk of them out. She and Harcourt needed to get this little errand over and done and back to the others with zero police or Spire attention.

"All right," she mumbled, her own voice sounding far away as she studied the manicured grass in her mind's eye. The place appeared clear enough, but she wished she could see to the side. There could be a parade just thirty feet away, but there was no way of telling until it was too late. Not that there were too many 3:00 a.m. parades, but that wasn't the point. "Here we go."

Neon filaments laced her fingers and Kate released the spell into the burning brazier. With the crackling of sparks, the wall of aether around them thinned. Towering trees coagulated around them, light streaming between wind-rustled leaves. Damp grass sprang beneath her feet.

Someone shouted.

Twenty feet away, beyond the wooden lounge chairs, a pair of men backed away, their eyes locked on the two people that had just appeared in the empty park.

"*Guten Abend,*" Harcourt said.

One of the men broke and began running away. Realizing he was alone, the second wheeled and raced to catch up.

The old man snorted. "Guess they didn't want to talk."

"We're just lucky they didn't pull their phones out and record us." Kate pushed the iron brazier over with her foot, dumping coals onto the grass, and sending up a plume of orange sparks. "We need to move." She twisted the lid off a water bottle and poured it out onto the hot metal, unleashing a cloud of sizzling steam. The chalk from their tiny seven-foot ring coated the grass.

"True. The Brotherhood searches for videos." He opened a second bottle and dumped it onto the embers.

"We still need to have a chat about that little spy network." Kate glanced over her shoulder making sure the park was still empty. A huge monument loomed behind her, silhouetted against the pale night sky— atop a jagged rock, a ring of green bronze figures, their hands clasped as they orbited a globe. She'd spent the better part of a day in this park as Master Boyer was handling some private business. It was among the clearest memories of Switzerland, at least of places that were safe to Travel to. Using one of the blankets, Kate wrapped the still-warm brazier and shoved it into her rolling suitcase. She picked up the five topaz stones from the ring and dropped them into her jeans pocket. "Let's get out of here before we're spotted."

Eight hours later, and after a whirlwind of errands, their cab stopped before one of the most powerful banks in the world. Laughing children played in the fountain square before it, geysers of water shooting up from smooth paving. A couple of policemen watched with passive eyes. Kate glanced toward them, her own eyes hidden beneath a pair of giant, plastic-framed glasses she'd picked up from a street vendor. After seeing the grand five-story building, with its imposing walls decorated with statues, she'd imagined an interior worthy of emperors—gilded marble and polished wood. Instead, she found herself in a nice and modern bank, like an ultra-sleek DMV.

Frowning, she took a seat at a minimalist bench and waited as Harcourt approached the long counter, briefcase in hand. After a few words, he was graciously ushered through a door by a smiling brunette. No one seemed to bat an eye that he was wearing a T-shirt and oversized blue jeans with his suit jacket and thousand-dollar dress shoes.

Nervously, Kate studied every face that entered for the next forty-five minutes, searching for any sign of recognition from the newcomers. Files that might have been found in Harcourt's Edinburg suite would have told the Spire that the remainder of their stolen funds were at the National Bank. Harcourt doubted they'd have cracked the datadrive's encryption yet, and if they had, they wouldn't expect such a brash move. But desperate times required some recklessness.

It felt so weird to be doing this, to think this way. The paranoia, the cloak and dagger, unknown enemies with silenced pistols. She felt like a character in some bizarre heist movie or spy fiction.

The tiny pistol tucked in her pocket felt huge. She fought the nagging urge to touch it, to make sure it wasn't peeking from her pocket or somehow visible through her pants. The gun was a last resort. Fleeing first, magic second. If the time came for the pistol, she was well and truly fucked, and the others were now trapped in Hollit.

Finally, Harcourt emerged from the back, escorted by a black-suited man with the smile of a car salesman and the wary posture of a Secret Service agent. The old man nodded, and Kate rose, her heart racing with the need to get out of here as soon as possible. The suited man gave her a polite nod and opened the door. He escorted them down the steps and opened the door to their waiting cab—not the one they'd arrived in.

She let a breath as they began to drive. "Everything go all right?"

"Perfect," he whispered. "Eyes front."

"Hmm?" she asked, turning toward him.

"Easiest way to spot a quarry is to look for whose looking for you."

"Sorry," Kate said, strumming her fingers on her lap. "I'm still learning this."

Harcourt grinned. "I'm only learning this side of it."

"So how you like being in the crosshairs?"

"The crosshairs are fine. Bit of a rush. It's the bullet that sucks. But you say that like you've been in the Brotherhood's sights before. You never have."

"Yeah, but I never knew I wasn't in them until I *was* in them. And *thinking* you are, and *knowing* you are both suck."

"Don't lie." Still facing forward, his blue-gray eyes turned her direction. "You're getting a rush out of it."

She glanced out the side window as the cab turned a corner. "I'll tell you once we're gone."

"That's not a denial."

"Have I called you an asshole today?"

"No."

"You're an asshole."

Two blocks later, they turned again. A sea-green Vespa rounded the same corner, its rider's face hidden beneath a tinted helmet. The same Vespa had taken the last turn, as well. Kate forced herself to breathe. She rubbed sweaty palms along her jeans. *So what? They made a turn. No big deal.* It wasn't like they were on side-streets, this was a major thoroughfare.

Crossing the river, they rode several more blocks before turning again. Tires rumbled over the brick street. Kate glanced again. A long red trolleybus dominated her view, but no Vespa. Kate let a sigh, but then the little scooter veered into view. "Shit."

"What?" Harcourt whispered.

"I think we're being followed."

Harcourt grunted but didn't look. "How many?"

"One. Woman on a Vespa."

"They won't move alone, and we'll be gone by the time backup comes. Don't worry. Eyes front."

They pulled up to the curb beside Hotel Stabba, a simple three-star nestled between the other buildings. Kate kept her eyes to the curb as she stepped out. She held her breath, waiting for a shot, but the little scooter hummed past. She strode quickly beneath the stone awning and opened the door. Harcourt behind her, they bypassed the slow elevator and headed up the stairs to the second floor.

Hotel Stabba occupied the renovated shell of two smaller buildings, cramming as many rooms as they could fit into the space. Halfway up the hall, the floor stepped up two feet as they entered what would have been the neighboring building. Kate already had her key out when she reached the door.

She looked back. The hall was empty. They slipped into the tight little room, dominated by a single bed. The chalk wards she'd inscribed earlier still marked the door and the frame to the single window. A black plastic bag, tightly wrapped in tape, covered the smoke detector like a mafia murder victim.

Kate stepped into the tiled bathroom. A trio of olive green backpacks rested on the floor beside other supplies crammed into the white chalk circle stretching from wall to shower. She tossed a handful of cheap white towels to Harcourt. "Here."

He began cramming them beneath the door, sealing the wide gap.

Kneeling onto the smooth tile Kate lit the brazier. Thick hazel smoke filled the cramped room. She blew through circled fingers, fueling the blaze hotter.

Briefcase in hand like a man rushing onto a leaving subway car, Harcourt slipped in across from her. "Ready."

Her eyes watering from the smoke, Kate wove her magic into a glyph and dropped the muslin bag into the bowl. With a dazzle of sparks and smoke, aether welled around them, and once again they entered the Abyss.

Kate dropped to a sitting position and rubbed the tears from her eyes. The air in the circle was clearing up, slowly, save for the perfect column of smoke rising from the iron bowl like the stalk of some great mushroom. "What are you grinning about?"

Harcourt's smile broadened. "We did it."

"We nearly got caught."

He harrumphed, shaking his head. "Even if that rider was following us, which we can't be sure of, we made it out. No kicking down doors. No gunshots. Tell me you can't enjoy that."

"You're a weird guy. You know that?"

He shrugged. "They shot me. I can enjoy slipping through their fingers."

"Yeah but if they shot you again, I can't patch you up." She eyed the black briefcase. "Show me what we got."

He popped the mother-of-pearl tabs and opened it. "Two kilos of gold." He removed something from the case and held it up. A transparent plastic strip unfolded from his fingers, rectangles of gold running its length, each in their own sleeve like a package of condoms.

She accepted it. "Got some weight to it," she said, bouncing it in her hand. In the firelight, she could read the individual serial numbers stamped into each hundred-gram ingot.

"That's just half. Have you ever seen that much gold?"

"Sure, but I've never held it."

"Then by all means." He offered her the other one-kilo strip. "We have just as much silver, but that's just not as impressive, now is it?"

"Yeah, you should have started with that and then worked your way up to the gold." She handed them back. "We'll need to be careful selling that off. No clue what the exchange rate is and can't let anyone know how much we have."

"Of course." He locked them back in his case. "We'll divide it up. Let everyone take care of some, to be on the safe side."

"We don't have any champagne to celebrate, but..." Kate reached over and removed a plastic bottle from the cardboard flat. "...how 'bout a nice room-temperature Coke?"

He blew an amused snort. "That's probably worth more than the gold."

"What can I say," she said twisting off the red cap, releasing a hiss. "I'm a big spender."

They floated through the misty aether for several long minutes, passing the bottle back and forth. An elemental crept near them at one point, resembling a grotesque snail covered in seeping boils, its shell the skull of some enormous predator. It looked as if it were going to collide with them, but the mindless creature diverted, diving down through the mist and out of sight.

"I have a question," Kate said.

"About the Brotherhood's network?" Harcourt asked, his gaze fixed to where the snail had disappeared.

"Two questions, then."

He smiled. "Of course."

"Evan. Does he know about the yeng beetle? That it's killing him?"

"Ah." Harcourt gave a mournful nod. "He does."

"How long?" she asked.

"Three..." he shook his head, "...maybe four years if he doesn't remove it."

"Can he?"

"Yes and no. If he does, the scarring returns, lessened, but still there to some degree. His lungs might retain some of their restored strength. The fire did a lot of damage." Harcourt's thumb stroked his own scar like a child soothing a dying pet. "His hand will wither away. The transformation is surprisingly quick, but putting the beetle back on takes a full day to restore him back."

"And you need him able."

He nodded. "I suggested he remove it early on, before we came for you. He did and has refused to since. He says he can't perform his job in that condition, which is true. But I think he'd rather pay the cost than be that way again."

Kate's lips tightened. Evan was a dead man, and he knew it. Without the beetle, he'd have had sixty or more years of life. No telling how long life expectancy would be in a half century. Now he had four years at most. This one day of waiting in a Hollit hotel room while she and Harcourt had run off to Bern had cost him the equivalent of two weeks life.

"As far as the Brotherhood," Harcourt said, changing the subject. "Their search network is very extensive."

"So, you going to tell me about the spies now?"

He shook his head. "Their agents are only one facet, and a small one. The Brotherhood's largest resource is the Net. In fact, I'm certain it was a Net search with my name that tipped them off."

"How? You guys own Google, too?"

He chuckled. "No, but we do own many, many sites. Sites that practitioners use. It allows us to keep track of who's doing what."

"What sites?"

"Osiris-Morri, for one."

Kate blinked. "Wait, what? No way."

Harcourt shrugged. "Easily half of the magical supplies purchased online come from the Brotherhood. Crystals, herbs, cauldrons, raw materials, even that brazier, and your all-natural chalk... Osiris. They track purchase patterns, install cookies on your computers, and you happily give us your addresses and phone numbers in return for free shipping."

"That doesn't make sense," Kate said. "The Spire hunts practitioners. So what, you stock them up, wait for the credit card to clear, and then kill them?"

"I've told you. The Brotherhood is only concerned with practitioners who pose a certain threat. They couldn't care less who's realigning their chakras or making love potions. Practitioners use our services, and in return, we watch them. We flag certain searches to find out who's making them. That's how Jim tipped them off."

"You fuckers sold my email address, too, didn't you? You know how much SPAM I got last time I bought something there?"

He laughed. "You said we were evil."

"It's not funny. Hunting us is one thing. People who send SPAM are a whole other level of asshole." Kate's gaze lowered to the iron brazier, eliciting a disgusted chill along the back of her scalp. It was from the Spire. She leaned closer and blew into the embers, focusing energy and speeding their course along. First chance she had, she'd pick up a replacement.

Harcourt's eyes followed a city-sized mass, slowly tumbling through the aether. It looked like thousands of cubes randomly fused together. Tiny lizard-like shapes scurried over it, diving into the jagged crags. "So now you know. I don't feel bad sharing these secrets. They did shoot me, after all. But don't judge them all by the actions of a few."

She snorted. "I'll believe that when I see it."

"How about this?" He removed a slender red binder from the case and offered it over.

Kate flipped it open, finding a typed letter followed by pages and pages of scanned images. She stopped at the image of a yellowed coastal map, the city of Marseille circled in red. "What is this?"

"A gift from a friend. After you and Mr. Stevens mentioned France, I had one of my contacts look into it."

"Contacts? In the Spire?" she asked, voice rising.

He nodded. "I *do* have friends. Just because management doesn't approve of what I've done, doesn't mean my old co-workers don't. The official verdict is that if Candace has left our world, then she's no longer our problem. Our, jurisdiction, if you will, only extends to Earth. I'm hardly the only one who disagreed with that."

"Just the only one dumb enough to act on it."

The old man smiled, his little teeth glistening in the brazier's light. "That's right. I hadn't expected them to get back with me so quickly, but the binder was deposited in my box only hours before we were attacked in Scotland."

"You think they could have warned us about that," Kate said.

"They had no means to. Communication is by letters and couriers."

"They could have tri..." Kate froze as she flipped the page. Candace's face peered sternly back at her from a grainy, sepia-toned photograph.

"Holy shit." Squinting, she read the cursive note in the lower corner, likely penned when the picture was made. "Eighteen sixty."

Harcourt let a long breath. "Appears she's older than we thought."

"You haven't read this?"

"There wasn't time."

Kate squinted at the summary written on the first page, everything in crisp bullet points. Dancing shadows beneath brazier's red glow made it difficult to read. She brought her fist to her lips and blew. Light welled between her closed fingers. She opened her hand, and a tiny white light, not much more than a Christmas bulb, floated up above her. "Looks like she was some hedge witch. Marie Marchand. Born in eighteen-thirty-six. No tower affiliation."

"Self-taught?"

"Appears so." Kate tapped the page. "She'd tried to join the...*Tour des...Chuchotements* in eighteen sixty-four. They turned her down."

"Any reason why?"

"Yeah," Kate gave a humorless laugh. "Said she wasn't good enough. She must not have liked that because the tower's meeting hall burned down later that year. Eight dead. Appears the Spire looked into that. Listed Marie as a suspect, but no one ever found her. Your *friend* here thinks she might have done the same thing in Berlin. Nineteen eleven. Similar story, but no pictures." Kate flipped the page. "And again, in Belgium."

Harcourt leaned closer, trying to read the page upside down. "Definite pattern."

"Yeah. Everyone told her she wasn't good enough. But she knew one trick, one effective spell to buy her the time to keep trying."

19

THE TRAIN TO ETOP

The exchange rate for gold was total shit. The silver was worth slightly more on Hollit than Earth, or Terra as Outworlders called it. But the speed at which gold back home had inflated meant it was worth roughly a third here. Kate didn't mind, it was still more than enough to keep them going for a while. Once this was all over, she planned to spend a few years shipping Coke over for gold and then selling the gold for more Coke. Viatores always tried to keep that activity at a minimum, careful not to draw the Spire's attention out of their fear of crashing the economy. But she figured she couldn't get in their crosshairs any more than she already was, so she might as well get rich.

They were navigating the market near a bakery, the aroma of hot sweetbreads filling the tight streets. Backpack snugly loaded with her new brazier, Kate was mentally spending her future millions when Evan stopped abruptly in front of her.

"What in the hell is that?"

Kate followed his pointing finger to a small, paved clearing with a fountain. A statue of a nude woman with a bowed serpent's head stood at its heart, water pouring from her outstretched arms. A ghostly, masculine figure stood before it, its translucent flesh silvery white. Turning his head, the figure gaped, mouth open. Pale eyes scanned the market and its people.

"I was wondering when we'd see one of those," Kate said.

"Ye see tha', too?" Nate asked.

"Everyone does," Jim said. "Dream Walker."

"You've seen them before?" Kate asked, trying to sound casual.

Nate nodded.

"But what is it?" Evan asked.

"Dream Walker," Jim repeated. "Somewhere, some dude's having an out of body experience. He's new at it, judging by the lack of clothes. Probably thinks this is all a crazy dream. Then tomorrow, he might remember some image or song he heard and introduce that to his own world, thinking he made it."

"And that's normal?"

"Oh yeah," Kate said. "Some worlds, they're easier to see than others." Her eyes flicked to Nate. "Back home they're harder to see. Only very special people can notice them."

The figure straightened as if seeing something off to the left that caught his interest. He streaked toward it, a blur of motion and was gone.

"Whoa!" Evan exclaimed.

Kate patted his arm. "Come on. You look like an outsider enough without you gaping at the phantoms. We got a train to catch."

Smooth alabaster columns ran the circumference of the three-tiered station, giving it the appearance of a giant's wedding cake. It was the second-highest building in Arin, still a good thirty feet lower than the Grand Kelsut's golden teat. Gold-hued escalators carried them up to the highest platform where they waited beside the helical track. A steady breeze coursed through the open area, ruffling Kate's robes. Dull bronze eagles ran along the platform's outer rim, their extended wingtips forming the rail. Nate and Jim were leaning against one of them, enjoying this commanding view of the city, while Kate kept herself safely away from the edge, arms folded against the chill.

After twenty minutes of shivering, a distant hum signaled the train's approach. The other two dozen passengers began shuffling toward the tracks, bags in hand, as the train slowed to a stop with a metallic hiss. It consisted of three cars, the ones on either end tapering to a bullet point. Twin rings around each car rotated with the track, allowing it to stay level within the spiraling tube. Passengers exited the far side, their murmurs and footsteps echoing down off the high roof. Once the sounds thinned, polished doors slid upward, and the crowd surged on board.

The five of them managed to secure a small booth together, their luggage occupying the sixth seat. It stank of old sweat and overripe fruit with a metallic tang. A wide hexagon of gauzy silver fabric hugged the curving outer wall, its corners affixed by quarter-inch glass posts. Evan tacked a Red Gate icon above the single door, affixing it there with a glob of putty.

Other travelers shuffled past the arched doorway, gazes noting the seat filled with packs, but then averting once falling on the foreign-skinned occupants. A little girl, maybe five, with lime robes and cobalt skin openly ogled them, her mouth open in a curious gape before her father hurried her away. After ten minutes an electric gong rang, and the train began to move.

The silver hexagon stirred, and then the image beyond the train's metal walls came to life like a flickering electronic window. No, she realized, the flickering wasn't a technical glitch, but the stuttering of the passing curved rails, like when moving quickly past a wooden fence.

"Hmm," Harcourt said, bobbing his head side to side. "It's not a screen."

Nate followed his lead, changing the angle at which she looked at it. "Wicked."

Kate tried it as well, discovering that the perspective changed, just like a real window.

"I wouldn't touch that," Jim warned.

"Why?" Evan asked, his fingers hovering millimeters from one of the stubby glass posts.

"Seriously? You were a *stick a fork in a wall outlet* sorta kid, weren't you?"

Evan's fingers retreated. "So it'll shock me."

"Hell if I know, but I don't wanna find out the hard way."

They rode for more than an hour before passing through the mountains, the passage marked by a towering stone edifice of a man in a cylindrical hat, carved into the granite mountainside. Its features were worn, the face completely broken off from either wars or the passage of millennia, but it still commanded awe. Lush forests of umbrella-shaped trees stretched beyond the range. The train stopped in a small town before continuing on, the shadows long beneath the low-dipping sun.

Kate watched the world through their monitor before finally falling asleep. She stirred during the next two stops, but awoke to the sight of infinite ocean.

They were crossing a bridge, a high one judging by the ships passing beneath them. The golden red of the never-setting sun danced across the rippled surface. It stretched forever, no curve, no distant boats sinking below the edge, just flat and endless until they were too small to see. Cloud-fringed peaks shone in the low light, but Kate had no way to gauge how distant they were. Fifteen miles or five hundred, it just depended on their size.

Nate and Jim were asleep on the bench opposite her, their heads cradled in the maroon, cushioned rests. One of Nate's long hands lay in her lap, the other arms stretched out, the back of her hand resting against Jim's thigh, assuring her he was still there. A strange pang pressed at the bottom of Kate's throat. Loneliness? Harcourt was still beside them, sleeping, the red binder of Marie Marchand open in his lap. She thought of the way Evan had selflessly offered to give him the yeng beetle even at the loss of his hand and flesh, the risk of needing an oxygen tank to breathe, but he'd offered it to save the old man's life. Who would have done that for her?

"*You don't get her*," Candace's voice echoed in her memory. Once, that statement of selfless courage, rescuing Kate and charging off to save her tower mates, had earned Kate's eternal love. Candace had died saving her. The ultimate sacrifice. Now, the awful truth embittered that memory.

Don't be stupid, she scolded herself. *Here you are, a Magus whining like a little girl. "No one loves me." Who do you love? Who would you give everything for?*

Master Boyer. My tower mates.

This isn't about you, this is them—avenging them. Stop your whining and focus on what you have to do.

Kate swallowed away the lump. She looked out the monitor window and watched the passing mountains. Christ, she needed a bump.

Towering black obelisks lined the last few miles into Etop. Wasp-like vehicles zipped along the highways to and from the great city, their scintillant wings soaking up the rising sun's rays. A titanic pyramid stood at the city's heart, a mountain of polished stone and glass, like if the Las Vegas Luxor had eaten everything else on the strip. The city stretched out in a perfect grid, save for the X of angled roads stretching out from the pyramid's corners and dividing Etop into four pie-wedge districts.

The station where they arrived was bustling. Musicians and jugglers carved out their own little arenas against the walls or in the middle of thoroughfares, forcing the crowd to condense as it moved past them. It stank of smoke, rotting trash, and hot grease, made worse by the sticky, humid air.

"Everyone, watch each other's packs," Jim warned. "I've already seen one pickpocket."

There were more non-Hollitians than Kate had remembered. A group of Torbans shuffled past, their skin tattooed with elaborate mazes of metallic ink, like circuitry, and then coated with a fine layer of white ash. A woman with bronze skin and ribbon-braided hair peddled frozen treats to a group of children before her refrigerated cart. Ghostly Dream Walkers glided among the crowds, impervious to the physical barriers that hadn't been warded.

"Don't stare," she reminded Evan, though Kate couldn't help gawking herself at the sheer diversity of populations, the races all the analogs of human from their perspective worlds.

At Nate's urging, they stopped at a tiny cafe. Kate purchased a shuka— a kind of flat-bread wrap stuffed with various vegetables, goat cheese, meat, and a vinegary syrup.

"Careful with those Hollit burritos," Jim warned around a mouthful of protein bar. "No telling what's in them. Get yourself the shits."

Nate paused mid-chew, seeming to reconsider the half-eaten shuka.

Kate arched her brow. "So says the guy who couldn't wait to get his first dehod kebob."

"Yeah, but I know what's in it, and it was well-cooked."

"Don't worry," Kate assured. "We're stocked up on antacid." She took a large bite, savoring the tangy juices, and tried not to think what kind of meat it was.

Eight blocks later, they reached the District of the Gods, packed with grand temples and monuments, each vying to outshine its neighbors. Many familiar symbols adorned the high walls and towers—crosses, crescents, and ankhs. Evan glanced nervously at an enormous jade swastika above one temple until Jim assured him the symbol's origins were far older than the Reich which soiled it. At the district's heart, facing a fountain square, stood the Templum Aetheris, or Oritur Aer Portus as most called it. The domed building stood a hundred and fifty feet high of violet-streaked marble. It was a near-perfect twin of the great Pantheon in Rome, though Kate had no idea which of them was older. A dense group of people crowded the covered platform before the great double doors. Most cradled bags and trunks of every make, many brimming so tight they looked to soon burst. Raised voices laced with exhaustion came from all sides, many of the words Kate caught, but most were so thick in their dialectic accents she couldn't begin to understand them. But the mannerisms of frustrated passengers were universal.

The back of Kate's scalp cinched as she crossed the powerful wards infused into each of the three steps. She pushed her way to a black-framed sign and immediately understood. The price of passage to Dhevin had quadrupled. Many others, Lumit, Ahl, Torba, and Zash had been indefinitely canceled. Kate noted the time for the next crossing, about two hours, and headed back to where the others waited.

"What's that about?" Jim asked. He clutched a handful of curved goggles he'd found at a nearby shop.

"Cancelled flight," she said. "But we're okay."

"Cancelled? Did something happen to the Viatores?"

She shook her head. "I don't know. But another thing is there are no return trips. One-way only."

He shared a look with Harcourt. "Viatores been vanishing back home. Maybe it's been happening everywhere else, too."

"As long as we can get to the Athenaeum, we'll be fine. Maybe even get some answers as to what's going on."

20

DISCIPLES OF YELLOW

A bronze bell tolled three times, and the imposing double doors of the Templum Aetheris swung open. A hooded figure in dark robes stood at the entrance, towering a full foot above the tallest of the waiting travelers. The slender nose of its bird-like mask protruded a full two feet, tapering to a sharp point.

The crowd of displaced and angry people shied away, parting before the lanky and masked giant. Kate had never seen one of the Netru, the Viatoric priests of the Demhe. She couldn't tell if it was male or female, only the commanding presence emanating from it.

A line queued before the steps and travelers shuffled toward the doors, on their one-way passage to Dhevin. Taking the lead, Kate fell into line and started up the steps, the crawling tingle of wards humming along her skin. The travelers dropped their payment into a flower-shaped cauldron of polished stone as they entered, the coins chinking by the handful.

Kate tried to catch the Netru's eyes beneath the bone-like mask, but she gasped at the realization that what she'd mistook for black robes was, in fact, swirling mist. It wasn't aether, but it whirled and flowed across its form in the same living manner, only a few wisps trailing away at its shoulders. The priest turned its head toward her, the emerald-green eyes registering her awe, and then the slender nose dipped sharply toward the offering bowl. Kate dropped the golden coins onto the growing pile and headed inside.

Few spoke as they entered the temple, and those who did only in hushed whispers. Their low voices and shuffling footsteps echoed across the huge chamber. A single beam of sunlight sliced through the smoke, leaving a star-shaped shadow on a polished wall. Craning her neck, Kate noticed the single hole at the top of the dome. A metal grate covered the thirty-foot oculus, its shape the Heptagram of the Viatoric Ipsissimus. One square, six rings, and twin seven-pointed stars—Kate had spent years dreaming of the day when that sigil would blossom before her open fingers. Then three years more knowing that it never would. Now, seeing it, the dream rekindled. One day, that symbol would be hers.

A dozen enormous mosaics adorned the walls, each depicting land-scapes from various worlds. One stood out among the rest, not a scene, but a symbol, gold on a black background. The tiles were new, pristine and lacking the smoky patina of centuries. The swooping glyph seemed to move, making it impossible to take it all in. Kate took a step back, a strange vertigo overtaking her. The symbol slid into focus, but now the world around it warped.

Even having never seen it before, Kate knew without a doubt in the world what the symbol was—the Yellow Sign. A terrible weight, like a steel ball formed of pure hopelessness, welled in her stomach, pulling it down-ward. If the sign was displayed, then Carcosa had its king, or queen as the case may be. Kate forced her eyes away, breaking its oppressive spell.

Jim grunted behind her. Kate glanced back to see if he'd noticed the sign as well, but he was looking at the nine other Netru gliding through the crowd. Four wore identical smoky robes as the doorman. The remaining five were clad in gold, the fabric so gleaming that it nimbused in the hazy air. They carried what looked like rifles with red-enameled stocks and glass cylinders on either side of their silver barrels. The red chrome of their masks protruded from beneath their cowls, wedge-shaped and lacking any feature but vertical eye slits. Those hidden eyes tracked the newcomers, lingering on each and every person like vultures surveying the sick and dying.

In all her readings of the masked priests, she'd never heard of these other five. They only wore black and ivory-colored masks, but things had changed. Nate's wide eyes were locked on the golden symbol, white above the pupils.

Kate touched her shoulder, eliciting a jump. "Don't look at it." She turned to Harcourt and Evan, repeating the warning.

The crowd gathered in the heart of the great chamber, within an enormous inlaid gold and nickel ring. Arcane symbols of multicolored metals traced the edges, each color a different spell. Kate tried to look casual as she studied the artifact, the power thrumming from it like a great diesel engine. A spherical iron brazier stood five feet high at the circle's heart, the emanating heat like a physical force. The white smoke seeping from its angular holes smelled of cedar and magnolia. Kate inhaled deeply, committing the fragrance to memory.

The gold-clad guards closed the doors, locking them with a rotating lever. The smoke-shrouded priests gathered at one of the steel cases along the wall and returned to the ring, marching single file, each cradling a softball-sized stone in one hand and an engraved rod in the other. Circling anticlockwise, one stopped as they reached a rounded divot in the inlaid floor until they all stood towering equilaterally around the nickel ring. Careful not to draw attention, Kate pushed her way closer to see.

On some unspoken cue, the five Netru knelt and placed the stones into the depressions. Tiger-eye, she realized. The priests stepped into the ring, the crowd parting before them and they halted at the smoking brazier. Their long fingers flicked and wove in the familiar pattern, magic lacing. Their croaking voices unintelligible beneath the masks, they chanted. In one synchronized motion, they raised their rods above the grated orb. Some hidden mechanism opened and powder cascaded from their tips. White smoke erupted from the coals and aether whirled outside the rings, ushering them into the Abyss.

They traveled quickly, the dream reefs tumbling past like asteroids. Kate assumed the role of the wide-eyed first-timer, avoiding the guards' attention, oohing and aahing as she studied which of the inlaid glyphs glowed around the ring. She couldn't do it at once. That would be too obvious. Instead, she studied them in four quadrants and reassembled the patterns in her mind. She doubted it was enough for her to perform the traveling herself, but it was a start. She finished none too soon. After half an hour, the aether thinned, and a massive circular chamber solidified around them.

Three more of the golden guards silently waited outside the materializing ring. The silver ghost light of the inlaid floor faded and a rush of dry air whisked the smoke away. Kate scrunched her eyes from the sudden and painfully bright sunlight all around them.

Following the lead of several of the other travelers, Kate pulled her goggles on. Made from some soft, plasticy shell, they covered most of her face. Instantly the wash of light faded. Colors emerged. Beyond the circle of spiral columns, an enormous black city loomed on all sides, bright flags snapping in the breeze. What should have been a rainbow of house colors was now dominated by a lemon-bright yellow. Kate's toes curled as she spied the elaborate and subtly shifting glyph of the Yellow Sign emblazoned across a taut banner crowning a nearby tower like a ship's sail. Kell, the Scholars' Roost, and bastion of all knowledge, wasn't as safe as she had hoped. One of the Netru extended its long arm and Kate was swept up in the crowd now shuffling toward the exit.

21

CITY OF BLACK SPIRES

Amidst a flat sea of farms and undulating grasslands, the ancient city of Kell rose to a height of nine-hundred feet. Originally a basalt mesa, the city was carved in the same sense as Petra or Ellora, starting at the top and moving downward over the centuries as the population grew, the result being a wide variety of styles among the enormous towers, laced together with carved bridges and metal cables. In its early days, sewage was handled by copper gutters weaving down the structures. As plumbing technology improved, rendering the old ways obsolete, the downpipes whose placement had become incorporated into the elaborate reliefs, were replaced by a pneumatic tube system, carrying messages and small packages up and down.

Long-tailed birds swooped and chittered between the black spires. Over sixty avian species made Kell their home, nesting either directly on the basalt walls or inside the thousands of deeply carved niches—knotwork trimmings and the open mouths of forgotten gods.

One hand against the wall, Kate kept her eyes on her feet as she descended the spiraling stairs. Most appeared to have been repaired over the years, metal edge-caps textured for grip. Others were worn, smoothly bowed from centuries of use. While she noticed some, the concept of guard rails seemed to elude Dhevinites. Not that Kate would have trusted her weight to one, anyway, but without one she felt like she was out there, hanging by the edge. The six-hundred-foot drop made her head swim.

Thin nets skirted many of the towers every fifty feet or so, looking like vertical tennis courts. A faller landing on one seemed about as likely of it breaking under the strain or bouncing them off to a plummeting death. Neither struck her as appealing.

Kate pressed herself close to the neighboring wall as the wind strengthened, fluttering her robes and pulling on her pack. The worn carvings along the tower, their stained features smoothed away by many hands, told her that she was hardly the first to embrace them.

The icy blue sun dominated the sky, easily twice the size of hers back home. As a result, the Dhevinites' eyes were very small, hooded, and shielded below enormous eyebrows extending a finger's length to either side of their triangular faces. The feature was a source of great pride, being plucked and waxed, dyed and framed in tattoos. Kate recalled some social status accompanied each of the looks, but didn't know it. Master Boyer would have scolded her for such ignorance. Though she did remember one social class: Slaves. The lowest rank among Dhevin's population had no brows at all, the ridges instead scaled in tiny wired loops. A displeased master could grab the metal tab on either side and pull, ripping it out and blinding the slave with their own blood.

A pair of men rounded the corner ahead, shirtless save for long jackets, their ruddy brown skin oiled and decorated with scars. Unsure of protocol, Kate squeezed herself even closer to the tower's face, her pack rubbing against the stone. The lean man in the front furrowed his brow in an annoyed expression. They passed her on the outer side, a spicy waft of perfume as they hurried by, not paying the slightest attention to the drop beside them.

Kate followed the stairs down two full spirals before reaching a platform, joining three of the towers with a sort of market. The golden flag with the Yellow Sign fluttered above a round stand. Freshly cut metal rods showed that a statue had recently stood there, the stone still stained green from rain like a lingering shadow. A pair of slaves scrubbed white-scrawled graffiti from a wall, the huge letters runny. The first word was gone, but "WILL RETURN" was still plainly visible. Who would return?

"Bloody fuckin' hell," Nate groaned.

A tall woman with steely black hair and a skin-tight green bodysuit sang before a crowd at the far end of the platform. Not a bodysuit, Kate recognized, but thousands of tiny insects, scuttling across her red skin, their shells glinting in the sunlight. A few traced across her face and fingers, grooming the curling brows and painted nails.

"Don't stare," Kate reminded.

"Wha' the hell is tha'?" Nate asked, still wide-eyed and nose crinkled.

"Very expensive clothes," Kate said. "She's someone important, and we don't need to insult her."

"They're fuckin' bugs."

"Yup. Nice color, too. And they don't fuck on her, just the queen." She scanned the city, locating the Athenaeum two towers away. A capsule-shaped gondola glided toward it, and she followed the path of its cables to find the nearest station. Maybe they could get to it.

"So what happens when she sits down?" Evan asked. "Crushes them?"

Nate gave an exaggerated shiver.

"They move out of the way first," Kate said. "They sense her intention and act accordingly."

"So she sits bare-assed?" Evan asked with an amused grin.

"Yeah. And it's probably the cleanest ass you'll ever find. Syl mites eat any excess skin or anything else. It's like living inside a high-end spa. No calluses, excess hair, nothing."

"If you don't mind being covered in bugs."

Kate shrugged. She plotted a rough course: Two bridges, down one level and then to the station. "There is that. But you also never have to wash your clothes. Just put them back in their jar when you want to wear something else. You can get them as a necklace, too. Trim your beard, always have perfect hair and skin above the neck. You might like it."

"I'll pass."

"You're missing out." She pointed to a gray-hued elevator tube. "We'll take that down."

They crossed the suspended market and joined the growing line outside the lift's metal-lined doors.

"Is it just me," Harcourt said, his voice low. "Or are people staring at me?"

"Price of beauty," Kate said, eliciting a chuckle from Nate.

"No," Evan said. "He's right."

Kate eyed the waiting crowd. While they were packed nearly shoulder to shoulder, everyone was giving the old man a wide berth. He could have spun his arms around and hit no one but Evan. Most were silent, though a few spoke in low whispers, sidelong glances flicking Harcourt's direction.

"It's the yellow," Nate said, noting the bright lemon color visible inside the bell sleeves and between the leg slits.

Frowning, Jim gave her a questioning look, but Harcourt spoke first.

"She's right. No one else is wearing it."

Kate looked around. Aside from the flags, and several bell-shaped blossoms hanging from one of the vine-laden towers, there wasn't a scrap of yellow anywhere. *Well, shit.* If Candace was behind the banners, and the Netru's cutting off of worlds, the last thing they needed was to get busted breaking some color edict. "Jim, you brought safety pins?"

"On it." He shrugged off his pack.

"Next we need some new clothes."

Jim drew a plastic baggie with spools of thread and needles inside. "Agreed."

"I'm not wearin' bugs," Nate said sharply.

"We couldn't afford them." Kate shook her head. "We can get away with Hollitian garb for a while. It's a lot more diverse here. But not *these* clothes."

Evan moved behind the old man, blocking him from view as Jim began pinning the slits in Harcourt's robes shut.

"Not enough to make this tight, so small steps or you'll pop one," Jim said.

Harcourt was rolling his sleeves inward to mask the brilliant yellow. "That's going to make stairs difficult."

"We'll figure it out." He pinned the bottom of the front slit. "Turn around." Harcourt did, and Jim started on the back. "If we're getting new clothes, Katie, the rest of us need to fit in, but for the Athenaeum you might want to look a bit more formal."

Kate looked down at her red robes with their mismatched sleeve. The heat from the pale sun was making her sweat and compared to the perfumed Dhevinites, she probably smelled like a horse. "Good point."

Despite the most valiant attempts at homogeny, language is organic—ever-changing. Even the Trade Tongue, used across a hundred words, morphs and adopts regional variances. Dhevin was no exception, and its particular dialect made it difficult to understand. But by the time they'd crossed two towers and found a clothier, Kate had learned several important things.

Kell was only one of the many Dhevin nations to surrender to the Golden Empress. The coup had been swift, nearly bloodless. Those who had resisted, mostly senators and their families, were now hanging en masse from the Gallows Roost, a slender tower at the southern end of the city. While rumors of the empress had begun the previous year when the Netru had adopted the golden garb, the sudden power shift had occurred only a week before. Conversion to Terran time placed that a single day after Kate's magic had been restored.

For the most part, life hadn't changed, though travel outside the Empire was impossible. The new leadership fell to the surviving successors of the old. Yellow was forbidden to anyone outside the government. Three days had passed since the empress had made her only appearance, a parade from the Templum Aetheris to the citadel. Citizens had crowded the windows and overlooks to glimpse their conqueror, but had only seen a gold-robed figure, her face hidden beneath a simple, pallid mask. Kate shuddered at the news the empress had been flanked by a dozen grotesque and blind dogs. A golden beacon shone from the citadel upon her arrival, shining toward the heavens. Six hours later it was gone, though no one had seen her leave.

Kate resisted the urge to pry the clothier any deeper. Comments such as "strung bastards up" and the "living goddess" only told her that those stationed below the highest social class supported their new matriarch. The gnawing paranoia was bad enough without accidentally outing herself as a dissenter.

"We're well and truly fucked," Jim whispered once they'd left. He cast a glance back over his shoulder. "But even if the Golden Empress is real, like actually from Carcosa, we don't even know if it is Candy. No one saw her face."

"We're not fucked until we're caught," Harcourt answered. A warm breeze ruffled his gauzy green shirt and billowy trousers.

"I'm willing to take the step of faith that she's the real empress," Kate said. "The Netru seem to believe it."

Harcourt grunted in agreement. "And if it isn't Candace, then maybe she's near the empress."

"Wonderful," Jim said, sarcasm dripping from his voice. "So what do we do?"

"Keep to the plan." Kate leaned her head into the wind, allowing it to press her wide-brimmed hat on instead of ripping it away. Between the hat and the huge goggles, she felt like a low-budget Audrey Hepburn.

Nate snorted. "The one where we go to the library and say, *excuse me, where can I find the directions to Carcosa?* Tha' one?"

"That's the one," Kate said. They followed an arched bridge, one with an actual handrail, thank God, coming to a triangular platform where one of the cable gondolas made their stop.

Evan eyed a needle-like spire peeking between the stone forest. Rows of corpses, their wrists and ankles bound to the wall behind them, decorated the top like some grotesque thistle or bushel of bananas. They were all nude save for the cage-like, pewter masks. Buzzards hopped and feasted among the dead while orbiting kingbirds gorged on bloated flies. "So how did she take the city in a single day?"

"Faith," Kate said, pulling her eyes from the gruesome display. "Belief in Carcosa's rule runs deep. The King in Yellow, or Empress in this case, reigns supreme. If she controls the Netru, she controls all communication between worlds. If they say she's empress, then she's the empress."

"So, she's what, a god now?" Evan whispered. "How do you kill a god?"

"She's not a god, no more than a pharaoh or any other *divine* ruler. She might be the newest to wear the Crowned Mask, but she's hardly the first."

"So how do we do it?" Jim asked.

"No clue," Kate said. "That's why we stick to the plan." Her eyes returned to the Gallows Roost, the masked dead ranging from children to the elderly. One misstep and she'd join their grisly ranks. "I need to go alone."

"What?" Jim asked. "Katie, I don't know if you've been paying attention, but we're in the lion's den here."

"Exactly. We'll find a room. If something happens to me you'll still be safe."

"You mean trapped here. You heard that woman. No one leaves the Empire."

"But you'll be safe. I'm the only one that can do this, and there's no need to risk everyone. If something happens... Just trust me. I can do this."

22

ENTRY DENIED

Framed between thirty-foot statues, the iron double-doors of Kell's Athenaeum formed a perfect equilateral triangle. Elaborate half-reliefs of hooded monks and strange creatures adorned the blackened metal. Kate stared at them for a solid three minutes, marveling at the insane details captured within. Every stitch in their clothes, the tiny engravings on the ring of a raised hand, a stray hair across a down-turned face, was perfectly molded as if the artist had made the figures life-size and then shrunk them down. There were no visible hinges, and only a subtle misalignment revealed the seam along the middle.

Power thrummed from the portal like a bottled storm. She'd lost count at around twenty protective wards, each one stronger than any at either Whittaker's or Cù-Sìth, not only capable of repelling elementals, scrying, or incorporeals, but even flesh. These wards weren't simple spells, but deeper, older, their bindings sowed with the lifeblood of willing sacrifice. Somewhere inside her, either intuition or submerged memory from her studies, Kate knew that each of the detailed ten-inch figures cast into the iron were those who had laid down their lives for this protection. If there'd ever been a barrier erected that might stop a god, the Athenaeum's doors were it.

She glanced back over her shoulder. No one was paying her any active interest—simply a newcomer, a tourist ogling the masterwork. She could walk away now, and no one would remember her. To pull the silver dangling chain would out her. Only the worthy could enter the Temple of Knowledge, and stepping through those doors would announce her existence to not only the world, but to her enemies.

Kate had dreamed of this, the yearning fantasies fueling her studies. But now, at the precipice of triumph, she hesitated. The Athenaeum was Switzerland—neutral, immune to governments and tyrants. No one, not even the Kings or Queens in Yellow had ever held power over the librarians. They were the check and balance. But times had changed. Candace, if the Golden Empress was Candace, had seized Dhevin the moment Kate's powers had returned. While such a move must have been planned over years, there was no doubt in Kate's mind that the timing was related. The restoration of Kate's magic had led to the two hundred corpses rotting atop the Gallows Roost. Not only them, but the countless more at each Dhevin nation. Their blood, though unintentional, was on her hands, and if Kate refused to pull that silver chain, she'd not only spit in the face of her fallen tower mates, but those unknown victims.

Kate straightened. Clenching her teeth, she pulled the chain and a distant bell tolled beyond the iron doors. Resisting the urge to look back to see who might be watching her, Kate stood straight, confident, her palms sweating and scalp pricking. The great doors slid open from the middle like curtains or robotic moth wings, widening just enough for the hefty, white-robed man to step through.

He was hairless, his skin the color of dried blood, his face decorated with elaborate tattoos. His hooded eyes, hidden behind amber-hued spectacles, zeroed in on Kate. He politely nodded. "May I offer assistance?"

Kate stepped closer. "I wish entry."

"Do you carry letter of referral?"

"No, and I have no patron."

The corner of the librarian's lip gave the slightest twitch. "Apologies. Without advocate or credentials, entry is forbidden."

Kate extended her hand, her fingers already weaving. Seven interlocking squares blossomed from orange light. One by one, five disassembled into rings as the heptagram laced into existence, the librarian slapped Kate's hand with a hard *smack*.

Kate clutched her stinging fingers. "What the fu—"

The librarian seized her shoulder, his grip tight and painful. He pulled her close. "Silence!" He wrenched her inside, shot a furtive glance out the open door, and then with his free hand touched a jeweled stud beside Kate's head. The great door slid closed.

"You're hurting me," Kate growled, her fingers drawing the magic to knock the fat fuck across the inlaid floor.

"Apologies, mistress." He released her and looked around like a guilty child. The enormous room extended all the way through the tower, ending at a high window on the opposite wall two hundred yards away. But the tower's exterior wasn't that wide, a hundred yards at most. A forest of pillars filled the chamber, many supporting small platforms at odd intervals. Winding stairs led up and down to the other levels, partially visible through the cutout floors. The weird, Escheresque architecture hurt her brain. Books and scrolls packed the shelves honeycombing every surface. Tablets stood displayed on stands beneath pale lights. Tiny dumbwaiters, heavy with leather-bound tomes, floated up and down the walls like busy ants.

"Forgive," the librarian whispered, "but you cannot ever do that in public. Ever!" He glanced back again.

Several of the other white-clad eunuchs were watching, hairless brows arched with curiosity. A woman with ankle-length braids and a silvery sylmite bodysuit looked up from a nearby table, her lip curled in a contemptuous glare. A quartet of men in bright yellow sat at a platform sixty feet away.

"But how—"

"Shh," he hissed. "You can't be here. If anyone saw what you are, we'd both hang upon Roost. You must leave. Go to Atoq Bridge. Midnight. Change clothes, your appearance, talk to no one. Understand?"

Kate nodded.

"I am Durio. They will tell you I sent you. No." He paused, his small eyes darting back and forth. "No. They'll ask you for key. Speak to no one unless they ask you for it. It's important."

"All right," Kate said. "My name is—"

"No," his thick hand came up as if shielding him from her words. "I can't know it. If they capture me, I can't betray it. We might have been seen. Leave now. Go. Atoq Bridge. Midnight."

Durio touched the stud again, and the iron doors slid open. He took her by the arm, softer this time but still firm. "No advocate, no entry." He pushed her outside like an angry bouncer. Kate stumbled, her left heel threatening to go out from under her. "That is law," Durio said, his over-acted expression a little too cold. Without another word the doors scissored closed.

Kate's cheeks felt hot. What the hell had just happened? A few passers were staring at her. *Play along,* some part of her brain whispered. Kate slap-brushed her shoulder where he'd grabbed her and redirected her frustra-tion to the iron doors. "Fuck you!" she spat, loud enough for her audience to hear. Wheeling, she stormed away, praying that no one was following her.

23

BLIND DATE

Once the sapphire sunset had faded below the horizon, shops shuttered, streetlights ignited, and clouds of striped bats poured into the night sky. Not the entire city had retired for the evening. Noodle diners, bars, and brothels rolled out the lights. Hoots and music echoed up and down the chasm streets, melding into an excited white noise. The smell of tobacco and opium smoke tinged the redolence of flowering vines.

Avoiding those night-thriving districts, Kate made her way through the Carved City, down the twisting steps toward Mydorn Square. A shallow pool dominated the platform, fed from a waterfall fifty feet above. A narrow channel ran from the basin, over the edge to a platform below. Submerged lights cast shimmering patterns across the neighboring towers, giving the graven statues a subtle illusion of movement. Her bootsteps ticked across the open square, pink tiles dividing its surface into rentable vendor spaces.

Huge white letters in still-drying paint read 'KAMRE WILL RETURN.' A few unlucky feet had found the graffiti, the ghosts of their misstep stamped across the market. Kate had seen the message three times now. No mention who or where this Kamre was, but after Durio's impassioned warning, she figured it was best not to be asking questions that might draw notice.

The gnawing paranoia of being alone needled at the back of her skull.

Was Evan back there? Turning to look for him would only expose his presence. She just had to trust he was still following. Thirty feet above, from the vantage of a shadowed flying arch, Jim and the others were silently watching as Kate crossed the square and entered the tunnel of Atoq Bridge.

Irregular cubicle-like shops, their doors and windows shuttered, lined either side, leaving just enough room for two people to walk abreast. Two stories up, a slanted roof shielded the sky above. A light globe burned thirty feet ahead, the only illumination inside this sloped passage.

Lizard brain kicked in the moment she entered the bridge. Dark passage. Lone woman, meeting a stranger. Fight or flight mode cycled up, ready to drop into either gear. *Please say Evan's close.*

No, she scolded herself. *You're not some powerless girl anymore. You're a magus. Stop acting like you need their protection. They need yours.*

Kate drew a breath, collecting her energy and calming her pounding heart. Shoulders back, she strode the rest of the way to the lone streetlight. Musty smells filled the passage—mildew, pigeon shit, and old sweat.

A man with a square cap stepped out from the shadows ten feet away. His slender eyebrows extended perfectly flat for several inches past his face before curling upwards. Tiny black eyes gleamed in the light. "I am Pamor." He shot a furtive glance up and down the bridge. "Durio sent us."

On cue, one of the shop doors creaked opened just a few feet behind Kate. She spun as a second man emerged, his face hidden beneath long shadows. His broad shoulders nearly filled the passage.

"We must go," Pamor said.

A fearful warning skittered up Kate's spine. She looked back and forth between them. "What's the password?"

Pamor's huge brows creased. "Password?"

"Yeah. He'd told me you'd have one."

He shook his head. "He didn't tell us."

"Then you better go back and get it from him." Kate moved her back against the wall, the men on either side of her.

"Durio is dead."

"What?"

A soft jingling echoed ahead. Pamor turned. A third person was entering the tunnel bridge. The opposite side from where Kate had.

Pamor slipped a hand into the pocket of his long jacket.

The newcomer stopped twenty feet away. Beneath the open, knee-length vest she wore something resembling lizard skin. Syl mites encircled her throat in an undulating pattern of glistening violet against her smooth, rust-colored skin. A few sparkled in the light's glow as they traced up her face, grooming the tightly curled eyebrows. Slender, crimson-dyed dreadlocks draped her back and shoulders, each one capped with a tiny golden band.

"Dahn Livia," Pamor said, his shoulders relaxing.

"Pamor," she replied with a nod. Her eyes flicked between the men and then to Kate. "Do you have key?"

All at once, the big man behind Kate lunged as Pamor yanked his hand from the pocket, a blocky object in his fist. Light gleamed off polished metal. It looked like one of those old broom handle pistols, but with a stubby, flat barrel.

"No," Kate yelled as an encircling arm pinned her elbows to her sides. Bad move. Her hands were still free.

The newcomer dropped to her knees, her own gun emerging from beneath the vest, but Pamor's pistol was already dipping toward her.

Kate motioned her fingers, emerald light welling. Her attacker heaved Kate back as the spell released. The brilliant beam of green light punched through a door beside Pamor's ear.

Yelping, he sprang away in surprise, the cap tumbling from his head.

The woman lifted her gun. The slit-like barrel looked like some novelty toy that fired nickels. It buzzed like a vibrator on a tile floor.

Pamor jerked. Tiny red dots bloomed across his back. His pistol clattered to the floor, and then he collapsed backward, gurgling.

The big man wrenched Kate around as if to run, but Evan was standing at the bridge's other entrance, a silenced pistol in hand. The man drew a curved knife.

Fuck this. No one was making her a hostage. Kate threw her shoulders forward pulling the man with the motion.

He grunted but didn't fall or let go. His sandaled feet peeked between her legs. Kate drew her power and released a loud "Ka!"

The man's ankle snapped with a wet pop, the bones along the top of his feet splintering like dry twigs. Screaming, he crumpled.

Kate managed to catch herself without landing on the man now clutching his mangled foot. Hooking her middle finger, she twisted her hand open in a quick snapping motion. The fallen knife flew up into her grip.

Evan was hurrying toward her, pistol raised in both hands.

The woman had her weapon up as well, that coin-slot barrel aimed at Evan. It hummed faintly.

"Stop!" Kate shouted, throwing up her hand. "He's with me."

The woman lowered her gun, pointing it at the maimed attacker.

Evan kept his trained. "You all right?"

"Fine," Kate panted.

Pamor coughed frothy red, his eyes staring toward the ceiling. Blood oozed from a fist-sized hole in his chest. It looked like hamburger, a mulching of flesh and cloth.

"Who the hell are you?" Kate asked.

Keeping her gun on the wounded man, her eyes flicked to Kate. "I am Livia. We must leave. More will be coming."

"Who sent you?"

"Durio. And if these shit sons are here, then he is dead."

"What's this about?" Kate demanded.

"You," Livia said. "There is bounty for any Viatores not loyal to empress."

Pamor spasmed, let a final wheeze, and went still.

"What about him?" Evan asked, nodding to the brute with the smashed foot.

Livia's pistol gave that loud whir, and the brute's face disintegrated with a thousand miniature explosions. He slumped against a shop wall. Tiny hair-like needles jutted from his exposed cheekbones and rims of his jellied eyes.

Evan's pistol was back up and trained on Livia, his finger on the trigger.

"What about him?" She lifted her hands in a sign of surrender. Her thumb came off the pistol grip, and the muted humming ceased. "He intended to kill you for money. No loss. No witnesses."

Kate touched Evan's shoulder. "Ease up."

He removed his finger from the trigger, but held it there until Livia holstered her pistol beneath her vest.

Livia turned. "Come."

"Where are we going?" Kate asked.

"Safehouse."

"Where?"

"Ruins point of safehouse if I say." Her gaze flicked up and around. "Many listening ears and many purses eager to reward them. Follow me."

"We have friends with us," Kate said.

"Terran?"

Kate nodded.

"Then bring them. You can't use that," she said to Evan who was picking up Pamor's fallen gun. "Maybe we can unlock it. What good is revolution without guns, yes?" She turned and continued on, her gold-capped locks jingling with the motion. "Come. Quickly, or we shall wear masks upon gallows."

Jim was the first down the steps once Kate and Evan emerged from the covered bridge. He froze as Livia's slender hand snaked beneath her vest, but Kate assured her that Jim was her friend.

"What happened? We heard shouts," he asked once Livia's hand retreated from the folds.

"Someone attacked me," Kate said.

His eyes flicked to Livia. "Who?"

"Bounty hunters, I think."

"Bounty?"

Nate and Harcourt rounded the corner, hands steadying the hidden weapons beneath their clothes.

"Sounds like Candace put a price on any rogue Viatores," Kate said. "Someone spotted me at the library and tracked me down."

"Christ," he said. "Where are they?"

"Dead." Livia scanned the arches and balconies above. "And we will join them if we don't hurry."

They followed their new guide down the twisting steps and a maze-work of bridges, avoiding lit paths where curious eyes might see, moving ever downward to the filthy, dank streets at the roots of the chiseled, black towers. Dripping trash and leaves hung from the taut wire mesh canopying the canyon streets. An effluvia of rotted vegetation, dead vermin, and bird shit flowed through the narrow valleys like clinging smoke. Kate breathed through her mouth but the taste, or at least her imagination of taste, was somehow worse.

Evan walked in the rear, warily assessing every nook and corner.

"I bloody well pray we're not going down there," Nate hissed as they stepped around a corroded metal grate. Rancid water trickled between the thick bars, carrying the filth somewhere deeper—a kingdom of rats and roaches where sunlight never invaded.

Kate nodded, not wanting to draw enough breath to voice her agreement.

While Livia probably didn't speak English, Nate's meaning was unmistakable. She didn't react in any way. Turning at the base of one spire, she led them into a tunnel. Humming lights flickered along the door-lined passageway. Carved and painted graffiti marred the black walls, including the now familiar proclamation of Kamre's return. They emerged on the far side and to Kate's eternal relief, up one level to an elevator that carried them back to fresh air.

Shoulder to shoulder in the lift, Jim leaned close to Kate's ear. "This little midnight tour is fun and all, but are we going anywhere?"

Kate elbowed him. "If you'd seen the last two guys, you wouldn't mind the long way either."

The elevator's door slid open about three hundred feet above the street. Livia lifted a hand, telling them to stay. She peeked out and looked around before motioning them to follow.

Eventually, they entered a shallow alcove, and Livia knocked twice on a metal door. Three seconds later she knocked again and a bolt thudded. The door cracked open, revealing a mirror. A small reflected eye scanned them once, zeroed on Livia, and the door opened.

"*Zad zad fashat*," a Dhevinite man said, his voice husky. Triangular tattoos crowned his brows. His wooly gray hair was shaved into narrow stripes. He held a pistol down against his side and a square hand mirror in the other hand.

"*Lara zad meban.*" Livia pushed her way inside. "Durio *mear*."

The man groaned.

Livia motioned her head, and Kate followed her inside, her ears popping as she crossed the threshold. Two wards, she deduced—scrying and lower elementals.

The smell of onion and boiled vegetables filled the long apartment. A single, inset light burned from the carved, arched ceiling, illuminating the brightly frescoed walls. An assortment of books, cups, weapons, and dirty dishes littered a round table near the back. Two other men stood off to the side. The large one clutched a shouldered rifle, its flat, coin-slot barrel up but not pointed at anyone. His veiny forearms were immense and tattooed in the same curling lines as his brows. The other man was thin, bald save for a single braid running down his head like a bound Mohawk. A pink tongue slid nervously across his lips, a pistol gripped in his hands.

Once Evan had made it inside, the stripe-haired man closed and barred the door.

"More than we expected," the man with the rifle said in heavily accented Latin.

"I was thinking the same thing," Kate said.

The doorman turned, now standing between them and the only exit. "Who killed Durio?"

"Esteemed Senator Pamor," Livia said, each word heavy with bitter sarcasm.

The man's lip curled as he gave a soft spitting sound.

"I put him down." Livia nodded to the rifleman. "Lower your weapon, Vorsis. You as well, Saso."

Vorsis, the big guy with the rifle, shook his head. He motioned to Kate. "You're Viator?"

"I am."

"Prove it."

The skinny guy, Saso, touched the big man's shoulder. He'd already pocketed his own pistol. "Relax, Vorsis."

Vorsis shook his head, his eyes still locked on Kate. "Both Durio and senator are dead. I must know she's real."

"Fair enough." Kate extended her right hand and gathered her power. The glowing glyph of her rank wove itself before her splayed fingers.

The doorman let a heavy breath, somewhere between relief and awe. Saso smiled widely, the glyph's orange light gleaming in his hooded eyes.

Vorsis lowered his weapon. "Apologies. I had to be sure."

"I understand," Kate said, dispelling the glyph. "So now that you know who I am, it's time you told me who you are and what this is all about."

24

ENEMY OF MY ENEMY

Introductions were made over vibito, a honey wine mixed with berries. Astius, the doorman, was the oldest, a former soldier with a nasty limp. His son, Vorsis, still belonged to Kell's army, though several ill-advised comments after the Golden Empress' takeover had branded him a dissident. The small man, Saso, was a Lumitor, studying to ascend to Magister Arcanus. He was a fidgeter, his fingers hungrily exploring the table edge as if hunting some secret Braille message.

"You are sisters, yes?" Saso asked once Kate had introduced the others. "Kate and Nate."

"No," Kate said. "They're shortened nicknames. I'm Katherine and Nate's Natasha."

"Oh...understand. But tower sisters?"

"No."

Saso picked at the table's lip. "Do all Terran women possess *ate* names? Jate? Bate? Rate?"

"Do all Dhevinite men ask stupid questions?" Nate asked.

"Only him," Astius growled with a shake of his head.

Sipping his drink, Harcourt turned to Livia. "What about you? Joining a resistance and clandestine meetings seem unusual for a woman of your obvious station."

Livia sighed heavily, her dark eyes focusing on some distant time. "My brother-in-law was senator. Empress hanged him and his family, including my nephew Dox. He was nine." She swallowed bitterly. "I searched Roost until I found them. Each separate from one another, and too high for me to reach them."

"And they didn't come for you?" Harcourt asked. "You were his family."

She shook her head, her gaze returning to the present. "My husband died some time ago. It was his relations, though I remained close, Auntie Livey. I'd have joined Senator Kamre, but he escaped before I could find him. We have weapons, thanks to Vorsis, and information, including what Durio smuggled from Athenaeum, but we have no way of reaching Kamre."

"And that's why you need me?" Kate asked.

"You need us, as well," Astius said. The old veteran tapped his finger on the table like a miniature gavel. "Durio saved your life. Got killed for it." He tapped again. "Livia also saved your life back at bridge."

"That last part's up for debate," Kate said, nodding to Evan who was quietly listening, but couldn't be catching much with his shallow grasp of Latin, let alone the Dhevinite's particular flavor. "But you're right. Durio did save me, and if you're plotting against the empress, then maybe we can help each other. What do you need?"

"In past two years, many Viatores have gone missing or been killed," Livia said. "First it was believed to be rival nations, but we later realized it was not isolated to Kell or even Dhevin, but everywhere. Then gold-clad Netru appeared. Whispers of Carcosa's return began to circulate within towers and government." She shook her head. "No one imagined it was actually real, merely Demhe priests flexing their power to strengthen their monopoly. Then Zash was cut off. No warning. All transport simply ceased. Some of our remaining Viatores traveled there themselves, seeking answers. Most never returned, but those that did told stories of verl hounds and monsters patrolling aether and also of empress.

"Shortly, other worlds were cut off and disappearances increased. Saso's mentor vanished around that time."

Saso nodded. "I heard it. Barking and growls coming from his room. His door was locked from inside, and by time I got in..." he sniffed, "... nothing. He was just gone."

The memory of howling monsters sent a cold chill along the back of Kate's neck.

"Master Hestius of Athenaeum, was first to voice concern to Council," Livia said. "He believed invasion imminent and urged preparation." She shook her head. "Most thought old eunuch mad, insisting bedtime story coming for us. But Senator Kamre took notice. And following archivist's advice, he prepared, hoping to repel Golden Empress. But she came faster than anyone anticipated. Hestius and Kamre escaped in first hours of takeover, several soldiers and practitioners accompanying them."

"Where did they go?" Harcourt asked.

"Far from this world. We..." she waved her long fingers at the others, "...missed ride and were trapped. Other supporters were found, tortured, and executed. None of them knew where Kamre had fled."

Harcourt leaned back in his seat. "Do you?"

"We hadn't. But when Durio sent word he'd found rogue Viator, he offered this." Livia lifted a green pneumatic canister. She twisted the lid free and removed a bundle of rolled pages decorated with multi-colored inks. "We have information that must reach Senator Kamre. You're only one that can take us to him."

"You must help us," Astius said, more of a statement than a plea. "Empress moves around, making attack against her nearly impossible. By time we know where she is, she has already left. She rarely uses Templum Aetheris to travel between realms, so we can't anticipate where she'll appear or leave. But..." He tapped his finger hard against the tabletop. "We know which world she'll strike next."

"Where?" Kate asked.

"Iziba. It's next one on Durio's map. He estimated three weeks at most. If we can get this information to Kamre, he can strike once she arrives."

Kate accepted the papers, the magic of an inscribed spell tickled along her fingertips. The first few pages were covered in tightly-written script, various notes and dates. A large, folded map came next—the amorphous shape of the Abyss with its spiraling octopus arms and empty void at its heart. Several points were marked in red, the lines between them forming an unfinished nine-pointed star. Iziba, circled in white, lay precisely where the next point would fall, the line's path sketched with a dotted line. The final five pages were cut from a book, instructions on casting a circle. "He's on Soonat."

"Sounds familiar," Jim said, craning to get a peek.

Kate flipped through the rolled papers. "Old world. Never been there."

"Can you do it?"

She rotated the page, studying the symbols surrounding the ring. "No problem. I'll need some supplies."

"We'll collect those for you," Vorsis said. "Safer if you remain here."

"That works for most of it, but I need red tourmaline, five perfect pieces about this big," she said, pressing her thumb to her index finger.

Astius grunted. "Saso can procure those." The old veteran nodded to the skinny Lumitor, who was absently twirling a coin between his fingers. "Can't you?"

Saso nodded. "Definitely. I know where to go."

"Bring me ten," Kate said. "I'll select the best five."

"Of course." Saso sniffed.

A sudden awareness woke at that sound, the sleeping need inside her opening its eyes. Sniffles, the nervous energy. He was a practitioner, masterless, in mourning. She knew that story all too well.

"How long do you require?" Astius asked.

Kate pushed the growing hunger away. "How many people are we taking?"

"Only ourselves and some supplies."

"How much?"

Astius' lips tightened. He motioned to a stack of wicker crates near the wall. "Seven of those."

Kate sat silent for a full minute, calculations running through her head. Nine passengers plus their gear. The circle to carry them comfortably would need to be twenty-one pedes—just over twenty feet. Plus an additional Roman foot for the outer ring. At that size she'd need to inscribe the glyphs three times—four to be certain. They'd each have to be perfect, her destination firmly in her mind and she'd never been to Soonat. She gulped back the last of her drink. "Give me five days."

25

CURIOUS MINDS

Chalk in hand, Kate squatted on the polished floor scratching the glyphs along the inner ring. Taking her time, she drew each stroke with painful care. She looked back at the unfurled pages behind her, its edges held in place with empty cups.

Shit. She'd gotten the last one wrong, the intersecting lines too low. Kate rubbed out the offending mark with a rag and started again. When it came time to cast this for real, there could be no mistake.

Evan and Vorsis sat on a mint-colored settee pressed against the wall with the other furniture, making room for Kate's circle.

"Simply press latch here," Vorsis said, flipping over a pistol in his hands, "and magazine opens." A soft click and a tiny hatch swung outward.

Evan did the same with the gun he'd taken at the bridge.

"This is grinder." Vorsis removed what appeared to be a smooth ivory wheel from the magazine chamber, a metal axle running through its middle. "When trigger is pulled, it lifts into oscillating blades, firing stream of slivers. Very fast. They don't do much individually but en masse..."

"Yeah," Evan grunted, inspecting the wheel. "I saw. What's the range?"

"Range?" Vorsis asked.

"How far do they fly, at least where they can still damage?"

"Ah. Little one like this would be thirty kundra."

"Thirty what?"

"Umm." Vorsis scratched his nose. "About twenty paces."

Evan's lips tightened into a frown. "Not very far. What about those bigger ones, like you had?"

"Forty paces. Those have much bigger grinder." He held his fingers out to demonstrate, forming a circle the size of a tea saucer. "But, for this." He gripped the pistol. "Press thumb here." The weapon emitted its muted hum, a little higher pitched since the magazine door was open. "That starts grinder spinning. Give moment to get up to speed and then fire."

Evan tried the same, but nothing happened.

"It's not attuned to you," Vorsis said. "I can fix that. Then it will be *your* gun."

Kate continued inscribing the chalk glyphs as the men talked weapons and gizmos. Despite different races and from vastly different worlds, soldiers always found their common bond.

At her third attempt, Kate finished the circle. Knees aching, she rose, inspecting her work. It was good. A little bunched on one side, but passable. Jim would have made his computer-perfect, but this was good enough. She'd need to do it at least five more times before she'd know if she was ready to do it for real. Once the muscles had memorized the motions, she'd know for sure.

She eyed soup on the table, unsure how long it had been there, or the last time she'd eaten. Her stomach clenched at the reminder, and Kate decided to remedy that little matter before starting the fun task of wiping up the chalk and starting over.

Nate scooted her chair as Kate approached, giving her room. She twisted a silver ring back and forth between her knuckles as she studied the Frankentome.

As Kate had expected, the soup was cold. Dollops of oil had coagulated along its surface like milky lily pads. She stirred it, breaking the film and began eating the room-temperature noodles.

"I found some info on Soonat," Nate said.

"Hmm?" Kate grunted.

Nate flipped to a dog-eared page. "It's not much, just a page and a half that was printed on the back of a page we wanted. But it looks to be a weird one."

Kate swallowed a mouthful. Dhevinites *really* loved their salt. "This the eclipse thing?"

"Naw. Now that was in there. Since we don't know where we're headed, I can't tell from the conversion table if they'll be in eclipse or not. But I found this." She read, "Travelers must free themselves of all magnetic paraphernalia prior to entering this plane. Even a simple compass needle might pose harm."

Kate slid the binder over and read the warning scrawled in flowing calligraphy. The page ended before any explanation for the warning was given. The rest of the printed pages had been left at the Balmoral, and Harcourt's computer was now useless. They'd tried it in Switzerland, and as Kate had feared, it was fried. Candace had stolen the original book, so this cryptic scrap was all they had.

Kate closed her eyes and searched her memory for anything she'd read or heard during her time at Onyx Tower. Master Boyer had mentioned his single journey there when he was but a Magus. But he'd discussed so many worlds in that last year, feeding her conviction to study the Viatoric path. Magnets? He'd told her of the hidden sun and their alien technology, vastly different, yet eerily parallel to their own world's. There was something, just on the edge of her memory, close enough to touch, but too far to seize, like a teasing cat outside the reach of petting fingers.

Surrendering, Kate shook her head. Whatever it was, they'd have to be —and then the memory came. "Batteries."

Nate's brow creased.

"Magnets," Kate said. "They're volatile there. Soonati use them like batteries."

"Magnets? As in regular magnets?"

"Yeah. You could like power Jim's flat off the stuff on his fridge." She turned toward the men who were still playing with their deadly toys on the sofa. "Vorsis, there aren't any magnets in those guns of yours, are there?"

He shook his head. "None, Kate."

"When we go, we need to be sure we have no magnets on us at all. We'll need to double check each other just to be safe."

"Explain." he said.

"Because they could explode."

His long brows lifted. "Understand. Will inspect each other's equipment to be certain."

Nate was frowning when Kate looked back, her gaze absently on the cluttered table, her lips pouted thoughtfully.

"What?" Kate asked.

"I was just thinkin'. If Soonat has technology like we do, and ye said it was old, is it the first dream world?"

"How do you mean?"

"I mean like back home. Did cavemen dream up this other world and then it evolved beside ours?"

"Doubtful. It's the same age, if not older. Our worlds probably influenced each other's but neither dreamed up the other."

Nate blinked. "Terra isn't the first?"

Kate caught a laugh before it could escape. '*Never laugh at curious minds*,' Master Boyer had scolded. Mocking ignorance only discouraged the questions to cure it. If a release was needed, it was saved for behind closed doors where the senior practitioners would share their amusements over late-night drinks—The Teacher's Lounge as Dennis used to call it.

"No," Kate said, a slight pang at the memory of her old tower mates. "Our world isn't the first at all. Just like the rest, our universe is just the coalesced dreams and concepts of those before us and those around us. Just like the song says, 'Life is but a dream.'"

"Then which one is the first?"

"Welcome to the Great Riddle. No one knows. Older accounts spoke of worlds predating ours, but they're gone now."

"Gone?" Nate asked. "They blow themselves up?"

Kate shook her head. "If they blew themselves up with nuclear war or something, the universes would still be there. There'd be remnants. But they're just *gone*. Either torn apart back into the aether or they left the Abyss entirely. Here." She pushed aside the cold soup and unfolded the map.

"This is Terra." Kate pointed to a green spot just inside one of the outer arms. Her finger moved to a similar dot on the far side of the Abyss. "And this is Soonat. These are both moving away from the center, toward the edge. The further they go, the less attuned they become. That's why in younger worlds people travel back and forth between them and why Dream Walkers are easy to see. Eventually, we'll hit the edge and then..." She shrugged. "Who knows?"

Nate circled Terra with a silver-ringed finger, a few chips of violet polish still clinging to her nail like paint on an abandoned house. "So, we used to be here?" She slid her finger deeper into the black mass.

"Um hmm."

"And we had ghost people walkin' 'round and travelers from other worlds, just like Hollit?"

"Oh yeah. Chariot of the Gods and all that. Look at mythology, gods coming down, and crazy alien images. A lot of it was true. But those people are gone, or at least stopped coming by."

"So God left us?" Nate asked.

"Well...no. They weren't gods."

"But they dreamed us. At least their dreams made the world."

"It's not like someone said, 'Oh and I'll make this world with planets and galaxies and a little wet rock with people on it.' Those concepts just sort of came together out of the aether."

"So where does God fit in? Where did all this..." Nate stirred her hands above the map, "...come from?"

"Um..." Kate shifted in her chair. She'd just wanted some salty noodles and to rest her knees, not a theology session. "That's the Great Riddle. Some think God was the first dreamer. Others say the aether is God, just too big for us to see and we're simply his dream. Some think he's out there waiting for us to find him. I don't know. Just believe what you want. That's what Master Boyer said."

Nate tongued her cheek, her dark chocolate eyes toward the map but seeming to look through it. "And where's Carcosa?"

"There's the question." Kate leaned over the map. "If it's real, and I'm beginning to think it is, Carcosa's here." She tapped the vacant eye at the black cyclone's heart. "Either in here, or along the edge—sort of an event horizon, both inside and outside the Abyss. Viatoric scholars referred to it as the hub."

"So, how'd they lose it?"

"No one knows. Records refer to its power and the kings, but always in the past tense, as if it was always lost."

Nate frowned and flipped through the binder. "Speakin' of kings. There was somethin' about a blue one." She stopped at a scan of a stained and worn page, most of the words stained and unreadable. A short entry read 'The Three Kings of Hali.'

Kate nodded. "Yeah. Three kings. Red, yellow, and blue. Sort of a trinity, each representing one of the different paths of the Art. Yellow was the most famous because it represented the Viatoric path."

"And what happened to the other two?"

Kate shrugged. "The Yellow King devoured them and crafted his mask from their bones."

Nate's brow lifted.

"That's the story. Master Boyer called it a fable, and I never thought otherwise. Three Kings, three paths, Maiden-Mother-Crone, Father-Son-

Holy Ghost, the Three Fates. There's lots of trinities. Each king ruled a city-state along the cloud shores of Hali, Carcosa being the greatest."

"A lake of clouds." Nate touched the round void, her fingertip caressing the perfect emptiness. "Once this is all over, I want to see it."

Kate grinned. "So do I."

26

OBSIDIAN AND ICE

"Here we go." Gathering her power, Kate blew through her circled fingers, igniting the jagged pale wood within the brazier. It wasn't hazel, but some native wood she couldn't pronounce—chalroughtem? shalrootem?—something like that. Saso had assured her it would work. The scrawny Lumitor had brought her ten polished marbles of red tourmaline. Each of them appeared perfect to her—she really needed to work on her gemology—so Kate had selected the five that seemed to feel the best.

They were now equally spaced between the two outer chalk circles, the glyphs and runes scribed with as much power and precision as Kate had ever done. While she'd cast gating circles before, those were for worlds she'd already seen, and with Master Boyer's oversight. For her first journey into the truly unknown, she needed absolute perfection.

Blinking, she looked up from the flickering fire. The rings filled the room from one side to the other. Furniture pressed against the far walls, barricading the locked, metal door just in case anyone tried breaking in while they were away. Three stacked piles of gear and luggage took up half the real-estate inside the circle. The eight others stood around, away from the edges, lest their feet smudge the chalk lines. Livia and Vorsis watched her with fierce intensity, jaws set and tense with the nervous trepidation of a first-time flyer when the jet's engines begin to rev. Saso and Nate both watched with her every move, heads slightly hunkered like stalking cats, eyes locked in that all-too-familiar expression of a hungry student. Evan was watching the door, his back to her. Only Harcourt and Astius appeared relaxed. While sharing very little in common, the older men both carried that same passive interest that only came from a lifetime of brushing death and accepting when they weren't in control.

"You ready for this?" Jim whispered beside her, the open tea box in his hands.

"Definitely," she said

Jim grinned. "Good." He lifted the box toward her. "Let's get out of here. I need some open spaces."

Kate removed one of the freshly-loaded packets of herbs and reagents. Focusing her power, she wove a glowing glyph and unleashed it as she dropped the bag. Purple and silver sparks crackled from the fire. The aroma of salt and wisteria filled her senses. Smoke hit the low ceiling and spread toward the walls. She'd never cast in a room lower than the vessel and wondered if the resulting bubble would remain low during their journey.

Wispy aether bled from the shadows beyond the circle, swallowing the light. Her chalk ring ignited with an internal glow, and the floor faded to that black mirror nothingness as they entered the Abyss.

An inhuman wail greeted them, that madman wolf cry of nightmare.

Kate whirled, gooseflesh prickling along her back.

"What was—" Evan started, but Jim shushed him with a sharp hiss.

Afraid to breathe or move, Kate scanned the misty darkness.

Another howl sounded, further away. Was it the same one?

Yips and barks came from somewhere high above. Craning her neck, Kate could just make out three canine forms loping through the mist, headed toward the last cry.

"W...what do we do?" Nate breathed, her trembling voice barely audible over the crackling fire.

Two more baying cries rang out in succession, even further away. Another joined in, so close that every hair on Kate's arms stood on end and pressed against the insides of her sleeves. Wet snuffling came from behind her. Kate spun to face it, her fingers weaving emerald light.

The verl hound charged past, so close that Harcourt could have reached out and touched it. The old man sprang backward, falling over one of the wicker crates and spilling ten of the needle shotguns across the ring.

Vorsis drew his pistol, but paused. It made no hum as his fingers wrapped the grip. "*Garn!*" He dropped it. The pistol clattered on the mirrored floor as he pulled a wedge-shaped knife from his belt.

"Quiet!" Kate hissed throwing a hand up. "Shh"

The verl hound stopped. Its enormous baby's head turned toward them. The nostril flaps where its eyes should have been, flared wide. Evan raised his pistol while Astius drew a knife. Kate's fingers wove, threading emerald light.

The beast snorted a low chuff. Then a distant howl drew its attention, and the creature raced away into the aether, barking and yipping like an idiot child.

The sounds of the racing pack grew more distant, until finally fading away. No one spoke.

Kate released a heavy sigh and reabsorbed the power from the green glyph.

"Have they gone?" Astius asked, his knife still before him.

"I think so," Kate whispered.

"We must hasten," he said. "Get away before beasts return."

She shook her head. "Not yet."

"Why?" Jim asked.

"They can't hear, or see, or smell us in our bubble," Kate said. "At least as long as we're careful. But if we go too fast, they might see our wake and follow it. We'll wait until we know they're gone and then I'll speed us up. Until then, keep your voices low."

They floated in silence for several long minutes, eyes and ears transfixed on the curling aether. A single scream rang in the distance, but so faint that if Nate and Saso hadn't flinched Kate would have questioned if she'd imagined it.

"It's like an old submarine movie," Harcourt mumbled to no one in particular.

Livia and Vorsis looked at him, their long Dhevinite brows raised.

"Never mind," Harcourt said.

Kate waited another ten minutes before she pushed more of her power into the smoldering bowl, increasing their speed. Normally, travel through the aether moved as if from a sailboat, the dream reefs and swimming inhabitants sort of gliding past. Now they moved as if a car on the autobahn.

The others all noticeably relaxed—shoulders drooping and weapons being holstered away among a symphony of sighs.

"I take back my laughing at those in Scotland," Evan said.

Nate gave an enthusiastic nod. "Damn right."

"Christ, that was too close," Jim breathed. The beads of sweat dotting his forehead glistened in the firelight. He released his white-knuckle grip from a baggie of asafetida grass and pushed it back into the tea box.

"They weren't looking for us," Kate said. "They were just there."

"They patrol empress' domains," Astius said.

"But we didn't see those on the way in," Jim said.

Kate shrugged. "We were with the Netru then. They're allowed to pass. The hounds were looking for anyone trying to escape." A modicum of pride welled in her chest. Had her circle not been absolutely perfect, the verl hound would have smelled her at that close of range. *'You're a natural,'* Master Boyer said in her memory.

Harcourt and Livia started to repack the guns into their crate, but Vorsis shooed them away and did it himself.

After several more minutes, Kate increased their speed even more. They raced through the Abyss, all but the largest of reefs blurring past. Even then, the journey to distant Soonat would take hours. To her relief, the bubble had inflated to its full fifteen-foot height once they'd entered the aether. With no bathroom but a pair of improvised chamber pots, fresh air would be at a premium.

Nine hours. Nine hours they'd rocketed across the blackness. Evan was getting pretty good at pido, a sort of Dhevinite backgammon that Vorsis and Astius loved. Saso had slept most of the journey, claiming a headache. Astius had finally delivered a sharp kick to save them from the young man's snoring. Most everyone had taken a brief nap but Kate. She had to maintain focus, no matter how passive, and feed wood to the brazier. Too much would smoke them out, and it wasn't like opening a window was an option.

While Kate could have pushed their speed even faster than she had, she'd been unsure of the toll it'd have taken. Now, as they approached their destination, she felt the high cost of their speed but knew she could have halved their travel time without laying herself out.

She peered into the dancing flames, her eyes unfocused and taking it all in. Her magic flowed, and a vision blossomed in her mind. She'd never seen the paved platform, not with her own eyes or even a photograph. The image was infused with the spell she'd read, landing coordinated for the first-timer. Bright azure stone, hexagonally shaped and closely fit. Beyond that, just off the platform at the edge of her image, spindly weeds peeked out from black sand.

Whiteness bleached the image, nearly washing it out. Kate grit her teeth. *Damn.* She'd assumed that they were close enough to Soonat for her to catch the picture of what it looked like now. But eviden—

A white wave rippled across the mental picture, and Kate realized the truth. This *was* what the landing site looked like now.

The realm of Soonat held some similarities to Terra. A round planet floating within a seemingly limitless space. However, the rules worked very differently. The orbiting moon worked in close synchronicity with the sun, the result being a rolling eclipse that slowly moved along the sky. From the ground, the eclipse lasted sixteen months, bringing darkness and cold. At any time, one-fifth of Soonat was beneath the corona sun—a twenty percent chance, and they'd just won the seasonal lottery.

"Okay," Kate said, breaking the spell. "Change of plans. It's winter."

"Bloody hell," Jim grumbled, the term sounding weird from him.

"Let's get dressed, and hopefully there's shelter nearby," Kate said.

"Preferably one with loo," Livia said. She'd been the only one of them not to use the improvised toilets, leading Kate to wonder what kind of camel bladder the woman possessed. Kate had squatted above the bedpan twice.

They'd prepared for this possibility, bringing cold-weather clothing just in case. Although finding real winter gear in Kell was about the same as finding it in Mexico City. Long sleeves and the lightest of jackets were the best they'd collected.

Kate pulled on a second pair of pants and swapped her sandals out for her tennis shoes with two sets of socks. Nine people dressing at once within the circle might have been funny had she not been one of them. There were no walls to lean against, and the burning fire in the middle of it all made for a more significant obstacle than she'd expected.

Livia unstoppered an etched bottle and pressed it above her breasts. The silver syl mites flowed down her shoulders and throat, seeming to pour inside.

"Here," Jim said offering Kate a scarf made from one of their old blankets. She wrapped it around her neck and ears, tucking the ends down beneath her jacket.

There was a sort of Hobo-chic to how everyone looked—exotically cut clothing mixed with blanket scarves and homegrown sock mittens.

Now properly bundled, or at least as well as she could, Kate knelt before the burning bowl again and drew up the two images. She focused on the second one. Snow glistened before her, no trace of the blue pavers. Wind whistled in the distance. She blew into the flames and in her mind, snow flew outward as if caught in a helicopter's down blast. Muted blue shone beneath a layer of clinging ice. Kate blew again, the fire blazing hot against her face. More snow whisked away, leaving some of the stone exposed.

Once satisfied that it was as clear as she could manage, Kate wove her fingers, focusing a beam of power into the brazier. The flames brightened and crackled. The blackness outside the circle dimmed to gray, lighter and lighter until fading to blinding white. Cold blue stones, snow embedded in the cracks, formed beneath her knees. Frigid wind burst through the smoke walls finding all the weakest places in her bundled clothing. Kate drew a breath, a dagger of icy air entering her lungs.

Shivering, she looked around, her first glimpse at this alien world. It was twilight dark, the ring of sunlight visible through thin clouds. Jagged mountains of black obsidian rose on all sides. Wind-swept snow skittered across their smooth glass slopes. It was a valley, maybe five miles across, a frozen lake at its heart. Rows of ice-crusted trees stood off to the left, many broken beneath the winter's weight. A few specks of green, needle-leaved trees, decorated the otherwise colorless landscape.

"There!" Evan said, pointing to a round building with a high conical roof fifty feet away.

"We'll check it out." Vorsis placed a hand on his sidearm.

"Make sure they're friendly before pointing a gun at them," Kate said, but he and Astius were already moving. The old man's limp was even more pronounced as he trudged through the knee-deep snow.

Jim heaved on his frame pack. "Gather everything up."

"Should we not wait for their return?" Saso asked, his breath pluming into clouds.

"We'll know if it's safe by the time we get there, but I'm fucking cold, and that's the only shelter."

Kate gathered her pack and Samsonite and hurried after the others. The brazier would be fine for now, but it was too hot to move, and she couldn't bring herself to extinguish their only warmth. Snow crunched beneath her shoes and pushed its way up her pants legs where it found skin.

Astius and Vorsis had made it to the building and were circling it around. Dull silver shutters sealed the windows spaced every few feet along the wall. They'd completed their perimeter check by the time the others arrived.

"No tracks. No smoke," Astius reported. "Sounds quiet. There is wood stacked on far side beneath tarp."

"No sign of Senator Kamre?" Livia asked.

"None," Astius said.

"It's not like they were expecting us," Kate said, her arms folded against her chest for warmth.

"Durio said we would find him here," Livia snapped, more to herself than anyone.

"Let's see if anyone's home."

Hand on his holstered sidearm, Astius ascended the three obsidian steps to the door. He glanced back to Vorsis who was behind him, but to the side, his knife out. The old veteran rapped on the polished wood door.

Nothing.

Astius knocked again and after a minute pulled the brass handle. The door slid sideways, the motion knocking clinging snow from its face. His head off to the side, he peeked through and finally looked inside. "Hello?"

He stepped inside. Vorsis moved up the steps to cover him.

"Empty," Astius called. "There's food and fireplace."

"Wonderful," Livia shot, starting up the steps. "Let's get inside. I'm freezing."

A faint tickle ran along the back of Kate's ears as she stepped through the door and out of the wind. "Alarm enchantment," she said nodding to the glyph scratched above the inside door frame.

"Then someone knows we're here," Jim said. The glyphs were fairly simple, often used for not only security but to keep sneaky novices out of their mentor's liquor cabinets. They didn't last long, two years at most. The building itself was small, maybe sixty feet across. The walls rose to six feet before angling up into the steep, pointed roof forty feet above. A brushed metal chimney came down from the tipi point and into a large stove, or boiler, judging by the pipes leading down under the floor. Smaller rooms stood on either side. One, a bathroom Livia declared before excusing herself, and the other a dry pantry.

"This looks promising," Vorsis said, examining a white plate mounted beside the door. He slid a cylindrical knob upwards, and tubular lights along the ceiling braces came on.

"You shouldn't be touching things if don't know what they are," Astius said.

Vorsis snorted. "It's light switch. They're pretty much same everywhere. Not like they've changed in three centuries."

"And you don't know how their electricity works," Astius growled. "You'll cook your balls off before you can give me grandson. Why don't you and Saso go fetch rest of gear?"

Kate took care of the fire, one of the benefits of being a sorceress. By the time the others had lugged the last of luggage and crates up the hill, the cabin was comfortably warm.

"So, what now?" Harcourt asked from a wooden chair.

"We wait," Livia said.

"For who?" Harcourt asked. "Kamre? How long? What if he doesn't come?"

"Durio said he would."

"But Durio's dead."

"I don't require reminding," she spat.

Harcourt lifted his hands. "What I mean is that things have changed. They might have changed here. What do we do if Kamre doesn't come?"

"He is right," Astius said, his hands extended before the hot stove. "If Kamre doesn't come, or if someone else does, we require plan."

"Hollit," Kate said. "I can get us to Hollit if we need to."

Livia scowled, making an ugly grunt in the back of her throat.

Astius didn't seem to notice. "Once you've warmed up," he told Kate. "Prepare circle for Hollit just in case we need to leave quickly."

Twenty minutes later, just as Kate was finishing up the circle, a faint whine sounded in the distance.

Astius moved to one of the windows, cracking them open with a little slide lever. "Something approaches."

"What?" Evan asked.

"Shit if I know."

Kate hurried to one of the windows, squeezing in beside Nate. She couldn't see anything through the metal slats, but the sound was definitely getting louder, pitching deeper into the bass.

A wedge-shaped craft glided over the ridgeline. It looked like some pregnant stealth bomber, with no tail fins or engines she could see, and painted white with hideous purple and green zigzags. The plane circled once, slowly, and then hovered down onto the blue platform, the clinging snow scattering from the down blast. Four stubby legs inflated out from the bottom as it rotated down. It landed facing away from them, its arrow-head nose toward the lake.

A ramp door in the back opened, and five bundled figures emerged. Not a millimeter of skin visible. They spread out into a V-formation. Four carried short-barreled rifles while the one in the lead carried only a holstered pistol.

"What do we do?" Jim asked, echoing Kate's sentiment.

"Keep your weapons ready but do not draw," Astius said. "Kate, move to back. Vorsis, far left. Evan take right. Everyone else, on me. Let me do talking. Saso, get door for our visitors."

Rubbing her fingers together, Kate moved behind the stove where she could still see. If something did happen, she had cover and, unlike the rest, she didn't need a gun. Jim's hands were at his side, his fingers moving. If he had to, the Lex could throw up a shield or push an attacker away. Evidently Practitioners weren't in the old veteran's training.

Saso pulled open the door and moved away as the newcomers reached the steps. The leader stopped just outside the door. Livia's head was in the way, so Kate moved to the other side of the chimney pipe for a better angle.

The leader pulled off his goggles—rust-red skin, black eyebrows extending beneath his tight hood. Dhevinite.

The man stepped inside, the soldiers filing in behind him their weapons across their chests. Two appeared female by their builds.

"Welcome," Astius said.

The man looked them over, his gaze lingering on Harcourt, Nate, and Jim. "Who are you?"

"Refugees from Kell," Astius said. "We bring news for Senator Kamre."

"Who sent you?"

"Durio of Scholar's Roost."

"Who is your Viator?"

"Tell me your name first," Astius demanded.

"Lieutenant Tompii of Maurus, and I asked you question."

"She is behind us," Livia said. "Now bring us to Senator Kamre. We carry urgent news for him."

Tompii tapped his hooded head. He spoke quickly, his voice low. From his pocket, he removed a gold and blue rod, like a fancy pen. He held it out, slowly sweeping it across, lingering on everyone's faces for two to three seconds. When he got to Livia, he stopped. He muttered something short, an acknowledgment and tapped his ear.

"Dahn Livia," Tompii said with a slight bow. "Senator is pleased to see you." He tucked the little rod back into a breast pocket. "Apologies for precautions, but I'm sure you understand. Please come with us. Kamre is eager to meet with you."

27

KAMRE

S eated in a comfortable chair with cup holder armrests, Kate watched through the angled window at black, snow-covered peaks passing beneath them. The airplane was nothing like what she'd expected— padded chairs, footrests, and even a dedicated air vent. Mostly empty, the plane looked to comfortably seat sixty people at max capacity.

Kate was trying to articulate what it reminded her of when Jim whispered, "It's a bloody tour bus."

That was it, she realized. The speckled gray upholstery, perfect for masking stains, the little screen in front of her displaying what was directly beneath them, all of it screamed tourist, not military.

The soldiers sat in the rear, beside the doors. Now that their winter masks were off, she could clearly see that they were all Dhevinite, ruddy, tattooed skin and sweeping eyebrows. Tompii sat in the middle, a greenish-gray device hanging from his ear. Like the plane, or whatever this thing was, the technology was too advanced to be Dhevinite. In fact, not even their guns were the Dhevinite needle shotguns, which made Kate wonder if those would even work here. It was all likely Soonati technology, but she hadn't seen any of them. Likely the pilot was Soonati, she guessed, but had no idea where the cockpit was. Kate didn't even know what the people of this world looked like. Their excerpt in the Frankentome hadn't made it that far.

They crested a high spine of mountains, and a valley opened before them. Ahead, nestled in the endless tapestry of white and black, four perfect circles of green shone like portals to a living world. Kate leaned toward the window for a better view.

Close together, they were of varying size and in no discernible arrangement. The largest, filled with leafless trees, could easily have fit three football fields. Beside it, and only a little smaller, appeared to be tilled farmland. Tiny figures moved around a cluster of tents like busy insects. Next was the smallest, only two hundred feet across. Kate made out some irregular stone structure emerging from a blanket of vines. Colored lights lazily moved within an oval pool. But the final circle drew Kate's attention from all the rest. There were plants and trees, and even a smaller pool, but much of it was paved. At its heart stood a great tower of black obsidian, rising eighty feet or higher above the snowy valley like a defiant king.

The plane slowed and hovered down onto the concrete platform, the tower huge and looming outside Kate's window.

Two dozen or more men and women hurried toward it. Most were Dhevinite, but a pair of ashy Torbans pushed their way amongst the crowd. The rest were something else—lean, with high, sharp cheekbones and long faces. Their gray skin gave them the appearance of living statues or stylized department store mannequins, sort of an androgynous elegance. Hair color ranged from white to pale blonde. Their green and yellow cat eyes shone like cut gems set in slate.

The plane touched down with a slight bounce and the humming engines instantly silenced.

Lieutenant Tompii rose as a female soldier activated the ramp release. "Follow."

Kate hadn't been sure what to expect when they'd ascended the wide steps and entered the black glass tower. She wasn't surprised by the wards, the air feeling heavier as she crossed the threshold, but the dark wood, thick moldings, and warmly painted walls of a country English manor were nowhere near what she'd have guessed. It wasn't a perfect match. The round doors, bamboo furnishings, and slender white neon lights shattered that illusion. It smelled of cut flowers, tobacco, and carried a weight, as if this building and everything inside had been here for eons.

After removing their shoes in a posh entryway, Tompii led them into a semicircular room where several people waited.

"Livia," A man said, stepping forward. He was Dhevinite with long curling brows nested beneath golden tattoos reminiscent of fish scales. His short dreadlocks grayed at the temples where they met the arms of his wire spectacles.

Stepping forward, Livia accepted the man's hand, sandwiching it between both of hers. She bowed her head. "Senator, happiness to see you."

"It broke my heart to leave so many behind. Who brought you? How did you come?"

Livia released the Senator's hand with a broad sweep toward Kate. "Kate Rossdale, Magus Viator who knew empress."

All eyes locked on Kate, many narrowing in mistrust at that latter part of Livia's introduction. *You wanted to be a big shot*, she thought. *Here you are.* "I'm intimately experienced with her betrayal. She's no friend if that's what you're worried about."

"I am Igna Kamre." He stepped toward her, a ringed hand extended. "And if you have Livia's trust, then you have mine as well. Gratitude for bringing her to us."

Kate accepted it, trying to mimic Livia's one hand beneath, one above, head bow.

"This is Ipsissimus Jengta Vephar," he motioned to a bald, gray-skinned Soonati in white velvet printed with swirling red leaves. "Our host."

Jengta nodded. "Welcome to my home." The feminine voice echoed strangely, like two people speaking at once. No wrinkles or lines marred the Soonati's skin—just smooth and eerily perfect. The intricate sigil of an Ipsissimus Lex hung from her neck. Cast in seven shades of gold with twin triangles of clear and black crystal, the medallion radiated power—not magic, though Kate didn't doubt that it was enchanted, but the power of authority.

"Thank you," Kate said.

"Who was your mentor, Kate Rossdale?" A plump, bald Dhevinite asked. Deep wrinkles stretched from the corners of his small, dark eyes, set beneath hairless brows, their tattoos more elaborate than even the senator's. She guessed him as Hestius, Master of the Athenaeum of Kell.

"Ipsissimus Jake Boyer."

Hestius' gaze lifted, searching his memory. "Onyx."

"You knew him?" Kate asked.

"Remember him, yes. Few artists achieve such rank, fewer so from distant Terra. We mourned his demise."

"You knew about that?"

He nodded. "Rumors only. All knowledge passes through Athenaeum. If I recall, Viatoric pupil was cause of his demise, yes?"

"No." The smile fell from Kate's face. "He was murdered by a woman posing as his student. She stole my powers, destroyed my tower, and let me take the blame."

Hestius didn't flinch at Kate's anger. "Understand. And what happened to this betrayer?"

"She's now ruling your world."

"Ahh." He turned to a short Dhevinite in a black leather vest. His gray mustache extended as far out as his eyebrows, almost like a frame. "Your suspicion was correct, Thetish. Empress is Terran."

Thetish's mustache bent, his lips curling into a smile. "That means she is mortal."

"Of course, she's mortal," a tattooed-faced woman huffed. "All of Carcosa's rulers passed eventually. Mortality was given."

"I mean that killing her will be easier knowing that she is Terran." Thetish scowled.

"Killing is easy. Problem is knowing where to find her," the woman said.

Thetish's lips peeled back into a mean grin, he drew a breath to reply, but Livia spoke first.

"That is our reason for coming. We know location of empress' next invasion."

"Where?" Kamre asked.

"Iziba. Durio gave it three weeks."

"Two weeks now," Vorsis corrected.

"Where is Brother Durio?" Hestius asked, his gaze searching the newcomers.

"Dead," Livia said.

The old librarian blinked, his lips tensing into a pale line. "Understand."

"Do they know what Durio discovered?" Thetish asked. "About Iziba?"

Livia shook her head. "No. I don't believe they knew about that."

Hestius frowned. "Explain."

"They killed him to find me," Kate said. "He died protecting me."

"But you can't be sure they didn't glean information," Thetish said.

"He didn't surrender how to signal me," Kate said.

"But you can't be sure what he did or did not disclose." Thetish's moustache twitched, a condescending edge flavoring his words. "Not unless you attended his interrogation."

"No."

"It is all we have," Livia said. "We must at least consider it."

"Agreed." Kamre turned to Jengta. "With Kate Rossdale, we have four Viatores to move our troops. If possibility of ambushing empress exists, attempt must be made."

Jengta gave a single nod. "Agreed. But we haven't much time." Her slitted cat eyes moved to Kate. "But our guests are surely exhausted from their journey from Dhevin. Let us play hosts before we play generals."

"And this is our library," Jengta said, pushing open a mirrored door.

With everything Kate had done today, she should've been exhausted. She had been earlier, and even asked for coffee with the futile hope that it existed in this realm. No such luck.

Her host had offered tarshu. Not knowing what tarshu was, but not wanting to appear rude, Kate agreed. The steaming drink came in delicate porcelain cups with no handles. Using a pair of tongs, Jengta dropped a single mint-colored cube into the hot water where it dissolved into a sizzling green beverage that smelled vaguely of grape candy.

It tasted like sugar-caked gym sock, but seconds after that first hesitant sip, the foggy weariness whisked away. By the end of the cup, Kate was about ready to climb the walls—like Ritalin on hyperdrive. The energy wasn't jittery, but sharp—laser-focused, her brain hungry for something to do. Kate's inner speed-freak marveled at the casual way Jengta had taken two cubes of green magic in her cup.

Stepping through the narrow doorway, Kate's hand went to her mouth at the sight. The room was long, the left wall following the tower's curve. A twenty-foot ring of inlaid brass dominated the parquet floor, a smaller one nested inside it. The clean circles contrasted the clutter of books, scrolls, and wicker boxes piled across every surface, forming canyoned pathways like the claustrophobic lair of some literary hoarder. Pale squares of light hovered above strange computers on one table, the opaque screens displaying foreign words and geometric patterns.

"Hestius brought much of this when they arrived, and we haven't had time to do more than catalog all the works," Jengta said, traversing the narrow path. "It required Thetish two trips to transport all the soldiers and books.

Kate glanced back to Thetish, who had taken a branching path toward a desk. He and Nari, the tattoo-faced woman, were the only Magus Viatores that Kamre had convinced to flee Kell, making several trips to carry the senator's entourage and one-hundred and ninety soldiers—many, as Astius had whispered, too old to still serve or too young to protest. Then there were the refugees, wives, husbands, children, and friends of people important enough to grant passage. The fifteen slaves Kamre had brought didn't get a choice. But Jengta had demanded their permanent freedom if she was to offer her house's protection. The liberation was largely moot, Kate decided. They were here, on another world than their own and with little choice but to join the army or continue serving the same tasks they'd performed before.

"Ah," Jengta said, stepping past a packed bookcase. "Syn, I want to introduce you to someone."

Kate rounded the corner to see a lean Torban man standing within an alcove. Looking up from a book, his strange blue eyes met hers, their black pupils wide and flat like goat's eyes. Slender lines of metallic ink traced along his face and down his neck, turning at sharp angles, both emphasizing and defying his natural contours. Piercing rings ran the length of his hooked nose like jeweled steps. Fine dust coated his bluish skin, likely the source of the medicinal smell filling the space between the bookshelves. The silks of his fringed robe were woven with a mesmerizing pattern of colors and textures, like it was made of a hundred individual ribbons, each strip its own masterpiece.

"This is Kate Rossdale," Jengta said. "Magus Viator of Terra. Kate Rossdale, this is Syn, Magus Viator of Torba."

"Pleasure to meet you," Kate said. "Just call me Kate."

Syn pressed his palm flat against his chest. A mazework of hair-thin copper lines traced up each of the six long fingers. He gave a single nod. Tiny bells jingled from delicate chains strung between his earlobes and nostrils. "It is a great pleasure, Kate," he said, enunciating each syllable, his voice like a purring panther. "I have encountered very few from your realm. I look forward to hearing of it."

"Likewise. I've never spoken with a Torban before."

Syn nodded again, as if Kate had confessed something of great significance.

"We need everything we have on Iziba," Jengta said.

Syn's head cocked. "Iziba? Binary suns. Spheroid. Oxidation accelerated." He blinked. "Things rust."

"Yes. Do you know the glyphs to reach it?"

"I do not," he said.

"The empress is headed there. We hope to beat her. Nari knows the glyphs, but we have to determine where in Iziba the empress will arrive."

The bells tinkled as Syn nodded again. "I understand. We will begin at once."

28

CRESCENT OF GOLD

"Lookie what I found." Nate beamed as she hefted a blue leather tome onto the already enormous stack lining Kate's table.

Kate eyed the cracked gold letters along the four-inch spine. *The Lost Kingdom*. "Oh wow. Good work." She pursed her lips, hesitant to voice her next thought.

Nate shrugged. "I know we don't need it anymore, but I still wanna see Carcosa once this is done." She glanced back and added. "And diggin' through all the scrolls and everything kept me off of Thetish's radar for the last two hours."

Kate peeked past the wall of books. Thetish was kneeling inside the brass ring, chalk in hand, practicing his glyphs for the journey to Iziba. Saso crouched opposite him, slowly pacing along, the open Garat manuscript in his hands like a living bookstand.

"Watch feet," Thetish growled as Saso's toes encroached within five inches of the chalked symbols.

"Looks like he's busy," Kate said.

Nate snorted. "Aye, but if he thought I wasn't doing anything productive he'd make me fetch him water, or make Saso do it and have me lug his damned book because he's too good to do it himself. Seriously, is this what it was like trainin' at Onyx? 'Cause if it was, I'm real happy now I wasn't in a tower."

"No. We trained our students. We didn't treat them like slaves."

"*Garn!*" Thetish snapped—a Dhevinite curse that the Magus favored. "Nate, fetch cloth."

Kate lifted her head above the books. "I'm using her at the moment."

"Apologies, Magus Kate," he said with a nod. "Saso, fetch rag."

Saso hopped up and hurried across the cluttered room like a scolded dog.

"*Thank you,*" Nate mouthed. "So, do ye need anythin'? And I mean *anything* right now?"

"Sorry. Check with Nari and Syn."

"I have. They never ask for anythin'. Please, I don't care what it is. I'll go wash yer clothes right now."

"Have you seen if Jim needs help?"

"He's busy with Jengta, studying circles and mastering the laws of the universe or some shite. Trust me, he's happier than a butcher's dog while I'm runnin' gofer for an arsehole."

Kate nodded. "All right, then. Tell you what. I don't have time to go over that right now." She nodded to *The Lost Kingdom.* "So, run it over to Harcourt. He'd probably love something to do."

"Consider it done." She picked up the huge book and winked. "Thanks."

Smiling, Kate returned to the unbound pages before her, their surfaces meticulously inscribed with arcane symbols and the margins filled with little notes in Soonati writing, which she couldn't read. While Jengta's collection was certainly formidable, even before Hestius' stolen additions from Kell's library, very few of them were in Latin. None were in English, but instead a buffet of over twenty written languages, many as dead as the worlds that birthed them. She'd found one that she was pretty sure was an exact copy of the *Voynich Manuscript*, and just as indecipherable. Reading the spells themselves wasn't tricky. Magic, like mathematics, was a universal language. But minutia—the best wood, and herbs, the warnings of Abyssal territories crossed, the cultural and physical anomalies of the destination—were all lost to her. Thankfully, she had the others to help her with that.

Nari, having the most experience with Iziba, believed Candace's grand entrance would be in the city of Malto. Thetish warned that the city of Givita would be equally likely, but Syn had pointed out that Malto, while smaller, was considered the cultural heart, and the empress' history made that the likelier choice. Kate knew nothing about either, but agreed with Syn's logic. Voting three to one, the Viatores studied the way to Malto, agreeing to learn Givita as well, if time allowed.

Kate studied the glyphs again, allowing the infused power to enter her mind. Somewhere deep behind her eyes, she saw the long journey, the glowing ring. The spicy aroma of orange peel and hot metal tickled the back of her throat. Before her, or within her, it was difficult to tell, a brown floor emerged from the aether—her destination. Kate held the image, memorizing the curving paths of pale grout between the tiles and the sense of being there, at some distant place she'd never actually seen. The remembered shriek of a hawk cried out in the distance, and the vision turned away from the floor to sparkling sea stretching toward the horizon. She stood near the edge of a cliff, waves crashing far below. Warm, humid air caressed her face, pulling at her beard. A single white-speckled hawk soared above, across crystal blue skies, a limp weasel in its talons.

The image faded and Kate found herself again between the leaning canyons of the library, the smell of paper and dust, and Thetish's bitching at Saso. She looked at her cup, a green ring along the porcelain bottom. In the past four days, she'd become quite fond of tarshu. She'd been locked into *The Zone* for nearly the entire time. One cube could keep her going the rest of the night, but the distant cry of her muscles begging to be used drew her attention.

Kate rose to her feet. "I think I'll go for a walk," she announced to no one in particular.

Nari and Syn were near the back, engrossed in a whispered conversation. Thetish was standing in the middle of the circle, tugging his mustache like a Vaudevillian rogue as he scrutinized his completed work. Careful to give the chalked sigils a wide berth, Kate made her way toward the door.

The whirlwind of studying, planning, and working with other practitioners both above and below her station was both exhilarating and exhausting. She'd never imagined she'd experience that again, the sensation and bond of peer, mentor, and student. It felt like being in a tower, literally this time, she supposed. And like in a tower, while she might not admire everyone else she shared it with, there was still respect. And that, Kate decided, had been what she missed the most since Onyx's fall.

Bypassing the elevator, Kate made her way down the spiral steps, past paintings and photographs of gray-skinned strangers and exotic land-scapes. The ever-present aroma of cooking and the bustling sounds of voices and clinking pots drifted up from the second-floor kitchens. Half the servants being Soonati and the other Dhevinite had caused a few problems. Though Jengta assured that they'd managed to work through the lack of shared language.

Kate made her way down to the first floor. After locating her boots among the slots honeycombing the wall, she exited the sturdy door, her ears popping slightly as she crossed the warded threshold. Long shadows stretched across the great yard, hemmed in on all sides by a ten-foot wall of black stone. Birds hopped and twittered between trees, their branches studded with tiny buds anticipating the end of the twilight days.

The eclipse held fast for its entire journey across the overcast sky. But now, one hour before sunset, the moon slipped from its placement, allowing a brief crescent of golden light before plunging beneath the glistening horizon.

To her left, a single Dhevinite soldier guarded the three flying vehicles, including the bus that had carried Kate and her friends to this bizarre wonderland. The sentry carried a short-barreled brown rifle over his shoulder. As Kate had feared, the splinter guns they'd hauled from Dhevin didn't work here. Hopefully, they would on Iziba. Otherwise, it would make for a difficult attack. Like Nari and Thetish, she suspected the Abyss' toll on electronics would leave the weapons no more than glorified clubs no matter what world they visited next. That left them twenty rifles and a handful of sidearms. Evan had made sure no one knew about the pistols they'd brought with them in their inventory.

In two days, they'd know for sure. In two days, they'd know if they were too late or wrong in beating Candace there. But maybe, just maybe, if they did head her off, and once the deed was done, Kate would be free of the Iron Word and finally free of the undue guilt she'd borne for Candace's crimes.

"Kate!"

She turned at hearing her name.

"Where you off to?" Evan asked, jogging up beside her.

Kate tossed her shoulder back in a shrug. "Don't know. Just getting some air."

"You heading out there?" He motioned toward the stone archway, a wall of calf-deep snow piled against the edge like a window. The water of melted snow ran down a shallow channel, emptying in a pool to her right.

"I...hadn't thought that far ahead," she said. "I guess I should have gotten a coat."

"Give me a minute, and I'll bring you one."

"No need. I have enough people waiting on me at the moment. I'll just stay in here."

Evan smiled, white teeth visible between his lips. "Okay. So why don't I go grab us coats, and if you change your mind by the time I get back, then you can go out?"

She laughed. "I think I can let you do that."

"Great. Back in a minute." He hurried back toward the tower.

Kate strolled to the narrow pond. A golden, six-legged, softshell turtle clambered off the bank with a splash as she drew close. She stopped at the edge, her eyes following as purple insects skittered across the surface, though she wasn't watching them.

Two days. Would she get a chance to speak with Candace, confront her, tell her, *I know who you are?* Probably not. She was dangerous. Images of Harcourt's photographs flashed through her mind—a seated man, his intestines laid before his feet. There was no talking to anyone who could do that. And even if she could stand before the liar, the thieving murderer she'd once called sister, what good would it do?

I'd feel better.

Master Boyer had said there was no room in the Art for vengeance. He'd never held a grudge and was quick to forgive. But Kate wasn't him. Only after this festering cancer of hatred was excised would she even hope to move on. She smiled, knowing that Master Boyer would still pardon her for that. He wouldn't approve, but he'd always forgive.

Evan trotted back down the tower steps, long burgundy coats over his arm.

"That didn't take long at all," Kate said.

"I told you it wouldn't." His honey eyes flicked toward the arch. "So... you change your mind?"

"After all your trouble I could hardly refuse."

"It's no trouble." He offered her a hooded coat. "After you."

Kate pulled on the coat and cinched the belt tight. Her ears buzzed as she crossed the heavily warded archway and then the cold wind hit her face. A well-worn trail plowed through the snow, heading east before splitting, one toward the field and the other toward the orchard. Through one of the open archways, pairs of soldiers practiced with curved swords, the contingency in case their guns failed to work on Iziba.

Bypassing the clean path, Kate headed right, following a shallow trail, rounded and unused since the previous night's snowfall. Ice and snow crunched underfoot. A sudden breeze flapped her coat against her legs. Face down against the frigid blast, Kate hurried the thirty yards to the third courtyard.

The cold vanished the instant she passed the broken archway, and the sudden warmth stung her cheeks. No wards protected this garden, but whatever enchantment or technology shielded it from the winter's fury was still intact.

Kate stomped the melting ice from her boots. A small animal that looked like a chipmunk with a fox's head chirped angrily and scurried away, vanishing beneath a leafy bush. Following the step-stone trail past dainty, twisting trees and violet stalks of bamboo, Kate reached a clearing. A large disk of polished obsidian filled the space, twenty feet across and hewn from a single slab. Seven etched circles of varying size extended from the center, like a black monochrome target, the brazier the bull's-eye. Seven tapered pillars ringed the outer edge. Dull silver fire pots hung from each, unlit and supported by a twisting silver arm. One anchored a spectacular spider web, the weaver nestled at its heart, its abdomen as big and blue as a robin's egg.

"What is this place?" Evan asked.

"This? Ceremony ring."

"Well...obviously this. I mean," he waved hand toward the trees and small ruin of what might have been a stone house, "*this*. Do you know?"

"Jengta only called it the garden. There's a few grave markers that way, so I think that's more of what it is."

He grunted.

"For the rest of us," Kate motioned to the black disk, "this is the escape pod. In a pinch, one of us can cast a circle here. No wards to stop us coming and going. Brazier's loaded with white oak, and ready to go." She followed a path down toward a wide pool. Small, round fish, like stingrays, glided beneath the still water. Luminescent spots dotted their backs, glowing pale blues, and greens. A few meandered toward her as she reached the stone-lined bank, hoping for food.

"So why aren't you training with the others?" Kate asked after a minute's silence. "How often do you get a chance to learn sword fighting?"

Evan shrugged. "My job's to protect Harcourt. We worried that if I spent too much time with the soldiers, they might mistake me as part of their ranks."

"Then why'd you follow me out here? Harcourt's back at the tower."

"I'm to protect you, too."

"I'm pretty safe here."

"I didn't say it was hard work. But it's still my job." His gaze moved to a bright pink long-tailed bird hopping in a tree. "Besides. I get restless. Had to get out for a bit. Spend time with someone...someone I could understand what in the hell they were saying."

She laughed. "You could at least say you enjoy my company."

"There's that, too."

Kate's eyes returned to the school of glowing rays, their wing-like fins swishing and breaking the surface in the vain hope for treats. Their combined light lit the bank, overpowering the dim glow of the setting sun at their backs. She'd have to bring something for them next time. In two days she might not have the chance again.

"Where are you?" Evan asked.

Kate drew a breath. Released it. "Just we're so close to the end. If we head Candace off, then Kamre's soldiers will do the rest."

"That's a good thing."

"Yeah, but...what then?"

"Whatever you want," Evan said.

"Nate's still wanting to see Carcosa," Kate said. "So maybe we'll do that."

"Sounds like a plan to me."

"Yeah, but what next? What do I do? Baltimore? Move to Edinburgh?"

"I don't think any of us should be returning there," Evan said. "Probably best to avoid Scotland for the next thirty years or so."

"Maybe Hollit," she mumbled. Kate shook her head. For three years her life had been merely survival—the next meal, the next rent payment, the next fix. Long-term plans were a forgotten luxury, and now, as she found herself on the verge of completing her goal, the endless options terrified her.

"Just see the world, Kate," Evan said. "All of them. It's wide open for you. Run. See it all. You have this power and you just..." He shook his head. "Don't waste it."

A cold pain slid though Kate's guts like a dagger of poisoned ice. What the hell was she thinking, griping to him about the future? Of all people?

Harcourt's words echoed through her memory. *Three...maybe four years.* That was all Evan had. He was a dead man walking, his future a looming gallows and here she was, on the cusp of a new life, bitching about how many choices lay ahead.

Kate swallowed and forced a smile. "You're right. I should tour the worlds." She looked up at him, met those sincere golden eyes. "You up for it?"

Evan grinned, his perfect teeth as white as the snow-capped mountains behind him. "Sounds like a plan."

29

D-SQUAD

"There they go," Jim said, eyes fixed out the window.

From the warmth of the large tipi-like cabin, Kate watched the smoke from Syn's brazier envelop the crowd of huddled soldiers. Their obscured images distorted and faded. Then a passing breeze shattered the smoke bubble and carried it away, leaving the blue platform clean and empty.

Paranoid that travelers might be sniffed back to the tower, Jengta insisted that the convoy depart from the remote cabin where Kate had arrived. It made sense, but Kate just wished there'd been a better place for them to use—someplace warmer.

Kate turned to Astius, who was wearing a long white shirt, sort of like an Indian kurta, beneath his heavy jacket. "Once I finish the ring, you hurry down. Got it?"

Astius winked, the tattoos above his brow rippling with the motion. "We will be there before you have need to call us."

Behind him, forty-six soldiers triple-checked their gear, each of them wearing the Iziban clothing Nari had brought back the day before. Her recon trip had also discovered that the Templum Aetheris had closed, cutting the world off from the rest, and preventing anyone from announcing the impending conquest. The Golden Empress was coming. Kate just had to beat her there.

She looked to Jim and Nate. "Ready?"

"Damn right," Jim said, hefting the brazier.

Nate only smiled.

"Then let's freeze our asses off." Kate pulled a scarf up over her mouth and nose. Chalk in hand, she started for the door. A Dhevinite soldier slid it open, releasing a frigid blast. Kate ran out, down the shoveled slope, and onto the blue paving.

"Here," she said, offering Nate the long string affixed to her chalk. "Hold it down tight."

Nate pressed the knotted end firmly down into a divot at the plat-form's heart. Kate dropped to her knees and began drawing the ring.

She worked quick, circling almost the entire stage—forty-three pedes, by far the largest circle she'd ever cast. One mistake in the string's length or the angle she held the chalk and the ends wouldn't align. They'd have to scrub it off and start over.

The ends joined perfectly.

"Next," she called back, her words muffled beneath the scarf. The cold stung her eyes. It wormed through her thick clothes, meeting the sweat welling across her skin.

Nate pulled the string to the next knot and held down. "Ready."

Keeping her chalk straight up, Kate began the inner ring, forty-two pedes, pouring her magic into the line.

The chalk slipped on the uneven stones, sending a two-inch curving line downward. *Shit!*

Kate scrubbed the errant mark with her sleeve, getting most of the offending chalk. She closed her eyes, pushing away the cold, the frustra-tion, and the anxiety of all the people watching her. *You got this.*

She started the circle again. Her whispering lips brushed the inside of her breath-moistened scarf. "Alla tehru. Alla tehru."

A gust of wind skittered dusty snow across the platform, but Kate didn't slow, didn't waiver in her focus. "Alla tehru. Alla tehru." Her words faded as she neared completion, her jaw set and lips barely moving. "Alla tehru. Alla tehru."

The ends joined, and Kate released a breath.

Without even needing a cue, Nate released the string. Jim hurried inside the double-ring and set the brazier in position. Up the hill, the cabin's door opened, and soldiers filed toward them, Astius limping in the lead.

Kate began inscribing the glyphs, magic flowing down her arm and into the chalk. Snow crunched as soldiers encircled the ring, their boots only inches away from where Kate worked. Their bodies formed a human shield, protecting her from the wind. No one coughed or said a single word, the only sounds being the clicking of chalk on stone and Kate's whispered mantra.

Knees aching, she completed the first circuit of symbols and then started back the other way, pausing long enough to place the five spheres of moonstone equilaterally along the circle. Magic poured down her arm, sealing each glyph with the click of chalk. "Done," she announced, completing the final stroke.

Crawling to her feet, she approached the brazier. Jim had already lighted it and now waited with the muslin bag of herbs at the ready.

Astius barked a sharp order, and his troops all stepped inside, careful not to touch the chalked glyphs. Within seconds they had stacked the supplies and stood at attention.

Astius gave them a quick inspection and said, "Ready."

Fingers tracing in the air, Kate focused her power until the glowing symbol before her blazed brighter than the flames. She took the bag from Jim and dropped it into the fire. Her chest rose, and her head tipped back as she released the spell, the surge of magic hitting with an orgasmic shudder.

The tang of orange peel and hot metal and then aether swirled around them pulling them into the Abyss.

Kate dropped back into a seated position, her breaths coming in long gasps.

"You all right?" Jim asked.

She nodded, her words coming between pants. "Yeah...just...wow."

"Do you need anything?" Harcourt asked, moving up beside her.

"No." Kate swallowed. "I'm good. Just a circle this size...it's twice the diameter of the last one, but it takes four times the power."

"Hell," Jim said. "Can you keep it going for six hours?"

"I've still got a lot left. It was just...a lot at one time."

The soldiers murmured and shifted, their eyes peering through the rolling curls of aether. One Dhevinite woman whispered something to the men beside her, eliciting restrained chuckles.

"Astius," Kate said.

"Yes?"

Kate motioned to the melting snow that had blown into the circle or fallen off boots. "Tell your people to dab that up. Carefully. If it smudges the chalk, we're in trouble."

His eyes widened as he scanned his troops' ice-caked boots. "*Garn*." He shook his head. "At once." Astius belted orders to his troops, starting with the joking cadre.

Senator Kamre had assigned Astius to lead the team sent with Kate. He said it was because they already had a rapport. That was true enough, but Kate suspected it was because while the senator did listen to the old veteran's advice, Astius' age and bad leg had resigned him to the D-Squad. Kamre traveled with Thetish and the most capable troops. That was no surprise. Nari had carried the next most capable, led by Lieutenant Tompii as well as Livia and Vorsis. The Dhevinites were sticking together as if they were the only ones vested in this cause, while she and Syn got the scraps.

Kate peeled her gloves and held her hands up to the warm brazier. "Make yourselves comfortable. This is going to be a long ride."

A distant howl greeted them as they neared Iziba. Soldiers reached for their weapons and Astius hissed orders calming the ranks, telling them to settle down.

Kate clenched her hand, squeezing a faint tremble from her fingers. *They can't see you.* She leaned close to the burning bowl and focused on the memory of the curving chocolate brown tiles. A second image formed. The once white grout had chipped and darkened. A few of the tiles were cracked. The imprint of three chalked circles, almost perfectly stacked, showed where the other Viatores had landed. Kate rotated the picture around, lining them on top of each other. Her fingers wove and released the spell, and the aether whirled and dissolved with a rush of warm, salty air.

"Welcome," Kamre declared. He stood atop a stone platform thirty feet away wearing an orange kurta with black, striped trousers. The hood of a thin cloak concealed his short dreadlocks. Judging by the vine-covered ruins that surrounded them on three sides, his stage appeared to be a section of fallen wall. Soldiers stood on all sides, most congregating in the remains of some amphitheater, a few traces of rotted wood seats held on with gray ceramic brackets.

Behind her, the ground gave way to a sixty-foot cliff and to the ocean. Squawking, four-winged seabirds glided below. An enormous paddle-wheel ship chugged along far to the left, the light of the twin suns reflecting its white accordion-like fin like some origami shark.

Astius ordered his troops off to one side where they fell into formation away from any possible view of the distant ship.

"Sliver guns won't work," Vorsis said, strolling toward his father. "Rifles do, but they're underpowered. Jams might be issue."

"Pleased to see you, too." Astius clapped his hand on his son's shoulder.

"Figured that went without saying." Vorsis looked over toward Kate. "Good journey?"

Kate nodded. "I'm a bit hungry."

He pointed toward a half-wall covered in chipped paint. "Mess is back there. They should have something ready for all of you."

Evan pointed to a splatter of red arcing across the old stone. Tiny black flies swarmed above a crimson pool on the leaf-strewn ground. "What happened there?"

"Ah." Vorsis scratched his knuckles across his cheek. "That was when Kamre and Thetish arrived. Someone was here and saw them."

"The empress' men?" Kate asked.

He shook his head. "Just locals, I believe."

"So, they killed them?" Kate exclaimed.

Vorsis nodded.

"Why?"

"Liability," Kamre said, approaching. "Any witnesses of our arrival would endanger us all."

"But you didn't have to kill them," Kate said.

"We have no luxury of spare troops to guard prisoners," Kamre said. "We require everyone we have. I'm not proud of it, but two innocent lives are small price for our goal."

Kate shook her head. "I can't believe you'd—"

"Kate Rossdale," Kamre said. "I do not require your counsel or judgment. It is done and I wouldn't hesitate to do it again. Now gather your belonging and rest. We still need to get to city."

Face growing hot, Kate ground her teeth. She wasn't some fucking bus driver. She didn't work for him.

Harcourt touched her arm. "Let it go," he whispered.

Kate shot him a glare, the full bore of her anger aimed at the little man. He didn't cower. "I know. Not here. Not now."

"Understand journey took much out of you," Kamre said. "Once you've recovered, Nari needs to speak with you about next step. She's by old lighthouse. That way."

Kate snorted. She didn't need to recover, she just needed away from this murdering asshole. She'd lost her appetite. "Then let's get to work."

30

BENEATH CRIMSON STARS

The stars above Iziba burned red. A hundred thousand twinkling crimson specks strewn across the black heavens like unmoving embers. The city smelled of coal smoke, humanity, and the bitter-sweet aroma of cherry blossoms.

"There," Kamre whispered, pointing across the canal.

Kneeling behind a low, rooftop wall, Kate squinted at a tiered four-story building overlooking the arched canal bridge, sort of a wide, open-topped pagoda. The yellow glow of haze-shrouded gaslights cast deep shadows across its face.

"Appears promising," Lieutenant Tompii said, peering through his binoculars.

"Down," Kamre whispered.

A line of small figures crossed the bridge below, their furred faces hidden beneath protruding hoods, like the cornettes of nuns. Kate couldn't tell if they were men or women. They didn't speak, and thankfully none lifted their eyes to the rooftops where the plotting invaders hid.

"Can you take us there?" Kamre asked once the procession had passed.

Nari nodded. "I can get us to square below, but I've never been inside building."

"Good enough. Tompii, maintain watch. I'll accompany Viatores."

Kate clenched her teeth. The fear of being spotted was bad enough without the trigger-happy senator beside her. So far there'd been no fatalities this night—at least none that she'd been told of. Her condemnation of Kamre's action at the ruins was probably to blame for his joining her now. Izibans were smaller than other people, standing a head lower than those of Earth. Harcourt would probably get along fine. The rest stood out like giants.

Crouch-walking, they moved back to the small chalk ring. Nari touched up the simple glyphs and removed the vented lid from the small brazier. Kate wasn't very experienced with inner-world travel. She'd only performed it twice before her ill-fated test journey to Hollit. It was the most common type of traveling Viatores carried out, and Nari was a master.

Nari sprinkled a pinch of herbs into the burning coal, unleashing a plume of smoke. The world outside the circle faded. A moment's black, and then the glow of streetlights emerged from the darkness. Smooth flagstone formed beneath their feet and an errant cherry blossom tumbled past.

They were now a hundred yards from the roof. Gnarled trees lined the square, their branches heavy with flowers. Kate released a breath. The square was thankfully empty.

"Come," Kamre whispered.

Flanked by two soldiers, Kate hurried toward the tower, their footsteps clicking on the pale stone. The metal tips of Kamre's short dreadlocks jangled behind her. She glanced back in time to see Nari sprinkle another pinch into the brazier and with a surge of smoke and aether, she was gone, taking the incriminating chalk ring with her.

They stopped beside a flint-studded door. At its heart sat a Y-shaped keyhole framed in yellow ceramic. Kate felt the door. No wards.

Weaving her fingers in a hooking motion, Kate pressed her palm to the lock. Tendrils of magic felt inside, probing the wooden gears and porcelain levers.

"Someone approaches," Kamre whispered, peering around the corner.

"I'm working as fast as I can," Kate whispered without moving her lips. Her fingers worked against the door, her hand rotating.

"We must move," Kamre said.

"Almost got it." Kate slid her thumb across the wood, then pulled an invisible thread of magic. The lock clicked.

"Quickly," Kamre ordered.

They hurried inside. Kate glimpsed bench desks, wooden columns, and painted clay statues before the door pinched shut behind her. Thankfully, it was empty of people.

After two excruciating minutes, Kamre cracked the door and peered out. "Clear."

Kate cupped her hands before her mouth and blew. Light welled between her curled fingers, making them glow red. Opening her hands, she released a small, floating orb. Wincing from the sudden brilliance, she dimmed the light to nothing more than that of a single candle.

The orb floated into the room like a child's balloon, making shadows move.

"There," one of the soldiers whispered, motioning to a narrow staircase.

Kate called the light back into her palm. Closing her fingers as if she were holding a flashlight, she directed the beam toward the floor as they navigated across the room.

One by one, they checked the floors, verifying them empty. The second contained rows of long tables surrounded by floor to ceiling cabinets, like card-catalogs. The third housed an enormous half-assembled loom—pieces laid out on the floor like some IKEA project from hell. The fourth floor was open, balconies on all sides, a conical roof suspended above it by the five thick stilts. Nervous pigeons cooed from the rafters above.

Kate extinguished her light and carefully approached the edge. Across the canal and the wind-rustling trees stood the rooftop where they'd first arrived. She tried to see Tompii or any of the other soldiers looking back at her but couldn't. Good. This vantage gave a better view up the hill, past the slate-tiled roofs and two other canals to where she could just make out the upper dome of Malto's Templum Aetheris. Earlier that day the gold-robed and red-masked Netru had emerged from the building, declaring this world the empress' dominion.

Such an act had preceded her appearance in Kell by two days.

"Do what you require," Kamre whispered.

Kate left the balcony and inspected the open roof, committing it to memory. She closed her eyes, focusing on the sounds of tinkling wind chimes and the stink of pigeon shit. Removing a worn stick of chalk from the pouch at her belt, Kate inscribed a small sigil across the trapdoor's edge. Anyone opening the door and she'd feel it. More importantly, leaving her magic here guaranteed a connection. She could return to this very place when she desired.

"I'm ready."

Without a word, they hurried down the stairs and back into the night.

31

THE QUEEN IN YELLOW

Without working radios, Kate and the other Viatores earned the prestigious honor of lookouts. They worked in shifts, hiding atop their intended roosts and watching the Templum. Any sign of the empress' arrival and they were to travel back to camp and call for the attack.

Kate took the second shift.

Seven hours of the purest boredom huddled atop a roof, afraid to peer too far over the edge and be seen, and afraid to move more than an inch at a time for fear of a creak giving her away. There was no air conditioning and no toilet, save for the glorified bucket they used for long crossings.

Astius had assigned her a soldier named Bira as her escort. Bira had a shaved head, protruding brows dyed an electric purple, obsessively cracked her knuckles, and wasn't much of a conversationalist. They exchanged maybe fifteen words the entire shift, the rest being vague grunts and gestures. Probably for the best, Kate decided. No talking meant no one accidentally overhearing them.

But it was still boring.

At least she had shade. By the time Syn arrived at his rooftop post, the suns were reaching their zenith. Through the binoculars, she saw the Torban Viator raise a six-fingered hand, signaling that he and his escort had it from there.

Have fun. Then, without a word, Kate and Bira scooted back to the chalk circle and traveled back to camp.

Jim was already standing there with a bowl of noodles when the aether thinned. "Welcome back."

"That better be for me," Kate said, her stomach cinching at the smell of grilling food at the nearby mess tent.

"Of course. When Syn left, I knew you'd be back and hangry."

"I fucking love you. You know that?"

Jim shrugged. "Never doubted it."

Bira left with a curt nod, and headed to the mess.

"So any update?" Jim asked once Kate accepted the bowl.

"Nothing yet." She shoveled a mouthful, a dribble of watery soup running down her chin. "How 'bout here?"

"Tense. Everyone's on alert, ready to spring at a moment's notice. Which means no wandering around. No getting near the cliffs where you might be seen. Carry everything on you. There's been two fistfights already."

She grunted and continued eating. "What is this?"

"Nate made it. Don't even ask what they're cooking over there. Some sort of big-ass rats, possums or something, they found eating bamboo."

Kate curled her lip, the delicious aroma of meat losing its appeal. "We got any more of this, then?"

Jim smiled. "Better believe it."

Kate tipped the shallow bowl to her lips, drinking the last of her soup. "Give me a minute, and we'll go for seconds." She returned to her ring, tightly packed alongside three others with space for Syn's. She rubbed out some of the marks, and altered them so that it led back to the rooftop position.

Jim was carrying over an armload of cubed wood to load in the brazier when a sudden gust of wind blasted the empty platform beside him, and in a swirl of black aether, Syn appeared.

Three dozen conversations instantly silenced.

"She's here!" Syn called.

The tower groaned as the weight of fifty-two people appeared atop it. Pigeons scattered, fleeing their shaded roosts beneath the roof, gray and purple feathers spiraling down to the floor. Hunkering soldiers started toward the balcony's edge. Kate desperately wanted to join them, see the empress, see Candace and watch her die. But she couldn't. Not yet.

"Scrub it up," she hissed.

Harcourt, Evan, Nate, and Jim all began cleaning the glyphs from between the twin rings, careful not to actually break the chalked circles. Kate focused her power and began scribing new symbols, the sigils back to Soonat.

Horns sounded in the distance. Astius ordered his riflemen to the front, their weapons down but ready. They only had four of them. Kamre and Tompii's squads each had six rifles. Their teams were to be the spear-points.

Kate's ears buzzed as the other soldiers opened the trapdoor, activating her alarm spell. They stormed down the stairs.

Someone cried out below but was cut off.

Kate tried not to think of it as she worked.

Another blast of horns sounded, followed by a steady thumping of drums.

"She approaches," one of the riflemen said.

Kate focused on her work. If she fucked up, she'd have to start over, and she had to get this right. It'd take ten minutes for the empress to reach her. Kate could do it.

"That's it," Jim whispered, wiping away the last of the old symbols.

Kate's chalk ticked across the wooden planks, the cadence of drum beats growing closer. Finishing the first circuit, she reversed her direction, sealing the glyphs. She set the pieces of red tourmaline in place as she worked her way back around the circle, adrenaline fueling her magic.

The drums grew louder like the heartbeat of a waking giant.

Thump-thump. Thump-thump. Thump-thump.

Kate released her breath as she finished the final stroke. Done. Panting, she crawled to the balcony's edge between Evan and Jim and peeked over the railing wall.

She gasped at the sight, a sudden terror hitting her like ice.

Two hundred yards away, beyond pink-blossomed trees and low buildings, the procession crested an arching canal bridge. A dozen smoke-clad Netru walked in front, three abreast, carrying drums or banners blazoned with the Yellow Sign. The gold-robed guards followed, their red-stocked rifles across their chests. Behind them came two rows of hideous verl hounds, their eyeless faces scanning the crowds. There had to be twenty of them, all huge, larger than any of the ones at Onyx Tower, like brown bears. Golden chains encircled each of their fat, baby necks. A lone figure walked between them, dwarfed by the towering Netru.

Sunlight gleamed off her flowing golden robes. She carried her hands clasped before her, hidden inside wide sleeves. The only part of her not wrapped in brilliant gold was her masked face, nestled beneath a large hood. It looked to be ivory or bone, smooth and coming to twin points like devil horns or some strange crown. She moved gracefully, seeming to glide rather than walk, but something in the way she held herself, the angle of the shoulders, the faint tick-tick of her head as she glanced at her newest subjects, that exuding confidence was all too familiar.

Kate balled her hands into fists, hatred welling, washing away the cold of fear and doubt. Candace. The tower-sister she'd mourned, the betrayer, the two-hundred-year-old magic thief, strode before the city as a conquering goddess.

Fuck you.

The retinue behind her was twice the size of those in front. None of the crowd along the tree-lined streets, packing the balconies and canal barges said a word. No cheers. No cries. Only awe and fear. Even a few ghostly Dream Walkers stopped to watch.

"Ready yourselves," Astius whispered.

The parade entered a large square dominated by a needle-like green spire. The building balconies at either entrance appeared empty, but Kate knew they weren't. She held her breath.

Figures rose above the railing walls, rifles coming up in one motion.

A verl hound roared.

Twenty riflemen fired, their shots echoing across the city. A pink dome of latticed light bloomed around the empress, the geometric forms infinitely complex. It spun and writhed, deflecting rounds and sending them into the trees. Petals rained from the branches.

Kate's eyes widened. She'd never even heard of a shield that enormous, let alone one that could stop bullets.

Several of the Netru collapsed, orange blood spraying across the flag-stones. Three of the verl hounds staggered and dissipated in puffs of smoky aether. The rest scattered.

Shouts erupted below as Kamre's men stormed from the buildings. Civilians, caught between two forces, screamed and fled down side streets, some leaping into the canal. Others joined the fight, some charging the empress' troops, others going for Kamre's.

Kate shoved her fingers in her ears, the *boom boom boom* of the rifles beside her so loud it shook her teeth. One of the soldiers cursed and banged his rifle, ejected a jammed round, and continued firing.

Verl hounds charged the closing soldiers, smashing through the ranks. The golden guards raised their guns, firing back. Without cover, most were cut down before they could take a shot. One, a willowy giant favoring its left leg, fired up at the men beside Kamre. Kate couldn't see what came out of the barrel and she couldn't hear it over the cacophony of gunfire, but she witnessed the results.

The soldier exploded. No fire. He simply erupted in a geyser of red, head and right arm blasting away from his body. Blood and chunks of flesh showered the soldiers beside him and rained down the side of the building like confetti. Another rifleman exploded, then another before someone managed to hit the Netru marksman.

Soldiers in the square were screaming as the hounds ripped limbs and shook bodies like monstrous terriers. Kate clenched her fists, fighting the urge to help, to shoot her magic, not as if she would hit anything from this distance, but she could try. Kamre had ordered her not to join in, not waste her reserves if they needed to leave in a hurry.

Fuck it. Kate wove her fingers, launching an emerald beam down into the battle, missing a hound by inches. Following her lead, Syn fired as well, soon followed by Livia and even Thetish. Kate hit one hound, knocking it onto its back before a charging soldier ran it through with a curved sword.

"What's she doing?" Jim asked.

The empress spread her arms, fingers splayed toward the heavens. She brought her hands together in a clap, and a half-dozen black disks opened around the square, bleeding misty aether.

"No," Kate breathed. "That's...that's impossible."

Howls rang across the city, not just from the square, but everywhere. And then they came. Verl hounds clambered through the portals, pouncing on civilians and soldiers alike. Screams filled streets. People ran out of buildings, hounds snapping behind them. Each portal closed as soon as it birthed its horrific child.

Seizing the commotion, the remaining Netru soldiers focused their fire on the riflemen above. One hit a soldier near Kate. The woman screamed as her arm exploded from the bone, scalding flesh and steam splattered Kate's shoulder.

Yelping in pain, Kate whirled and realized it was Bira, her eyes wide and locked on the tattered mess dangling from the stump. Jim sprang toward her, his fingers already weaving silver light. Another soldier fell, his head coming clean off in a burst of skull and gore. Bloody dreadlocks plopped around them like scraps of rope, chunks of scalp still slinging to their ends. The stink of cooking meat filled the air.

Kate braved another look over the railing. Candace strolled through the square, her pink shield whirling around her. She thrust her hand through the dome of light and unleashed a brilliant white beam, thick as her arm, across the square and into the back of a fleeing soldier. The soldier went rigid, his head back as his organs—lungs, liver, heart, and coiled intestines—volcanoed out his mouth. His body collapsed, just a sack of skin and bone and bloody clothes.

The ranks shattered. A horn blasted from Kamre's tower.

"Retreat!" Astius screamed down at his men. "Get back here, you bastards!" He spun toward Kate, his finger stabbing toward the ring. "Take us from here!"

Kate scrambled toward the circle. Harcourt was already there, his witchhunter blade clutched between his hands like a holy relic. Kate dropped more wood into the brazier, enough to carry them anywhere but here.

Jim and Nate hauled Bira back into the ring. She was limp, her eyes closed. Astius had taken her fallen rifle and was now firing over the rail, screaming at his soldiers. Chunks of the railing as big as dinner plates buckled and steamed around him as Netru returned fire.

Bootsteps charged up the stairs below, and soldiers burst through the trap door, several covered in blood. A terrible roar echoed below, and a man screamed. Wood splintered. A verl hound smashed through the opening like a breaching shark, jaws snapping at a bald-headed soldier. The man fell backward and scrambled away on his hands.

Other soldiers rushed the beast, their swords before them. Evan's gun barked three loud shots, and the verl hound wailed and crumpled. The soldiers moved in and finished it off before it could stand.

"Fucking hell!" Kate cried, seeing the smear of chalk where the fleeing soldier had crossed it, ruining both rings and the glyphs. He looked at her stupidly, his hooded eyes bulging in terror and confusion.

"Fucking hell," she repeated. "Get out! Everyone out of the ring! Nate!"

"Comin'," Nate shouted.

Kate dug through her bag, dropped the chalk, picked it up and fished out the string." She shoved them into Nate's hands. "Tie this."

"What do you need?" Harcourt asked.

"Clean it up. All of it. Now!"

The old man began scrubbing the planks with his sleeve. Jim and several soldiers joined in, including the dumb fuck that had just ruined the last one.

"Here." Nate held out the tied chalk.

Kate took it, and Nate held the string down in the middle. Kate drew her magic and began to work.

Gunfire and shouts rained around her, but Kate didn't look up, didn't flinch. She only focused on keeping the chalk straight as she traced the giant circle. It was their only hope.

A meaty pop came from behind her, followed by wet splatter. Someone screamed.

"There!"

"I'm jammed."

"They come. Don't let them inside!"

"Done!" Kate shouted, finishing the first ring.

Nate pulled the string, held the second knot in place under both thumbs. "Set!"

Kate pressed the white stick against the boards and began the second circle, trying to ignore the raging battle.

"They're attacking Tompii's tower," Astius shouted. "Direct fire to keep them out until they can escape!"

"No! No! No!" someone began shouting.

Kate's grip tightened on the chalk to the point she feared it might break. Blood pounded in her ears and sweat dripped down her face, threatening to drip onto her work. "Alla tehru. Alla tehru."

"Tompii is down. They got him."

"Nari?" Astius asked, his voice high with pleading desperation.

"Can't tell."

"She's gone! They're scattering. *Garn*, they're butchering them."

Kate pushed the sounds away. She couldn't focus on who was dead and who was dying. The next Viator to die might be her. She had to finish the circle, or they were done for. "Alla tehru. Alla tehru. Alla tehru." She closed the ends of the second circle and began the first circuit of sigils.

A verl hound roared somewhere beneath them. Then the shouts and cries of soldiers charging to face it. Wood cracked to her right, and steaming splinters and specks of blood landed around her.

"They're coming this way. Be ready!"

"Come, bastards. Run!"

Kate couldn't tell if the shouts were meant to encourage or taunt.

Magic poured down her arm, her hand a blur of motion as she scribed the glyphs of passage.

Evan's silenced gun fired twice, only a foot behind her. *Chak, chak.* She realized he'd been pacing her around, acting as a human shield as she crawled on her knees.

Kate finished the first round of symbols, and began back the other way, sealing them. Jim was directing soldiers, carrying the wounded into the ring, making sure no one stepped or dripped blood onto the border.

"They're almost here!" a woman shouted.

"Keep them covered," Astius ordered.

Pounding footsteps raced up the tower. A half dozen soldiers came charging up, one slamming into Evan.

"Back!" Evan shouted. While none of the troops spoke English, Kate had no doubt they understood his order.

More soldiers hobbled up, carrying the wounded. A few with rifles raced to the shredded balcony to offer support. Other riflemen protected the trapdoor amongst the ring of swordsmen.

One of the support columns cracked, steam spewing from long fissures. The roof groaned, the weight of wood and slate tiles threatening to crush them. Gritting her teeth, Kate focused her magic into her work, a hot laser of energy down her shoulder and out through the chalk. The final sigil was in sight, inching closer with each stroke. She was too close now.

Soldiers were still shouting updates, reports of positions and the fallen, but Kate could no longer hear them. "Alla tehru. Alla tehru."

The roof groaned again. Raining tiles shattered along the balcony. The oily stink of smoke grew sharper. A verl hound roared somewhere below her, followed by the clangs of steel.

"Done!" Kate shouted, completing the final stroke with a flourish. "Get inside!"

Soldiers rushed into the ring, many leaping over the white chalked lines like crossing a great chasm. Kate scrambled through the mayhem to the brazier. Harcourt and Jim were hunkered beside it, shielding the fiery bowl from shuffling legs. Red smears coated Jim's arms like he'd washed his hand in blood and used his clothes as a towel. He clutched the tea box against his chest like a terrified mother.

Kate stopped beside the fire, her heart *thump-thump-thumping* in her ears.

Someone knocked painfully into her shoulder, almost trampling her down.

"Back!" Evan yelled, throwing out his arms. "Get back, God damn it."

"To circle. To circle," Astius was shouting, his words punctuated by rifle fire down over the balcony. Mangled and steaming bodies littered the deck. The railing wall was long gone, its broken remnants sagging out over the edge.

Kate's fingers wove before the brazier, filaments of power gathering strength.

Astius slapped one soldier on the back, ordering him to the circle. The old veteran fired twice more down to the street, and then across the courtyard to where a pair of golden-robed Netru stormed onto an empty rooftop. Flames engulfed the building Syn had occupied, a column of black smoke blocking out the suns.

Astius fired at the Netru, dropping one in a spray of orange. He looked back, confirming his soldiers were off the balcony and hobbled toward the circle. His body seized as a Netru shot him in the back. Rib bones buckled, some shattering through the skin. Red steam burst from the wounds, out his mouth and nose and Astius fell.

"No!" someone shouted. A soldier started toward him, but was held back by many hands. The Netru's silver-barreled rifle swung their direction.

Kate dropped the muslin bag into the fire and released the spell. Her head spun with the sudden rush of power. The sweet aroma of flowers and ocean air and aether whirled around them like an enveloping cloud.

The cry of hounds greeted them as they slid into the Abyss. Dark shapes loped and sniffed just beyond the circle's barrier.

One soldier raised his weapon, only to be slapped by an older man.

"You fire that, and we'll throw you out to get eaten," he snapped. "Understood? That goes for you all."

"Quiet!" Nate hissed. "Shut up, all of you."

Cold fear hammered through Kate's veins as the blind hounds turned their heads toward them. They circled and sniffed, trying to find the trail. No one spoke, the only sounds being the muffled cries and sobs of the wounded and shell-shocked, their brothers and sisters holding them tight, pleading with them to keep quiet.

The bubble inched through the pack, slower than Kate had ever traveled. A huge hound with red veins spider-webbing its hideous face lifted its head only ten feet from the circle's edge. Rifles lifted toward it. The beast's nostrils flared. It turned and raced off to the right. The rest of the pack followed, their forms vanished in the curling aether.

"Are they gone?" Harcourt asked. He still gripped the witchhunter blade, his knuckles white and bloodless.

Someone shushed him.

They floated in silence for five solid minutes. One soldier wheezed and died only an arm's reach from Kate. Jim was kneeling over a ragged claw slash across one woman's thigh. Nate was doing what she could to sooth another.

Over sixty people packed the circle. It reeked of blood, sweat, urine, and the sharp tang of fear. Two units should have been nearly a hundred soldiers, not including the support crews like Evan, Harcourt, and Nate. How many of the others had made it out? Were those hounds rushing off to devour them?

Kate swallowed and began to increase their speed back to Soonat. She had no idea what to expect.

32

REGROUP

A blast of frigid air greeted them back at Soonat. The chalked lines from two other circles already covered the blue platform as Kate and her passengers appeared. Around them, the jagged black glass mountains gleamed beneath the golden corona sun, like the fiery eye of God. Fresh footprints trampled the blood-speckled snow all around the platform. They led up toward the shelter, a flat trail of gray wind-swept smoke trailing from the chimney. The building's sliding door opened and soldiers hurried down to meet them.

"Gods be praised," Kamre said from the lead. "Carry injured inside. Transport is on its way."

Soldiers raced around, seeing to the wounded. Many of the ones with Kate didn't have winter gear, theirs being left behind in the confusion.

Kate swooned as she rose to her feet, but Harcourt caught her.

Evan moved to help, but the old man shooed him away.

"Help the others. I have her." He slid himself under her arm and escorted her toward the platform's edge.

"Here," Kamre said, removing his fur-lined coat and draping it over her. "How many could you save?"

"Fifty-nine," Kate said. "Thirteen are injured. Another died on the way."

"Fifty-nine?" Kamre sighed with a shake of his head. Smeared flecks of dried blood striped the gold tattoos above his brow.

"How many of Nari's people made it out with you?" Kate asked.

"With us? None. Syn saved eight. But he took heavy losses. Yours was largest group to escape." The senator, now general, returned his attention to his troops, helping to carry the wounded and be seen as a strong leader.

Kate and Harcourt marched up the trail to the shelter. The low murmur of three dozen conversations echoed beneath the steep roof. The heat of the blazing fire and packed bodies filled the room, stinging her cold cheeks as she stepped past the door. The stink of smoke and blood permeated everything.

A crude hospital occupied the rear portion of the cabin, the wounded laid out on blankets and folded tents. Kate smiled for the first time that day as she recognized Vorsis leaning over one soldier with red-stained bandages encircling one of her arms.

As if sensing her eyes, he looked up and nodded a greeting. Vorsis muttered something to the wounded soldier and came over, wiping his hands against his legs. "Good to see you made it out."

Kate gave him a hug. "I thought you were dead. When I heard about Nari..."

"Livia and I got out. Daring escape. We jumped rooftop to rooftop to reach Syn before he gated." He looked past Kate's shoulder, eyes scanning the newcomers. "Where's father?"

The relief in Kate's chest crashed. She swallowed, her eyes averting.

"No," Vorsis groaned, his huge shoulders slumping. "No. Please."

"I'm sorry, Vorsis," Harcourt said.

Vorsis pressed a fist to his lips. He opened his mouth to say something, paused and clenched his teeth. "How?"

"Netru rifle," Kate said. "He ordered all his men to the circle. He was the last one left when it happened."

"He didn't suffer," Harcourt assured. "He was a brave man."

Vorsis nodded absently. Kate reached for him, to hug again, but he pushed her away with a gentle hand. "Gratitude. I must...see to my troops." He headed to where Jim and two more of the Leges were treating the wounded.

Thetish and Syn sat near one wall. Syn gave an acknowledging nod, and Kate wove her way to them.

The Torban sorcerer pressed his hand against his chest. "It is good that you escaped." Redness rimmed his pale eyes. Streaks from sweat and God knew what else had washed away his usual coating of dust, revealing his cadaver blue skin beneath. Without the dust, the coppery tattoos almost glowed like hot circuitry.

"You as well."

"We nearly didn't," Syn said. "We had to ignite the asafetida to drive away the hounds."

"You cast while burning asafetida?" Kate asked.

He nodded. "Casting was profoundly difficult. The grass drained much of the power and refused to leave the vessel. I do not recommend it."

"I've never seen anything like that," Thetish muttered to no one in particular. His hollow eyes stared across the room. A smudge of black soot stained his rust-red cheeks. Dried blood speckled his sleeve. "No drawing circles, no stones, she simply gated them in." He shook his head. "How?"

"She is Queen of Carcosa," Syn said.

"She is not goddess." Thetish's distant eyes lifted to Kate, a pleading desperation behind them. "You claimed she was Terran. Mortal."

"She is. But she doesn't just have the power of an Ipsissimus, but many. And not just Viatoric, but all of them."

"We couldn't even hurt her."

"One bullet struck," Syn said. "I saw it."

"Did it?" Kate asked. "It punctured her shield?"

He shook his head, a stiff single motion to the side, jingling the hanging bells. "Just before. The initial shot of the volley."

"Much good it did," Thetish said.

"Yes," Syn replied. "She *can* be harmed. It took her time to heal. If she is an Ipsissimus Lex, that would make sense. She could do that. Then she called her hounds by some means we've never seen. I believe they were just beyond the veil, awaiting such a summoning, but that is only conjecture. She would have known an assassination attempt was possible and may have had her verls ready for such an event. If we were to surprise her, truly catch her unprepared, then it may be different."

"*May* be," Thetish snapped. He lowered his voice to a hissing whisper. "But you do not know. None of us do."

"Asafetida works against the hounds or anything else she can summon from the Demhe," Syn continued, ignoring the outburst. "We can use that. Possibly arm our soldiers with smoking censers, hurl them like grenades to stay her summonings."

"But that won't work on Netru," Thetish said. "And they..." He shook his head. "You saw what they did. Men exploding like clay bottles."

Someone shifted in the corner of Kate's vision. She glanced over to see Kamre there, the small eyes behind his spectacles quietly watching.

"But it can stop the hounds," Syn said. "Allow our troops to focus on the Netru."

"There's another option," Kate mumbled, not fully intending to voice the thought.

The Viatores' eyes lifted to her.

"There's a way to control the hounds," Kate said.

"Explain." Kamre said.

She shrugged. "I don't know. But I've seen it. Candace, before she was empress, she did it. If we could find the spell—"

"We could use them against her." Kamre nodded, ideas kindling behind his eyes.

"Yeah," Kate said. "In theory."

"Theory?" Thetish laughed, dry and without humor. "Our last theory almost killed us. Nari is dead." He swallowed. "They tore her in half."

"Surrendering, Thetish?" Kamre asked. "Is that it?"

"No!" Anger flashed across his face, his brows dipping in the middle, the expression exaggerated by their three-inch length. "I'm not. But we require more than hypotheses. Our last *theory* cost us dearly."

"It was desperate plan," Kamre said. "We paid for it."

Thetish snorted. His small, hooded eyes looked up at Kate. "And how do you still stand? Sit." He patted the bench beside him, his hand more flopping than slapping. "You must be exhausted."

"I'm fine, thank you."

Syn cocked his head, those creepy goat eyes searching her face. "Are you?"

Kate nodded. "I'm sleepy, but not drained."

"You just crossed the Demhe—a forty-three pes circle, and you're not drained?"

"No. I could cross again if I could stay awake long enough, so don't get any ideas."

The Torban's eyes narrowed. "Interesting."

"Explain." Kamre said.

Kate shrugged. "It's just that I'm very good at conserving my magic."

"Tell me, Kate, how large of a circle could you maintain?" Syn asked.

"No clue. Those last ones were the biggest I'd tried before."

"How large do you theorize?" Kamre asked. "Could you...double it?"

Doubling it? Eighty-four pedes, plus one for the outer ring. Kate's tired brain struggled to imagine how long it would take to inscribe. "Probably. If I could draw it perfectly. I don't know."

The senator chewed his lip, his gaze losing focus, probing some unseen thing beyond the walls.

"Lofty claim," Thetish said.

"I'm not saying I'm up for it right now, but if I were rested, yeah. I...I could do it."

Kamre lifted a finger, circling it around. "You could gate everyone in here?"

"Sure. Providing we could find a space big enough to both draw the circle and arrive. And that would probably lay me out. I mean inscribing a circle that huge could take hours."

Kamre nodded. He gazed across the room. "But it *could* be done."

A dreadful weight settled in her chest, her heart sinking into her gut.

"*Serves you right for bragging,*" Master Boyer laughed in her memory.

Kate rubbed her eyes. Right now, surrounded by the dead and wounded, and he was planning troop movements? What possible good could that do at the moment? "Could and should are different—"

"It's here!" a soldier shouted from the window. "Transport is here."

Relieved sighs filled the room as a sudden surge of energy filled the exhausted troops.

"All right," Kamre called, walking away. "Load wounded on board for first trip. Rest of you will catch next one. Leges, go with wounded. Now move!"

Kate nursed her second cup of overly sweet tarshu, wondering when it was going to kick in. Sure, she was awake, her blood pumping with the stimulant's rush, but everything still felt wrong, as if she was underwater—close to the surface without breaching it.

They all sat in a paneled room, most of them at a lacquered table, the rest spread out among stiff padded chairs. A holographic screen hovered before the curved wall, graphs displayed in floating light. The news was grim. Eighty-five dead or missing. Thirty-two wounded. Jengta and her little army of Leges had done their best on the injured and eighteen would be returning to duty. That gave Kamre ninety-seven soldiers—less than half of what he'd led two days prior.

Kate closed her eyes. The image of Bira's exploding arm played across the backs of her lids.

"Our number of commanders rivals our number of troops," Kamre was saying. "We require more."

"Now that empress revealed herself," Thetish said, "unleashing her verls on populace, we may find supporters in Iziba."

"Possibly," Kamre said. "Providing they don't blame *us* for that."

"Some undoubtedly will," Jengta said, her twin voices in different shades of exhaustion.

"We may be able to recruit any of their Viatores," Thetish continued, tugging his mustache. "They might jump at opprotunity for sanctuary."

"Are you volunteering to return?" Kamre asked.

Thetish nodded. "I'm most suited."

Kamre turned to Jengta. "What of your troops?"

"What of them?" she asked.

"How many can you spare?"

Jengta cocked her head, her green cat eyes studying the senator. "I have but sixteen, and I explained that they would not be joining you when we made our agreement."

"Things have changed," Kamre said. "This world is no safer than any other. People are dying."

"They are," Jengta said. "But do not mistake my offering of a haven as cowardice, senator. There are more than soldiers here under my protection—the young, the very old, the families and loved ones of those who fight. To join your campaign could out me and draw me under the empress' eye. Yes, you engaged the empress in Iziba without a single Soonati. And if that troubles you, please remember that there is not a single Soonati amongst the dead. No trace of our involvement." The Ipsissimus turned to Hestius, who'd been silent for the last half hour. "I have upheld my portion of the arrangement. This was not what we discussed."

The old librarian's gaze flicked to Kamre, his lips pulsing tight in an unspoken message to stay quiet. He looked to Jengta. "You are correct, my friend. We thank you for your assistance and apologies for any misunderstanding on senator's part. Arrangement is satisfactory." He nodded to Kamre. "Yes?"

The muscles in Kamre's jaw flexed, but he nodded. "Apologies."

"We may still be compromised," Livia said.

Thetish nodded. "Agreed. If empress took single prisoner alive...we should move."

"And you have suggestion as to where, yes?" Hestius asked.

Thetish's lip twitched. He looked to Kate and then to Syn, pleading for some form of help.

Syn provided one. "Hollit, maybe. The nation Erius has always accommodated Outworlders."

"They might even have soldiers to offer," Thetish added.

"Do you have anyone specific in mind, or do you speak in generalities?" Kamre asked.

"I may know someone," Syn said. "I will need to go to speak with them."

"Good," Kamre said. "Progress. Get me introduction, and I can handle rest. Bring your retinue when you go. I want you protected. Would you require more men?"

"Not necessary."

Kamre and Hestius began talking recruitment. Livia insisted more resisters could be harvested from Dhevin, but Kate was no longer listening. Instead, she heard the distant howls of remembered monsters. Men and women screamed, the hounds shaking them like limp toys. Arms and legs ripping free. Blood slinging across pink and white cherry blossoms. A white beam and a soldier's entrails exploding from their mouth.

"Kate."

Blinking, Kate straightened, trying to hide her lack of attention like a distracted schoolgirl. Everyone was looking at her. What was Kamre saying? "Yes?"

"You had said it was possible to control verls."

"Ah, yes." She knocked back the last of her tarshu. The empty cup rattled against the saucer as she set it down and Kate clutched her hand to hide the trembling. "At least that's what Harcourt said. Candace...back when she attacked our tower...she ordered the hounds away from me. She was keeping me alive so she could steal my magic."

"How had she learned this?" Syn asked. "Controlling verls, that is."

Kate shook her head. "I don't know. Harcourt told me a sorcerer named John Dee had claimed he knew how. We believe she might have learned the art from Dee's writings."

"I know this Dee," Hestius said, nodding. "His writings, that is. Athenaeum had several of his works. He was well known in his time."

"Do we have them?" Kamre asked.

The old eunuch frowned. "Not here. We only brought works related to Carcosa and Netru."

"And they're at Athenaeum, yes?"

"From last I saw."

"We need them back. Now," Kamre said.

Kate's attention drifted back to Malto, the screams and the stink of cooking meat. Eventually, it was decided that Kate would carry Livia, Hestius, and a handful of soldiers and family back to Kell. She and Hestius would never leave Livia's flat, but simply wait. Someone would carry a letter to the Athenaeum, requesting Dee's work. Meanwhile, Livia and the others would continue recruitment.

"Give us four days," Livia was saying. "Once Hestius and Kate have confirmed Dee's spell amongst books, we will return with any reinforcements we've gathered."

"Is that satisfactory?" Kamre asked.

Kate nodded. She half listened as other plans were debated, repeated, and cemented.

"Very good." Kamre slapped his hand down on the table, the sudden thump jolting Kate back to the present. "Begin your work at once."

Everyone rose and began shuffling away and breaking up into smaller conversations. Kate sat silent, the image of Astius exploding dominating her thoughts. The night before, she'd revisited the slaughter in her dreams. Had they really whistled like tea kettles when the steam erupted from their bodies, or was that the dream? She couldn't tell. The marriage of dream and memory had taken root.

She pushed herself up to her feet and left, half-aware of the former slave, now servant, hurrying to gather her empty cup. Tomorrow they'd be leaving for Kell and then four days of being trapped in that same damned apartment. Never once in all her fantasies and aspirations for Viator had she envisioned that her role would be VIP bus driver. She wasn't a leader or trailblazer. She was the pilot of Air Force One.

Kate avoided the minefield of private conversations, knowing that if she strayed too close, they'd try to draw her in. She touched her arm, remembering the heat of Bira's boiled blood splattering her. Long before that, it had been Heather's. Would that be it? Would she wear the blood of more before this was done?

And what of Candace? Did she ever reflect on the maimed and dead left in her wake? Probably not. That had been the trade. Candace had taken the magic and left Kate with the regrets. Why then should they still torture her? She had her powers back, why should she still endure the guilt?

Maybe they were still connected somehow. Maybe they always would be. Could Candace feel her? Did she sense her there on that balcony? Could Candace know her fear? It was possible. Three years Candace had siphoned off her magic. And what was magic if not her soul? She'd have to ask Jim.

Kate wasn't entirely sure where she'd been heading until she reached the library. Hiding behind a wall of stacked books, Saso sat at the far desk hunkered above an open tome. He looked up as she neared, his alarmed expression fading as he recognized her.

"Relax, Thetish is busy," she said.

Saso grinned. He licked his lips. "Am I that obvious?"

Kate snorted. "The way he keeps you running around, I'd be surprised if you weren't jumpy." She peered past him to the open book. A simple circle in metallic green ink dominated the page. "What are you studying?"

"Hymns of Dawn. Have you read it?"

"I haven't. Looks like a ward. Dream Walkers?"

He nodded. "I have to master five before I can test for Magister Arcanus."

"How many do you have?"

"Three."

"It's a good one to learn." Kate glanced up toward the door. "Listen, Saso, there was something I was wondering if you could help me with."

He straightened. "Of course."

"I was curious if you still had any blood dust."

"Pardon?" he asked through a fake chuckle.

"You heard me. Look." Her voice lowered. "I'm not going to bust you. I'm not going to tell anyone. But I know you've dusted. I'm just wondering if you have any to spare. I...I need it. After everything that's happened, you know?"

Saso bit his lip, his gaze flicking toward the library door.

"Like I said, I won't tell anyone. I know you understand. It's not like you're abusing it. Nothing reckless, just a little pick-me-up. That's what I need, too."

It was a lie, of course. Saso had been tweeked the night they'd met, the night Livia was supposed to be meeting a rogue Viator and possibly a trap. It was stupid for him to have bumped then, but the fastest way to a junkie's heart, if you're trying to score, is to compliment their control and prowess. Whether it was drugs, alcohol, or video games, the trick always worked. *No, they don't interfere with your life. You got it down. You're a pro.* It worked better if you could also compliment their abilities in bed, the two-front attack guaranteed a hook-up from the stingiest of users. However, Kate would never sleep with Saso, so she took the next best route to his heart.

"Tell you what; you help me out and I'll personally teach you a fifth ward, something that'll impress Thetish."

His eyes lit. "Truly?"

"Promise. Can you help me?"

He nodded. "I don't possess much."

"Don't need much. Just get me one good hit then promise me that you'll never ever give me more, even if I ask, and I'll train you."

"Agreed." He nodded, his smile practically glowing. "It will take me few minutes to fetch it."

"Then get it."

33

ONE HIT AFTER ANOTHER

Saso's concept of a normal hit was about Kate's idea of a full weekend. Back home, the crystal nugget would have cost her a hundred-fifty bucks. It also wouldn't have been that pure, blood red. Kate just stared at it for three full minutes, holding it up to the light like a jeweler. It seemed almost blasphemy to crush it.

But she did.

Kate ground it atop the blue marble tabletop in her bedroom until it was the consistency of talc—like something Syn might coat himself in. Even powdered, it still held that ruby hue.

She cut it into two massive rails and briefly considered saving one. It seemed wasteful to snort it all at once. But no. Saso said this was one hit, and by God, that's how she'd use it. She wasn't a junkie anymore, struggling to stretch it out as long as she could. No way, this was a one-time thing.

Armed with a homemade tooter from a broken pen, Kate snorted the first daunting line. The dust burned, her world filling with the aroma of honey-scented roses. Clenching her eyes, she fought away tears until the sting abated. There, in the darkness behind her eyes, colors exploded, a lattice framework of crackling magic, originating up between her brows and surging through her veins like geometric quicksilver.

Kate sucked a breath. She wiped the tears. Her body hummed, the rush of energy buzzing through each individual atom.

"Wow," she said to the empty room. This was nothing like the stuff back home—that home-grown bathtub shit she'd hocked her TV for didn't hold so much as a candle against this. With each breath the mounting power grew stronger, the lattice more intricate. "Oh wow."

She eyed the second line still waiting on the table. It appeared brighter now, almost glowing a brilliant crimson. Her fingers hesitated on the tooter. This was enough. Holy shit this was enough. The sensible thing would be to ride this out, save the rest for a rainy day, maybe four rainy days.

No, she scolded. One-time deal. She needed this escape, and saving it would ruin the point. She lifted the little straw in a silent toast to Astius and Magus Nari and then snorted the rest up her other nostril.

Once the sting had faded, Kate blinked her eyes and marveled at how beautiful everything appeared. The creamy pattern of her bed sheets, the magnolia blossom walls with their textured plaster, the gilded picture frames, they were all so beautiful. The sky-colored tabletop before her was a masterpiece of blues frozen in an eternal swirl. The tiny traces of red dust still clinging to the polished marble stood out like little Christmas lights. She licked those up, her tongue going numb with the bitter tang.

Kate rose from her chair, her back popping as the million tons of stress lifted away. She moved her arms, spinning them, care-free as a little girl dancing in the rain. She laughed at the thought.

Magic tingled along her fingertips, begging for release. Kate twisted her hand open, summoning a little silver box from a mantle across the room. It flew toward her, landing in her palm with a solid thwack.

What is this? she wondered. She'd never even noticed it before. Kate lifted the hinged lid to discover an assortment of glass teardrops, all colors and sizes, their hues so vibrant under the room's lights it felt like opening a pirate's chest of jewels. Kate set the box down on the table, its surface still glistening with her saliva from licking up the angel kiss, and began exploring her room as if she'd never seen it before.

It felt like that morning in Jim's, power coursing through her as she explored his quiet flat, though she was at least in her body this time.

Jim.

He'd be so pissed if he knew about this, his face scrunching up with anger in that way he did. But fuck him. What could he do about it? He couldn't hang anything over her this time, hold her magic hostage like some moral terrorist. She was a Magus Viator. Junkies weren't Magi. She'd carried him across the fucking Abyss, and now he had an actual Ipsissimus Lex teaching him. No way he could say shit about what she did to relax. He was just a Magister. What right did he have to lecture her anyway?

She shook away the thoughts, the rush of anger releasing. This wasn't any time to waste making herself mad. She felt good. Happy. Here she was, a Magus on another world, living in a glass tower. Getting upset now was silly.

Kate zipped her Samsonite up and realized she'd been cleaning. God, she had so much energy. She needed to do something, see someone.

Tisha.

Yeah, Tisha. Last time she'd spoke to her was on the phone back in Scotland. That was a lifetime ago. Tisha would be so proud of her. She had her magic again.

I should go see her.

It wouldn't be difficult at all. She had more than enough magic to hop home, drop by Whittaker's and say hi. She had no idea what time it was there, but Tisha wouldn't mind a wakeup call if it was too late. Terra was across the Abyss, but a one-woman ring at full speed, Kate could be in Baltimore in an hour...two tops. She was a motherfucking Concord of Viatores even without this little boost.

Kate dug in her bag, finding her topaz, chalk, and the herbs. It was a lot to carry, so she just shoved it all into Jim's tea box. With a flick of her wrist, she pulled the gold and blue rug from the floor, leaving nice wood planks. Kate started the circle when she realized her mistake.

No brazier. Damn. Jim probably had it.

Was it in his room? He shared it with Nate, giving a double-chance someone would be in there. A moment's anger, or jealousy—she couldn't tell—flashed in the back of her mind, but it was gone now. She wasn't jealous. That was just silly. Been there, done that. They could have their fun. She was off to bigger and better things.

But she needed that brazier first.

The best way would be checking the room. If it was empty, great. If not...she'd have to come up with something. Maybe tell them that Harcourt was asking about them? By the time they figured out he hadn't, she'd be long gone.

Happy with this plan—it was a good plan—Kate headed out to Jim and Nate's.

The halls were blessedly empty as she followed the curved passage up the slight incline. There was no light from under the bedroom door. No noises from inside. She was about to knock when Kate realized the problem.

The wards.

Shit. Even once she got the brazier she'd have to escape two levels of wards, the tower, and the outer wall. Escaping wouldn't prove too difficult, she guessed. But getting back would be impossible.

Kate stifled a laugh, imagining her surprise when she'd find herself stuck outside. She'd have to go to the tipi cabin and then bum a ride home, and that would lead to so many questions.

Wait.

No, she didn't have to use the cabin. There was the garden. No wards there and better yet, it had a brazier. "Ha!" she laughed, this time out loud and she slapped her hand above her mouth.

Someone moved inside the room. Kate hurried away before Jim or Nate might catch her. The drip was coming heavy now, numbing the back of her throat and awakening the faintest whiffs of flowers and honey with every sniff and swallow. After gathering her things, she headed down the elevator, avoiding any eye contact with the few servants and guards along the way.

The wards at the front door made her ears pop as she crossed the threshold. The sky above was dark, black winter clouds hiding the stars. Her shadow, cast from the tower's high windows, preceded her, stretching ahead toward the yard's exit.

Following the dark trail, she strolled toward the arch. The old familiar rush of sneaking out danced along the back of her neck. In those early days, when she'd just joined Onyx Tower, she, Heather, Jim, and some of the other lower-ranked students would sneak out, hit the bars, or go looking for fun. She hadn't known of alarm glyphs, let alone learned how to feel them, so it was always a surprise when some of the Lumitors and Magisters inevitably showed up to bring them back. Later, after some years and ranks, she was on detail to round up delinquent Neophytes and Initiates. After that, the senior staff would tuck off and raise a little hell. The students had no idea. The privilege of sneaking out was earned, and Kate had definitely earned this one. She'd be gone and back before the sun came up and no one would ever know.

It was at the moment Kate crossed the open gate that she realized one monumentally important thing she'd forgotten—her coat. While she normally loved the heightened senses from the dust, the frigid air hit her like a thunderbolt, searing her skin with instant pain, all warmth ripped away. Tea box against her chest, she ran through ankle-deep snow, feeling the trail more than seeing it, until she crossed the gate into the garden ring.

Falling to her knees in the soft grass, Kate rubbed her arms, her teeth chattering. Colored lights from the pond welled and dimmed as the glowing ray fish rose and fell within their prison. She briefly considered going for a swim. Even the cool water was still warmer than she was. It'd been years since her last skinny-dip, but decided against it.

Kate already had plans.

Eventually, she crawled to her feet. Melting snow soaked her shoes. *I really didn't think this through.* Some might have called it dust brain, but no, she'd just been too excited and hadn't remembered the snow. No problem.

She pulled her wet shoes and socks off and knocked the rest of the clinging slush free. Once she was away, she'd set them up beside the brazier to dry.

The grass felt glorious between her toes as she followed the trail up toward the ceremony platform. Orange fireflies blinked and hovered above the bushes and within the twisted trees like ghostly candle flames. Moon blossoms dangled from vine-laced branches, their crystalline petals sparkling like ice in the scant light. Kate's wet feet slipped a little as she reached the smooth obsidian slab. The brazier was still there, as she expected, loaded with fresh oak. She'd just need to gather more from the pile beside the ruined hut to use on her trip home. *No dust brain here. No, ma'am.*

She fetched a good armload. Inside a metal cylinder, Kate discovered packs of herbs and a bundle of colored wax pencils. She started to put those back when she paused. Chalk on polished glass would be problematic. Kate kept the pencils. Everything ready, she knelt and had started the first circle when a voice called out behind her.

"Kate."

She spun, the pencil dropping from fingers.

Evan was trudging up the yard.

Damn it.

"Whatcha doin'?" he asked.

"Me. Um. Nothing. Just couldn't sleep."

He stopped at the platform's edge, his gaze moving between the wood, the tea box, and wax stick, so white against the black surface it might as well be glowing. "What's this?"

"I..." She snorted an uncomfortable laugh. "I was just practicing a circle. No big deal. What about you? What brings you here?"

He hesitantly nodded. Even in the dim light, the expression that he wasn't buying it was undeniable. "I was coming to see you."

"Me?"

"Yeah. I was up in the library. Harcourt's poring over that book Nate gave him. Looked out the window and saw you booking it across the lawn and out without a coat. Wanted to be sure you were okay."

"Yeah." Kate's joy deflated, sinking into her stomach like a stone in slow motion. "I'm fine." It was just like Onyx Tower—five minutes of freedom and *bam*. Busted.

"And the coat?"

"It was a short distance. Figured I wouldn't need it. It's not like I was going for a stroll or anything." She laughed, but it wasn't believable, even to her.

He nodded again, and his attention moved off behind her. "Damn. Look at those fish."

Kate turned. They were spiraling now, like a dance, the glowing dots on their backs like swirling, colored stars. "Beautiful."

"Come on." He started toward the pond.

The rays broke their little ballet and started toward the bank, hoping for food.

Kate stopped beside him. Damn, she'd forgotten bread again. Stifling a sniff, she asked, "So Harcourt's found something?"

"Maybe." Evan's eyes never left the pond. "He's up there making notes. Wouldn't say what it was. Just that it was too early to tell."

"He found Carcosa?"

He shrugged. "Wouldn't say, and I didn't ask."

They stood in silence for several long minutes. Fighting the need to sniff, Kate rubbed her nose. She needed to get rid of him. Maybe she could ask him to fetch some bread and a coat for her. By the time he got back—

"So where'd you get it?" Evan asked.

"Huh?"

He looked at her then, directly into her eyes, now lit by the school of luminous rays at their feet. "The dust. I wasn't sure at first, but now that I can see your eyes... Saso, wasn't it?"

"My pupils?" She laughed. "It's dark. They get big."

"Not like that. You're high, aren't you?"

"No."

"Please don't lie to me," Evan said, his voice laced with pleading disappointment.

Kate looked away.

"Saso, right?"

She didn't answer.

"Yeah." He sighed. "He was strung out the first time we met him. How much did he give you?"

"Just one hit. Look, Evan, I know you don't approve but after everything that's happened, everything I saw... I just needed it."

"I get it." His hand lifted toward her shoulder, hesitated, and returned to his side. "I do."

"So...now that you know, I'll just get back to my practice. Nothing to worry about so you can head on back if you like."

"Nah. I think I'll hang around here."

Kate sniffed. No reason to hide it now. "That's not necessary."

Evan sat down on the bank. "I think it is."

"I appreciate that," she said, her brain tumbling over this new hurdle. "But I really wanted to be alone. You understand?"

"Um-hmm. But I'm not leaving until you do."

Kate shook her head. *Shit*. He knew. He might not have known exactly, but he knew. "Any way I can convince you to go?"

"Nope." Evan looked up at her and patted the ground beside him. "Sit with me. Easier than craning my neck."

Kate glanced back toward the platform and the half-started circle. *There goes that plan*. At that regretful acknowledgment, a little piece of her admitted that it probably hadn't been the best idea anyway. She sighed and took a seat beside him.

There, her fingers running through the thick grass, watching the fish and fireflies dance, the regret was forgotten.

"Beautiful, isn't it?"

"Yeah." She doubted it was half as beautiful to him as it was to her right now—the vibrant hues, the tracer flare to each blinking lightning bug like miniature fireworks. *Boom. Boom. Boom.*

He smiled and looked around giving a faint nod. "You know, if you could ever pick this whole place up, walls and all, and just set it somewhere back home, you'd make millions letting people just come in and see this."

The math started running through her head. There were stories, of course, legends, of Viatores transporting entire buildings, even a mountain once. Probably bullshit, but good stories. "I think it'd take fifty of me to do it."

"I don't think the world's big enough for two, let alone fifty of you."

"I'm not sure how to take that. Is that supposed to be a compliment?"

Evan grinned, wide and playful. "A little."

She snorted. "You're not very good at them."

"Not really."

Kate took the first step. She glided her hand across the tickling grass and held his, wrapping her fingers around it. His skin was warm, and he returned the embrace, squeezing her hand tight.

They sat there for some time, Kate pondering her luck. Had it been her way she'd be shooting across the Abyss, alone, and with plans of finding Tisha with no cell phone, money, and dressed in flowing robes like she'd escaped some low-end anime convention. Now she was sitting here, holding hands with the man who'd saved her and brought her this new life. "Where are you?" she asked.

"Just thinkin'."

"About?"

"Candace."

"Wow." She straightened. Her grip loosened on his hand but didn't release it. "You really know how to talk to a girl. You're batting a thousand."

"Tell me about her."

"Well...she's an evil bitch."

"I figured that part out. But what else? You knew her for years. What was she like?"

Kate frowned. "I don't know if I could say I even knew her at all."

"Tell me about the Candace you *did* know."

"She was smart, like creepy smart. Probably the brightest I've ever met. She could read a spell or take a single lesson, and grasp it. But she wasn't arrogant about it. It was just the way she was. Made it difficult for her to teach others. She always found that frustrating, having to break large concepts down into smaller parts or having to repeat herself. But unless she was your teacher, she was friendly. She could own a room when she wanted to. You wanted her to like you, you know?"

Evan nodded. "Was there any hint about her? Like what she really was?"

"I've been thinking about that since we saw that video. Jim and I discussed it. Candace spent a lot of time alone. But we'd chalked that up to her being a solitary for so long. Getting to Lumitor on your own takes some serious time, and she was smart enough, so we figured that was just her way." Kate grunted. "Hell, I don't even know if she really was Lumitor. She might have always been Magus. She was powerful."

"More than you?" Evan asked.

"Oh yeah. I'd been Lumitor for over a year before she joined us. That's the minimum you can serve Lumitor, and it wasn't until Candace that any of us believed it could be done in that time. She served one year. It took me two more."

"Maybe she was just that far along when she joined," Evan said.

"That's what we all told ourselves, too. So then we were both Magister Arcanus. The minimum there is three years, and once again, that should be impossible. She reached Magus Arcanus in exactly three. It took me four to reach Magus, and that would've been a record if it hadn't been for her. But I couldn't have done it if it wasn't for her."

"How's that?" Evan asked.

"She pushed me...or at least made me push myself. Like I said, Candace made you want to make her happy. She'd encourage you, and you didn't want to disappoint her. Mix that with the fact she cleared Magister in three years, so I knew it was possible. She continued Arcanus, and I went Viator, so it wasn't as bad that it took me four." Kate snorted. "Little did I know, she was pushing me to reach Viator just so she could steal it. But it does explain one thing."

"What's that."

"The spell she used. Everyone thought Candace would follow the Viatoric path. She was obsessed with the worlds and the Abyss. But she didn't. Not all practitioners get to choose. Five percent choice, the rest is just following the path you were meant for. But we'd all assumed she'd be Viator."

"But you said it wasn't all choice."

"But she could have. Dennis told me she met every qualification. Do you know how rare that is? Even then, she continued Arcanus. We'd thought it was pride. She could have reached Magus Arcanus faster, and she wanted to prove it could be done. But that wasn't it. The spell she used, the one that steals magic, required her being Magus Arcanus. That's why she did it. Candace knew exactly what she was doing. Even before I knew I could be Viator, she was already on her way to stealing it. I..."

"What?" Evan asked.

Kate's eyes narrowed, a new direction of hatred opening before her. "That last day. My test."

He dipped his chin, urging her to continue.

"I'd taken us to Hollit. That was the first test. Master Boyer let us celebrate by visiting the Arin Market. We were all dressed in Hollitian robes, of course, but Candace wanted a new one—bright yellow. Heather got one, too. She was always copying her. Like I said, you wanted to please her. Candace didn't seem to care. But she went out of her way to show it to me, twirling around, *'Don't you think it suits me, Katherine?'*"

Evan lifted a brow.

"Yeah." Kate snorted. "She called me Katherine. She called everyone by their full names. Jim was James. Ronny was Ronald. Hell, she called Master Boyer Jacob from time to time. Magi get to call Ipsissima by their first names, but she almost never called him Jake. But it was all right. She made it sound somehow endearing. No one could call me Katherine but her and my mother and even then, I made my mom call me Kate since I was sixteen.

"But don't you see? She was fucking flaunting it at me. *'I think it's my color.'* Bitch. Fucking flaunting bitch." Kate let a long breath. "And that right there is all you need to know. She was steps ahead of us from the very beginning. She groomed me just so she could steal my magic and twirled around in yellow, begging for a compliment hours before she did it. She's that fucking cold." Kate let out a growl. She hadn't realized how pissed she was becoming, but now the magic wasn't simply coursing through her fingers, but at her back, almost like she was spouting dragon wings from her shoulders. She could feel them, invisible but there, arcing up and over her. Maybe Nate would be able to see them.

"She's arrogant," Evan said.

Kate barked a bitter laugh. "No shit."

"No. I mean she has to brag. It's not enough that she does what she does, but she has to show it off. That says a lot."

Kate closed her eyes and breathed, releasing the anger. "I'm sorry, but I really don't want to talk about that bitch tonight. I'm not exactly in the right frame of mind to deal with her right now."

He squeezed her hand. "All right. What do you want to talk about?"

"You," she said. "You know everything there is about me. You read files and shit. So, tell me about Evan Derian. What's he like?"

So he did.

Evan told her about growing up in New Mexico. He liked skiing. He told her about joining the army, the plan being to serve his years then head off to college with the GI Bill. One tour turned into a second. Then a second tour ended with a hospital in Germany. But before that, Evan shared funny stories of his squad mates, especially his buddies Steve Sanger and Edgar Soto.

"Most of it is rushing and waiting," he said. "Always has been, Steve used to say. Ever since the first caveman grabbed a club and declared himself the leader, the rest of the tribe had to stand around and wait. It's why they call 'em grunts. Cavemen."

Kate chuckled. "That was bad."

"Still true. Hell, knowing what I know now, it's probably been the life of a soldier since before Earth was even dreamed."

They were laying in the grass a few feet up from the bank, Kate nuzzled against him, his arm below her neck. The lightning bug had retired for the evening, and the only light was the watery glow of the ray fish reflecting off the leaves and the few stars peeking through the moving clouds. The occasional rustling came from the nearby bushes, the nocturnal residents scouring for food.

Evan's chest swelled against her as he yawned.

"You getting sleepy on me?" Kate asked.

"A little." He yawned again. "You?"

"Nope." While definitely relaxed, her pulse was still thumping in her ears.

"Yeah, didn't think so."

"You're the one that volunteered to stay with me. If you're not up for it, you can go to bed."

"I'm good," he said.

"You know..." Her hand slid down his stomach and along his thigh. "I might be able to wake you up."

"Stop it."

Her fingers glided back up his leg, moving inward. "Stop what?" She found the swelling bulge, and he pulled her hand away.

"Stop."

"Why? Look at this place. Are you ever going to find a better spot for this?"

"Not tonight."

Kate huffed, a flash of anger igniting in her chest. "Why not? I know you like me. Admit it."

"I...like you. But not tonight. You're not in the best frame of mind."

She laughed. "So, because I'm a little high, you're turning down sex inside a magic garden beside a glowing fish pond?"

"That's right."

"You are such a Boy Scout. Evan, I'm not going to regret this tomorrow."

"Actually, I was a Boy Scout. But the answer's still not tonight. On a different night, probably a different story."

Kate ground her teeth, the sharp pain of rejection sliding between her ribs, probing around inside her. There were exactly two human women in this entire universe. Nate was spoken for, and Kate still couldn't get laid. *Fuck!* She clenched her eyes, fighting the tears before they could come.

"Hey," Evan said, his voice soft and tender. "I'm sorry."

"No," she growled, now angrier at him for being sweet. Damn it, she was the one throwing herself at him, and he was the one apologizing. Everything was so good, so perfect, and she just up and screwed it up.

"I didn't mean to upset—"

"Evan," Kate said, fighting to keep her voice calm. "I'm okay. You did nothing wrong." She rolled away, off his arm, her back to him. "Look, you're tired. It's probably best if you went back. I'll be fine."

"Or." He slid up behind her, his arm pushing it way back under her head. "We could stay here." He touched her shoulder and Kate's anger melted.

She pressed her back against his firm chest. He was still hard. Not fully, but it still felt good against her lower back—a little comfort that maybe she wasn't a total lost cause. "Are you sure?"

He wrapped his arm around her, his hand almost clumsy in avoiding her breasts as he pulled her into a hug. "We can just cuddle."

"Cuddle? Oh my God, you are a freakin' Boy Scout."

"Eagle. But if you don't want to..." His arm began to withdraw.

"No." Kate pulled it back, held it close. "No. I'm sorry. This is good. I can enjoy this."

His breath felt warm against the back of her ear. "Good."

Kate lay silently listening to whirring insects and Evan's light snoring for hours. Her brain was still running at Mach 3, but she wouldn't move. She didn't want to.

Shortly after falling asleep, Evan had rolled onto his back. Worried she might wake him, Kate remained still. Her mind rolled over their conversation—Candace's deceptions, her pushing Kate to become Magus just so she could steal it. Had Candace actually been Lumitor when she'd joined? Maybe she'd always been a Magus Arcanus and was just biding her time. And what had Harcourt found? She'd have to check with him in the morning once everyone had woken up.

One of those fox-faced chipmunk things tentatively approached at one point, its nose twitching. It got close enough that Kate could have grabbed it, but still, she didn't move. It had become her game. She always ended up in some strange game when she was especially dusted, and evidently, that's what it was for this time.

The foxmunk rose on its hind legs, possibly considering climbing onto her, but then Evan shuddered in his sleep. It squeaked and scurried away. As it vanished into a crop of bamboo, Kate realized she had another problem. She needed to pee.

Just don't think about it. She rolled a little, adjusting her position, but it only offered a few minutes reprieve. Her persistent bladder ached, uncaring that she was happy and comfortable. She moved again, and then again, but it only got worse. *Fine. You win.*

Carefully, Kate extracted herself from Evan's hold.

"No," he grunted, but didn't seem to have woken. He rolled away from her.

Barefoot, and with only the light of the sleeping rays, Kate crept to a discreet spot behind a flowering hedge.

"No," Evan said, louder this time. "Get bed back." Urgency laced his slurred words. "It burns."

Shit. All her talk of his time in the army. Of course he was having a nightmare. Kate quickly finished up and headed back. Just wake him, maybe a kiss on the cheek and they'd be comfortable and happy again.

Rounding the corner past a draping tree, Kate could see him in the shadows. He was sitting up now. Good. He was awake, probably wondering where she'd gone.

She was almost to him when he slurred, "Burns..."

Evan shifted, and suddenly his silhouette elongated, becoming too wide. It quivered with a wet sloppering like a dog above a water dish.

"Put it out."

Kate froze. It wasn't Evan. It was something dark and hunkered above him. "No!"

She raced across the grass, closing the distance. The thing flattened down atop him, melding them into a single form. Kate dropped to her knees, the elemental slithered atop Evan like a net made of seaweed. She clawed at the wet strips binding him, but they held fast, coiling harder.

He jolted and moaned. Some of the thing looked to be in his mouth, but Kate couldn't tell where the Evan ended and the monster began. "Damn you!" She pressed her fist to her mouth and blew hard, her cheeks puffing. Beams of light sprang from between her warming fingers.

Kate opened her hand, and an orb of bright white light floated above her, bathing the entire garden in daytime light.

The elemental squealed. It looked like a thousand interlacing worms, some as thick as her arm and others like wriggling hairs. Its skin grew translucent beneath the light's radiance. Oozing holes ruptured along its surface like leprous wounds, releasing a putrid, milky froth.

Kate tore at the writhing strands, now greasy with the foul-reeking jelly. They slithered and squirmed of their own accord, fleeing into Evan's ears, and nose, down his pants, lacing between his eyelashes, and fleeing to the shade beneath his shuddering body.

"Leave him alone, damn you!" She yanked at the tendrils, but it was as if they weren't connected at any one point, tearing and re-connecting however they wanted. She couldn't shoot it with her lance without hitting him. Whatever this awful foamy mucus was, it seemed to be shielding it from her light because the strands grew stronger, more substantial.

Evan began screaming, foam and wormy tentacles boiling from his mouth. He kicked and thrashed, but the binding tendrils held tight.

"I'm burning!" It was killing him! Evan's teeth slammed down, spraying inky goo, but the strands just reconnected.

Heaving him onto his side, Kate grabbed the clump of the mass nestled at the small of his back. She pulled, but the strands slid and writhed between her fingers.

Evan was shrieking some noise over and over, the tentacles in his teeth and lips making it difficult to understand but Kate soon realized what it was.

"Fire! Fire! Fire!"

The elemental swelled, gorging on his terror and pain. Kate couldn't fight this thing. There was nothing to grab, nothing to cut. Her fingers prickled with the power coursing within it and without even thinking about it, Kate seized onto that, the magic and not the flesh, and pushed.

The creature jolted as if she'd hit it with a taser. Kate yanked. The monster peeled from his skin like gooey spaghetti. It stirred in her fingers, the tendrils tightening on Evan and snaking up her arms. She jolted it again and wrenched her entire body backward, falling onto the grass. Evan howled as the elemental tore free.

Arms still out above her, the creature writhed and squirmed, its putrid froth running down her arms and dropping onto her face. Tendrils reached for her eyes. Kate surged her magic out from her hands, and the elemental squealed.

She rolled onto her knees. Kate came up, the creature down before her. The oozing tentacles wound between her fingers, preventing her from casting. The buzz of power coursed through it, tingling wherever it touched her skin.

Evan was still screaming, his voice warping and raw.

Kate jolted it again. Her knuckles cracked as the ropey body tightened around her fingers. Her eyes watered from the reek of rotting fish and painful memories. The shocking wasn't helping get it off her, and its faster recovery only fueled a growing fear that she was making it stronger with each surge of power.

The idea that she was feeding it latched onto something in her consciousness, some half-remembered lesson and Kate realized what she had to do.

Driving her fingers even deeper into the balling mass, Kate began pulling energy in, drawing it in through her fingers and palms. The elemental lashed and squealed, but Kate held fast, power coursing up her arms.

The beast's magic felt cold. It bristled up her veins like ice, melting as it went. Strange images flashed within her mind—a smoking censer, the tang of myrrh, a downturned face.

The elemental was shrinking in her arms, withering like a weed in the summer sun. The power coursed faster as it weakened and with it more visions, the memories of an alien mind—a field of pale gravel, no...a rooftop. She was on a rooftop, a small circle of smoke her prison. A trio of robed and grotesque figures surrounded her. She couldn't see the faces, the memory hadn't focused on those. Instead, it looked beyond. Towers of steel and glass rose in the distance, rectangles of light shining from planes of blackened mirror. While the elemental had looked at those spires with terrified wonder, Kate recognized that skyline. She understood the glowing sigils emblazoned across the skyscrapers. The figures were talking, laying out their orders—The Contract. Only the caster's name was known.

He had summoned it from the Demhe. But Kate knew the others. *That lying son of a bitch!*

Hatred and fear erupted up Kate's arms. It surged across her body like a scalding drug. Not just her own, but pure elemental emotions flooding her senses. It coated her tongue, filled her vision, and wailed inside her ears. The purest loathing and terror became her world as the creature dissolved in her hands.

Kate collapsed. More power than she'd ever fathomed buzzed within her. Hatred crackled down her bones. Fear squeezed her heart and lungs like the grip of some ancient giant. Gritting her teeth, she pushed herself up. They'd sent that beast, not for her but her friends. The horror of that revelation only fueled that seething fire. *I'll kill him.*

But no. They were too powerful. Too smart. She'd die if she faced them. The inarguable truth of her hopeless situation paralyzed her with ice-cold fear. The two emotions swirled and crashed, each one all-consuming.

A pained gurgle broke through her torment. Someone was screaming. *Evan!*

She whirled to see him. Evan lay on his back, his shirt torn open and wet with evaporating ooze and fresh blood. Scratches crisscrossed his chest, now a knotwork of grotesque scars. Bloody trails ran from a ragged tear at his chest. The golden yeng beetle lay in the grass, its metal legs curled together like a dead bug. A strip of torn skin dangled from one of its hooked claws.

"No!" The unnatural terror surging though Kate's soul seized on that image. Fighting the paralyzing fear, Kate crawled to him.

Evan was staring up at the sky. His hair was coming out in clumps. Patches of his skin swelled and deflated into pink burn scars. His right hand looked almost skeletal, skin over bones with nothing else.

"No! No, Evan. No." She picked up the beetle and pressed it to his chest. Nothing.

She pulled its delicate legs open, pressed it again, pushing them into the little holes from which they'd been wrenched. Her fingers fumbled opening the beetle's clockwork jaws, pressing them against him, but to no effect.

"No. No. No!"

Footsteps raced up from somewhere. The shadows of figures moved in the corners of her vision. Evan didn't stir. His goldie-brown eyes stared up toward the blazing light globe above, his uneven pupils wide and black.

Something grabbed her shoulder from behind. Throwing her hand out, Kate spun, the "Ka!" escaping her lips before she was around.

A crack of shattering bone. A soldier windmilled back and hit the ground, his arm twisted and blood spreading from a jutting bone.

Kate gasped. A dozen soldiers were racing toward her, their weapons scanning the gardens. More were visible through the broken arch, a line of bodies racing across the snow. Every window in Jengta's obsidian tower blazed with light. Alarms blared across the nighttime valley.

"I'm... I'm sorry," Kate stammered to the fallen soldier clutching his wounded arm. She could have killed him. Fear for what she might have done only fueled the rage toward herself.

A pair of rifles were pointed at her. Someone was yelling at her in Dhevinite, but she didn't understand.

Kate motioned to Evan. "I have to help him."

Soldiers flooded into the garden, trampling bushes. Woken birds scattered.

"Please," Kate begged.

Someone was kneeling beside Evan already, shouting orders.

"Kate!" Vorsis jogged up the hill, his short-bladed sword in hand. He barked something at the two soldiers on her, and they instantly lowered their weapons. "What happened? *Garn*, is that Evan?"

"They got him," she cried and crawled to Evan's motionless body. The transformation had accelerated, his hand now nothing more than a ball of browning skin.

Vorsis was beside her. "What did they do to him?"

Kate didn't answer, she was still trying to get the beetle to attach. There had to be some trick to it, a command word or something. *Damn it, where's Harcourt?*

"Kate!" Vorsis grabbed her arm. "Where are they?"

"Who?"

"Empress' men."

Kate blinked. "No. It was an elemental. I killed it." She pressed the yeng beetle hard against his sternum, driving as much of her magic as she could into the device. She had more than enough, but still, it didn't attach. *Wake up, Evan. Don't do this.*

"Katie," Jim shouted, racing toward her. He was barely dressed, his robes flapping. Nate followed close behind him.

"Jim!" Kate cried. "Help me!"

He pushed his way through the soldiers. "What happened?"

"They got him. Help him, Jim."

He was already beside Evan, his fingers weaving silver light.

"Who?" Nate asked.

"Dalton," Kate said.

"What?" Jim looked up, his glowing hands on either side of Evan's motionless face.

"Terrance Fucking Dalton. They did this." Kate spotted Jengta entering the gardens, a retinue of gray-skinned soldiers behind her. But her attention locked on the small figure hurrying behind them. "Harcourt! Harcourt get over here!"

The old man ran up the hill, his eyes widening as he spotted Evan's limp body. "Jesus, no!"

"Help him." Kate pleaded.

The old man pushed her aside. "Evan. Evan! Come on." He pressed the beetle against Evan's chest, but still, it didn't grab hold. "Evan!" He slapped Evan's face. "Wake up!"

Jim caught the old man's hand. "He's gone."

"No. He can't—"

"He's gone," Jim said. "I'm sorry."

Kate's head spun. She swooned, her world lurching drunkenly. *No. No, no, no!*

Jengta knelt over Evan, still staring at the sky. She shook her head and tended to the teary-eyed soldier Kate had wounded.

A thousand questions followed. No, it wasn't the empress. I destroyed the elemental. No, I'm unhurt. Jengta had declared Evan's death a heart attack. Fear had killed him. But Kate couldn't feel it. She was only watching, numb, her mind consumed with the memory of Dalton and Melanie Solomon, who had spilled her own blood to call the assassin. The elemental's hatred swelled. Fear washed away in a surge of rage. *I'll kill him. I'll kill them all.* Negotiating was no good. Hiding was useless. Amber Tower would never stop, and Kate knew what she had to do.

Jim was leading her by the arm toward the garden's exit, his touch tender and compassionate. If she didn't do this, the next attack might take him, too. It could take Nate, or Vorsis, or even Harcourt. Kate had to act.

She pushed her way out from Jim's hold and ran back up the hill. Someone shouted behind her, but Kate didn't hear it. Kneeling, she touched her thumb to forefinger before her mouth, and blew through the open ring. A blowtorch jet of blue fire shot from her hand and ignited the brazier.

"Katie!"

Still on her knees, Kate turned, spying the white wax pencil. She hooked the thumb to the side and the pencil launched into her grasp. Magic coursed down her arm as she began the first circle.

"What are you doing?" Jim demanded.

"Don't stop me, Jim!" The shallow carved trenches for the circle made this easy.

"Damn it, Kate. What are you doing?" His foot came down, blocking the path for the inner ring.

"Don't!" Kate snapped, her hand coming up and crackling with power. "I love you, Jim, but I swear I'll hurt you if you get in my way."

He must have recognized the fury in her eyes because his foot withdrew. "What are you doing?"

Kate continued the circle. "I can't let him get away with this. I won't lose anyone else."

A crowd was gathering. Someone was calling Jengta back.

"You're going to Amber Tower," Jim said.

"Damn right I am." Kate finished the second ring.

Jim stepped inside.

Kate's hand came up again. "I told you—"

"I'm not stopping you," Jim said.

"What?" the power fading from her lifted hand.

"Finish the circle, Katie."

Nate stepped in beside him. "Best be quick."

"You don't need to do this," Kate said.

Nate motioned to the closing soldiers. Thetish was among them his face twisted in indignation and arms waving. "Hurry."

Kate began scribing the glyphs. It was a small circle, only intended for her, but large enough for the three of them.

"Magus Kate," Thetish shrieked. "Stop this!" He ran toward the ring.

Jim heid out a hand. "I wouldn't do that."

"You can't leave," Thetish shouted. "Not from here!"

"I don't think you can stop her," Jim said.

"Where are you going?"

"Baltimore."

"What is Baltimore?" Thetish snapped.

Kate finished the first circuit, she started around the other way, sealing the glyphs. The symbols glowed with the flood of magic. Thetish and Jim yelled back and forth, but Kate pushed the distraction away. She set the topaz in place and turned to the brazier.

"Let me through!" Harcourt shouted shoving his way past the wall of observers. He stepped over the circle beside Kate.

"Don't stop me!" she said, removing the packet of herbs.

"I'm not," he panted. Sweat glistened across his skin. A sheathed witchhunter blade jutted from his belt.

With a blast of magic, Kate dropped the packet into the flames. Rainbow sparks. The smell of cinnamon and rain. Black aether exploded on all sides, and they launched into the Abyss.

34

I DON'T GIVE A DAMN...

The bubble shot through the black like a missile, a swirling vortex of aether stretching miles behind them. It jerked and shuttered, dodging unseen obstacles, passing them long before anyone knew what most were. Their sudden dips and swerves continued down their comet-tail wake like memories of movement.

"Jesus, Katie," Jim whimpered, his eyes wide, crescents of white above the pupils. "Slow down." The occupants huddled away from the glowing wax edges out of fear of being tossed out.

"No," Kate said.

"This can't be safe!" Jim pleaded.

"You wanted to come." Kate flicked her hand toward the Abyss. "Feel free to step out if you don't like it."

"I'm just saying we're going too fast."

Kate didn't reply. Until she was there, her hands wrapped around Dalton's lying throat, it wouldn't be fast enough. Blood thumped in her ears, the anger and hate so strong it pressed into the backs of her eyes like a pair of fingers trying to push their way out.

Harcourt sat, his hands stretched out against the circle's floor to give him as broad of a base as they shook. His thumb rubbing along his scarred finger, he flicked his blue-gray eyes up to the spinning tunnel behind them and then back to his shoes. "How do you know it was Dalton?"

"The elemental," Kate said. "I took it inside me."

"Ye what?" Nate asked.

Jim groaned. "Fuck me."

"What?" Nate asked.

"Katie," Jim said, his voice calm and almost relaxed. "Katie, you need to listen to me. These aren't your emotions."

"The hell they're not," Kate growled.

Jim lifted his hands. "You need to calm down. Don't embrace it."

"How the hell do ye absorb one of those?" Nate asked

"Because," Kate said, "despite what Senator Fucking Kamre and everyone else seems to think, Viatores aren't bus drivers. We are the masters of the Abyss. *This*," she yelled, swinging her arms, "is mine. Elementals are of the aether. They're nothing. Arcani might summon them, beckon favors or bind them, but to Viatores they're just batteries."

"And concentrated emotion," Jim said.

"You don't think I'd be pissed on my own?" Kate asked. "I know who summoned it. I heard the orders. I know everything it did as if they were my own memories."

"But, Katie, they're not *your* memories."

"Stop calling me that! Don't you fucking understand? I remember *everything*. I remember killing Evan. *I* killed him! I *still* feel it."

Jim opened his mouth to reply, probably something dumb as hell, but Harcourt set a hand on his shoulder.

"Then why him?" the old man asked. "How did Dalton get his hair or blood?"

"He didn't," Kate said. "The elemental was following me. But it wasn't sent to attack me. That would have violated our little truce. No, the bastard sent it after those around me. They described Evan to it, but it could have gotten any of you."

"Then why did it take so long?" Harcourt said. "It's been weeks."

"The wards," Kate said. "It couldn't get to us, so it waited." She met their confused expressions. "Think about it. Ever since that night I was attacked, we've all slept behind wards. Every night—the hotel, Livia's flat. We even placed a Red Gate on the train. It's been following us. Shit, Nate even spotted it when we first left Jim's apartment. That wriggling net-thing. It's followed us across the multiverse. And when Evan fell asleep in the garden..." Kate shook her head, swallowing back the guilt. It was her fault he'd been there. If she hadn't insisted on staying and just gone back with him. If she hadn't decided to try to visit Tisha. Hell, if she hadn't up and gotten high, Evan would still be alive.

Jim set his hand on her knee. "This isn't your fault."

Kate pulled it away. "Don't."

No one spoke for some time. Finally, Harcourt broke the uncomfortable silence. "Kate at this speed will you have enough strength to face him?"

"More than enough. This isn't my magic fueling us. It's the elemental's. Trust me, I'm good." She figured it was best not to mention that the dust was more to credit than the creature, but no need for that argument.

"I see." His gaze returned to an immense dream reef cruising past. Everything else was too small to be seen at this speed. Craters pitted its surface. As it glided behind them, Kate realized that it wasn't one, but two continental-sized reefs locked together in a tumbling orbit. Orange flashes of sinewy lightning arced between them.

"You didn't have to come, you know," Kate said. "Amber Tower's hardly the safest place. They blame the Spire for Magus Gregor. Former or not, you shouldn't be there."

Harcourt shrugged, his eyes still on the distant reef, barely visible through the misty black. "Believe me, I don't want to be."

"Then why are you coming?"

He turned, looking at her, his brows crinkled as though it were the most obvious thing in the world. "I have to." He touched his throat. "We're bonded. Talking you out of it would have been impossible. But I swore I'd prevent harm from befalling you, or Nate, or Jim. So here I am."

Kate frowned. The fear returned, lingering at the edges of her anger. What was she doing taking them to the lion's den? She grit her teeth, fighting the overwhelming emotion. Evan's dead goldie eyes flashed before her, renewing the hate. No, if she was to protect them, she had to do this.

No one spoke for half an hour. Kate focused on the flames, her fingers drumming her thigh.

"I may have found something," Harcourt said to no one in particular, his voice hitching a little.

"Hmm?" Jim asked.

"Carcosa. In that book Nate showed me."

Jim perked up. "Really?"

"Well, sort of. It's not Carcosa per se, but Hastur, a sister city across Lake Hali."

"But it's the same world?" Jim asked.

"It is, or at least a world joined with Carcosa's. I'm not quite sure how it works, but yes. Kate, do you know what losfur is?"

Kate blinked. She'd been staring at the flames so long she couldn't see outside of them. "What?"

"Losfur. It says we need five losfurs. I assume that's a stone, as it gives the size. But I can't figure out what that is." Tears glinted in the corners of the old man's eyes.

Kate shrugged. "Worry about it later." She returned to the flames. This wasn't the time to get distracted talking of Carcosa and Kate's shortcomings with gemology. For once, she didn't care about Carcosa or Candace. "Ten more minutes."

The dump of elemental hate had finally faded. But it had only stoked her own anger. The rage burning inside her guts was all hers, and with each passing second, it only swelled. Dalton would pay.

Kate drew the elemental's memory of the rooftop—the white gravel, the flat black of exposed tar paper, a dull silver air-conditioner. A second image swelled, transposing it. The gravel had been swept back over the tarpaper. No matter. The long shadows cast from pale silvery light told her that it was nighttime. Good.

The fast journey had drained all of the elemental's energy and most of the blood dust's magic. No matter. Kate had her own magic now, and it was only fitting that her true power be used for what she intended.

She blew into the flames, a light puff. White gravel scattered, exposing the black paper and a line of the hidden circle. A harder blow blasted away gravel and dust. Kate rotated the image around, selecting the best position. Aether swirled, and then the rooftop materialized around them.

Kate rose, looking around. They were alone. A half-moon glowed in the heavens. To the right, she could just make out George Washington standing atop his Mount Vernon tower. A small brick shed with a steeply pitched roof, and a dingy gray door stood off to her left. She started toward it, gravel crunching beneath her bare feet.

Magic tingled across her skin, the hair of her arms raising in warning. Two wards. Kate wove her fingers, green light welling between them. She fired the emerald beam into the upper corner, blasting a hole through the frame and destroying the pathetic ward. The next beam punched out the lower edge. With a loud, "Ka!" she threw her hand forward and the door shattered inward.

A shrill alarm began beeping. A light pulsed down the stairs before her. Kate started down.

Three more wards guarded the stairwell. She shattered each of them in turn. A landing brought the deafening alarm into view. With a "Ka!" she smashed it, slamming the little red box into the wall as if it'd been punched by a god.

"Kate," Jim shouted racing down behind her.

"Stay back." Kate destroyed another ward and with a hard, "Ka," obliterated the door onto the building's top floor. Splinters scattered across a polished inlaid floor and a thick Persian rug. She looked around, unsure where to go. The alarms on this floor were still blaring, their shrill beeps echoing up and down the passage. Paintings lined the wide hall, staggered between busts of Magi, some so old their models had been wearing powdered wigs. Everything was accented with golds and orange. Amber globes encased the lights, giving everything that yellowish hue that always reminded Kate of the seventies.

Jesus, she thought. *Overkill much?* Onyx Tower had used onyx, of course, but restrained—little accents here and there. They hadn't slathered everything in black stone like some goth-kid's cave.

She whirled as a door opened down the hall. A lean man, mid-thirties, came running out, wearing a sleeveless BRF Marathon shirt and olive green boxers. He froze, his eyes locked on Kate standing in the hall. His gaze flicked to Jim and the others storming out behind her, all dressed in their Soonati silks.

"Wade," she said, recognizing him. Magister Lex. Nice guy. Bad at darts.

A skinny woman, with short hair and chestnut skin, came in next. Shayla, that was her name. Lumitor, last Kate had heard. Wide-eyed, Shayla took a step back as she saw the intruders. Her fight or flight was commendably better than Wade's.

Kate straightened. "Please inform Terrance Dalton and Melanie Solomon that Magus Kate Rossdale has received their summons." She pointed to a pair of elaborately carved doors. "Is that the ceremony hall?"

Shayla nodded.

"Tell them I'll be waiting inside."

35

...ABOUT MY BAD REPUTATION

Despite the gaudy excess of the hallway, Amber Tower's ceremonial temple was tastefully restrained. They'd entered it on the second floor, a wide balcony overlooking the main chamber. Geometric patterns made up the waxed wooden floor—interlocking symbols of every rank raging from Neophyte to Ipsissimus. Concentric copper rings marked the center with a few along the outer edges. It smelled of incense and beeswax candles.

Several wards had guarded the doors and shuttered windows. Kate found and destroyed them easily. She didn't have to, but it felt good. It also passed the time.

Kate had positioned herself so that once the temple doors opened, they'd see her standing in the middle of the room, ready to face them. A good cinematic intro, she decided.

Whispered voices and the sounds of shuffling feet came from the passage outside, but no one had yet opened the door. Harcourt suggested that rousing Dalton and the ruling Magi would take time. It wasn't as if everyone lived here. If they didn't come in soon, Kate would have to break up their little party and ask where the restroom was. While the blood dust's magic was gone, its wrath in making her need to pee had only just warmed up.

The doors opened. Kate lifted her chin. Jim and the other rose from the benches along the walls.

Over thirty people filed in the room, most of whom Kate recognized. Maryland's most influential practitioners, and none of them looked too happy. Two of her old tower mates from Onyx, Ronny Clews, and Beth Finn, were among them. They all wore robes, white trimmed with various colors. Magi Robison and Grey had gold, while Magisters Finn and Ishii had silver. Kate assumed the rest of the colors signified rank. *Cute.*

Her gaze locked onto Dalton. His trim was silver. It matched those ugly-ass eyebrows that were now flat and stern like those of an angry schoolmaster.

The coven spread out in a semicircular line before her. Seven Magi. Nine Magisters. Magister Solomon stood on the right side, heart-shaped face framed with shoulder-length brown hair. Despite her attempts to hide it behind a stoic expression, the tightness at the corners of her lips betrayed her.

Yeah, you better be afraid.

"Katherine Rossdale," Magus Joe Robison said, his voice loud and clear like a judge. He was bald, sporting a pointed, salt-and-pepper goatee like some modern-day Musketeer. Stern eyes regarded her through square spectacles. "Please explain why you've broken into our house at two in the morning and threatened our tower mates."

"Sure. I was summoned."

"Summoned?" Robison asked.

"Terrance Dalton, Melanie Solomon, and to a lesser extent Gerald Hippler." She scanned the faces, spotting him near the edge. His trim was green. "Hiya, Jerry. Remember me?"

Hippler looked away.

"Summoned?" Dalton laughed. "Are you high, Miss Rossdale? I should have expected this from you, but Jim Stevens. Has she dragged you into her delusions?"

"You'll address me as Magus," Kate snapped.

Dalton snorted, his lips curled into a mocking sneer.

Kate extended her hand. She wove the orange threads of light into her sigil, pouring more magic into it until it blazed. All eyes locked on the Viatoric Heptagram. Some gasped. Magister Ronny Clews put his hand to his mouth, the anger in his eyes giving way to disbelief.

"I see your powers have returned." Magus Arianne Grey's hair was too red to be natural or even look like she was attempting it. "Congratulations." Kate had always liked Grey.

"I'd been cursed. My tower was attacked. My tower mates murdered.

And I've crossed the Abyss to find their killer only to have three of yours attack me. Has Amber Tower declared war on me?"

"Kate, what are you talking about?" Ronny asked.

"Candace," Kate said. "She's alive. She killed them. She murdered Master Boyer."

"Candy?"

"It's true," Jim said. "We saw her."

"Magus Rossdale," Robison said. "This is all fascinating. But what do you mean we attacked you?"

"I mean Terrance Dalton sent Hippler there to break into my apartment and beat me up. Failing that, he sent an elemental after me. I paid him twenty thousand dollars to stop. So he and Melanie there sent an even bigger elemental, not after me, but after my friends." She looked straight into Melanie's eyes. "Evan Derian died because of you. But you fucked up. Never send an elemental after a Viator. It told me who sent it. It showed me."

"This is insane," Dalton started.

"Shut the fuck up, Magister," Kate snapped. "The adults are talking."

Dalton's face contorted with rage. "How dare—"

Magus Bernard cut him off. "Magus, just to be clear, you're accusing our tower of murder."

"No, Magus. I'm informing you that three of your members are guilty of that. Now, if you're saying their actions were by the will of Amber Tower, then that changes things. Were they?"

"N...no," he stammered, obviously unused to anyone talking back.

"Good. Because let me inform you of a little bit more. We were attacked at the home of Ipsissimus Jengta Vephar. She has two other Viatores beneath her and a small army. I've removed every ward in your temple. If Amber Tower is declaring war, I can promise you war."

"I'm not familiar with an Ipsissimus Vephar," Grey said.

"Because she's lying," Dalton hissed. His smug demeanor had given way to fear.

"Because she's on Soonat, you single-world idiot," Kate snapped. "Jim, you're a Magister Lex. Please tell them about your new mentor."

"It's true," Jim said. "Jengta is on Soonat. She's been training me for Magus. We live in her tower, an actual tower. There's two more Viatores. Thetish, of Dhevin, and Syn of Torba. There's also an army."

"Swear it, Jim."

"I swear it's true," Jim said.

Kate smiled, wide and mean. "There you are. A Magister Lex has sworn. So ask your own. Ask Dalton to swear he didn't do what I've said."

All eyes turned to Dalton.

"Magister?" Grey asked. "Did you attack Magus Rossdale?"

"No," he said.

"Because he didn't attack me," Kate said. "Not himself. He had Hippler there beat me up. An Arcanus sent the first elemental, probably Solomon. She sent the second one at least. And that one was to go for my friends instead of me. Ask her about it. Ask her how she feels about his death on her hands. Ask Dalton about the twenty grand I bribed him with to leave me alone. Did he pay that to Amber Tower or was that set aside to fund that new tower I've been hearing about?"

"It couldn't have killed him," Melanie Solomon blurted, tears running down her cheeks. "It couldn't have."

"Shut up!" Dalton shouted.

"Heart attack," Kate said. "The man you killed had nearly died in a fire. And your elemental made him relive being burned alive until he went mad. You put him in hell."

Solomon wept, covering her eyes.

"Terrance?" one of the other Magi asked, a skinny man with deep diagonal creases down his scar-pitted cheeks.

Dalton only glared at Kate.

"Terrance?" Scarface asked again.

"This is ridiculous," Dalton said. "Are you actually going to listen to a known blood duster, who's violated our house, and making wild accusations?" He shot a finger at Harcourt. "Look at him. He has a *witchhunter* blade. And you want to take her word over mine?"

"We had to kill a group of Spire who attacked us in Edinburg." Kate grinned. "You wouldn't happen to know how they found us, would you?"

"I...I would never!"

"Right. Because sending others to do your dirty work isn't your style," Kate said. "Fuck this." She looked to the Magi. "Your people attacked me. They killed. They summoned it from your house. Were they acting on your behalf?"

"No." Robison looked to Grey. "Arianne, we know you're planning your split. Did you order this?"

Grey's head snapped as if he'd slapped her. "No. Never! We never discussed this."

"So, they acted on their own?" Kate said. "I've been challenged. If none of you are going to support them, I demand my retribution."

"And what's that?" Scarface asked.

"I think we know," Kate said.

"I won't allow it," Robison said. "Not murder."

"Self-defense," Kate corrected. "They attacked a Magus. What did they think would happen?"

"We didn't know you were a Magus," Solomon pleaded.

"So, you attacked someone you thought couldn't defend themselves? Then allow me to watch your execution." Kate opened her hand toward the Magi. "Go on. Burn them, flay them, whatever it is you do. But if you lack the balls, give them to me."

"I won't let you kill them," Robison said.

Kate clenched her teeth. Why the hell was this so complicated? "Then I demand a duel."

"You outrank all of them," Grey said. "It wouldn't be fair."

"Fine. I just traveled across the Abyss. My powers have been strained. Let all three fight me at once."

"Not Jerry," Solomon blurted. "He had no part of it. He was just following orders. I'll do it. But not him."

Kate ran her tongue across her teeth. Gerald Hippler looked like he was about to piss himself. "Fine. Dalton and Solomon, to the death."

"First blood," Robison said.

"What?"

"First blood. This is still our house. There will be no killing here, and I'll offer sanctuary to anyone in need."

"Then you *are* protecting them?"

"Not as tower mates." He looked to the other Magi. "I propose that Terrance Dalton, Melanie Solomon, and Jerry Hippler should be evicted from our tower. Their actions have caused harm and endangered our coven. We'll banish them. None of our family will have anything to do with them from this night forward."

The Magi nodded. Kate had long suspected Robison was the Ipsissimus and the way they didn't argue only verified that. Grey was probably the Ipsissimus for whatever new tower they were planning, but she didn't argue either.

"Even so," Robison said. "I can't in good conscience allow you to execute them. First blood. That's fair."

Kate ground her teeth. Dalton was babbling something, the fear now in full force. Solomon was visibly shaking, but she carried her chin high, seeming accepting of her fate. Kate's bladder felt like it was about to burst. Patience was spent, and she really wanted this diplomatic bullshit over with. "Agreed."

The crowd dissolved into murmurs and shouting debates.

"Just admit what this is," Dalton was screaming at the Magi. "You're sabotaging our secession."

Jim set his hand on Kate's shoulder. "Are you sure about this?"

"You're not?"

"Look, they deserve punishment. Just...this? Katie, if you kill them, we can't help you."

"Death happens in duels."

"Kate," he growled. "Don't. I don't want you being a killer."

"What do you think we're doing with Candace?" Kate asked, her voice rising so loud that some of the arguing tower members turned to listen."

"That's different," he hissed.

"Tell that to Evan."

Twenty agonizing minutes later, the duel began. The arena was set within the largest of the inset circles—thirty-five feet across. Kate stood along one side, Dalton and Solomon before her, all equally spaced along the ring. From the balcony above, Magus Robison declared the rules. It would begin on his mark. No weapons were to be used. Once blood was drawn, that party was considered defeated. Any further action against them would be met with swift reprisal. His hazel eyes, framed behind square lenses, had been focused on Kate for that last part.

Everyone but the Leges had moved to the balcony. It was safer. Jim had at least stayed down here with Kate, but everyone else was an enemy.

Kate didn't care. Whether it was the bravado from the dust or simply years of putting up with Amber Tower's shit, she wasn't afraid. She smiled at Magister Maya Ing, a heavyset girl who'd once tried to get Kate banned from Whittaker's. *Get ready for a show.*

At some unspoken signal, all the Leges surrounding the circle extended their hands. Lattices of pink light blossomed from their fingertips, the largest and most intricate coming from Grey. There weren't enough Leges to fully enclose the entire arena with radiant mesh. Only a few errant lines flickered from one shield to another, to another. The glowing arena stood fifteen feet high, curving in at the top and bathing the duelists in shifting light.

"Begin!" Robison announced.

Instantly the three combatants cast their own shields, their fingers curling into something like an eagle's talon around an unseen ball. Dalton's was the largest, of course, him being a Lex. It extended from the floor to about a foot above his head. But Solomon was an Arcanus. Hers was no larger than a trash can lid, the edges of the locking geometric shapes rougher and less precise than Dalton's. Kate's shield lacked any precision at all, appearing more organic than mathematic, the lines fuzzy and bent. Though the power of her higher rank made it larger than Solomon's, a full three feet from end to shifting end.

Solomon's right hand ignited with pale blue fire. Her shield dipped, her arm rising to cast, but Kate was faster.

With a loud "Ka," Kate threw out her hand. A pulse of distorted air shot from her fingers and slammed into the incantatrix's shield. The force was stronger than Solomon could have stopped even if her guard wasn't down. The pink shield smashed into her face, knocking her head back. Solomon's feet left the ground as she hurled into the barrier wall behind her. Light thrummed across the entire ring, absorbing the impact, and Solomon fell limp to the floor, blood pumping from a shattered nose.

Green flared in the corner of Kate's vision. She lifted her shield in time to catch a beam fired from Dalton. He withdrew his hand back through the opening in his own barrier.

While healing and protection were the strengths of a Lex, they did possess a limited arsenal. The emerald lance was one of the few truly offensive spells they could wield. A potentially lethal spell. Dalton wasn't taking chances.

Good. He'd been the first to cast one. Now no one could scold Kate for her response.

She wove her fingers, summoning her power. Brilliant green streaked from her hand, far brighter and thicker than his had been. It hit Dalton's shield sending a shock of ripples across it, but nothing more.

She fired again, and again, each shot powerful enough to drill a hole straight through him, but the Lex's shield absorbed every blow. The ozone tang of magic scented the air.

Changing her tactic, Kate stretched her third and second finger, looping them into a jagged glyph. Violet lightning crackled from her hand.

It climbed across Dalton shield, sending sparks. But the barrier was still too large for it to get around.

Dalton grinned, his teeth reflecting the pink light. His right hand tutted a sweeping motion. A black, smoky whip unfurled to the floor. He lashed it up and over his shield like a scorpion's tail.

Dropping to a crouch, Kate lifted her shield in time to catch the black lash. It popped, loud as a gunshot, the whip striking so hard that it jarred Kate's hand. Numbed from the impact, Kate forced herself to maintain the curving of her finger to keep the spell in place.

Damn. She hadn't expected him to know the Inquisitor Lash. Few Leges did, and even then, only the most powerful. Dalton must be at the cusp of ascending to Magus if he could use it reliably.

The whip reared back, readying for another strike. Kate scrambled out of the way as it came down with another ear-splitting pop. As she did, she saw that Dalton's shield didn't quite reach the floor. It was a small gap, merely inches, and too far before him to allow a clear shot to his toes.

Dalton's whip circled above him, the air humming with its speed.

With a "Ka!" Kate hurled a shock of force into the sorcerer's shield to no effect.

The whip came down, trailing black smoke. It struck Kate's shield with another crack. Pain shot through Kate's hand and her shield dissipated, the pink web consuming itself with a sizzle.

She shook her hand, desperate to restore the feeling in her fingers. Dalton's mean smile grew. She couldn't get through his shield, and he knew it.

The whip circled again, gathering speed.

Kate summoned all the magic she could. Ignoring the shield, she fired at the floor directly beneath it. "Ka!"

The wooden floor buckled and cracked. Splinters exploded out. The force rebounded up, sweeping Dalton's feet out from beneath him.

He cried out, the shield and whip dissolving as he fell forward onto the ruined floor. His left hand slid out before him.

Seizing the opening, Kate hooked her thumb. Aiming her power, she lassoed his forearms. She twisted her hand and pulled with all the ample magic she could force. Before any spilled blood from his tumble might drop, she was going to yank that lying motherfucker across the circle and strangle him.

But that wasn't what happened.

A wet ripping came from Dalton's pale arms. The flesh just below his elbows tore. It peeled down, exposing red muscle and white ligament. The skin of his right hand ripped completely free, inside out like a dishwashing glove and sailed into Kate's open palm with a wet plop. The other skin glove snagged on Dalton's pinky ring. It stretched, fighting the anchor. The gold band won the tug of war, and the skin snapped, leaving that one finger intact, the ring at its base.

Dalton screamed, shrill and horrible. Eyes wide, he rolled onto his back, his flayed and bleeding arms before him.

Disgusted, Kate dropped the sticky ball of skin in her hand. Dalton was still shrieking.

All at once the wall of pink lattice vanished from around them. For a solid three seconds, no one moved. Everyone, even Jim, stared at the scene in shocked terror. The sound of retching came from the balcony. Then Leges rushed to the skinned Dalton as he fainted.

Kate wiped her bloody palm across her thigh and looked up at dumbstruck audience watching from above. Most were watching the maimed former tower mate, but several more were looking at Kate, their once contemptuous expression now morphed into fear. In one brutal moment, her reputation as the failed sorceress was lost. Machiavelli would have been proud.

Nate and Harcourt were far to the side closest the stairs. Nate looked away, her eyes clenched and mouth contorted open in a disgusted grimace. Harcourt was smiling.

Kate smiled at Maya Ing who was hunkered over the moaning Solomon. "How you like me now?"

"Magus Rossdale," Robison called. "Are you satisfied?"

She slowly lifted her chin. "Sure."

He swallowed, not from fear or repulsion, but the look of a man having completed a distasteful chore—like putting down a dying pet. "Fine. Let us tend to them. But then I have questions we need to discuss."

36

UNLIKELY ALLIES

The procedure of reattaching Dalton's skin was fascinating in that way a car wreck was fascinating. With a detached, voyeuristic interest, Kate watched a trio of Leges, led by Grey, roll the bloodless skin back down the unconscious man's arm and begin working it with spells. Silver light strobed beneath the flesh like a cloud-hidden thunderstorm. A ribbon of pungent smoke swirled out from a metal bowl beside them.

Jim leaned next to her ear. "Was that necessary?"

"Well, it's probably easier than skin grafts."

He huffed, the breath tickling the hairs across her neck. "You know what I mean."

"I didn't kill him. And he's going to have some gnarly scars to remember me by." She chose not to mention that the flaying was unintended. Too many straining ears nearby. No, she decided. If people were going to say shit about her, let it be this. The Baltimore Skinner had a better ring to it than Junkie Sorceress.

Robison led them and several other higher-ranked practitioners away before repairs could begin on the second arm. They brought them to a lounge—couches, several overstuffed chairs, a large TV, and a kitchenette, sort of an upscale version of Jim's entire flat. A vase of stargazer lilies, their petals dusted with orange pollen, rested atop a side table, perfuming the air with their sweet fragrance, almost masking the sharp stink of burnt popcorn.

"Would anyone care for coffee?" Scarface asked, heading toward the counter.

Everyone said yes.

Kate seated herself in a brown ultrasuede chair. Jim, Nate, and Harcourt took the couch to her right.

Tugging his goatee, Robison waited until all the seats had filled, before starting. "Magus Rossdale."

"Call me Kate."

"Kate." He tapped the arm of his chair, seeming to organize his thoughts. "You'd said Jake was murdered."

Jake? It felt so weird hearing Master Boyer referred to by his first name. "I did."

"How?"

"Candace Cross," Kate said, her gaze moving to Ronny who was towering in the far corner, his arms crossed.

"But how? The stories we heard..." Robison swallowed. "We'd thought it was an accident."

Kate looked to her companions. Harcourt gave a subtle nod.

"I'd thought that, too." So, Kate told them. She told of the spell from the book of John Dee. She told her memories of that night, the all-encompassing blue, the way Candace had controlled the hounds. She told of going to Scotland, and the Spire, neglecting to mention Harcourt's affiliation.

"Hold on. I'm a little lost." Terri Kirpowski, a skinny Magus with long, graying brown hair, opened her hand toward Harcourt. "And how did *you* know about this spell? Who *are* you?"

Kate's stomach tightened.

Harcourt let a long sigh. "It's not easy for me to admit this."

Kate closed her hands, fighting the urge to wipe her now-sweating palms on the chair upholstery. Amber Tower still blamed the Spire for their master's death. If the old man so much as hinted he'd been a member, this would get ugly fast.

"I knew Miss Cross." Harcourt set his coffee on the table. "Of course, at the time, she was going by Leslie Mills. This was the early eighties in Chicago."

"The eighties?" Ronny laughed. "How old was she? Two?"

"About twenty-five, I'd thought. We called ourselves the Disciples of Hali. Nothing serious, mind you, just fun. Remember, this was before the AIDS crisis, so covens and why people joined them was a bit..." He gave an embarrassed smile, glancing at Robison and Kirpowski, who were about his age. "...different."

Kate listened, enraptured by the old man's story, the lies flowing so smoothly that she almost believed them herself. Harcourt told them of David Dourif and Erica Margolis, Leslie's partners over their little group. None of them were powerful. They barely knew what they were doing. It was more of a game, a social club with magic and drugs and sex. But to Leslie, it was more. For her, Carcosa wasn't fantasy.

"It was Erica who found the books." Harcourt shook his head. "I don't know where she got them. Somewhere in Europe, was all she said, and I didn't dig. Leslie was ecstatic. She said they were exactly what they needed to reach Carcosa. The spell came from one volume. It didn't even have a title. It had been torn apart and reassembled, not even in order. There were two other sections, chapters, really, that had been cut from the original work and bound separately in their own volumes.

"It was about that time that the disciples began to break up. Leslie's obsession had begun dominating our activities. It wasn't exactly what we'd signed up for. As people left, she became more and more aggressive. Erica told me about the spell Leslie had found in the book. Told me what it could do. She said one of those smaller books contained a counter-spell, just in case Leslie might get ideas. I'd found myself in a bit of trouble with the law at that point. It made a good excuse to get out of town. So I did."

"And you took the book?" Robison asked.

"No. Less than two months later it arrived in the mail. Erica wrote that things were moving along. They'd made real progress, but Leslie was beginning to scare her. Shortly after that, their apartment burned down. David died in the fire. Erica was found a week later. Cut her wrists in a motel bathtub, they said. No one ever saw Leslie again, but I knew. I knew what she'd done."

"And how did Kate fit in?" Scarface asked. "That was decades ago."

Harcourt pressed his fist to his mouth, conveying heavy regret. "I hadn't thought of Leslie in years. My dabbling in the Art ended with the Disciples, but I remained involved in the...life. A collector, sort of an armchair scholar, if you will. Eventually, I heard of a relic authenticator who'd lost her magic. It dredged up old memories. I did some digging, learned what I could, and once I was convinced my suspicion correct, I contacted Miss Rossdale."

"And you believe this Leslie is also Candace?" Ronny asked.

"He showed me a photograph," Kate said. "Jim saw it, too."

Jim nodded. "It was her. And the spell to cure Kate worked. Candace stole her magic, killed Master Boyer and everyone else."

Kate told them about their journey, the Golden Empress, the missing practitioners (a subject that spurred a few glances between the members of Amber Tower), Kamre's resistance, and the failed assassination. No one interrupted her. Any unspoken reluctance to believe her tale was quickly quashed by Jim's corroboration—the silent nods and occasional additions by a respected Magister Lex were good enough for them. She resisted any mention of Marie Marchand. That detail would only bring more questions as to where she'd gotten that information.

"And that's it," Kate said. "The hunt is still on."

"And you're going to Carcosa?" Magus Grey asked. She'd arrived halfway through Kate's story.

"That's the plan," Kate said, readying herself for the declarations that it was a myth.

Grey exchanged a look with Robison and the other Magi.

"I want to come," Ronny said.

"What?" one of the other Magisters laughed.

"I want to come with you," Ronny insisted. "If Candace killed our tower mates, I want to help you."

"Me too," Beth Finn said above the sudden din of voices.

Kate blinked. The idea that anyone from Amber would actually want to join them hadn't even entered her mind. Ronny was skilled. He'd joined Onyx only four years after Kate. Finn had been one of Kate's first students when she was still a Lumitor. She was full-figured, just shy of overweight and with deep laugh lines she'd regularly exercised. Kate looked to Jim who nodded his approval.

"Your allegiance is to Amber Tower now," Magus Robison declared, silencing the room. He removed his glasses, idly cleaning them with his robe sleeve. "You can't simply leave and go traipsing across the Abyss for revenge." Robison slid his spectacles back on and turned to Kate. "Not without me. Jake was a friend. And if what you said about missing Ipsissima is correct, then it's possible she kidnapped Master Gregor as well."

"Kidnapped?" a plump Magus named Reed asked.

"Of course," Robison said. "If she's stealing their power, then she has to keep them alive."

A new surge of conversation erupted.

Robison leaned close, his commanding voice now pleading. "Kate. Please. Let us help you."

Kate turned to her companions. Jim was staring at her like *Don't look at me.*

Harcourt nodded. "We could use all the help we can get."

"Fine," Kate said. "If anyone wants to come, you're going to need coats. Also," she added, looking at her bare feet, "does anyone have some shoes I could borrow?"

"All right," Kate said, rising from the completed circle. Amber Tower had a good supply of hazel wood, which now smoldered in the brazier behind her, the haze filling the chamber in which she'd won her duel. Its smoky aroma masked the sharp tang of the solvents used to clean the blood. She clapped her hands. "One last time, No one has any magnets, right? I don't want to have someone's pocket explode because they forgot. You don't need any credit cards. There's no American Express off-world."

The soon-to-be travelers shook their heads. There were five of them, more than Kate had expected. Others had wanted to join, but Scarface— now named Patrick Morrison, once introductions had been made—had insisted that no more should risk themselves. Crossing the Abyss wasn't a field trip.

The rest of Amber Tower, who were still awake at this ungodly early hour, crowded the balcony for a good view. None but a cherished few had ever witnessed a Viatoric passage, and most of those who had were going with her.

"No electronics," Kate said. "Leave your phones, watches, anything you'd like to have later, leave it here. None of you have pacemakers, I assume."

A slight chuckle from the audience above.

"If you want a photo, you have to use film. If you use film, you have to develop it yourself. Taking it to the store for prints is a fast-track to meeting the Spire."

No one chuckled at that.

Kate scanned their faces. Magi Robison and Morrison had secured supplies. Magus Grey had been a surprise, but she'd insisted on joining if there was a chance at finding Gregor. She'd also had a pair of old trainers that fit Kate, though a little loose. She tried not to think of her own shoes, probably still in the garden where Evan had died. Then there were Magisters Ronny, and Beth Finn. Kate hadn't spoken to Finn since their time at

Onyx. In those final two years, Kate had been too engrossed in her own studies to have maintained their bond of mentor and student. Finn was as short as Ronny was tall.

"Okay then," Kate said. "Let's do it. We have a long trip."

They loaded up their bags, three pounds of coffee, two flats of Coke, a case of protein bars for Jim, a waterproof tub loaded with books from their archives, and several other effects. There were also four guns, including Magus Morrison's beautiful, inlaid shotgun, and few boxes of ammo for their other pistols.

Kneeling before the brazier, Kate drew her magic. There wasn't enough to do the rocket ship speed they'd traveled last time. The duel had taken a lot more out of her than she'd expected, and the first faint throbs of the dust's comedown squeezed at her temples. It'd still be hours before sleep. She dropped the herbs into the fire and released the spell. The world beyond the circle dimmed and blew away in a rush of aether.

37

CIRCLING HOUNDS

"My God," Grey breathed. She turned a full circle, eyes wide.

"Welcome to the Abyss," Nate said, a smile to her voice.

"I... I never thought I'd see it." Grey's hands trembled, but not in fear. It was like a child suddenly waking up in Disneyland.

Kate clenched her eyes. The headache was stronger now, each heartbeat a distant thunder. "Just don't get too close to the edge."

Jim set a hand on her shoulder. "Are you all right?"

"I'm fine." Kate forced her eyes open. "Been a long day."

Magus Morrison removed a green, silver-capped thermos from his bag. He grinned, those deep, scarred creases making him appear ghoulish in the firelight. "I brought coffee."

"You and me are going to get along wonderfully," Kate said.

Morrison unscrewed the top and poured the steaming contents into the lid cup. "I've always found it good to take care of the driver on a long trip."

Kate accepted the proffered drink. "I wish more Leges were like you."

"Hey now," Jim said, an indignant edge to his voice and his brow arched. "I think I do a fine job taking care of you."

"Yeah, but you only gave me tea. That's why *he's* a Magus Lex."

Jim snorted. "For someone who hates being called a bus driver, you have a skewed way of lookin' at Leges."

Kate blew across her drink. "Just callin' it as I see it."

"And what do you think of Arcani?" Robison asked.

She shrugged. "They're all right. I used to be one, but...had to give it up." She winked. "Speaking of which, now that we're out here, I want to know, are you really just a Magus?"

Robison's mustache lifted into a coy smile. "I had to give it up."

Kate lifted her cup. "Nicely played. You'll be very popular where we're going. With you and Jengta, that gives us two Ipsissima " She looked to Grey. "Or is that three?"

Grey turned her attention from the misty Abyss. She shared a look with Robison and then narrowed her eyes at Kate. "How did you know?"

"Losing my magic made me *real* good at gauging people, and that shield spell was a little too impressive for a Magus."

There, surrounded by the infinity of flowing aether, they traveled, the novice passengers marveling at the reefs and elementals. They talked, getting to know one another. Kate mostly listened, the headache mounting. Harcourt and Robison seemed to hit it off the most. Had the sorcerer but known who the old man really was. But Harcourt cranked up the charm, sharing jokes and stories of his past that Kate could only wonder of their truth. Jim was catching up with their old tower mates, sharing gossip and adventures from the years since they'd last spoken. Nate looked about as uncomfortable as Kate had ever seen her. Positioned at Jim's side, Nate simply watched these new companions, speaking only the minimum whenever required.

With everyone there—Jim, Nate, Harcourt—Kate kept expecting to see Evan. More than once, a hint of movement from one of the others in the corner of her eye made her look up, momentarily convinced he was there. But he wasn't. She'd never see Evan again. The weight of that singular truth pressed inside her guts, trying to find a way to fit, to become her new reality. How long would his glimpsed phantom haunt her? Now, when painful memories assaulted her dreams, would they be of Master Boyer's death, or be dredged from the elemental's stolen memory of killing Evan?

"I'm serious," Jim was saying. "Whole world's flat as a board. Horizon just goes on forever."

"I assume it's on a turtle?" Finn asked, grinning.

"Of course," Ronny added. "Turtles all the way down." He laughed a high, giddy chuckle, his mouth in a wide smile. God, Kate had missed that laugh.

A distant howl ceased all conversation. They floated in complete silence for several long minutes. No second howl ever came, but the conversations resumed much quieter after that.

Despite being the resident coffee-addict, Morrison was the first to nod off, soon followed by Ronny and Nate. Eventually, everyone fell asleep, Grey being the last, the novelty of the Abyss finally losing out to exhaustion. But Kate couldn't sleep. Even if she didn't have to remain conscious to keep the bubble intact, the lingering blood dust ensured she'd be awake for a while.

The steady drain on her magic only fueled the welling headache. She had enough to halve the remaining voyage time but feared what it might do to her pounding skull. The thumping behind her eyes was bad enough as is. Immersed in the silence of the Abyss, broken only by the crackling coals and occasional snores, Kate lulled herself into a trance, a sort of waking sleep, dreamless and safe from bitter memories.

Hours passed.

A keening howl yanked her from her daze. Kate wheeled, her blood pressure spiking in sudden fear. Jim and Nate bolted upright. The others were beginning to rouse.

A second wail came from behind them. That woke everyone up.

"Where are they?" Ronny asked, his head swiveling.

"Quiet," Kate shushed. "Everyone stay calm. We're almost there. Go ahead and get your coats on."

"They've never been near Soonat before," Harcourt whispered, scanning the curling darkness.

Kate shook her head. "Not that we've seen. It could be a wandering pack."

His blue-gray eyes met hers. "You don't think that."

"No. But a couple of hounds doesn't mean they found us. Occupied worlds were teaming with them."

"So they're still hunting?"

"I don't know." Kate glanced to Nate who was quietly listening in. "But it's what I'm hoping."

No one saw a hound, thankfully, but a warbling wail came from nearby. What would she do if they were there? What if Candace's forces had come and gone while Kate was away, and these hounds were just chasing down survivors? She could escape in the circle, but how far could she go? Her reserves were low enough and the dust crash imminent. Kate pushed the fear aside.

She dropped the last three hazel chunks into the brazier. If they did need to escape, she needed to make sure it could do it. Swallowing, she cleared her mind and gazed into the coals, summoning the image of the blue platform. It was clean, spotless. Someone had gated from it since the last time she'd seen it. Kate wove her fingers, and with a rush of cold, the frozen landscape emerged around them.

The Alarm Enchantment on the cabin door tickled the back of Kate's neck as they hurried inside. Someone had cleaned it since her last visit, the furniture put away, blood scrubbed from the floors. She commandeered the bathroom while Amber Tower hauled their effects up from the platform.

That final surge of magic pushing them through the veil and into the world had done it. The comedown had fully arrived. Her entire body ached. The pain in her skull extended from just behind her eyes, down her brainstem and into the space between her shoulder blades, like a single, ballooning channel pressing against all sides. Plopping herself onto a bench, she stared toward the floor as everyone bustled around her. She noticed the reddish brown of Dalton's blood still on her crumpled clothes. She'd tried washing it out back at Amber Tower, but evidently not as well as she'd thought. *I must look like total shit.*

"Here," Jim said, pushing a bag of dried food into her hand. "When's the last time you ate?"

Kate looked at the colorful wafers of alien fruits. She remembered enjoying them once. Now they held no appeal at all. "I don't know."

"Eat," he ordered and then returned to plundering the pantry, divvying out rations to everyone else.

With a few quick gestures, Robison ignited the stove. By the time it was warm enough to chase the chill from the building, the whine of the wedge-shaped transport echoed across the mountain valley.

Heaving herself up from the bench, Kate approached the door to see four bundled soldiers hurrying toward them, their rifles shouldered.

The leader stopped. "Kate?" It was Vorsis.

"Hey."

His shoulders relaxing, Vorsis raised his hand.

The troops lowered their guns.

He touched his hooded ear. "It's Kate. Yes." He scanned the faces now crowding the door behind her. "She has brought people with her."

"What were you thinking?" Jengta demanded. The kindly demeanor that she'd held during all the introductions vanished the instant the servants had escorted her new guests away. "Do you have any idea the risk you've put us in?"

Kate's eyes watered, not from fear of the Ipsissimus' anger, but from the pain of Jengta's loud voices. It was like two people shouting at once. "I'm sorry."

"Sorry?" Jengta's eyes narrowed, her pupils nothing more than black paper cuts across vibrant green. "You knew I forbade any traveling from my home. Syn told me that your spell sent a thunderclap across the Demhe."

"Really?"

"The empress is hunting for us, and you send an alarm to tell them where we are?" Jengta shot her finger up, twirled it around. "Even now, her hounds are circling, trying to catch our scent. So tell me, Magus, for what possible reason did you endanger the lives of everyone here?"

"They attacked Evan."

"And you had to leave, at *that* moment? You couldn't have waited, or told someone where you were going? You couldn't have gone to the relay station? No, you simply left with no regard for anyone but yourself."

Kate swallowed. She was too tired to be mad. "I'd absorbed an elemental. I was out of my mind."

Jengta looked at her for a long time. "That wasn't the only reason." She leaned forward and sniffed. "Hemapulvis."

Kate opened her mouth, about to deny it but Jengta cut her off.

"Your sweat stinks of it. Do you not think I've smelled it before—blood dust, you call it? It's poison. I will not abide it in my house."

"I'm...sorry. I—"

Jengta raised a ringed hand to silence her. "I don't care for excuses. If you weren't needed, I'd remove you from my house as I have with Saso."

Kate blinked, her gaze flashing downward.

"I thought as much. He didn't confess he gave it to you, but I smelled it on him during the chaos of your departure."

"What happened to him?"

Jengta shrugged. "He's folded into the soldiers. Medic. His journey into the Art is over. Syn has taken Senator Kamre to Hollit to negotiate a new base of operations. Thetish was to have left for Iziba to recruit, but in your absence, he's stayed. We needed a Viator here, and you weren't."

"I'm sorry."

"You were to have escorted Livia and her agents to Dhevin. Hestius has given her a letter for his followers at the Athenaeum to release all of Dee's writings. The recruitment and securing these works is critical to our success. You need to go."

"Now?" Kate blurted.

Jengta frowned, a strange expression on her smooth, slate-colored face. "Yes."

"I can't. I'm drained and feel like shit at the moment."

"Because of your poison?"

"Yes," Kate said. "It's a hangover."

Jengta's head cocked. "And this pain is why you want to delay us further?"

"I don't *want* to. It's just that I can't."

"Simple enough." Jengta rose from her chair and approached Kate. "Be still." She pressed her fingers into Kate's temples. Her long thumbs moved in sweeping circular motions.

A soothing warmth spread into Kate's pounding skull. Kate sighed, the pressure behind her eyes melting away. The calming wave rolled down the base of her skull and relaxing each vertebra before spreading out to each of her tight joints.

Kate blinked her eyes. The pain was completely gone. "Thank you."

Jengta shoulders slumped. She returned to her chair, one hand against her forehead. "I've taken your pain, Magus. Now do what I've ordered. You have one hour to rest before you leave."

38

VOICE LESSONS

The aroma of stewing onions, bat meat, and noodles filled Livia's cramped apartment. The door locked and windows shuttered against spying eyes made the unmoving air sticky and hot.

By the light of a hooded lamp, Kate leaned over an ancient book, studying the crisp writing, penned in white and red. The words were Dee's, but the writing wasn't. Whatever scribe had learned the spells, imbuing them into these near-perfect reproductions of Dee's grimoire, had lacked the flair of his penmanship. Perhaps it was the obsessive perfection to each letter, the angles as precise and uniform as if they'd been typed.

She jotted notes onto a pad beside her and flipped the page, coming face-to-face with a three-color rendition of a verl hound. This was it. While a brilliant sorcerer and scholar, Dee's artistic skills were crude at best. The nameless scribe who'd copied the image was worse. The skewed proportions, its back flat as a tabletop, the claws just a trio of hooks emerging from bulbish paws. No matter. The words, meticulously written below and above the image, were all that mattered. Gripping her pen tighter, Kate leaned closer and began to read.

After carrying Livia and five other Dhevinites across the Abyss, a journey that took twelve mind-numbing hours, Kate had passed out. She slept for nearly an entire day. Once rested, she headed back alone.

It had been her first solo trip across the aether. It was lonelier than she'd imagined, the silence oppressive. There, lying on her back with nothing but her thoughts, she mourned Evan. Once the tears finally came, she sobbed, begging him for forgiveness.

She arrived at Jengta's amidst a whirlwind of activity. The hounds outside Soonat had become more plentiful, but Syn had returned from his expedition having secured a new headquarters, a monastery on Hollit called The Order of Shezmu.

Joined by Thetish and fifty refugees, Kate accompanied Syn back to the flat world. There, beneath the sea-green sky, she wandered the paved courtyard, surrounded by lion-headed statues and overlooking a terraced vineyard, until she'd committed the place to memory. Thetish left for Iziba. Syn returned to Soonat to shuttle more refugees, and Kate traveled back to Dhevin to spend the next week trapped in a tiny flat that reeked of sweat and boiled vegetables.

The first four days were uneventful. Kate paced the apartment, unable to go out as Livia and her conspirator army of wives and minor nobles headed out each day to recruit.

"We've found twenty more soldiers," Livia had told her their third evening over dinner. "They're spreading word, so it may be more soon."

"We don't have that much room in here," Kate had said around a mouthful of salty bread. "It'll take us two trips minimum."

Livia shrugged. "Too many troops is acceptable problem to have, yes?"

"If they're spreading the word, it could get to the empress' people. How much are you telling them?"

"Everything," Livia said with a smile. "Our brave battle in Iziba—near victory. We simply require more forces to meet her when she arrives on Ryzut."

"Ryzut?"

"According to Durio's map, that's next world she'll conquer."

"Ah," Kate said. "So if the empress does hear, she'll be expecting us to attack her there." She picked at the crust of her bread. Then she looked up at Livia with a tilted smirk. "But we're not going to Ryzut."

Livia raised her spoon, offering a conspiratorial smile. "Misdirection is its own breed of magic. And in this, I am Magus. While False Empress readies herself for Ryzut, we shall storm Carcosa."

Kate nodded a salute.

Thetish had laid claim to Harcourt's book that mapped the path to Hastur. He'd chastised her for not knowing about Iosfur, the dream pearls found only inside the Demhe. Once he was done, Syn, and finally Kate, would learn the path.

But gathering dream pearls required stepping directly into the Abyss, exposing oneself to its denizens. No one wanted to brave the expedition until Kate had learned to control the hounds. And after six days of boredom in the carved basalt apartment, the books arrived.

Kate read the instructions carefully. Unlike other spells she knew, this one required no finger gestures or scribed symbols to focus the magic. Instead, she found detailed instructions in channeling it into her voice.

Closing her eyes, she moved the magic within her toward her throat. It was a simple trick. Shifting energies was the fundamental training for an Adeptus. But the practice was mostly aimed at directing it to the hands, eyes, or the seven energy hubs. Yes, there was a hub in the base of the throat, but not the vocal cords—or more precisely, the space between the vocal cords.

Pressing her fingers against her neck, Kate breathed a single tone. "Ahhhhhhhhh." The magic was there, but not where it needed to be. Releasing the energy, she started again. Kate drew the magic to her voice box, circled it around twice clockwise and then twice anticlockwise. Carefully, she slid the ring of magic inward spreading it like a drum head across her windpipe.

"La-la-la-laaa." There. She had it. But only an instant, the words passing through the warm membrane and infusing with magic. "La-la-laaa. Do-ray-meeeee."

"Pardon?" Ammia, an older woman with white dreadlocks and faded purple tattoos around her eyes, stuck her head out from the kitchen.

"Nothing," Kate said, the magic gone.

"Were you singing?" Her lips parted into a curious grin, exposing the ivory teeth, too perfect and gleaming to be real. Despite her grandmotherly demeanor, Ammia had been a decorated warrior in her youth.

"Sort of," Kate said.

"Good." The old woman nodded in approval. "Livens place up." She withdrew into the kitchen, humming her own upbeat tune.

Kate returned to the book, eyeing the terrible illustration, ruby ink dripping from its fangs. She had the spell, but there was no way to test, know if it was right, until she faced one up close. There'd be no room for error.

39

THE GARDEN OF GODS

Ryzut fell without incident. Spies, who watched the Golden Empress' procession, reported that she was escorted by twice the Netru as she'd had in Iziba. Whether Candace had been relieved or disappointed that no one had attacked her, Kate could only wonder.

Kamre's army had swelled to over four hundred. In addition to the newly recruited Dhevinites and Izibans, the monks of Shezmu had offered their service.

Unlike the familiar Hollitian robes—black for men, vibrant colors for women—the monks were clad in the deepest of purple, almost the same hue as their sun-darkened skin or the once eggplant tips to Nate's now scruffy hair. Pale yellow, like aged paper, peeked from beneath the folds along the inside of the dark garments. Each carried a pair of lion-headed sickle blades, one for each of Shezmu's dominions—the knife for harvesting wine grapes, the sword to slaughter wicked gods. Fulfillment of this second task had only been regulated in the eradication of small cults. The killing of an actual god, self-proclaimed or otherwise, was too irresistible for the priests to forgo.

Kate wondered how much the Shezmu priests of Ancient Egypt had resembled their Hollitian counterparts.

Shielding her eyes from the low morning sun, she emerged from the white stone barn, now serving as their bunkhouse. The smell of wood smoke and rain-wetted earth carried on the morning breeze.

From beneath the shade of her lifted hand, her gaze followed the glinting line of the spiraling train track that ran the mountains' spine across the vineyard's valley. At the base, near the banks of a stream still nestled in the mountain's shadow, soldiers trained in little circles, swords clanging in mock combat. Several more practiced with large, insulated shields to stop the Netru rifles. They moved in formation like Roman legionaries. Crows cackled and circled above on ebony wings, voicing their displeasure at the intruders who'd invaded their feasting grounds.

A horn sounded from a tower behind her, two urgent blasts. At once the training soldiers put away their weapons and melted into the fields like workers as a train sped into view.

Kate's attention moved to the crowd within the courtyard beside her, all eyes turning her direction. Most were monks, their dark violet robes now traded for dun-colored gauze, wrapping them like mummies. None of them had owned pants, and their flowing vestments wouldn't be congruous for their cold destination. All wore their sickle blades, but some carried bows. Others held spades and picks. Kate doubted how useful they'd be. Dream reefs weren't like mountain fields.

The crowd parted as she approached. Thetish stood at the center of a wide chalked ring. Only a few arcane glyphs decorated the space between the outer bands.

He raised his hand as she stepped across the circle. "Magus Kate, are you ready?"

"As much as I can be."

Thetish's waxed mustache lifted into a humorless smile. "It's your neck."

Kate winked. "Wouldn't have it any other way."

He snorted, evidently unimpressed with a little bravado, and signaled to Vorsis.

All at once the twenty soldiers and thirty monks entered the circle, carrying enough supplies for a ten-hour expedition. The soldiers wore crossbows slung over their shoulders. Since no one was entirely sure how well firearms would act in the Abyss or eventually on Carcosa, Kamre had ordered their training in the primitive weapons.

"What are you doing here?" Kate asked as Jim scooted his way up beside her.

"I'm on medical and support with Grey. Besides, the Iron Word requires I come with you."

"You and I aren't bound."

Jim shrugged. "No, but I am to Harcourt, and keeping him alive means I have to keep you alive, so it's all the same, isn't it?"

Kate snorted. "And what about you?" she asked Nate.

"Naw. I'm comin' because I wouldn' pass it up. But if it makes ye feel better, sure, I'm here for ye."

"My hero."

"And don't ye forget it," Nate said.

Kate spied Grey huddled beside Ronny and the other Leges, trying to stay out of the way. Despite being crammed shoulder-to-shoulder, the red-haired Ipsissimus was grinning, her bottom lip pinched between her teeth.

"You look happy," Kate said, pushing her way past the back-slung crossbows.

Grey's smile widened at its discovery. "And you're not?"

Kate shrugged. "That's different. I'm here to do the undoable. This all goes according to plan, you'll be sitting around twiddling your thumbs."

"I'll be watching the Abyss."

"I'd figured it might have lost some of its sparkle for you by now."

"I can't imagine it'll ever grow old. Honestly, Kate, once this is all done and behind us, I would gladly call you tower sister."

Kate paused. "Are...did you just invite me into your tower?"

"I did. You would be a welcome addition to any coven."

"Just because I can take you into the Abyss," Kate said.

"That's a plus to be sure, but don't think that's the only reason. You're fearless, Kate. I think everyone could learn from you."

"Trust me, I'm not fearless."

Grey cocked her brow. "I'm not implying you don't get scared. Of course you do. But you're fearless, nonetheless. That's what makes a Viator. They're brave enough to break the veils of reality. Do you think anyone could have done what you did? All the shit you took, and you still endured. I'd be honored to take you into my family."

Kate swallowed. A strange pressure welled in her chest, moving up into her throat. Grey was a Lex, the highest form of Lex. An Arcanus might stretch the truth for a compliment, but not her. Grey never said anything she didn't mean.

Kate blinked away a sudden urge to cry. "In Amber Tower?"

Grey gave a noncommittal smile. "Or Citrine."

"You're calling your new tower Citrine?"

"That was the vote. I think you'd find more than enough of us eager to learn from you."

Citrine? Kate wasn't sure if she could get used to that. It felt wrong to swear to anything but Onyx, even if Onyx was forever gone. "I tell you what. Let's put a pin in that discussion until all this business is over and done."

"I can agree to that. Just remember, when Robison comes offering you a seat at Amber, I asked first."

Kate glanced to Ronny who was staring at his shoes, trying really hard to act like he wasn't listening. "I don't see that happening."

"I do," Grey said. "I've known Joe a long time. He's planning to whether he knows it or not. But I invited you first."

"Firsties?"

"Dibs. It's a law as old as magic."

Chuckling, Kate side-stepped her way back to the brazier.

"Don't let your head get too big there," Jim whispered once they were away.

Kate jabbed him with an elbow. "Whatever."

"Yeah, well you don't see them getting into a bidding war over me. Tell you what, if you do decide to join a tower, don't do it till they grovel. Maybe offer you a car or somethin' to make up for all the piss you took."

"Sure. You want to be my agent?"

"Damn right, I do."

"We're ready," Thetish announced.

Taking her position as Second, Kate knelt beside him. Thetish's ceramic brazier looked like polished eggshell, as thin as paper, but stronger than steel. His long fingers wove the glowing glyphs with more of a sweeping grace than Kate could, his entire arm moving in sort of a liquidy dance. She offered him a short silver rod with a bulbous round end like a baby's rattle.

Thetish thumbed the lever along the side, and the bulb opened like a metal flower, dumping the herbs into the fire. Sparks sputtered with the smell of spring rain, and they slid into the Abyss.

Having never traveled the Demhe before, most of the monks gasped and gawked, their eyes wide with wonder. Without coordinates scribed into the ring, the bubble sat motionless, misty aether floating around them.

"So you know where we're going?" Kate asked.

Thetish nodded. "I saw promising one on my last voyage from Iziba. We'll retrace path and see if it's still there." The sorcerer wove his fingers, twisting filaments of light between them like a cat's cradle. The bubble jolted. A few murmurs of surprise as people staggered, and then they began accelerating like a subway car from a dead stop.

Kate studied Thetish's movements, the casual intensity in which he manipulated the magic. She'd never just piloted her way through the Abyss before. It was always with a beginning and end coordinate, a set path between them like rails. The speed was all she'd controlled. Thetish meanwhile, had dedicated years to free-form travel, exploring the secret realms outside of concrete destinations. Joyriding, though he'd likely scoff at the term.

They traveled for nearly an hour, moving deeper into the Abyss. They passed several small reefs, but none large enough for their needs. A dozen low conversations in four languages filled the bubble, their participants all scanning the gloom as they passed the time.

A Soonati soldier pointed out into the mist, her jade-colored eyes fixed and wide.

Several gasps followed. Kate twisted around to see.

"What the hell is that?" Grey breathed.

A cluster of greenish blue light, haphazardly arranged in rows cruised along beside them at the very edges of sight. Flashes of pink and yellow swarmed lazily about it.

"Oh wow," Ronny said. "Now that deserves a camera."

"Is tha' an elemental?" Nate asked.

"Not exactly," Kate said, her eyes riveted to the enormous shape. It looked almost like a colossal tadpole or prehistoric fish, but with three sweeping fins equilaterally spaced along its length. The greenish lights dotted along its ridged body, like little runways. Judging its scale was nearly impossible with nothing around it, but Kate guessed it to be the length and breadth of a jumbo jet. "It's an Abyssal Whale."

"Wait, there's whales?"

Kate nodded. "I've never seen one."

"Because you don't explore," Thetish said. "Once, near Dhevin, I witnessed herd of two dozen." He veered the bubble closer.

Several passengers cried out, reaching for weapons.

"Oh, stop it," Thetish scolded. "Just...look at it." A strange reverence accented his voice.

"My God," Kate breathed as they neared. It was easily twice as large as she'd first guessed. The great, wing-like fins rippled, the lights dancing across them. The swarming yellow and pink lights weren't part of it at all, but something else. A school of puffy balls with pulsing, luminous hearts, orbiting the whale like tiny fish, though each was probably the size of a basketball.

"While fear and ugliness seed elementals," Thetish said, to no one in particular but loud enough for everyone to hear. "These are born of virtues —love, happiness, innocence. These are everything we are that is good. Never fear them. They protect the Demhe, consuming ugliness."

"They eat elementals?" Nate asked.

"Oh yes," Thetish breathed, the lights shining in his eyes like stars. "Magus Kate, witness it and know that we are not masters here. We are... nothing but travelers in garden of gods."

"Do they get bigger?" Grey asked.

Thetish nodded. "Much. And there are entities even larger than them."

"Like what?"

"Nameless powers that don't wish to be seen, and that no one should see," Thetish said.

"Have ye seen 'em?" Nate asked.

"No."

"Then how do ye know they're there?"

"I've heard their piping across Demhe. I've seen whales flee and I had no desire to witness what could frighten them."

They followed the whale for some time, keeping a safe distance as it twisted and corkscrewed through the mist. Then without warning, it vanished, the lights winking out in a wave beginning at its tip and down to its tail. A minute later it came back, the lights reappearing in the same fashion.

"There," Thetish said.

Kate realized that the whale hadn't vanished at all. It had passed behind something.

A great shape emerged from the swirling aether, an enormous reef, several miles in diameter, slowly tumbling through the misty void.

Thetish raised his hand in silent thanks to the whale and slowed the bubble, maneuvering beside it. Kate's pulse began thumping in her ears.

"Are you ready, Magus?" Thetish asked.

Kate rubbed her sweating palms across her jeans. "I suppose I am."

"You'll do fine," Jim said.

Trying to steady her racing heart, Kate touched the witchhunter blade fixed to her belt and the soft bulge inside her jacket pocket. She had everything she needed. Chin high and back straight, she approached the circle's edge. All eyes watched her as she looked out across the Abyss.

There's nothing to fear. And with that thought, Kate stepped across the glowing border and into infinity.

Her stomach lurched in a moment of weightlessness, like the sensation of a fast car cresting a hill. Cold enveloped her, not air as if stepping into a freezer or outside one of Jengta's gardens into the snow, but more like sliding into still and frigid water.

She fell for only a moment, but imagined ground beneath her, and she stopped with a jarring of bending knees. *You're not going to freeze*, she told herself, but the thought only lessened the cold to an uncomfortable chill.

Turning her head, expecting to see Jim and Nate watching her, she saw only aether. Perhaps the dark curls eddied slightly more where the bubble should have been, but there was no other trace of it.

A moment's panic flashed down her spine, lizard brain jump-starting her fight or flight. She was alone in the endless Demhe, no food, no water, no way out. No, rational brain reminded. The bubble was still there. She was a Viator. *This* was her realm. Until this moment, she'd only watched the Abyss through a window. But now, now she was truly inside it, floating in a sea of aether.

And there's fifty people watching you right now, she realized. *Wipe that scared look off your face and act like a Viator.*

Kate turned back to the reef, huge, its features hidden in shadow. Imagining steps beneath her feet, she walked toward it. The sensation was incredible. The dreamed floor wasn't solid, but slightly yielding like walking across a plush mattress. It formed instantly as her foot descended, filling no more space than she needed to step, and then evaporated away the instant her weight left it. She stopped before the reef and blew into her hands. Light welled between her fingers and Kate released the glowing orb.

A sudden burst of colors erupted from the titanic reef. Blues and golds and sparkling reds glistened across its surface, seeming to dance in the moving light. In this world of black and grays, a single light had revealed the hidden beauty. The orb continued higher, at least it felt higher as there was no real *up* or *down* here. More and more of the reef came into view. Tiny rivulets of white mist coursed along its surface, forming ponds and miniature falls.

Faint lights shimmered around her. Not lights, Kate realized, but reflections, like the way a dog's eyes glowed in the headlight of a passing car. The little lights moved, swimming in the aether, some fleeing the ascending light globe, others chasing it. Curious will-o-wisps. Whether they were infant dreams, the souls of the dead, or a billion sleeping dreamers across a thousand worlds, Kate could only wonder.

A rounded peak jutted from the dream reef's side. It seemed the best vantage to look out for elementals and hounds. Now that she was exposed, the light globe shining like a beacon and her scent drifting on the unfelt currents, they would come.

Cresting the hill as she neared, Kate realized that the reef's shape wasn't random at all. It was a head, the peak a hooked, aquiline nose, easily eight hundred feet high. Lakes of white mist filled the hollows of its eyes and open mouth, its lips rimmed in glistening minerals like sea-tumbled glass. Carefully, Kate stepped to the side, shifting the gravity around her. A moment's vertigo, but then the reef was below her.

With one cautious toe, she stepped down onto the jagged surface. It didn't crunch or give in any way—hard and immobile as a diamond. Settling her weight down, Kate smiled. She was the first person, possibly the first living creature to have ever set foot on this infant world. With luck, they'd harvest one of its seeds.

Kate raised her hand in the direction of Thetish's bubble. Vorsis appeared, seemingly out of nowhere, he fell, further than Kate had, before slowing to a floating stop. Another soldier followed, and then another. Leges came next, each releasing their own light globes like flares. Some walked toward the reef, others swam. Two flew. One terrified Dhevinite crawled.

They broke into teams of five, each with two workers, two soldiers, and one Lex. Each group claimed their own section of the nose—gravity being wherever they chose, so the slope wasn't a problem. They kept close, all within a hundred feet of each other and all in Kate's line of sight.

She scanned the aether for movement, both dreading and praying to hear the howl that had poisoned her dreams all these years. Never in her life could she have imagined that she'd ever want to see a verl hound. Metal clinked as picks and spades ineffectively assaulted the terrain. Eventually the searchers merely moved in circles, scouring for any signs of pearls.

Attempting to shift her stance, Kate realized that her feet were stuck. Her shoes had sunk a centimeter into the ground. She pulled her right one free with a squelch of rubbery suction. Then she extracted her left shoe. While hard on initial contact, the reef softened like potter's clay beneath the steady pressure. She'd need to keep moving in order to not get stuck. Eyeing the two footprints now clearly imprinted on the giant's nose, she wondered what form, if any, those fossils might permanently leave on the gestating universe.

Voices cried out. A monk held his fist aloft in triumphant excitement. Several more circled around him fighting for a glimpse of something in his open hand.

"That's one," Kate said. Fourteen more to go. This was going to be easier than she thought.

One of the Leges, a gray-skinned Soonati named Chachory was heading toward her, almost flying with long, gliding steps. "Magus Kate," he said, his creepy twin voices high with excitement. He stopped beside her, though his chosen gravity was about thirty degrees different. He thrust his hand toward her, a globular pearl resting inside it like a sacred offering. "We found one."

Kate plucked the pink iridescent stone from his open palm. Faint bands of blue and silver ran across the smooth surface. She rolled it between her fingers. The dreams and concepts of a thousand souls had coalesced into this singularity, wrapping it layer by layer into something beautiful. It had floated for untold ages through the aether until landing atop this reef to seed. Was this blue skies, or green? Was this four-limbed mammals or two-headed birds? The only way to know would be planting it and waiting an eon for it to bloom.

"Too small," she said.

"Are you certain?"

Kate nodded. "They must be the size of a sheep's eye. I'm sorry."

Chachory's shoulders slumped as Kate placed it back into his hand, as if it weighed twenty pounds. "What do we do with it?"

"We'll keep it for now. Give it back to the person who found it."

"At once, Magus." He left, his pace much slower than his arrival.

Shifting her feet so they wouldn't stick, Kate returned her attention to the aether. Nothing moved in the distant curls. This might take longer than she'd hoped.

───────

Three exhausting hours passed before a second pearl was found. As the cheers erupted down the slope, the hair along Kate's neck prickled upright as a distant howl answered the call.

Other heard it as well, their heads swiveling from the celebration and toward the misty black. The cheers lowered, then silenced as a second howl rang. Closer.

Soldiers clambered for their weapons. Vorsis shouted orders. The groups of searchers hurried together, circling up like old-fashioned wagons. Somewhere, within Thetish's invisible bubble, Kate knew that crossbows were being readied. She scanned the aether.

There'd been movement before, a shy elemental had circled twice, but now something genuinely awful was stalking them. A bark, sounding like a madman's yip, came from her left.

Kate spun to face it, but there was nothing but a whorling of freshly disturbed aether fifty yards away.

There! A dark shape galloped through the mist, coming up from the opposite direction from where it had first howled. Archers tracked it, their bows raised. Kate had to meet it before it closed in. She only prayed it was alone.

Kicking off where she stood, Kate glided down to where the searchers huddled. It was more of a controlled fall than flying, sort of moving the world around her.

The circling verl hound retreated off into the aether.

"Hey!" Kate shouted after it. "Come here, you ugly fuck."

The creature emerged from the mist, but stood there at the edge, its head moving side to side like a cobra. Kate focused her magic into her throat. She opened her lips to call it, but then the beast charged.

Its malformed infant's head came into full view of the floating light globes. A webwork of red and purple veins ringed the flared nostrils of its eyes. Its lipless mouth opened in a screaming howl.

Cold fear shot down Kate's chest. "Stop!" she commanded, but the magic wasn't there. The beast was coming closer. Archers scattered to the sides for a clean shot from behind her.

She gathered her power again, circling it one way around her vocal cords and then the other. The hound was thirty feet away, one good leap and it'd be on her. Bows creaked. Sensing something, the verl hound veered sharply to the right with a sudden surge of speed. Bowstrings twanged. Two arrows sailed past it. Screaming a howl, it dove toward the warriors.

"*Stop!*"

The hound slid to a halt. A half dozen archers stood ready, arrows trained. A row of soldiers stood before them, weapons raised to receive the charge.

The hound turned its head toward Kate.

"*Sit!*" she ordered.

The beast shifted as if unsure. It turned and started toward her, its bulbous head bent in a curious stance.

"*Stop there,*" Kate said, trying to control her fear. The words themselves meant nothing. The beast couldn't understand them, but the intention had to be pure—uncontaminated by fear or doubt.

The hound stopped.

"*Sit down.*"

The verl hound plopped onto its haunches, sitting on nothing at all. A string of white drool oozed between its fangs and fell. Its eye nostrils flared with two sniffs, eliciting more frothy drool.

Now what? Kate took a tentative step toward it. The verl hound cocked its head, but remained impassive. She continued closer, not slowing. If it caught the faintest whiff of doubt, the spell would break. A musky stench invaded her senses, but Kate maintained her focus. She held an upturned hand toward the beast.

It bent forward and sniffed. The crystalline teeth parted, and a mottled purpled tongue lolled out.

Revulsion knotted inside her guts. *If it licks me, I'm going to puke.*

The hound leaned closer. Hot, wet breath panted across her cold fingers.

"*Lay down,*" she ordered, enunciating the thought more than the words.

The beast did, looking like some sort of demented sphinx. Kate laid her hand atop its waxy head. With a needy whimper, the hound pressed against her. Had anything ever given it affection before, she wondered.

No. This wasn't affection. It was dominance. The beast enjoyed her touch, not for the kindness, but to appease its master.

Taking a step back, Kate removed a baggie from her jacket. The hound perked up. Not removing her eyes from the beast, Kate reached inside the bag and drew out a half-frozen toovakaru, a furry, spotted lizard notorious for eating the monk's grapes.

Eye nostrils flared, the verl tracked every millimeter of movement as she lifted the dead toovakaru up by its nubby tail and held it out.

The hound opened its maw, the jaws stretching wide like a bulldog. It snatched down onto the lizard, yanking it from Kate's hold. Three wet crunches, toovakaru guts squelching between its teeth, and then it was gone.

The hound looked up at her, its vein-webbed brows raised in a hopeful expression. Its tongue licked the blood and fur from its teeth. The offering accepted, the bond was sealed. Kate's jaw tensed at the thought of Candace sacrificing her friends for this ceremony with the same cold manner she'd given it this pest.

While this didn't buy eternal loyalty, the beast considered her its dominant pack mate. "*Go now*," she ordered. "*Leave.*"

The hound spun onto its feet and raced away into the gloom, off to chase elementals and scavenge the Dreamlands.

Kate released a breath. Looking back, she spied Jim halfway to her, his lips tight with fear and hand gripping his witchhunter blade.

"You all right?" he asked.

She nodded.

"If that'd continued any longer, I was going to have a heart attack."

"You? You should have seen it from my angle."

"No thanks." He squeezed her shoulder. "Good work."

Kate nodded, her attention returning to the misty expanse. "We need to get another lizard-rat."

No more hounds came that day, though their cries and yips were heard, followed by a shrill scream. After eight hours, the expedition headed back to Hollit, a single usable pearl in their possession.

Kate cast the circle the following day while Syn stood watch over the prospectors, hoping a hound might come. None did, though a particularly nasty elemental tried to sneak up on them. The expedition ended without a pearl to show.

Syn took Thetish out for the third day. Three verl hounds caught the scent. Overwhelmed, Thetish couldn't exert control in time. Soldiers and Leges put them down, losing two of their ranks in the process.

And it continued, two Viatores out while one stayed behind in case they were needed. Days stretched into weeks. The world of Rish fell into the Golden Empress' domain.

"How did you fare?" Kamre asked the moment the aether blew away on their arrival.

Soldiers and prospectors filed past, stretching their legs.

Kate blinked, her eyes stinging from the sudden daylight. It had been her eighth day to stand watch, freezing her ass off, and the warm air felt wonderful. She wanted to lie on the sun-warmed courtyard stones and sleep. "It was good. Five hounds. I controlled them all."

"Very good," Kamre said with a nod. "Very good. You have bested Syn's record. Any pearls?"

Kate accepted a steaming cup of tea from one of the robed monks—the Hollitian Welcoming Party as Jim liked calling them. "We found one."

Kamre released a sigh. His lips parted into a wide smile. "That gives us ten. We can leave for Carcosa."

Kate glanced to Thetish, who was nursing his tea by the brazier, his legs stretched out before him. Dark bags hung beneath his small, tired eyes.

"We require fifteen," Thetish said. "Five for each Viator."

"Ideally, yes," Kamre agreed. "But you had seriously underestimated time required to collect these stones. Three Viatores isn't necessary to transport us all. Magus Kate claims she can carry our entire army herself."

"But that would lay me out," Kate said.

"Yes, and if we need to leave before you've recovered, Magi Thetish and Syn could do that. There's no need for fifteen pearls."

"I'd feel a lot better if we had fifteen," Kate said.

"As would I, but we don't have luxury of time. Each day that we wait only increases our chances of being discovered and diminishes our supplies."

"Senator," Thetish said, his voice calm and without emotion. "I would have words with you privately?"

"No, my friend," Kamre said. "Decision is made. Rest. In two days, we leave for Carcosa."

40

HASTUR'S TEMPLE

They assembled at sunrise. Three hundred eighty-two soldiers, thirty-one practitioners, and a handful of support staff waited along the very edges of the courtyard, filling the entryways of adjoining buildings. Some talked, others waved their goodbyes to loved ones who watched from second-story windows. But all maintained a safe distance from the enormous three-tier circle dominating the ground. At ninety-two pedes, the largest of the chalk rings was only a hand's breadth from the northern and southern sides. The smallest, at ninety pedes, would carry the army to a world that few even believed in.

Simply drawing the circles had taken Kate four hours, and that was with Livia and Grey's assistance. With masterful care, the two Ipsissima Leges had precisely measured dotted markers across the stone to be sure the great rings went down exact on the first try. Then came the herculean task of scribing the glyphs. Even after the monks had covered the completed circles with waterproof tarps once she'd finished, the paranoia of some unforeseen, late-night rain destroying all her work had made sleep difficult.

"Are you ready for this?" Jim asked as Kate completed her inspection to ensure that nothing had been smudged or inscribed incorrectly in those final hours when the end had been in sight.

"I want you to promise that the next time I mouth off how I can do the impossible you punch me in the teeth."

"Gladly, but that still won't stop you."

"I love you, too." Kate nodded to Kamre standing at the circle's edge.

On his order, eight troops carried a short wooden bridge across the lines. Kate held her breath, watching their feet, but the troops stepped over the chalk with infinite care.

"Watch your step, you fat-footed oafs!" Thetish shouted. "Slowly! Slowly!"

The bridge in place, spanning the border, they began hauling in supply boxes on wheeled carts, one after another. Once they'd stacked two U-Haul's worth on either side of the circle, the signal was given, and everyone else crossed the bridge, entering the ring.

Kate waited as they filed inside, segregating themselves by races. There were, of course, some who did it intentionally but most probably didn't realize they did it. However, a small portion defied that inclination, mostly soldiers who had fought side by side, their shared experience now over-riding any racial barrier. The other humans, all eight of them, gravitated toward her.

"Here," Morrison said, extending a cup of steaming coffee. He'd grown a short beard since the night they'd left Amber Tower, and it suited him, concealing his scar-pitted cheeks. The dusting of gray at the corners of his lips gave him a scholarly air, like a cute college professor.

"You know you're my favorite, right?"

He winked. "Bribes do that."

Careful not to burn her lips, she blew across the cup and eyed the black nylon holster on Beth Finn's thigh. "Morning, Wyatt Earp."

Finn patted the plastic pistol butt. "Howdy, partner," she said in an exaggerated drawl.

"You know how to use that?"

Finn grinned. "This is the part where I'm supposed to say, *I hope I don't have to.* But this is the first time I've gotten to wear it for real outside the range."

"Just don't shoot your foot off, "Quickdraw," Ronny said.

Finn snorted.

"Magus Kate," Robison said. "Could I ask a favor?"

Kate sipped her coffee. "What's that?"

"Jim's normally your Second for this, but I was wondering if I could have that honor." He smiled a sheepish, schoolboy smile, the morning's sun glinting off his glasses as his head lowered by millimeters. "He said it was all right."

She glanced at Jim who only shrugged. "You know what to do?"

Robison nodded. "I did it for Jake once. Many years ago. It would make me very happy to do that again...in his memory."

You mean on the voyage to kill his killer. But Kate knew the Tower Master was too proper to verbalize such sentiment. "I'd be honored to have you."

Kamre shouldered his way through the crowd to the space around the burning brazier. Syn and Thetish flanked him on either side. "We are ready."

A sudden terror knotted in her stomach. This was it. The largest gating ring she'd ever seen, the lives of four hundred souls. One mistake, a single error, and they might all find themselves trapped in the Abyss, unable to escape and hunted by horrors.

Drawing a breath to calm her nerves, Kate handed Morrison back his cup and knelt beside the burning wood. No one spoke or shifted their feet as she wove the glyph between her fingers. Among the sweeping arcs of pink-threaded light, a single lapis shape emerged: the Blue Sign.

Robison crouched beside her, his eyes transfixed on the pulsing sigil and a large muslin pouch in his hand. Accepting the bag, Kate dropped it into the flames.

Violet and red sparks erupted from the coals, sizzling across the ground. Kate straightened, her head back with an involuntary cry as the magic surged into the iron bowl. It mounted higher, waves upon waves of power. Robinson's hand found her shoulders before she could fall. The smell of burnt rubber, her mother's laughter, and then aether consumed the world beyond the chalked walls.

Kate gasped. Beads of sweat dotted her forehead.

"Katie," Jim said, crouching beside her, his voice drowned by the thumping in her ears. "Are you okay?"

She nodded. "Just...give me a minute." Magic pulsed with each heartbeat, coursing down an invisible tether and into the flames.

"You are pale," Syn said, concern almost lacing his emotionless voice.

"This was too much for her," Thetish hissed, his whispered voice rising. "We must return. Senator, I told—"

"No." Blinking her eyes, Kate shook away the fog. "No, I got this."

Syn knelt before her, his pale goat eyes watching her from across the still-sputtering brazier. "Are you certain? There's no shame if it is too much."

"Thank you." Magic bled from her with each pounding heartbeat. *Thump. Thump. Thump.* "I can do it."

They traveled in silence for some time, the travelers shifting their feet and watching their pilot through side-long glances. Eventually, the dam broke, the whispers and mumbles giving rise to dozens of conversations in five languages. The furry-faced Izibans spoke quickly, their voices like little birds. The Soonati, with their double-voices, spoke in hushed tones near one of the supply piles, the lilting of their language almost musical.

Kate didn't speak, she only stared into the magic-devouring flames, counting the hours. A herd of whales had emerged from the darkness. Afraid to look away from the brazier, lest the distraction break her concentration, Kate could only listen to the gasps and exclamations of wonder as Ronny and Jim gave her the play-by-play of the giant creatures' passage.

The excitement continued long after the whales had vanished beyond the misty curls, but the first baying howl ended all discussions. A second wail followed, and soon an entire pack of snarling verl hounds raced past, chasing a small elemental. More barks echoed across the infinite gloom, dozens, maybe even a hundred hounds, yelping and keening all around them.

"So many," Nate breathed.

"If they're all here," Kamre said, loud enough for the soldiers to hear, "then perhaps empress is home."

"Or perhaps such a hoard is normal for Carcosa's borders," Syn muttered. "No one knows from where they originate."

A muted debate ensued as to the verls' presence, but Kate shushed them.

"Do you want them to hear us?" Her eyes unfocused, she stared into the orange coals and opened the valve of magic. Her shallow reserves of power flooded into the flames as the image of interlocking wood planks formed in her mind. The face of whose memory she now conjured reflected up at her: a sharp-nosed woman with black eyes, her name lost to history. A second image appeared, this one a jumble of grit and shattered squares. Dried grass protruded from between the broken ceramic tiles and chunks of fallen masonry.

Kate blew.

Dust swirled, some of the tiles slid and tumbled, revealing even more wreckage beneath. A kangaroo mouse bolted from its burrow and hopped away. Lacking the magic to clear the site properly, she muttered,

"Everyone hold on." She wove her fingers, etching the Blue King's glyph before releasing it into the hungry flames. Sparks popped, and the aether whirled.

Jagged shapes emerged from the mist on all sides. Soldiers yelped in surprise, stumbling as mounds of broken roof tiles and fallen columns pushed their way up through the circle's floor. A stack of boxes crashed, spilling its contents. A thousand crunching pops sounded as the weight of Kamre's army came down onto the debris-littered floor.

The instant they appeared, four trios of soldiers broke from the ring, checking their perimeter. Magus Morrison slid his shotgun from its soft case.

"I wouldn't fire that until we know it works here," Harcourt warned.

Dizzy from the strain of magic, Kate lifted her gaze. A semicircle of empty, stone benches rose before her. Towering statues, their features worn from time, ran the stadium's perimeter, their arms cocked above their bent heads to brace the roof which had long-since collapsed. Each wore a mask etched with a different expression—joy, anger, sadness, ecstasy. Beams of yellow light cut across the top, casting the long double-shadows of setting suns.

"It's a theater," Harcourt said. "And we're the players."

"Hastur's temple," Syn said, his voice breathy with reverence. "God of Shepherds and the Stage."

"I have to see," Kate muttered, staggering to her feet.

Robison and Grey tried holding her down, pulling with gentle hands and telling her to take it easy, but Kate swatted them away.

"Where are you heading?" Kamre demanded.

Kate pointed up the slope of seats, where one of the squads now ran. "I want to see it."

"Stay here. You're too weak. Let scouts report first."

"Don't ever call me weak," she mumbled. Careful not to slip on the strewn wreckage, Kate started up the daunting stairs.

"Katie," Jim said beside her, "are you all right?"

She nodded.

Behind her, Kamre was shouting orders. "You men, clean this up. All of it. We require space for circle home."

Huffing, Kate reached the top of the broken wall. A brisk wind brushed her sweat-slicked face. The ruined city of Hastur stretched before her, a gridwork of crumbling, roofless buildings and weathered obelisks. Ferns and tufts of long grass protruded from the cyclopean masonry.

Patches of lush blue clover grew in the shadows of buildings, like splatters of cobalt paint. They rustled in the steady breeze. Gnarled, leafless trees jutted here and there, the broken paving stone and masonry heaved away and tangled in their twisted roots. The bare branches didn't so much as tremble in the wind, and their bark glistened in the low sunlight like rough-hewn flint.

Movement drew Kate's attention. A striped lynx stood on a nearby wall. Its eyes were the same golden hue as Evan's. Kate's breath caught as she held the cat's stare, neither of them moving. Then the lynx snapped its attention to a trio of soldiers coming around the corner, and it fled into the ruins.

"Would you look at that," Morrison said.

"Whoa," Robison breathed.

Kate turned. On the other side of the stadium, just beyond a row of buildings, a sea of milky fog stretched to the horizon. Cloud waves broke against corroded metal poles and silently lapped against the rock-strewn shore as sleek gulls circled above.

"The misty lake of Hali," Jim said. "Christ, I can't believe it."

"Believe it?" Beth laughed. "I decided I was dreaming weeks ago. All of you are in my head."

Far to the left, the cloud lake blazed orange and lavender as a crimson sun sank beneath the horizon. Beside it, a second, dimmer sun was just beginning to set. Kate's gaze slid to the left, following a line of green uprights nearly hidden in the Hali's mist. Far beyond, shrouded in the darkening haze of lead-colored clouds, a city loomed on the distant shore. Slender towers thrust to the heavens above wide domes. A pale, golden beam, like a single ray of afternoon sunlight, shone up into the sky, encasing the largest of the spires.

Kate's breath caught in her throat. "Carcosa," she whispered, almost afraid to say it aloud.

Harcourt followed her gaze. "And the Yellow Queen appears to be home."

41

RELICS OF THE DEAD

"Scouting reports show ruined fortress *here*." Kamre stabbed his finger onto the map harvested from the Frankentome. Consisting of little more than a collection of squiggly lines and colored dots, Kate had written it off as useless because it offered no sense of scale or even labels. But on their first day, after the twin suns had risen, Nate discovered a cracked and worn mosaic along the cloud shore. There, in tiny chips of colored glass and clay, it depicted not only a map, but told them where they were on it.

After waking from a ten-hour coma and with one hell of a magic hangover, Kate had spent her entire day inscribing a new circle on the cleaned stadium floor. Meanwhile, Kamre's forces had set camp in the ruin of a pillared palace two blocks from where they'd arrived.

"We'll leave at sunset," Kamre continued. He sat on the wide base of a marble column, his generals and advisors on the cracked floor before him like school children. "Move along this valley until we reach it. Syn will inscribe a new circle there, which can shuttle troops back to this location if we have to fall back."

Futherio, the purple-skinned High Priest of the Shezmu Order, clicked his tongue. "Risky. We should send the Viator with five men to the ruin, and then have him transport the rest there."

Kamre shook his head. "We can't."

Another click. "Why?"

"Risk," Syn said. "At most, I could only carry half the forces. That requires four journeys—two each way. Each time we disturb the aether only increases our potential of being caught."

"And Viatores are too important to place at spear point," Kamre said. "I want them protected in rear."

Kate tightened her lips, holding back a frown. Keeping their precious bus drivers safely in the back meant that the fight would be done by the time she got there. She wanted Candace for herself, let that bitch know it was *her* who found her.

"Once rested," Kamre continued. "Syn will hold that position with four troops while we continue, circle lake, and here," he pointed to a penciled X, "Thetish will inscribe second circle. After that, we will cross plain and storm Carcosa."

The other generals nodded, muttering their agreements.

"What about me?" Kate asked.

Kamre smiled. "You'll maintain position here."

"Here?" she blurted, her high voice echoing off the stone walls.

"You're too valuable. We can't risk you being injured or not having enough magic to carry us all out, even if we succeed. No, if empress drives us back, Thetish and Syn can carry us here and you, refreshed, can travel us away. If something happens to you, they can attempt it separately."

"You just want me to sit here while you face her?"

"We all have our responsibilities."

"I accept that," Kate said, her voice rasping with venom. "But for all of you, she's a *thing*, a faceless monster. But I *know* her. She attacked *me* personally. So, don't think I'll just sit and wait while you go after her."

Kamre's already red face darkened. Anger flashed in his eyes. "This is too important for your vendetta. You *will* stay here. Otherwise—"

Hestius lifted a pudgy hand. "Apologies, senator." He turned to Kate. "Magus, we understand your anger. You have suffered greatly at her hand. But you understand how much we need you, yes? How grateful we are for everything you've done?"

"I do."

The old librarian pressed his palms together like a priest at prayer. "I swear to you. You will not be alone. Livia, myself, and many more will be here with you. We are not soldiers. Let them fight. Our duty is to world."

"That's fine," Kate said. "But you all seem to forget that there's more that I can do than ferry everyone around. I'm a Magus. Do you understand what that means? I've battled sorcerers before. I'm not helpless."

"True." Hestius nodded. "But pallid mask adorns her face. She isn't sorceress. She is power unto herself. You have done your part in her fall. You carried us across Demhe and history will immortalize you."

"I don't give a shit about history," Kate snapped. "I want—"

Harcourt touched her arm. "It's fine," he whispered.

Kate wheeled. "What?"

"Let it go," he said like a patient father, his blue-gray eyes pleading.

"A frontal assault already failed. We need magic to beat her. Catch her off-guard."

"And we have magic," Hestius assured.

"You can't win this argument," Harcourt whispered. "Let it go."

"But—"

"That's an order."

Swallowing back her anger, Kate nodded to Kamre. "I'll stay here." She didn't speak for the next twenty minutes, brooding, as the generals laid out their plans. Harcourt knew how much she wanted this. So what if he was her boss? Fuck him and fuck his Iron Word, the coward. It took an Ipsissimus Lex to absolve her of it, and she just happened to know one. Jengta wouldn't, but Grey would.

"Gather your forces." Kamre rose, tucking Kate's map into his pocket. "Departure upon hour."

"Come on," Harcourt said.

"Don't you fucking talk to me right now," Kate growled.

The old man's kindly face hardened. "Some battles you can't win, and that was one of them. Hate me all you want, but follow me." He turned and left, not so much as waiting for a reply.

Asshole. Clenching her teeth, Kate followed him into a long courtyard with a recessed floor. Soldiers were already scrambling as orders were barked. The aroma of onion stew and bird meat filled the air. Unable to make cooking fires for fear of smoke, the resident Arcani had heated metal grills. Once again, Kamre had reduced world-altering power to menial duties.

Amber Tower had carved out a small corner beside a broken four-armed statue, now serving as a bench. Beth Finn had pronounced it Camp Terra.

Robison was the first to see them approach. "Looks like we're heading out."

"Not all of us," Kate grumbled.

"We're not leaving?"

"You can, but I'm to stay here until it's over."

Shaking his head, Jim looked at Harcourt. "You were right."

"Right?" Kate asked. "You knew they'd do this?"

The old man filled a clear camping cup from a metal jug. "You might know magic better than me, but I know people and politics. They had no intention of risking you, and you'd have no intention of staying put. So, we made a plan."

"It might have been a good idea to have warned me, too."

"I couldn't be sure, so why upset you? Besides, your poker face is for shit."

"So we're doin' it?" Nate asked around a mouthful of Jim's protein bar.

Morrison grinned, a dangerous excitement like a teenager getting the car keys for the first time.

"Doing what?" Kate asked, voice rising in frustration.

Harcourt waved away the questions. "Let's let our friends leave first. After that, Magus Morrison has something to show you."

Kamre's troops marched at sunset, their bootsteps echoing down Hastur's empty streets. As the red faded from the sky, colorful ribbons of faint violet fluttered across the heavens. The aurora brightened, shifting to indigo, then blue, green, and all the colors of the spectrum dancing above and casting eerie shadows.

Kate flinched as the first howls sounded in the distance. But they weren't the madman screams of verls, but actual wolves calling to the tinseled night.

"Will they attack?" she asked.

Ronny shrugged one shoulder. "No one's even seen them. But they're definitely in the city."

"And we're going out there?"

"So, you'll face down actual monsters," Finn asked, amusement coloring her voice, "but wolves are what freak you out?"

"Being hunted is being hunted," Kate said. "At least in the Abyss there's nothing for them to hide behind to sneak up on me."

"Don't worry about them," Morrison said. "If we're in a group they shouldn't attack."

Kate snorted. "Maybe back on Terra. But we don't know these wolves. These might have two heads or be twelve feet tall. Maybe they're invisible."

Harcourt sipped his water. "And is that going to discourage you from seeing what Morrison has to show you?"

"No. I was just mentioning it."

"Good." He glanced up at the aurora, the rainbow hues sparkling in his ice-chip eyes. "Let's give it a little while longer and then head out."

They waited half an hour until the vibrant ribbons faded from the heavens, leaving only the faintest glow like some eerie twilight. Black stars filled the non-color sky like a hundred-million pinholes across a tattered screen. An owl screeched, the ruffle of feathers, and Harcourt nodded that it was time.

"Where are you headed?" a young Dhevinite soldier asked as they approached the door. He looked no more than sixteen, his upper lip fuzzy with a boy's mustache. Kamre had left four soldiers to keep watch over them. Only two carried the tall, insulated shields.

"For a walk," Kate said.

"Now?" he asked, adjusting his hold on the large crossbow. Kamre had taken the rifles on his campaign once it was determined they worked in this world.

"Aside from the arena to here, I haven't seen the city."

"There are wolves," the boy said.

"We're armed," Morrison said, patting his shotgun.

The boy nodded. "Sound carries. Empress might hear shot across lake."

"I'm an Ipsissimus Arcanus," Robison said, his posture straightening. "Do you understand what that means?"

The guard nodded, his copper-capped dreadlocks jingling with the motion.

"Then you know nothing will hurt us. Don't worry." He bobbed his nose toward the packs and bedrolls still laid out around the four-armed statue. "We'll be back."

Seeming comforted with knowing they weren't leaving all together, the guard stepped aside. "Caution. Empress can see all."

"Then it doesn't matter," Grey said as they shuffled past.

From the light of the black-speckled twilight and the three tumbling moons, they followed the stone streets canyoned between ruins, their footsteps loud in the silence of the dead city. The buildings loomed black in the pallid light. Bat-like lizards and night birds circled above, silhouettes on silent wings.

Nate flinched as they passed a rubble-strewn doorway, her shoulder squaring up for only an instant.

"What?" Kate asked, her fingers coming up and gathering energy.

Nate blew a growling breath. "It's nothin'. Just a phantom."

"Like citizens?"

"Naw." She shook her head. "Shapes. They don't keep form. Their faces keep changin'. No big deal. I've never seen *this* many, and they keep poppin' out and vanishin'."

Grey was very pointedly listening to this exchange. She licked her lips but didn't speak. Probably filing that conversation away for later. Perhaps the red-haired Ipsissimus was hoping to recruit more than just Kate.

After climbing a steep ramp from a fallen wall, they passed through a broad square, and reached a deep canal. The paved trench stretched eighty feet wide, the arched bridge across now shattered by time. Reeds and shrubby trees lined the muddy trickle along its bottom. They rattled in the wind, carrying the smell of wetness and decay. A small, furred animal scurried into the high grass with a rustle of dried leaves.

Something caught Kate's eyes, an out of place smoothness among the debris. Peering down, she realized that what she'd mistaken for rubble from the collapsed bridge was also bone, the jumbled skeleton of some enormous animal, its skull as broad as a coffee table with a quartet of curving tusks.

Following the trench, they reached a misty bay. Stone piers stretched out over the Hali. The muddy stream vanished beneath the clouds. Nate stared across the harbor, her eyes focused on things Kate could only imagine. Spirits wandering the lanes and docks where ships and commerce once thrived? Jim took Nate's hand, giving it a reassuring squeeze.

Far in the distance, beyond the roofless palaces, the steady beam of the Golden Empress stretched to the heavens above Carcosa.

Morrison motioned the shotgun toward an imposing facade with spiraling columns. "The map we found was over there." He bobbed the twin barrels toward a corroded brass ladder along the dock. "What we didn't show them is down here."

Kate followed him down. Her steps pinged off each rung until she reached a black gravel beach. A stone wall to their right, the spit of shore extended only ten feet at the widest to where the cloud waves lapped, the rocks coated in ice at their furthest reach. Animal skeletons lay along the shores, their sprawled shapes glinting with frost in the faint light. Moving past the remains of some long-necked bird, she realized that it wasn't ice, but crystals coating the delicate bones and shoreline.

The cloud lake's beauty warping into fear, Kate distanced herself from the silent waves.

Small crabs scuttled away, hooked pincers raised, their legs ticking off the stone. They vanished into the lake.

"This way," Morrison said. He led them into a wide arched inlet beneath the port.

Stepping in behind him, Kate's nose curled at the stink of bird shit. A huge shape dominated the alcove, its features masked in shadow.

Pebbles crunched as the others stepped in beside her, blocking most of the light from outside.

"I think we can risk this now." Robison blew into his hands. Light welled between his curled fingers. He opened his hands, releasing a tiny light, no brighter than a candle, but enough to make Kate blink away from the miniature brilliance.

The vault extended maybe forty feet deep. Tiny brown bird nests speckled the sloping walls like barnacles. A stone shelf, about four feet high and wide ran along each side. It appeared clean of rubble, except for a shadowy pile in the far corner. Three boats rested on the gravel before her, some dull brown metal glazed with bird droppings and dust.

A second light flared to life. Finn released her own miniature light globe, and Kate realized that it wasn't three boats but one, a single craft with a pair of huge pontoons on either side.

Kate glanced over to Harcourt who was smiling this smug, cat-ate-the-canary grin. "You're kidding me?"

"I know, right?" Ronny patted one of the metal floats, a dull *thump-thump.* "It's awesome." He laughed his high little chuckle.

Harcourt, still grinning, said, "Why would I kid? This is perfect."

"You can't be serious," Kate hissed, fighting the urge to yell.

The smile vanished. "Deadly. You said we have to surprise her. I agree. She's not going to expect this."

"Am I the only one that saw those bones back there? You want to actually take *this* out over *that* lake?"

"Why not?" Morrison wagged a finger toward the ceiling. "There's a hundred murals up there that show these things sailing the Hali. The mast is broken, and I don't know if we could fix that in time, but we could paddle it right up to Carcosa."

Kate stabbed a finger at a substantial rent along the closest float, the straw of some animal nest peeking out from the gash. "It's broken. We'll sink right to the bottom, if there *is* a bottom."

"Easily fixed."

"What about him?" She nodded to the cluttered corner, which she could now see housed a broken skeleton and a small camp, a hammered copper pot still dangling from a tripod. "Why didn't he fix it?"

Morrison shrugged and scratched his beard. "Lacked the tools, who knows. Maybe he was too injured."

Kate opened her mouth to reply, but paused. "That's the first human skeleton I've seen. And that wood...it's not all rotted away. How did this guy get here?"

"Who knows," Morrison said. "He's been there maybe twenty years."

"That was before Candace came. This is a dead world."

"Dead?" Grey said. "There's life everywhere. The wolves, the birds, all still here."

"But *people*," Kate growled.

Grey shook her head. "We haven't seen any. But there're signs."

"Old burn marks up in the city," Jim said. "Campfires and the like. All old, but way newer than the rest of this."

"And we're not concerned about this?"

"If there are people here, they're hiding," Morrison said. "But nothing shows anyone is still here. Might be nomadic, or maybe they only recently died out."

Kate looked again at the jawless skull resting on its side, the forehead too large, a bony crest along the top. She shivered, a nameless dread skittering down her spine. Hastur wasn't dead. And if not, what about the other cities? Were Carcosa's descendants still scraping an existence in the ruins of the three kingdoms? Or were these travelers from somewhere else, the progeny of some failed and forgotten expedition?

She swallowed, chasing away the thought. "So," she said, turning back to the boat, "you got a welding torch or something in your gear?"

Robison snorted. "Kate, you might think of Arcani as some path you had to briefly follow on your way to Viator, but there was a lot you could've learned had you only committed to it." He smiled, that waxed mustache lifting on either side. "I *am* the blowtorch."

"How long?" Harcourt asked.

Robison stepped around the wreckage. He kicked at a cup-shaped anchor. A crab hurried away. "You said Kamre is attacking in three days?"

The old man nodded.

"That gives us two." His lips tightened. "We can do that."

"We don't have the choice."

42

RIDING THE STORM

Two nights later, as the auroras faded from the pale skies, they hauled the boat out from its drydock.

"Don't touch the mist," Kate warned as Ronny hurried before her, his hands around one of the outrigger's braces.

His toe came down into the cottony lake, sending white curls puffing away. Crystal gravel crunched beneath his boot. Carefully, he lowered the metal pod onto the rolling mist. Jim was on the far side, guiding the starboard outrigger. A smooth, gleaming weld ran along the outside. A patch from another harvested wreck now covered the big puncture hole. Robison's handiwork didn't worry her as much as the rest of the boat. But the bald sorcerer's glowing confidence did some to ease her mind.

The pontoon sank into the clouds, confirming her worst fears, but then its weight lessened. The grinding of metal on the gravel lake bottom faded and then silence. By the time the boat was half-way in, it floated atop the Hali.

"Load up," Morrison ordered, his voice a whispered shout. Grey took the lead, followed by Morrison, then Harcourt and Finn. Jim and Ronny held the rear, clutching the tie-knobs on the outriggers' ends.

Careful not to let the mist touch her, Kate climbed on board. 'S.S. Amber' the boat read across the stern, the words inscribed in black marker. It wasn't Kate's first choice of names. Hers would have been Onyx's Revenge. But Morrison had found it, and he won the naming privileges. Tingles prickled her nape as she crossed a faint ward. Red planks lined the interior, most showing no sign of rot. She stepped over three benches before taking a seat. The boat could easily seat twelve. More if they squeezed.

Once they were all safely aboard, Jim and Ronny pushed off with a pair of cut poles and Finn and Robison paddled.

The Amber glided through the clouds. No swishing of oars or waves sloshing against the hull, just silence, save for thunder rumbling in the distance.

Mist curled and wafted around them, the eddies from their oars spinning out miniature tornadoes. Occasional columns and shapes formed across the surface like faces or people, but then dissolving the moment Kate registered them. Nate was pointedly staring at her feet.

Following the shore, they paddled out from the bay until the vast lake opened before them, the golden beacon glowing in the distance.

They reached the first of the metal poles standing twenty feet above the surface. A layer of crystals skirted its base, thickening to more than a foot where it disappeared below the waves. Two paths of poles stretched before them, spaced every fifty feet, one leading to Alar, the other to Carcosa. They followed the second. Corroded chains dangled from a pair of hooked arms at their tops. Each arm supported long-dead lamps of blue and yellow glass.

Jim's whispered question broke the silence. "What if we get there before the army?"

"We wait," Harcourt replied. "The empress' men will be focused on the army."

"And if they're not?" Grey asked.

"If not, we find another place to land. You and Morrison can shield us from any fire."

"That's a lot of guesswork," Kate said. "I don't want to know what happens if we sink or go over the side."

"Everything is guesswork, Kate. It's gotten me this far. Once Kamre's men storm the gates, all eyes will be on him. We have no sail. We're riding low. And no one will expect us to cross the lake."

"Because it's insane."

"Exactly."

Kate turned her head in time to see a woman with flowing hair rise and then dissolve a dozen feet away, her head arching back in an almost sexual throe before dissipating. "I have no idea how you talked me into this."

"Because you're as insane as me," Harcourt said.

Jim laughed.

They'd traveled for over an hour, switching rowers once, but seeming no closer to the distant city. A warm wind began to blow, stirring the mist lake and causing the chains to rattle and bang against their poles. Dark clouds rolled across the pale heavens, plunging them into darkness.

Lightning flashed, a skittering web-work across the sky, followed by a rolling boom.

Ronny scrunched in the middle of his seat, arms tucked against his sides. "You realize we're in a metal boat, right?"

"The wards are good," Robison said.

"Against capsizing?"

"Then what do you suggest? We're miles from shore."

"I don't know," Ronny said, his voice rising. "Just...what do we do?"

"Keep going."

The cloud lake churned around them, the waves growing higher. Lightning flashed far beneath them, igniting the Hali in a purplish light. Thunder rumbled, its vibrations coming up through the little boat.

"You're fucking kidding me," Kate said, gripping her bench. "We're sandwiched between two storms."

A thick bolt shot down from the sky. It met another rising from the lake, forming a single tether of jagged light. A warm drop struck Kate's shoulder. Another hit her thigh, and then the heavens opened. Rain sheeted down.

It pinged off the hull and outriggers but passed through the rolling cloud wave, each strike sending up a tiny puff of mist. Their visibility shot, the wind and waves pushed them sideways. Morrison and Jim worked the paddles, struggling to keep the poles in view. They drifted further away, lost in a sea of storm.

"Everyone, hold on," Morrison shouted. Rain was pouring down his short beard.

Kate and the others began scooping water out from the boat. It filled as fast as they worked. A huge wave sent her sliding, banging her hip painfully into the side.

Ronny lifted his hands. A disk of pink light bloomed above them, deflecting the pelting rain.

"No!" Harcourt shouted. "They'll see it."

"That doesn't matter if we sink," the skinny Magister yelled back.

"It's meaningless if they know we're coming!"

"He's right." Grey waved her hand downward. Soaking red hair clung across her forehead. "Rain's the least of our problems."

Ronny ended the spell and continued bailing. Lightning struck one of the poles ahead. Electric fingers arcing down its length, descending deep below the surface, down to infinity.

"There!" Morrison shouted. He started paddling toward it.

Another wave surged toward them, writhing figures in the oncoming cloud. The boat lifted, almost straight up. Kate gripped the sides, her head down between her knees. Her improvised bailing cup tumbled away. The Amber crested the wave, and tipped downwards, everything sliding toward the front.

Lighting flashed miles below, an immense plane of purple light. Kate opened her eyes in time to see something huge against it. Backlit by the brilliance, an enormous centipede, long as a city block, wriggled in the depths, its silhouette burned into her vision even after the light faded.

Dizzy from the height and horror of the depths, she clenched her teeth and held on. Howling wind whipped her wet hair.

"Almost there!" Morrison called above the tumult. "Keep bailing!"

Releasing her white-knuckled grip from the hull, Kate furiously scooped the ankle-deep water out with her free hand. Another wave came, but she held on. The tiny pistol tucked into her waistband jammed into her back as they slammed down. Gritting her teeth from the pain, she continued to work. They struggled their way closer to the pole, fighting the waves.

The world flashed in purple brilliance. A deafening boom shook her teeth. Lightning danced along the portside outrigger, but splayed away from the open hull as if hitting an invisible wall. Rain sizzled across the steaming pontoon, now listing awkwardly to the side, stretching further and further away. Kate only stared at it, not comprehending what she was looking at. Then the horrible realization that the rivets holding the front brace had popped.

"Get it! Get it! Get it!" Morrison shouted as Grey tried to lasso the front cleat with the anchor chain, tie it down before the pontoon might break away.

Her ears ringing from the blast, Kate found her lost cup. Scoop after scoop she hurled over the side as the rain poured from the sky.

The storm raged for half an hour, tossing them up and down, banging them until they were battered and sore. Then it ended as quickly as it had come. The clouds opened, revealing that pale night and glittering black stars. Exhausted, Kate took Jim's oar. Blood trickled from her stinging knuckles. She skinned them when a wave had slammed her against the deck. Jim slumped on the bench, his chest heaving. With Nate's help on the other oar, they paddled to the closest pole.

"Closer." Finn leaned out, a section of remaining chain in one hand. She swung it around and caught it. "Good." She wrapped it around one of the knobby boat cleats.

"Let's just catch out breaths," Robison said, cleaning the water from his square spectacles.

Kate sighed. She slid down onto the deck, her back against the bench. Far behind them, the storm raged above Hastur. Her lips against her stinging knuckles, she wondered how those still behind were faring. The chalk circle they'd spent an entire day inscribing was most assuredly ruined. Even if Candace pushed Kamre's forces back, chasing them across the lake, there was no way Kate could redraw it in time. Escape was gone.

"That should hold." With Ronny as his spotter, Robison precariously crawled backward along the outrigger brace. "Another storm will take it out."

"Well," Ronny said, brushing his hands. "I don't care if they do have extra boats there. I'm not crossing this again."

Nate snorted. "Fuckin' right."

The rest mumbled their agreement.

"How much longer do you estimate?" Harcourt asked.

Kate eyed the golden beam, like a celestial tower, shining above Carcosa. She'd been terribly wrong in judging the sheer scale of it. It wasn't some large city across a lake. The towers and domes weren't low against the ground. They were enormous. A colossal metropolis looming above where the great lake Hali emptied into the infinite Abyss. "I'd say we're less than a quarter of the way. We wouldn't have made it by dawn even if the storm hadn't hit."

"Fight'll be over by the time we get there," Morrison said.

"No," said Harcourt. "If we misjudged the distance, then so did Kamre."

I suggest we take it slow. Let them catch up if they need to. No use wearing ourselves out getting there early."

Kate rubbed the itchy pink skin across her knuckles. While Robison had patched the Amber, Grey had patched the crew. She picked up her oar. "Then let's get to it."

43

THE COURT OF THE DRAGON

K ate guessed they'd crossed the halfway point when the fiery hues of sunrise ignited within the Hali. The twin suns rose in the distance, springing from the same point they'd descended, coming up like a pair of bouncing balls. The air grew thick and wet. A steamy fog rose from the cloud lake, shrouding them in a sticky haze.

They rowed through the mist in silence, the only sounds being the occasional click or rasp of their oars against the hull. The seemingly endless procession of slender poles with their dead lamps glided out from the mist before them, one after another as if they were caught in some infinite loop replaying over and over.

They worked in shifts, catching quick naps as they could.

"At least no one should see us coming," Finn said, her words the first spoken in...Kate couldn't remember.

"True enough," Ronny said, manning his oar. "I just hope we'll see the city before we run straight into it."

The twin suns burned through the haze like a pair of colorless disks. As the first began its descent, falling level with its companion like a pair of owl's eyes, a bell tolled in the distance ahead.

"Listen!" Robison leaned forward, his hand to his ear.

The bell rang with quick, metronome timing, echoes chasing between strikes.

Clang-clang-clang-clang.

"The attack is starting," Robison said. "We have to be close."

They paddled faster. The bells continued, growing louder. Fear and excitement raced along Kate's spine, spreading through her veins and making her skin prickle, the hairs lifting on end.

Grey pointed up ahead. "There!"

A dark shape loomed from the fog, stretching wide before them, featureless in the gray gloom. Then jagged spires emerged, higher and higher with each second. Leaning forward, Kate searched the silhouettes trying to spot anything moving along them. Nothing.

A shadow fell to her left. Kate turned to see more buildings now blocking the suns. The city wasn't just before them, it was beside them. The trail of poles had led them straight into a bay. They were in the lion's den.

"Docks over there," Harcourt said. "Find a spot to land."

The bells were still ringing somewhere ahead. Everyone peered through the mist, looking past the ghostly forms rising and falling from the Hali. A stone jetty emerged to the right, standing fifteen feet above them. The crystals from eons of lapping waves encrusted its base.

"Stairs," Kate said, pointing to steps rising along one side.

They paddled closer. The towers and arches just beyond the docks came into view. Slender windows with dagger-tapered tops lined many of the buildings. Chipped and faded paint clung to the elaborate reliefs and scrollwork adorning every surface. Nothing, not even the worn steps before them were spared the decadent decoration. Two gold-trimmed black banners, each three stories tall and emblazoned with the Yellow Sign, stood on either side of a flower-shaped gate.

Morrison rose at the bow, stretching for a twisted metal ring mounted beside the steps. "Little closer."

A faint whistle and then a loud pop. Morrison's arm exploded at the shoulder. Steaming blood and shredded flesh splattered Kate's legs.

Finn screamed.

Magus Patrick Morrison tumbled over the side, his head gonging against the pontoon, and then he was gone. No cry, no splash, just the lingering stink of burnt meat.

"Down!" Jim screamed.

A pink lattice of light bloomed from Grey's hand, enveloping the bow of the boat. Another whistle and the shield surged brighter with an unseen impact.

Beyond the shifting web of pink geometry, Kate spotted the gold-clad Netru near the gate, its rifle aimed at them.

Grey's shield pulsed from two more quick shots. She thrust her hand between the moving strands of the magical web, firing an emerald lance. The green light nimbused in the fog, making it appear as thick as Kate's thigh. It missed by inches, shattering a part of the gate wall beside the Netru.

It tucked behind a column, robes swishing with the movement, and returned fire.

"If he hits the floater, we're fucked," Nate yelled, trying to fold herself under her bench.

Ronny threw his oar onto the floor and grabbed Morrison's padded shotgun case. "He won't." Before Kate could figure out what he was planning, Ronny sprang from the boat and out from behind the safety of the shield. His left foot pinged off the blood-spattered outrigger, and he landed on the steps. He huddled there, out of the Netru's line of sight and slid the shotgun free.

"Wait!" Kate leaped after him. Her foot slipped on the metal pontoon. She lurched. A child's face appeared in the cloud waves beneath her, its mouth open in a silent scream. Redirecting her momentum, Kate hurled herself at the steps.

She came down hard, banging her shin. A crackling pop sounded beside her. A perfect circle of gray lichen blackened and curled. Kate ducked before the Netru could correct its aim and she pressed herself beside Ronny.

"The hell are you doing?" Ronny cracked open the gun, verifying it was loaded.

"That's what I was going to ask you."

He clicked the shotgun closed. "You're our ticket home."

"And this isn't Call of Duty, dumbass. Stay down." Curling her fingers into a claw, Kate cast her own shield. It wasn't anything as bright or as large as Grey's, but hopefully enough to stop that weapon. She rose.

Two shots pounded into the shield, their impacts distorting it. Kate caught her footing before she could fall down the stairs and thrust her hand through, releasing her own lance. The brilliant beam slammed into the column, blasting away shards of stone. The Netru dove to the side, out of Kate's line of fire but straight into Grey's.

The guard looked up in the last instant, realizing what he'd done. Grey's emerald beam skewered him, punching a clean hole straight through his chest. Orange blood sprayed out its back, and the Netru crumpled, its rifle clattering onto the ground.

"Everyone all right?" Robison asked. "Beth?"

Finn was curled against the floor, her shoulders convulsing with sobs.

"Everyone out of the boat," Harcourt ordered. "We don't know if anyone heard that."

Nate tossed the chain to Ronny who pulled the boat against the pier.

Scanning the windows and open doors for movement, Kate followed the stairs up to the top, emerging into a wide square. The etched paving stones beneath her feet weren't stone, but crystal, each irregular block perfectly fitted. Faint colors, blues and purples, glowed deep within them like gemstones encased in ice. The harbor appeared abandoned, the buildings dark and empty. Yet, it was clean—swept and devoid of rubble. A few puddles remained from the previous night's storm. Bells continued to ring.

"Slow down." Jim hurried up beside her, Nate at his heels.

"Jesus," Nate breathed, craning her neck up toward the closest spire, a twisting corkscrew rising into the murky haze.

Jim drew his witchhunter blade. "Any ideas where we're going?"

Kate pointed beyond the open flower gate. Shrouded in fog, a golden pillar of light stretched to the heavens. "That's a good start."

The boat now tied, the others joined them. Harcourt clutched his own dagger in his scarred hand, a silenced pistol in the other. Smeared crimson stained Finn's forehead and hair, the skin pink from where Morrison's flash-boiled blood had scalded her. Tears framed her puffy eyes, but beneath that, a growing rage burned. She clutched her black, squarish pistol in one hand, her trigger finger straight along the side.

"Let's move before someone gets here," Robison said. "Leges on the outside. Keep your hands free for shields."

With Grey in the lead, they hurried past the dead guard. Ronny paused beside its fallen rifle.

"Don't touch that," Jim warned.

"Looks simple enough." He set the shotgun down and touched the glass cylinders on either side of the five-foot barrel. "Not broken."

"Don't," Jim said. He glanced back at the gate. "Come on."

Ronny hefted the weapon up, grunting little. "I'd rather be on this end of it."

"No!" Kate snapped.

"Why?"

"Kamre seized one in Iziba. It exploded when a man test-fired it. Ensures no one but Netru can use them."

Ronny's lip curled into an uncomfortable sneer. Carefully, as if it were a live cobra, he set the Netru weapon backed down, grabbed his shotgun in one hand, and hustled to where they waited.

Through the gate, they entered another square, this one lined with broken, nude statues. Their arms were long and delicate, their faces smooth and featureless except for vertical eyes with a jeweled V set above them. Most of the jewels were missing.

None of the roads from the square appeared to lead directly to the lighted tower.

"This way," Grey said, selecting a wider road nestled in the shadow of a cracked dome.

They jogged down the crystal streets, tremendous shapes looming above them in the gray haze. Kate searched for any signs of movement, but the empty windows and gravity-defying arches were still.

Stopping at intersections, Grey peeked around corners before signaling them to keep going. The roads turned and tangled with no logical sense, following them across overpasses and dark tunnels through angular buildings. The bells had stopped ringing.

Beneath the echoes of their running feet, the faint *pop-pop* of gunfire sounded in the distance.

"Damn," Grey said as they turned into a circular dead-end. Cracked and shattered mother-of-pearl tiles clung to the walls, casting distorted and broken reflections. "Back to the last cross street."

They hurried back, the street curving around a blocky tower. Ronny was in the lead, and he slowed as he rounded the next corner.

"What is it?" Kate asked. The lane before them split, veering to the left and right. A stained fountain of an open-mouthed man adorned the corner of the wedge-shaped building before them.

"Which way did we come from?"

"From the right," Finn said. "I remember that road."

"But that other road wasn't there," Robison said, nodding to the left.

"How do you mean wasn't there?" Jim asked.

Kate glanced up the left-most street, strewn with rubble and ancient facades. "He's right. That wasn't there before."

"No, you just don't remember it."

"I remember that fountain," Kate said, "and it was flat against the wall."

Jim opened his mouth, the protest on his lips, but paused. He looked to the fountain of the open-mouthed man, a wide basin beneath its chin. "Son of a bitch."

"That's impossible," Grey said.

"We just sailed across a cloud to a city older than Earth. Impossible was a long time ago. The streets are shifting." Kate pointed to the golden tower of light. "Keep that in sight, and we'll make it. Take the left street."

Seven blocks later, the street came to a slender and broken bridge of teal glass. A milky stream of mist ran beneath it. The tower stood directly ahead, rising behind the tops of ruined buildings, so close now that they could see the windows and columns studding its side.

"No way," Kate said.

Nate shook her head. "Ah, hell naw."

Robison peered up the flowing cloud canal. "There's another bridge a little ways up. We'll go around to it."

They jogged back up the street they'd come down, a narrow passage hemmed in between a pair of windowless buildings. Golden bars stretched between their upper floors like a jungle gym. Red and lavender streaked the gash of sky above, heralding the first sunset. The distant gunshots were louder now, but with the streets' distortion of echoes, Kate couldn't begin to guess how close they were or even which direction.

They turned the corner, making it a half block before Finn yelled, "Down!" A pink shield latticed before her, covering both Nate and Harcourt, its brilliant light reflecting off the neighboring buildings.

Gold glinted ahead, a red-masked face bringing up its weapon. Grey's larger shield unfolded, blocking Kate's view. The pink threads pulsed. A section just in front of Kate's chest surging brighter as the first shot hit it.

Grey thrust her hand out and released a green beam, blasting a hole in the wall beside it.

Returning fire, the Netru ran across the street and into a darkened building.

"Eyes on the windows," Harcourt ordered, crouching behind Finn, his pistol raised. "Don't let it get above us."

They fanned out, the Leges, Grey, Ronny, and Jim, keeping to the front, their interlocking shields aimed ahead. Robison and Kate fell back, theirs aimed up toward the building. Finn, her shield the weakest, took the rear. Together they formed a loose Roman Shield turtle with Harcourt and Nate huddled in the middle.

Robison's shield thrummed, three shots hitting in quick succession.

Crimson flashed in a second-floor window, but was gone before Kate could react.

"Two more!" Ronny shouted as a pair of golden guards turned up the street ahead.

Purple lightning crackled from Robison's hand, streaking down the lane and dancing along the darkened window as a red mask peeked out. Kate couldn't tell if he'd hit the soldier.

Jade light flashed beside her as the Leges fired at the soldiers ahead. Grey summoned one of those smoky black whips, but far longer and thicker than the one Dalton had used. It cracked like a gunshot, shattering a stone beside one of the Netru's heads.

Firing back, its rifle whistled sharply with each shot. It tried to crouch behind a hunk of broken masonry as Grey's whip lashed down, but too late. Its head exploded in an orange spray like a shotgun blast.

The Netru in the upper window peeked out, getting one shot and vanishing before Robison or Kate could fire back.

Harcourt's pistol barked two quick shots. He was on his knees, firing around the edge of Jim's shield. One round struck a Netru's knee peeking from behind a doorway. The giant stumbled out and was instantly skewered by Jim's emerald lance, taking it right through the abdomen. Falling to its knee, it swung its rifle up. Two more pistol shots and it crumpled.

Running bootsteps sounded ahead. Five more Netru charged around the corner, laying fire as they scattered.

"There's one behind us!" Finn yelled. Her shield warped and shook as shots hit it like sledgehammer blows. Her spell faltered, and the pink shield vanished.

Swinging her arm down, Kate threw hers up in front of the young sorceress in time to catch a shot aimed for Finn.

"We're going to get overrun," Jim shouted. He pulled his hand back through his shield as shots pelted in from two directions.

Robison unleashed another blast of lightning up at the window. The Netru peeking out jolted and burst into flames. "Maybe take one of the buildings. Make them come to us."

The Netru coming from the rear fired as it ran across the lane to a broken statue, the shots thrumming off Kate's shield. It dove behind the cover before she could even cast back.

Crouching behind it, its gun protruded from behind the statue's leg. Kate thrust her hand through the shield, grabbed the three feet of the exposed barrel with her mind, hooked her thumb and yanked. The gun ripped from the Netru's grasp, clacking off the stone, and then sailed toward Kate. The startled guard stumbled into view. Kate released her hold on the now flying weapon. Her fingers arced the quick glyph, and an emerald lance sent the weaponless Netru scrambling back for cover.

"There," Robison said, nodding to the yawning black arch of a darkened building.

Seeming to understand the intention, one of the Netru charged out from cover, its long legs launching it across the open span toward the doorway. Grey's whip came down, too late and cracking nothing but air with a puff of black smoke. Ronny thrust his hand out from his shield, green light lacing between his fingers.

His exposed hand exploded in an eruption of red mist and white bone. Ronny shrieked, shrill and horrible. He fell backward onto the street, his shield spell vanishing as he clutched the stump halfway down his forearm, a pair of shattered bones jutting from the ragged flesh.

Grey stepped in to close the gap in their fortifications. Ronny was curled on the ground, screaming, one leg kicking, and blood everywhere. Nate and Finn were trying to help him, shouting his name and trying to get him to unwrap his body from the gruesome wound.

Howls erupted across the city, a symphony of wailing madmen. Kate's heart caught in her chest, a stabbing pain of fear going right through her.

"Fuck me," Jim groaned.

A black disk irised open in the street fifty feet before her, strands of aether curling out like curious tentacles. Then the verl hound charged out.

"Cover me," Kate shouted, dropping her shield.

The old man hunkered behind her, his pistol up, braced across his other hand still clutching the witchhunter dagger.

The hound's nostril eyes flared. It roared. Its teeth, like jagged, broken glass gleamed in the pink lights of the other sorcerers' shields. Claws clicked across the paving stones as it barreled toward her.

Pushing the panic down, Kate focused her magic to her throat. She circled it twice clockwise around her voice box.

Seeing that Kate had dispelled her defense, the hunkered Netru jumped from its cover behind the statue and made for its fallen weapon.

Harcourt fired.

The Netru staggered and scrambled back as the second shot rang out.

The hound veered its course, aiming itself toward Harcourt.

Kate circled the magic twice the other way. The verl was almost on them, its forelegs lowering for a running lunge.

"*Stop!*"

The hound skidded to a halt only five feet away. It looked at her with those sightless nostrils, foam dripping from its lips. It was hers. Now for the blood offering to seal the pact.

Kate pointed at the Netru peeking out from behind its broken statue. "Kill the Red Masks."

Poor choice of words. Color meant nothing to the blind beast, but it understood her meaning. Roaring, the hound wheeled and charged the cowering soldier. Evidently surprised by the hound's change in loyalty, the Netru didn't react until the last moment when it raised its arms to shield itself. Those huge jaws opened, seizing the Netru and shaking it. Fanning blood splattered the wall. The Netru didn't cry out or make any noise, just the *thump-thump* of its flailing body slamming the ground and going limp.

Kate wanted to look away, hide from the brutal death she'd caused, but refused to remove her eyes from that monster in case loyalties shifted again.

Its giant baby head smeared in orange blood, the verl hound tore the guard's arm off. It started trotting off like a dog with a bone, made it four steps, paused and turned toward the other Netru who were still firing from down the road. The mangled arm tumbled from the hound's mouth, plopping on the crystal pavers. The beast howled and charged past the sorcerers huddled behind their shields and took down the closest Netru with a flying leap.

Seizing the confusion, Grey took down another with her whip as Robison launched balls of blue fire at another. Side by side the two Ipsissima moved forward, raining death.

Finn was providing cover as Jim worked on Ronny's arm, lacing the stump with silver light. Ronny was on his back, deathly pale, his eyes glazed as Nate knelt above him, her forehead against his. At least the wound had stopped bleeding. The scent of cooked meat churned Kate's stomach.

She scanned the streets for more hounds or Netru reinforcements. Sweat ran down her face, despite the growing chill. Lengthening shadows stretched across the fog-shrouded streets.

A Netru rifle shot killed her hound, blasting it apart in an explosion of aether. Robison killed the final soldier with a forked emerald lance and held his position as Grey began tending Ronny's wound, removing the poisonous cooked blood from his system and taking away the pain.

"What do we do with him?" Harcourt asked.

"What's that supposed to mean?" Grey snapped. "He's coming with us."

"What?" Ronny asked, groggily from his back. "I...can help."

"We're charging into a fight," Harcourt said. "It's dangerous for him and suicidal for us."

"What do you suggest? Leave him? With those hounds around here?"

"No," Ronny pleaded, his one hand reaching for Grey.

"She's right," Kate said. "They'll smell him."

"Wards then," Harcourt said. "Can you ward him? Would the Red Gate work? We can get him later. Take care of him then."

"It's possible," Kate said.

"I'm not leaving him," Grey snarled. "He's my tower mate."

"Agreed," Robison said. "He's coming with us. Nate, you and Harcourt help him. If we find a place that's safe we'll reconsider, but not until then."

Wrapping Ronny's mutilated arm in the remains of his shirt, Nate and Harcourt helped him up, holding him between them. With Grey back in the lead, they continued up the lane, past the carnage of fallen Netru.

The clatter of claws drew Kate's attention up a side street. A pair of hounds emerged from the gloom. Gathering her magic, she seized control and offered them the corpses of the dead before sending them out for more victims.

The element of surprise lost, they moved within a fortress of joined shields, a glowing tank of pink spider webs. It caught the initial shots of a charging guard, which Grey dispatched with brutal efficiency.

The pops of distant gunshots were coming louder now, definitely inside the sprawling city. Ghostly fingers of the coming aurora danced across the fading sky like translucent ribbons. Hurrying between a pair of black, iron statues—Netru with their arms raised to the flickering heavens—they crossed an arched bridge spanning the cloud canal.

The city beyond was different from what they'd seen, not just cleaned but restored. Fresh moldings trimmed the windows and doors. Vibrant flowers, their colors crisp even in the fading light, circled the many obelisks and fountains that bubbled apple-scented water.

The bloodied remains of a Netru guard lay sprawled at the entrance of one square, surrounded by bloody paw prints. They crossed the open area, wider than any of the squares they'd seen before, passing a central statue of a human woman, her extended arm before her, palm toward the colored heavens, like an orator.

Ronny gave a pained growl. Kate assumed it was his injury. His head rolled drunkenly to the side, but his eyes were hatefully affixed on the marble image. Looking closer, Kate realized the statue—eighteen feet of masterwork detail—wasn't just of any woman. It was Candace. A strange pinkish hue to the white stone colored the statue's cheeks and the veins in her arms, giving it an almost semblance of life. She stood like some great Caesar before the Senate. Marble lilies, each of their petals delicately thin and tinged with that same internal color, mounded at her feet. Rage boiled in Kate's gut. With all the pain and death left in her wake, Candace was portraying herself as some triumphant hero, a goddess displayed before a dead city of mute worshipers.

"This way," Grey said, motioning them to a wide avenue lined with spiraling columns. A high fence of red metal sealed off the street, save for an elaborate gate adorned with a curling gold dragon. The great glowing tower loomed only a few more blocks ahead.

A quartet of hounds raced across the open square. Kate managed to seize three of them, but the fourth continued its charge. Finn winged it with her own weak emerald lance, but Robison finished it off. The near-constant use of their magic since their arrival in the city had sapped the other practitioners' powers. Kate's reserves were fine, barely touched, but the brilliance of even Grey and Robison's shields had noticeably dimmed.

Kate sent the trio of verl hounds after the dead and then off to find more of the red-masked Netru. If they bore any grudge for the loss of their pack mate, she couldn't tell.

"Hold on," she said as they reached the gate. Black gemstones glinted in the gold dragon's fierce eyes. A faint tingle danced along the nape of Kate's neck, tickling the backs of her ears. "Dispel your shields."

"What?" Grey laughed. "Why?"

"Because they're disrupting my senses. There's wards here."

"Then get rid of them."

Kate narrowed her eyes at the fiery-haired Ipsissimus. "Gladly. I just need to know where they are. So dispel your shield or take it over there. Either way."

"Kate," Robison said, his voice grave, "without a shield, if one of those soldiers fires on you..."

"Then I hope they miss or one of us sees them first." Kate dispelled her own shield and left the huddle.

Jim was watching her with open terror, his lips tight and bloodless. The glowing tank shuffled twenty feet back, leaving Kate entirely out in the open. Exposed. She felt like a soldier in a war movie, that poor bastard who drew the shortest straw and had to storm from the trench alone, crossing No Man's Lands beneath the sights of enemy machine gun nests. Would she hear the shot, or would it just be over? One moment there, the next an eruption of steam and blood?

Shaking the paranoia away before it clouded her judgment, Kate approached the wide arched gate. Shallow etchings flowed up the twisted metal bars and circular latch. Power thrummed from the golden serpent and its faceted eyes. She held her hand just beside it, feeling the magic. They were wards, yes, dozens, but not against people. Elementals couldn't pass. Neither could incorporeals, verl hounds, wyrds, and a whole host of other entities that Kate had only heard of. But above all of those protections, the most powerful were dedicated against scryers. No form of divination outside of physical eyes could pierce the enchanted barrier.

She checked it again, taking her time. These enchantments were only a couple of years old. Why would Candace, who loved using her verl hounds, specifically ward against them?

A clatter came from the stepped street beyond. Flinching, Kate peered through the bars, but saw nothing but empty windows and a small, wooden-wheeled cart. Twin rows of angled, inset blocks ran up the steps, forming a pair of ramps that the cart's wheels could follow. Sweat beaded her brow. Her hands were slick, the paranoia of being out in the open flooding back.

She glanced over her shoulder. The others were intently watching her. Kate licked her lips, looked at the thick disk of the latch, and touched it, a grazing tap as if checking for an electric charge. Nothing. She twisted the cold metal. It rotated as smooth as any bank vault dial. A faint click that she felt more than heard and the latch stopped. Holding her breath, she pushed the gate open. It swung wide on silent hinges.

Releasing her breath, Kate stepped through. Her ears popped as she penetrated the wards, but nothing more. She lifted a hand, signaling the rest to follow.

"What is this?" Robison asked as they drew near.

"I don't know." Kate pointed to the cart half a block ahead. "We can carry Ronny on that."

Grey's shield crackled and vanished as she tried to push it through the open gate. She stopped cold as if her extended, clawed fingers had run into a solid wall. Grey took a step back, and the shield reknitted before her.

"Dispel it and just walk in," Kate said. "It's protected against enchantments and just about everything but us."

"Why?" Grey asked.

"I *don't* know. But the hounds can't get in here."

The corner of Grey's mouth tightened, a subtle twitch of her unease, and she ended her shield. She stretched a leg though as if stepping over a puddle and seemed to relax as nothing happened.

Finn closed the gate as the last of them filed through. Even with the wards, none of them argued about re-forming their shield tank as they made their way up the stepped street to the cart, dispelling it only once they arrived.

It was smooth, carefully constructed, and new. A pair of carved dog heads capped the long pull handles, the space behind them darkened by oily hands.

"Here ye go, Skinny Malinky," Nate said, guiding Ronny into the bed.

"Whose is this?" Harcourt asked, touching one of the whittled dog heads.

"Ours now," Kate said.

"It's too short for a Netru."

Kate paused. The old man was right. "Has there—"

"Whoa," Jim yipped, his shield springing before him and bathed the road in a pink glow.

Kate spun, fingers already threading jade filaments, but paused when she saw the head emerging from a cracked door.

It was a woman. Short black hair covered her chocolate brown head. Simple silver hoops hung from her ears. She had two large moles, one above her left eye, the other below it. Those eyes were fixed on them, not in anger, but more of a cautious fear.

"*Quem é você?*" the woman said, her voice soft and barely breathed.

What is that? Spanish?

"Hello?" Robison said.

"English?" the woman asked.

"Yes," Robison answered.

The woman blinked. She vanished behind the door. She was saying something, and then the door opened. A man was with her, but not human. Golden rings traced up the bridge of his corpse-blue nose and along his brows framing almond-brown goat's eyes. A Torban, though not dusted. Metallic tattoos gleamed across his flesh like a city roadmap. He held a menacing chisel down at his side in a six-fingered hand. A gold cuff encircled his wrist, its face decorated with the Yellow Sign atop a black stone. He wore a long shirt and trousers of bright, lemon yellow.

"Did she bring you?" the Torban asked in accented Latin.

"Who?" Kate said.

The Torban blinked, seeming puzzled at the answer.

"No," Kate said, realizing what he's asked. "We came to see her."

His hand tightened on the chisel, but he didn't lift it.

"There's more," Nate said.

Other faces, emerged in the windows around them, watching through the glass panes. They were every race, a few Kate had never seen. Some were curious, others afraid.

"We don't mean you any harm," Robison said. "Our friend is hurt."

The Torban's eyes flicked to Ronny slumped in the cart.

"Are you who for the bells sound?"

"Yes."

The Torban's blue lips tightened.

"Joe?" a voice called up the street. A skinny black man with a bushy beard, and dressed in an identical yellow outfit as the Torban, stepped from a doorway. "Joe? Did she get you, too?"

"Elliot?" Robison asked. "Holy shit!"

"Master Gregor!" Grey exclaimed.

Only at that name did Kate recognize the wild-eyed man coming toward them. He looked almost nothing like the Tower Master she remembered. Not just the madness in his eyes, but the age. Gregor was in his sixties, but this man looked no more than thirty.

"I don't believe it," Robison said, throwing his arms around the once-old Ipsissimus. "We thought you were dead."

More of the watchers were emerging now, whispering and hesitantly stepping from their doors. They were all the same age as Gregor.

"Mostly. Though I don't look it." Gregor said. "Did she...did she rob you, too?"

"No," Grey said. "No. We brought ourselves. Or, Magus Rossdale brought us."

"Rossdale?" Master Gregor's teary eyes moved to Kate. "Rossdale. I remember you. Katherine? Jake's pupil?"

"Yes," Kate said.

He laughed. "I knew I recognized you. She robbed you too, didn't she? Candace? It was her wasn't it?"

"She did."

"I knew it. I knew it. When she stole my power, I knew it." He hugged Grey. "Where are the others?"

"There's an army attacking from the other side," Grey said. "This is all we have. We lost Patrick Morrison."

Gregor's smile dimmed.

"Did Candace bring you here?" Robison asked. "Did she..." He motioned to Gregor's face.

Gregor nodded. He swept his hand to the timid, yellow-clad crowd. "She brought all of us. The walking dead."

"You're all Ipsissima?" Kate asked. "Ones she robbed?"

"Oh, yes," Gregor said. "Most of us were, but we're all equals now. Prisoners in palaces, and we'll live in them forever. Forever young and hostage. She calls it our punishment for our arrogance."

"Punishment?" Robison asked.

"Because every tower told her she wasn't good enough," Kate said. "She's punishing them for shit people did to her a hundred years ago."

"How many are you?" Harcourt asked.

"I don't know you?" Gregor said, as if he wasn't sure. "Forty-one. We lost Sarshesko, last week. She fell and broke her neck. Her victory against our captor. Don't think I haven't considered it, myself."

Forty-one, Kate repeated. Candace had the power of forty-one practitioners. Ipsissima. And that wasn't including those she might have left on their home worlds before she started bringing them here. "Tell me where she is."

"In her tower, of course." He glanced up as if suddenly afraid. "She might be seeing us now." He clutched Grey's shoulder. "We have to go before she comes. Take us away from here. Take me home, Arianne."

"We will," Kate said. "But after we kill her."

Gregor barked a high laugh. "Kill her? She wears the Pallid Mask."

"I don't give a shit what she's wearing. It's just a crown."

"It's not!" he hissed as if she'd just blasphemed in church. "It's not an object. It's a force. A power of her and she of it. No one can kill her. She's the Yellow Queen."

"Watch me. Tell me how to get to her."

44

THE PALLID MASK

"He'll be safe here," Gregor said. They'd laid Ronny on a narrow bed suspended from the ceiling on golden threads, so thin they were almost invisible.

Now that they were out of the firefight, Grey and Jim were carefully tending the tall Magister's wound, the smell of anise and burnt sulfur heavy in the air. A retinue of the formerly greatest practitioners in the multiverse were running about, fetching bandages, water, and food for their guests, or merely doing lookout.

Kate glanced across the palatial home. A solid amethyst chandelier floated near the ceiling, though, she suspected, it might be suspended by more of those gold threads. The ceiling itself was a moving kaleidoscope of color, much like the aurora shining outside and through the windows. Everything was big, sized for something like a Netru and strangely retrofit with the same detail to gold and master artistry. Yet there was almost no furniture, eerily Spartan like a new house. Most of what there was appeared to be homemade, possibly by the same craftsman who had constructed the cart outside, the one they'd stained with Ronny's blood.

The howls and gunshots were louder now. Flames burned in the distance, visible across the rooftops.

"Once she's dead, your powers will return," Kate said. "But not at once. It's overwhelming when it happens and will lay you out."

"This is suicide," Gregor said. "You can get us out of here, any world you want."

"And she'll find us. Or she'll find more practitioners to rob and keep here. This is our best chance. She's focused on the army."

"There is another way," Robison said. "In the harbor. We have a boat. It can't carry all of you. In Hastur we have reinforcements. If you can cross the city, you can escape."

"Brave the hounds and then the Hali?" Gregor asked.

"Yes. That's how we got here. It wasn't easy. If the attack goes poorly, the other Viatores will meet there. They can take you away."

"Where?"

"You said you don't care," Kate said. "On Hollit, the Order of Shezmu. We have a book there that can cure you."

Gregor snorted. He touched his own gold cuff inscribed with that hellish glyph. "You know we could never make it to Hastur."

"Then wait," Harcourt said. "If we fail, we won't be the last to attack. Others will come."

Gregor ran a wet tongue across his lip, swallowed, his disappointment screaming. "I just want to go home."

Something exploded in the distance, the windows trembling with the shock.

Robison patted his old mentor's shoulder. "I want you home, too."

"And I can't talk you out of this?"

Robison shook his head. "Before I'd seen everything she'd done—the suffering, the murder—you could have. We have to finish this."

"Can you tell me how to get to her?" Kate asked.

Thick streamers of purple light fluttered across the skies, casting strange shadows and glinting off polished stone. Forgoing their shields, so the light wouldn't give them away, they crouch-walked up the wide, steep street. Ahead, beyond a curve, a wedge of pale yellow shone across the lane, like sunlight through an open window.

The sharp stink of smoke tickled the back of Kate's throat and made her eyes water. Deep beneath the stench of burnt wood and tar, she caught the faintest hint of asafetida grass. The howls and pops of gunfire had moved further away. Whether it was Kamre's forces being pushed back, or simply them navigating the maze-like streets, Kate couldn't say.

"Hold on," Grey whispered and peeked around the bend. "Shit."

"How many?" Harcourt asked.

"Four, no five of the goldies. Maybe twenty hounds. They're not looking this way."

Kneeling behind her, Kate braved a peek. Ahead, fifty yards beyond another dragon gate, the twisting white spire of the Empress' citadel rose to the heavens, encased in a tube of golden light. Verl hounds paced the paved yard, paying close attention to where the firing was coming from. These weren't the little ones they'd seen before, hounds the size of lions. No, these were the enormous hounds with the golden chain collars. Candace's elite. A trio of Netru stood by the great, pointed doors, their long, wedge-shaped masks giving them the look of patient vultures. Another patrolled to one side. She couldn't see the fifth one, but there was no reason to doubt Grey's claim of it.

"There's the building he told us about," Kate said, nodding to a tall, narrow palace butted beside the gate. "Most of the way looks good, but you might be spotted getting into the door."

"We'll just have to hope they don't see us," Harcourt said. "Or smell us."

Kate shook her head. "If the hounds could smell us they already would. I think the dragon gate is masking us."

"Then let's get to it." Harcourt checked his Rolex. "Three minutes. It'll take you twenty seconds to get to the gate." He nodded to Finn, lifted his pistol with the big black tube sticking out the end, and they hurried around the corner.

While they had several firearms, the need for stealth required the two silenced pistols. Harcourt claimed to be a good shot. Though he insisted he'd never been an assassin for the Spire, Kate would never believe him. Robison offered to take the second. He'd shot before, giving him a serious advantage over Nate, but Finn had interjected.

"I've been shooting my whole life," she'd snorted. "I'll take 'em down faster than either of you." Now, with that pistol up and ready in both hands, and her backup strapped to her thigh, Finn followed the old man, keeping low.

They crouched for a few seconds behind crystal doorsteps, and then scurried across the open span and into a covered doorway.

Kate waited, her heart speeding as if she were sprinting. Five Netru. Twenty Hounds. One mistake, and they'd never get through the tower's door. *Even if you pull it off, you still might not get inside*. She silenced the thought. There was no time for doubt.

She checked her watch. One minute to go.

The seconds crawled by, each tick taking longer than the one before it.

"Thirty seconds," she said.

Everyone tensed.

At twenty seconds remaining, Kate and her companions started toward the gate, running on bent knees. They stopped at the crystal stairs. The golden dragon gate was thirty feet away. Kate checked her watch. Eight seconds.

They hurried out into the open, charging straight for the gate.

One of the Netru jerked its head toward them. It loosed a cry like a crow's call and lifted its weapon as Kate reached for the disk-shaped latch.

A burst of gunfire, that metallic *chak-chak* of suppressed weapons, sounded from the second floor of the building to her right. Two of the Netru crumpled.

Kate yanked open the gate and stepped through, drawing her magic to her throat the instant she crossed the barrier. Another Netru collapsed mid-run, its body sliding across the ground.

The blind hounds were scattering, trying to figure out what was going on. Several spun toward Kate, this new smell seeming to appear out of nowhere. They charged.

A fourth Netru fell, orange plumes blossoming from its chest. The fifth one, who was standing on the far side of the yard, was limping for cover, dust and shards of chipped crystal from missed shots exploding around it.

A dozen snarling hounds were charging Kate, their mouths open and streaming drool.

"*Stop!*" she commanded.

Seven of the verl hounds froze. Another one slammed into one of the halted hounds, sending them both sprawling. The enchantment broken, they both clambered to their feet and ran toward her.

A green beam streaked from Kate's left, spearing the closest charging hound and blasting it apart in a burst of aether. Its gold chain clattered to the ground. Gunshots from the balcony above took down two more.

Kate pointed to the Netru hiding behind a twisting pillar, trying to get a shot between pistol strikes. "Kill the red masks."

The six hounds turned and charged the hunkered soldier. Kate didn't watch, she only turned her attention to the other hounds racing toward her through the clouds of thinning aether left from their fallen pack mates.

She managed to seize two more, giving them the same offering of Netru. They ran toward the bloodied dead before the high gate, when the doors opened. A gold-clad Netru stepped out in time for a leaping hound to slam into it and carry them both inside. Ignoring the recently dead, the other hound scrambled in behind it, vanishing behind the door.

Kate turned her attention to the last verl hound, a big one with two bullet holes already in it. The hound leaped, jaws open. Then Grey's emerald lance speared through the hound's open mouth, out the back of its pink, veiny head, and the beast exploded into black mist.

"Go!" Jim said behind her.

Drawing the gold shackle from her pocket, Kate ran across the yard. More gunshots took down the last of the untamed hounds, but Kate didn't look, her eyes locked on the ten crystal steps and the open door beyond them. Other footsteps pounded behind her. She raised her hand into a claw, a pink shield unfolding before her. Who knew how many Netru were inside.

One of her hounds, a squat but hulking monster with Netru blood across its face and paws, scrambled in through the open door before her, howling as it went. The other hounds had run off, hunting quarry in the streets of Carcosa.

She darted around a dead Netru, sprawled in a pool of orange blood.

The door was close now. Pale light glowed inside.

Master Gregor had confirmed that the empress' tower was well warded. His time without magic had made him sensitive like her. Crossing the threshold was a death sentence, but Candace had issued a key to her captives. The golden shackles they wore allowed them passage. Opening them, breaking the seal, would destroy them and whoever was wearing them. But a little grease and an Ipsissimus Lex to heal a skinned and broken hand had allowed them to slip Gregor's off.

Her fingers through and curled around that hard, sharp-edged loop, Kate ran up the stairs, taking them two at a time. Closing her eyes, she dispelled her shield and dove through the warded entrance.

A shock prickled her skin, the gold cuff pulsed hot in her hand, and she was inside, nearly slipping on blood.

Kate activated her shield and scanned her surroundings. A vast oval room stretched before her, easily fifty feet high, its coffered ceiling thick with gold. A white light, like a miniature sun, floated in the middle, illuminating the graven busts peering out from a hundred portals along the ceiling's rim. While unique, some hooded, others in various poses of neck and chin, all of them wore the pallid mask of the Yellow King. Intricate stone inlay covered the walls behind columns of polished stone. Doors ran along the outer wall, some open. Before her, an orange smear trailed twenty feet across the black floor to a mangled corpse. Far to the left, a verl hound feasted on a dead Netru. Its grunting and slobbering chomps echoed off the hard, stone walls. A golden chain collar on the floor told that one of the hounds had died. There was no sign of the third one that had entered.

She turned back to the door. Grey, Jim, and Nate were waiting at the bottom of the steps. Across the open courtyard, lit by the now blue aurora, the two sharp-shooters were hurrying this way, Robison offering support. Kate tossed the shackle out to Jim. He caught it, but didn't run inside.

Scanning the thick, stone door frame, Kate searched the myriad of protective wards hidden beneath. Some were ancient, their power as strong as anything at the Athenaeum of Kell, but others were new, products of Candace's restoration.

Along the right side, beneath a scrollwork of lilies and hidden faces, she found the Death Ward. Drawing her power, Kate wove her fingers and blasted the spot with a brilliant emerald lance. Stone chipped away with a crack like a hammer blow. It took two more shots before the ward was destroyed.

Kate searched the door again, finding a second lethal ward in the floor. The thick, black marble took three solid blows before the enchantment cracked. She destroyed two more wards, not lethal, but still dangerous, before she said, "Okay. Jim."

Jim entered first, the cuff firmly in his hand.

"Did you feel anything? Did it get hot or tingle?"

"No." He tossed it out to Nate, who came in next, followed by the others.

There was no reason to risk it without the shackle, but if they needed to make a quick escape or if Kamre's men arrived, those wards needed to be gone.

Grey cast her shield and motioned to an archway to the right. "This way."

Beyond the arch, they started up a spiral staircase. The steps were large, gently tapering toward the central hub, their intricate etchings worn smooth with centuries of use. Floating lights along the ceiling lit their way as they circled round and round.

A pulse rippled across Grey's shield as they reached the top.

She pushed her way inside, taking another shot from a Netru kneeling in a long passage. Grey was about to stick her hand through, but seemed to think better of it. She twisted her hand, the fingers flowing, and a smoke whip emerged from her thumb. The Netru got off one more shot before Grey lashed the black tendril over the shield and soldier's arm, snapping it like dried spaghetti. The rifle fell from the Netru's grip, and Kate finished it off with a lance.

They ran past it, taking a second stairway up. Kate's legs ached from the climb, but she continued onward. Candace was here. Now. The golden haze of light just beyond the tower's narrow windows declared her presence. But she was a Viator. She was twenty Viatores and could escape the moment she realized they were inside her fortress.

A verl hound screamed somewhere below them. Kate only prayed it was one of hers.

They killed two more Netru at the next landing, catching them off guard as they fired off the balcony.

"There!" Kate said, motioning to a wide arch across a columned chamber. They filed into a circular room, its top seeming to stretch to dark infinity. Eight spirals of iron pyramids ran the shaft's length like the grooves in a gun barrel.

Gregor had told them that the path to the empress' chamber was at the top, two thousand steps above. There was no way they could make that and still be standing, but Carcosa's builders weren't primitives.

Robison approached a raised platform, like a gold and blue podium. "Here."

Kate inspected the star-shapes dial, about four inches across. "No wards." She twisted it to the right, clicking it one notch, and then spun it all the way to the left.

The floor shuddered. A soft hiss, and then the platform began to rise, slowly rotating with the iron tracks.

Necks craned, they watched the tube above them, shields ready for movement. The ticks of rolling gears clicked beneath them, a metronome on fast forward.

Tic-tic-tic-tic-tic.

"We understand the plan?" Harcourt whispered.

"Grey and I out front," Robison said. "Jim on the left. Beth on the right."

The old man nodded. "The moment we can, split. Don't huddle up."

"You seem to know a lot about fighting Practitioners," Grey said.

Harcourt shrugged. "No one's fought anything like this."

"Nate," Jim said, "keep hold of your dagger. Stay in the back." Since neither Nate or Harcourt could cast, they each clutched the witchhunter blades at their sides. Kate carried the third, the one that was to have been Evan's.

The silenced pistols were spent. None of their other ammo could fit them. No matter. They'd served their purpose.

Tic-tic-tic-tic-tic.

The first of the open doorways above slid closer. They pressed themselves near the wall on either side as it passed, ready to strike anything that might peek its nose in. Nothing did.

There were no windows to the outside, no hints as to how close Kamre's forces were. They couldn't be far. Had he seen Kate's verl hounds, the ones attacking the defenders from behind? Was he even still alive? Had the attack been stopped, the survivors now fleeing across the plain?

Focus, she scolded. *What's happening out there doesn't matter. Not now. She's up there.*

Kate recited her mantra as they rose, the floors sliding past, becoming fewer and fewer. *Alla tehru. Alla tehru.* A faint wedge of light, fifty feet above them, illuminated a graven sunburst capping the end of the shaft.

Her grip tightened on the witchhunter handle. Almost there. *Alla tehru. Alla tehru.*

This final archway was larger than the other, taking up one-fourth of the shaft's wall. From their perspective, it seemed to slowly revolve like some inward-shining lighthouse. Eyes above, everyone shuffled into position.

"Wait for Kate's signal," Harcourt whispered behind her. "Then go through the moment she does."

The door was ten feet above them. The dagger's handle grew slick in Kate's hand.

Closing her eyes, she focused on her senses.

Tic-tic-tic-tic-tic.

Her heart hammered in cadence. There was so much magic around her, this place itself emanated power. *Focus.*

Tic-tic-tic-tic-thump.

They stopped. Kate leaned forward. "No wards." And at once they charged.

Three quick pulses pounded Grey and Robison's shield. A pair of Netru were hunkered behind an arched stone brace, their barrels peeking out.

The two Ipsissima barreled toward them, their joined shield filling the passage. The Netru kept firing, but hesitated as the pink lattice barreled toward them like an oncoming train.

"Now," Robison said as the giant soldiers backed from their positions, their hooded heads turning. He and Grey thrust their hands through, Grey lancing one with an emerald beam and Robison unleashing a burst of purple lightning. The Netru fell, dead or dying and the practitioners charged past, stepping over them.

The passage curved, one side opening into a flower-shaped arch. Master Gregor had said this was Candace's sanctum, her throne room where she would observe the battle below.

Rounding the corner, the archway opened into a great domed chamber. Three rows of gilded, blue stone benches ran along either wall. Across the far end, golden light spilled from seven great arches leading to a railed balcony that overlooked the city and the black cloud shores of the Demhe.

Standing at the room's heart, above an inlay of the dreaded Yellow Sign, the Golden Empress waited for them, encased in a luminous dome of pink geometry. The bone-white mask of her face held no expression.

They charged.

Power surged down's Kate's arm. She wove her fingers, readying the spell. Her ears popped at the last instant she neared the archway, and she knew the mistake. Of course it was warded. The gathered magic vanished from her hand.

Grey in the lead, her brilliant shield winked out and came back up a second later. The green light lacing between her fingers extinguished. As her foot touched the floor, the empress flicked a gloved finger.

Grey's freshly-formed shield slammed back into her as if she'd been hit by a truck. She sailed backward through the archway, her foot nearly hitting Nate's head. Grey struck the wall behind them with a meaty slap and fell limp.

From her other hand, a blinding beam of emerald light streaked from the empress's fingers. Robison's shield came up in time to catch it. The lance slashed through it like tissue paper, ripping the man in half from navel to collarbone. He loosed a gurgled cry and fell, blood and organs spilling across the polished floor like a dropped egg. The beam continued past but winked out the instant it met the open archway, the magic negated by its ward.

Jim and Finn cut to either side, their shields up as if they'd do anything against Candace's power. Harcourt hurried behind Jim, Evan's old pistol up and firing.

Boom-boom-boom.

Bullets ricocheted off the Empress' shield, striking the walls. She thrust a hand out, unleashing a white beam that burned into Kate's vision. The beam curved mid-air, missing Harcourt but striking the witchhunter blade in his off-hand. The slender steel crackled and exploded. Red-hot metal blew every direction. The gun fell from the old man's grasp. He collapsed only feet from the cover of the benches, clutching his face.

"Shit!" Kate started toward him, but Jim was already there.

"Come on." Dropping his shield, Jim reached for Harcourt, who was rolling on the floor, legs flailing. A second white beam struck his chest. Jim's spine straightened. A geyser of blood and organs erupted from his mouth and eyes.

"No!" she screamed. Something wet hit her cheek.

Jim's emptied husk plopped on the floor like a disused garment.

"You fucking bitch!" Kate screamed, unleashing an emerald lance. It did nothing against the empress's shield, but Kate fired again, rage fueling her magic. "Fuck you, Candace!"

The empress paused. Her head cocked to the side, in an insectile motion. The eyes beneath peered at Kate, anger giving way to amusement. "Katherine?"

"Fuck you!" Kate sobbed. She couldn't breathe, her lungs refusing to inhale. They were dead. All dead. Two seconds in the door. The coppery stink of blood filled the air. What in the hell had they been thinking?

"It is you." The mask did nothing to hinder that all-too-familiar voice. Candace laughed, beautiful and menacing. "I thought I'd lost you. But here you are."

Finn popped up from behind one of the benches, pistol out in both hands.

Boom-boom.

Candace flicked her hand Finn's direction. Finn had already dropped for cover. All three rows of benches slammed back against the wall.

"I'd thought that looked like Jim." Candace continued as if she'd just swatted an irritating mosquito. She shook her head. "Pity. Impulse, you know. I should have stopped to be sure." She took a step toward Kate.

Kate's hand came up, violet lightning arcing between her fingers.

"What are you going to do, Katherine? You can't hurt me." She continued, a casual stroll like nothing mattered. "I could have killed you already."

"Marie Marchand."

Candace paused.

"Leslie Mills," Kate said, desperate to buy herself time, her brain scrambling for a plan.

"Very impressive, Katherine. But what does that give you? Those names are dead now."

"You're no god. You're not even a Magus. You're just a thieving hedge witch who was never good enough."

Candace laughed again, like a mother before an ignorant child. "Look around. I'm more than you could *ever* imagine, an empress of worlds."

"S...show me," Kate stammered, her voice hitching from grief and anger. "Show me your face."

Candace continued closer. "This is my face."

"Beneath the mask! Show me your face, you evil bitch!"

"I wear no—"

Something flicked past Kate's shoulder. Nate's witchhunter blade sailed from the open arch. It struck the pink dome, deflecting its course, but the shield winked off. The blade crackling with pink light as it tumbled to Candace's feet.

Pouring her ample magic into her hand, Kate unleashed the lightning. The room flickered in the purple glow. It streaked toward Candace, branches extending, then drawing together and curving into the pale mask. The magic sputtered and vanished with no effect. The mask was like a witchhunter blade, drinking spells.

Shaking her head, Candace kicked the dagger way. The shield sprang back up around her. "Stop it," she scolded. "I won't kill you, Katherine. I won't kill your friend back there. No, you're going to live here."

"Steal my magic again?"

"Mm-hmm. I can't wait to hear how you stole it back. We have all the time in the world, Katherine. I can keep you young forever." She was now fifteen feet away. Her shield extended all the way to the floor. There was no getting under it.

Kate took an involuntary step back. "Stealing years? Giving them to me?"

Candace nodded.

Harcourt groaned from the corner.

"It was my mistake not fetching you once I'd found Carcosa. Brought you here to my city."

Kate licked her lips. Even if she could get through that shield, no spell could overcome that mask. She remembered the way Grey had sailed through the anti-magic barrier. The magic that had sent her was canceled, but not the momentum.

Surging her magic down her arm, Kate threw the witchhunter blade. Underhanded, not a good shot, but enough. The dagger flipped through the air, dispelling Candace's shield and thumping handle-first into her chest.

Seizing the opening, Kate hurled her hand out, unleashing every ounce of rage and magic in one loud "Ka!" She didn't aim at Candace, that would do nothing against the mask. She aimed at the floor just before her.

Stone tile buckled and shattered, pieces shotgun blasting up and into Candace's shins. The empress let a surprised yelp and fell forward, her legs coming out from under her.

She started to fall face-first, but froze, hanging in the air for only a moment like a tangled marionette before rotating around and righting herself. "Katherine, I—" Candace's eyes locked on the tiny stainless .32 now in Kate's hand. The pistol, a gift from Dennis, the hollow point bullets gifted from Evan, both men now dead.

Boom-boom-boom. The sharp recoil pounded into Kate's palm.

Two rounds stuck. Crimson blossomed from Candace's chest. Stunned, the empress brought her hand up, fingers beginning to curl.

Screaming in the purest hate, Kate continued to fire.

Boom-boom.

The first round struck the bony mask, knocking Candace's head back. The next bullet found her exposed throat. Blood sprayed across the ruined floor. Candace grabbed her neck, red squirting between the gold-gloved fingers.

Boom.

Candace fell onto her back. Her legs flailed.

Click. The gun was empty.

Candace gurgled. Blood ran from beneath the mask. Her fingers worked, silvery threads forming between them, the power of untold Leges mending the wounds.

Kate dove for the witchhunter blade, knocked aside by her assault on the floor. Grabbing it, she lunged at Candace, whose blood-smeared hand was coming up. Kate rammed the dagger into the empress's chest, the slender blade punching through her sternum like flimsy wood. A wet glove slapped Kate's cheek, clawing at her face and seizing her hair.

Candace's eyes blazed with fear and rage. She yanked Kate closer, their gazes locked together.

A hot buzzing shot across Kate's scalp, and down into her skull. The world warbled, losing substance, the only foundation those two hateful eyes before her. The energy hub at the top of her head flared, a surge of pure power exploding like a lightning bolt. Magic blasted down her body, striking each of the hubs in succession. Yellow numbness coursed through her veins, working at the edges of her vision and along her tongue. There was nothing, no sound, no heat, cold, fear, or even time— only yellow.

Something stirred within her, an alien sensation pushing its way through the cracks, an oily, yellow intelligence. Candace.

Screaming, Kate clenched her hand, barely registering the dagger in her grip. She ripped the blade free and rammed it in again.

A choked gasp and Candace's hands fell from Kate's head, releasing the spell. Her eyes unfocused and rolled upward. The tower shuddered, its tremor rippling out across the multiverse.

Panting, Kate sat up, straddling the dead demigoddess. Her head swam as her senses returned, pushing away the lingering yellow, like waking from a dream. Blinking the tears from her eyes, Kate looked down at the fallen woman, blood pooling across the broken floor. The electric hum of magic thrummed from the pallid mask, its pristine whiteness marred by a gray streak of Kate's bullet. Sliding her fingers beneath the mask's chin, Kate pulled.

The mask didn't move. She tried again, pulling upward and side to side, yet it held firm.

Swallowing, Kate pulled the dagger free with a wet slurp. She slid the slender blade up under the mask, finding resistance. She sawed to the side, breaking whatever was holding it on and peeled the mask away. Something crunched like a breaking stick, that was still too green to be brittle, and the mask tore free.

Candace Cross lay before her. Her pale, waxy face was thinner than Kate remembered. Her once-blonde hair was silvery white, and her eyebrows were completely gone. Jagged nubs protruded from her cheekbones like the roots of broken antlers from where the mask had grown.

Kate rose, her eyes locked on the dead woman she'd once called sister. "Burn in hell."

Boom. A gunshot slammed into Candace's side.

Kate sprang back. Finn was crawling from the pile of benches, smoking pistol in one hand, her other arm bloodied and against her chest.

Finn fired again.

"Christ," Kate yelped. "She's dead already."

"Fuck her anyway," Finn slurred. She wiped the blood pouring from her broken nose with the back of her pistol hand.

Behind her, Nate screamed. She was curled up beside Jim's body, hands over her eyes, a long horrible shriek rising from her open mouth.

Harcourt was slumped against a bench, one blue eye watching Kate from a torn and bloodied face. He smiled, those little teeth smeared in red. Then his head slumped back.

"They're scattering," Finn called from the archway, pistol clutched in her hands. The golden light outside was gone. Black stars twinkled above Carcosa. She limped out onto the balcony. "I can't hear any hounds. Are they gone?"

"I think so." Dropping the mask to the floor, Kate checked on Harcourt. The old man was still breathing. "Beth, get over here!"

Finn raced back to tend to the wounded.

In the hall, Grey was alive but unconscious, the back of her head bloodied. Finn did what she could to wrap it. None of them were Leges, but hopefully, there were still some surviving healers in Kamre's approaching forces.

Kate wrapped her arms around Nate and pulled her close. The sobbing woman folded against her. "It's over," Kate whispered, her teary cheek against Nate's hair. "It's over."

45

CRIMSON AND CLOVER

A half-dozen conversations ended as Kate pushed open the door and inhaled the aroma of sage and old wood. Ignoring the curious watchers, she adjusted the pot beneath her arm and approached the bar. Tisha was digging for something behind the counter, her curly hair now a vibrant purple.

Kate slid the leather briefcase onto the stained bar top and then set the heavy pot beside it, letting it drop that last quarter inch with a solid thump.

"You break my bar and I'll..." Tisha's scowl melted into a wide smile as she looked up, a pair of copper mugs in her hand. "Well, it's about damned time."

"Hey, girl. Glenlivet. Double."

Tisha's brow cocked above her thick tortoise frames. "That's all you have to say to me?"

Kate shrugged. "This is a bar."

Tisha snorted. Dropping the two cups down on the counter with a clang, she came around the side. "Come here," she said, giving Kate a hug. "How the hell have you been?"

"Good. Really good."

"I'll say. You wouldn't believe the shit I've been hearing."

"Like what?"

"Oh, well let's see. Last time I talked to you was, what, nine months ago? You were asking me for Dalton's number, then I hear from several reliable sources that you showed up in Amber Tower like a fury, skinned that motherfucker alive and then magicked away with three Magi and your old tower mates."

"I didn't skin all of him."

"Yeah, I heard that, too. Everyone came in all, '*What's up with Kate? She got her magic back. She tried to kill Dalton.*' All that."

"And what did you say?"

"I told them I didn't know. Then, some of them show back up last month with Magus Gregor, and they won't say shit except that people died and that you were some Sorceress Badass Hero. Ronny Clews is missing a hand, and no one knows why. So..." Tisha cocked her head like an impatient mother. "What have you been up to? And if you don't tell me, I swear to God I'll ban your skinny ass."

Kate laughed. "Well, we can't have that. But, not here. It's a long and... difficult story."

Tisha sighed, seeming to accept that. "Better be tonight."

"Promise." Kate nodded toward the pot resting on the bar. It was milky crystal, but with a deep, crimson hue, like a ruby encased in ice. "Got you a present."

"Nice." Tisha touched the smooth crystal, traced her fingers along the shallow carvings up to the thick, cobalt blue clover draping over the top. "Beautiful. What is this?"

"Honestly?" Kate shrugged. "I don't think it has a name."

Tisha shot her a sidelong glance. "Where'd you get it?"

"You won't believe me."

"I don't know. Try me."

"Tonight." Kate set her feet on the old brass bar rail. "So how 'bout that drink?"

"Coming right up." Tisha circled back around the bar and poured a pair of serious Scotches. She lifted one. "Welcome home."

Kate clinked her glass in a toast and sipped the whiskey. Damn, she'd missed that burn. While the distillers of Torba might make the best drinks she'd ever found, nothing in the world compared to a drink in Whittaker's.

"Okay," Tisha said, returning to the copper mugs. "Let me take care of these, then I'm going to call Tiny, have him take over, and then you and I can go out. I'm ready for story time. Deal?"

"Deal." Kate watched her friend saunter to the other side of the bar where a thick-necked guy was openly ogling her. Not sexual, though. Not contempt. Something else. Kate didn't recognize him.

His eyes averted the instant they met Kate's.

Baltimore Skinner, she thought. Kate sipped her drink again and then picked it up. Taking the chrome and mother-of-pearl-latched case, she slid off the bar stool and wandered to the back where the old wingbacks rested.

Mr. Lacroix looked up from a small hardback, the cloth at its corners frayed and discolored with age. "Welcome back, Kate."

"Thank you." She sat down in the chair across from him, setting the case on the round table between them. "This is for you."

He touched his glasses, but didn't break eye contact. His expression still friendly, but a wary tension pulled at his lips. "For me?"

She nodded, sipped her drink, and whispered. "It's done. What Vogler wanted to do. It's done."

The color drained from his fat cheeks. "I don't know what you mean."

"Of course you do." Kate leaned closer. "Don't worry. I always liked you. You were one of the only people that showed me kindness after my incident. He didn't betray you, by the way. He refused to. But I've had a few months to really consider who it was that was always nice, never took sides, never shut anyone out, and was always ready to listen. I figure that sort of setup would be ideal for a spy."

Lacroix swallowed, his chins rippling with the motion.

Kate sipped her Scotch, letting the fat man sweat. "I won't tell anyone. Just pass this along to your friends. Let them know it's done."

"What is it?"

"Everything he took. At least what's left. The money..." She shrugged. "Gold. More than enough to make up for it. Maybe a little extra for your trouble. Call it a peace offering. Two of the daggers were lost, but that's it. There's a letter explaining it all."

The fat man nodded. "And what about our friend?"

"He didn't make it, either. We made it though, to that place he said exists. We were there, and that's where he's buried."

"I see," a shadow of regret in his eyes.

"He was a bastard, but he was also a good man. He did what he thought was right. I'm doing this for his memory. Understand? You won't have any problems with me. In fact, I'm honestly happy to know you're around."

Lacroix's brows arched. "An odd sentiment."

Kate shrugged. "Not really. People think you're the bogeymen, but you're police, making sure no one steps out of line. I'd rather have that than the alternative. Who knows, maybe we can help each other out sometime."

"Does this mean you're moving back?"

"No." She shot back the last of her drink, let a breath at the burn. "But I'll be swinging by from time to time, so I hope this absolves me of any of my sins."

"Good luck, then." He accepted the briefcase, grunting a little by the weight of seven pounds of gold inside. "Consider the slate cleaned. I'll make sure of that."

"I'll be seeing you." Kate rose and headed back to the bar.

Tisha was already on the phone, securing the rest of her night off.

Once Kate returned to Soonat, she'd tell Harcourt how it went. He and Nate, her newest pupil, were enjoying the springtime bloom now that the eclipse had ended. Jengta said it would be beautiful, and Kate looked forward to seeing it for herself. First, she needed a night with her best friend.

THE END

Thank you for reading! Did you enjoy?

Please Add Your Review! And don't miss more urban fantasy novels like, FROSTBITE by Joshua Bader. Turn the page for a sneak peek!

SNEAK PEEK OF FROSTBITE

With a name like Fisher, it's only natural for me to be attracted to large bodies of water. I'm easily impressed by anything deeper than a bathtub. I grew up in Denver until I was 14. It's a great city, especially for nature lovers, what with the ever-present mountains and an environmentally conscious population. Water, however, wild, free-standing, blue-as-the-sky, shiny-as-a-mirror, water was not Denver's strong suit. The "lake" within walking distance of my childhood home would barely merit mention as a puddle in other places of the world. Fortunately, in the ten years since my dad sent me packing, I've gotten to see plenty of those other places: West Coast, East Coat, Gulf Coast, Great Lakes.

In the era of quick status updates, where everyone can define themselves by a short list of labels and in 140 characters, my status depends greatly on the perspective of the person describing me (and their degree of relatedness to me). I've never used Face-space or Five-corners, so I'm at the mercy of the people who do when it comes to labeling. The ones that have floated back to me are "world traveler," "professional vagabond," "dabbling wizard," or "lunatic-just-short-of-civil-commitment." My dad once used the phrase "career criminal" when he thought I was out of ear shot. Those labels all fall short of the one I prefer: Colin Fisher.

The lake stretched out in front of me was a prime example of everything that pond in Colorado wasn't. Lake Thunderbird was man-made, but that didn't make it any less impressive to the eye. The way the wings of the lake wrapped back around me created the illusion that I was on the edge of an island beach, rather than a hundred yards from a State Park parking lot. Sitting against the thick oak trunk, staring out across the charcoal blue waters, I felt a million miles away from all my problems. That thought, unfortunately, reminded me that I was really only 682 miles away from my most pressing issue. It would be a nine-hour drive, if I pushed straight through.

Going home to Colorado was the last thing I wanted to do. My mom died when I was 14. Dad and I did not deal with her death too well. When we weren't crying, we were fighting. Most of the time, we fought because one of us had caught the other one crying: machismo at its dysfunctional peak. Adolescent males are crazy to start with, but the grief made me a royal pain in the ass. In my defense, my father could have been a little more supportive, more understanding. There's no use rehashing that argument now, I suppose. There's not enough time left to finish it.

When school let out that summer, my dad sent me to live with my aunt and uncle in Boston. The plan was I'd come back in the fall, once things settled down, got back to normal. I don't think my dad or I ever realized that without Mom, there was no normal. If we had tried, maybe we could have come up with a new normal, but we didn't. The last time I saw him in the flesh was at my high school graduation...in Boston, not Denver. I celebrated my twenty-fourth birthday three months ago, which made me a Cancer. My dad had cancer and was either dying or already dead.

My thoughts wandered like the wind-chopped waves on the lake, dancing through graveyards of memories better left buried and undisturbed. The book I brought out there with me was lying in the brush beside me, untouched. Most museum curators would kill me for carrying it around, let alone setting it down in the dirt, leaves, and dried mud. I'll have to add them to the long list of people who sternly disapprove of my behavior. I picked up this peculiar tome in Charleston, chomping at the bit to read it. It's not every day that I found a 17th century commentary on faeries of the Rhine plains for less than ten bucks. The owner of the antique store couldn't read Yiddish and thought of it as a cute decorative paperweight. I thought of it as a feast of knowledge, waiting to be devoured, and I suppose both of us were right, in our own way. I probably would've finished studying it already, if I hadn't called home to Boston that night.

I went to Harvard for three years. That was part of the initial allure of spending the summer with Uncle James and Aunt Celia in Massachusetts. By getting a feel for the area while I was still in high school, my dad thought it might reduce the stress of transition later. He always thought I had Ivy League potential. I guess it worked a little. My freshman and sophomore years were great. Then Sarai disappeared. I dropped out after the second semester of my junior year, a ripe old burnout at the age of 20. I've often wondered if my dad would have put a "My son is a Harvard dropout" bumper sticker on his car if I sent him one. As failures go, it's impressive: aim for the stars; when you crash, you'll make a bigger crater.

I reached for the book, anxious to face the road again and be done with it. My legs were stiff, but responsive, as I rose. In my wild gypsy days, I've mastered the art of sitting under a tree for long periods of time, without letting body parts fall asleep. The walk from the lakeside to my car, Dorothy, was all too short. Dorothy's hood stretched on forever, a giant silver space-age yacht cleverly disguised as an '86 Ford Crown Victoria. Spare me the save-the-world speech: I had her converted to bio-diesel five years ago. It's possible to be environmentally responsible and still drive a tank.

I deposited the book onto the passenger seat, unceremoniously dumping it on top of the other unread treasures I'd acquired in the last week. My dad was lying in a hospital, parts of him slowly devouring other parts of him, but I still couldn't force myself to hurry. My traveling routine was what it was: drive for two to three hundred miles, refuel, cruise around the town to see if anything catches my interest, then find a safe place to park the car for the night. Interest for me comes in two forms: money and knowledge. I love old books and I don't mind a little manual labor to acquire them. I've been stretching my runs to 400 plus miles lately, near the edge of Dorothy's fuel limit, and skimping on the work, but this was still the way I operated. I'll get there when I get there. The fact that I didn't want to watch my Dad die had nothing to do with my refusal to break routine...okay, maybe a little. Maybe a lot.

I took a deep breath, my eyes panning over the grandeur of the lake one last time, before turning the key in the ignition. I didn't want to leave, but the road awaited. Nothing happened when I turned the key. I grimaced, frustrated by Dorothy's sudden rebellion. Soon, she'd be the only family I had left in the world and she was trying to jump ship, too. When I noticed that the headlight knob was turned all the way to bright,

I let my head crash down on to the rim of the steering wheel. I cried for far longer than a man can safely admit.

———

Don't stop now. Keep reading with your copy of FROSTBITE available now.

Read more amazing stories from Seth Skorkowsky at www.skorkowsky.com

And discover even more urban fantasy novels like City Owl Press' FROSTBITE by Joshua Bader.

Getting hired to be a personal wizard for a billionaire may just become a death sentence.

Colin Fisher is a young man with a lot of problems on his plate: a dying father, a dead car doubling as a home, and a mysteriously disappeared fiancée. You'd think with a magical inclination he'd be able to turn it all around, but not so much.

Yet his bad luck appears to be on the way out when the CEO of a multinational corporation offers him a job. It's a sweet gig as a personal wizard with a fat paycheck. It just has one catch. The paranoid CEO isn't a mere hypochondriac, he's been hexed with an authentic ancient curse.

Now Colin is the only thing standing between his new boss and a frozen bundle of fangs, claws, and rage. If he can't stop the cannibal ice demon in time to save his new boss, it'll be back to living out of his dead car. That is, if he even survives the battle.

Please sign up for the City Owl Press newsletter for chances to win special subscriber-only contests and giveaways as well as receiving information on upcoming releases and special excerpts.

All reviews are **welcome** and **appreciated**. Please consider leaving one on your favorite social media and book buying sites.

For books in the world of romance and speculative fiction that embody Innovation, Creativity, and Affordability, check out City Owl Press at www.cityowlpress.com.

ABOUT THE AUTHOR

Raised in the swamps and pine forests of East Texas, Seth Skorkowsky always gravitated to the darker sides of fantasy, preferring horror and pulp heroes over knights in shining armor.

His debut novel, Dämoren, was published in 2014 as the first in his Valducan series. He has now released several urban fantasy novels and sword-and-sorcery short story collections.

When not writing, Seth enjoys cheesy movies, tabletop role-playing games, making YouTube videos, and traveling the world with his wife.

www.skorkowsky.com

 twitter.com/sskorkowsky

 youtube.com/SethSkorkowskyAuthor

ABOUT THE PUBLISHER

City Owl Press is a cutting edge indie publishing company, bringing the world of romance and speculative fiction to discerning readers.

www.cityowlpress.com

Made in the USA
Middletown, DE
17 July 2021